Gore Vi... dimension of human
of the fantas... genius of Chekhov . . .

A man's life—and heart... are in Terence
Rattigan's unforgettably m... ...ke Browning
Version . . .

This century's finest triumph of classic tragedy in
Riders to the Sea by John Millington Synge ...

Thornton Wilder's dazzling mastery in expanding
the possibilities of the theater . . .

These are but five of the dozen milestone works
that make up a multifaceted world of emotion and
insight in

THE MENTOR BOOK OF SHORT PLAYS

*RICHARD H. GOLDSTONE is a member of the
English faculty of City College, New York, where he
teaches modern drama. A graduate of the University
of Wisconsin with a Ph.D. from Columbia, Professor
Goldstone has written for THE NEW YORK TIMES
BOOK REVIEW, THE SATURDAY REVIEW and
many other major publications.*

*ABRAHAM H. LASS, formerly principal of Abraham
Lincoln High School in Brooklyn, New York, is widely
recognized as an anthologizer as well as an authority
on college and college admissions. Mr. Lass is the co-
editor of 21 Great Stories, The Secret Sharer and
Other Great Stories, and Masters of the Short Story,
all available in Mentor editions.*

The Mentor Book
of Short Plays

edited by

RICHARD H. GOLDSTONE
and ABRAHAM H. LASS

A MENTOR BOOK from
NEW AMERICAN LIBRARY
TIMES MIRROR
New York and Scarborough, Ontario
The New English Library Limited, London

Library of Congress Catalog Card Number: 69-17925

 MENTOR TRADEMARK REG. U.S. PAT. OFF. AND FOREIGN COUNTRIES
REGISTERED TRADEMARK—MARCA REGISTRADA
HECHO EN CHICAGO, U.S.A.

SIGNET, SIGNET CLASSICS, MENTOR, PLUME, MERIDIAN AND
NAL BOOKS are published *in the United States* by
The New American Library, Inc.,
1633 Broadway, New York, New York 10019,
in Canada by The New American Library of Canada Limited,
81 Mack Avenue, Scarborough, Ontario M1L 1M8
in the United Kingdom by The New English Library Limited,
Barnard's Inn, Holborn, London, EC1N 2JR, England.

First Mentor Printing, February, 1970

5 6 7 8 9 10 11 12 13

PRINTED IN CANADA

To Betty, Janet, *and* Paul
and in memory of George Goldstone, *pioneer in the study of the one-act play and teacher to both editors of this volume*

Contents

MENTOR BOOK
OF SHORT PLAYS

Introduction

The short play is the Cinderella of the theater. For over five centuries, short plays were relegated to parts of the church service and to churchyards; to school halls and town centers; to converted barns and little theaters. In the nineteenth and early twentieth century, the short play was the special province of amateur groups; it was largely ignored by professionals.

But like Cinderella, the short play has after long neglect come into its own. Since the first World War, and particularly during the past decade, the theater public has displayed as much interest in performances of short plays—even in the commercial theaters of New York, Los Angeles, and Chicago—as it has in the traditionally more popular full-length plays. In the past few years, contemporary dramatists like Harold Pinter, Edward Albee, Neil Simon, Eugene Ionesco, Samuel Beckett, and Robert Anderson have been assiduously composing short plays which are being successfully produced on and off Broadway.

The short play is as old as drama itself. Known in ancient Greek times as a satyr play, the short play traditionally rounded out the tragic trilogy which Athenian audiences in the fifth century B.C. attended during the festival of Dionysus. The majority of the plays of ancient Greece and Rome have been lost. The earliest short play extant is a fragment by Sophocles called *The Trackers*—a play, surprisingly enough, about cattle rustling. The only extant short play by Euripides, which we have in its entirety, is *The Cyclops,* a comical adaptation of an incident in *The Odyssey*—the encounter between Odysseus and Polyphemos.

Between the fall of Rome in the fifth century A.D. and about 1100, if there was a living theater, no record of it remains to us. It is not until the medieval and renaissance periods of European civilization that a substantial body of short plays emerges.

In about 1200 the popularity of drama in England began—probably with the playlets first performed as an adjunct to the Roman Catholic church service. These little plays, called *mysteries*, dramatized those parts of the liturgy having to do with the life and death of Jesus, and with mankind's salvation. Another form of little play, the *miracle play*, was based on an incident in the life of a saint. Because these playlets proved to be both uplifting and entertaining, they were soon expanded and performed either in the courtyard of the church or on the church porch. Eventually they were moved to the public square or marketplace, though they did not, for a long time, lose their essentially religious or moral character.

At the onset of the English renaissance, that is to say during the reign of Henry VIII, another type of short play, the *comic interlude*, came into being. The interlude was performed at the royal court, presumably during the progress of a banquet. Another form of the interlude devised during Henry's reign was the educational-didactic short play written in Latin by the preparatory-school masters for the edification of their students. A great many of the interludes that survive are of unknown authorship. Others are known to be the work of John Heywood, a court musician before he took up writing, and of Nicholas Udall, successively headmaster of Eton and Winchester.

As drama flowered in England during the Elizabethan and Jacobean periods, the popular and ubiquitous short play gave way to the full-length tragedies, comedies, and melodramas of Kyd, Marlowe, Shakespeare, Ben Jonson, and Webster. It was not until the late seventeenth century that Molière reestablished the short play in the French theater, placing the stamp of his genius on the farce-comedy—a genre of short play that in time was to absorb the talents of Anton Chekhov and Bernard Shaw. The farce-comedy is, of course, still very much in vogue in today's theater. Where the short play of the sixteenth century was intended to be either didactic or merely entertaining, Molière's short plays were pointedly and amusingly satiric. For two hundred years following Molière, the short play remained principally satiric comedy.

In the twentieth century, however, the short play began to cover a wider spectrum than that of comedy. It attracted a great number of serious and intense writers of drama, whose work embraced a broad variety of dramatic forms and moods. During the first World War, Susan Glaspell and Eugene O'Neill wrote their early plays for the Provincetown Players. The Provincetown Playhouse was only one of several regional theaters which began exploiting the full potential of the one-act and the short play. Among others, the Carolina Folk Players in Chapel Hill were especially notable.

The advent of radio and then of television provided an additional impetus for exploring the possibilities of the short play. So great became the need for twenty-five- and fifty-minute plays that writers began turning to the inexhaustible resources of the short story, successfully dramatizing writers such as Dickens, James Joyce, William Faulkner, and Ernest Hemingway.

Most recently, the permanent place won by off-Broadway theater has resulted in American premieres at the Cherry Lane Theater and the Provincetown Playhouse—both in Greenwich Village—of celebrated one-act plays by Samuel Beckett, Eugene Ionesco, Harold Pinter, and Edward Albee.

All these recent developments have challenged the former absolute supremacy of the full-length play, and the general theater public, ever since Noel Coward's series of one-acters in the 1930's, *Tonight at 8:40,* has accepted an evening of one-act plays as readily as it had accepted the conventional full-length play.

Each of the plays selected for inclusion in this volume has a vital dramatic impulse, each one was written for performance, and each has proved itself stageworthy and absorbing. Not all, however, were written for the theater. Three were created for production on television, one for radio. Of the remaining eight, at least two have had Broadway productions: two were first performed by the legendary Abbey Theater of Dublin; and one, Rostand's *The Romancers,* has served as the book for the long-running off-Broadway musical *The Fantasticks.*

The plays we have chosen here reflect the varied dramatic forms and possibilities inherent in the short play. The realistic drama finds expression in Granberry-Hart's *A Trip to Czardis,* Lady Gregory's *The Rising of the Moon,* Terence Rattigan's *The Browning Version,* and Paddy Chayefsky's *The Mother.* Melodrama is represented by Reginald Rose's *Thunder on Sycamore Street.* Gore Vidal's *Visit to a Small Planet* is a fantasy—not unrelated to science-fiction—with an underlying social commentary. The plays of Anton Chekhov, Edmond Rostand, Thornton Wilder, Tennessee Williams, and William Inge are comedies in various styles. Synge's *Riders to the Sea* is an authentic example of modern tragedy.

All of these plays have a relevant dramatic immediacy for today's readers and for today's audiences. Some of the plays dramatize anxieties and attitudes peculiar to the 1960's. Others "merely" dramatize one aspect or another of the unchanging human condition. All, however, have one element in common: they have proved themselves in performance. And they are vital, incontrovertible evidence that the short play remains, after twenty-five hundred years, a flourishing and exciting literary genre.

R.H.G.
A.H.L.

Reading a Play

Some of us read plays because—quite simply—we don't have access to a theater where we can see plays produced. But more of us read plays because we are both challenged and absorbed by the printed record, *the text,* of a dramatic work. We study the text of plays we have seen in the same way that we study maps of places we've been to and journeys that we've already taken. We want to see where we've been.

A play is obviously more than words. It is an event. It is actors speaking, gesticulating, and reacting. It is dark and light; sound and silence; music and speech. Above all, it is spectacle. All these elements the reader must create for himself. Though they are in the text, they are, in a sense, beyond the text—reachable only through the reader's imagination.

Never underestimate the power of imagination. For instance, we can conjure up Helen of Troy better than Homer could. In *The Iliad,* in Book III, when Helen hears that the Trojans and the Achaeans are behaving strangely and that Paris and Menelaus are going to fight a duel over her, Homer tells us that she wraps a white veil around her head and goes out to see for herself. She comes up to the Scaean Gate, where old King Priam and the Trojan elders are sitting on the tower. Homer says that when the old men look at her, a hush descends. "Who on earth could blame the armies for suffering so long for such a woman?" they ask each other softly. "She is the image of an immortal goddess."

Is Helen fair or dark, tall or slight? No matter; in our

"mind's eye" she is a goddess, far lovelier than Homer can describe.

Hearing and Seeing

Homer, of course, gives us the clue, in the hush, in the tone of the old men's voices.

In a play, the dramatist uses words as clues for the director, the actors, all the artists of the theater who will re-create his meaning in their production.

The reader, too, must interpret the clues. For instance, he must *hear* what lies under and between and above the words. The line may be, "I know he's waiting for me." But is the character speaking the line afraid? Angry? Indifferent? Anxious? She is one kind of person, he's another—the situation between them can be anything at all. One meaning can be achieved by special stress or emphasis; another by pace or pitch; a third by a pause. Tempo can make a difference.

At the beginning of Synge's *Riders to the Sea,* Cathleen and Nora are anxious; they speak in restrained, low tones to the reader's inner ear. In *Thunder on Sycamore Street,* when Arthur looks up at Joe, turns and stands next to him, and takes off his eyeglasses and flings them into the crowd, we are prepared for the stage direction *strong.* This underlines the force not only of Arthur's voice when he says "Throw the next stone at me, neighbors; I live here too," but of Arthur's coming of age as a man, pinpointed later when the stage direction says his wife moves to him "knowing that Arthur is no longer a grown-up child."

Tempo adds enormously to dramatic vividness in Terence Rattigan's *The Browning Version* when Crocker-Harris picks up the phrase that Gilbert tells him is the school's epithet for him, "the Himmler of the lower fifth," and repeats it three times. In his varying emphasis is made clear his terrible understanding of himself as others see him.

The reader also wants to be able to "see" in his mind's eye what would be visible on the stage during a performance. It is not only the costumes, sets, colors, that he should try to bring to mind. Gestures, groupings, pantomime, movements, entrances and exits—these are the life and heart of the play's development.

For instance, it is diverting for the reader to see a stylized set (as for *The Romancers*) or exaggerated period costumes (*A Marriage Proposal*) or a variation in lighting effects to deepen a mood (*The Browning Version*)— but it is of the essence of good play-reading for him to see "close-ups" or "pan shots" that bring character and conflict into sharp focus.

One instance of the importance of really *seeing* what is happening occurs in Lady Gregory's *The Rising of the Moon*. During a good part of the play, the Ragged Man and the Sergeant are seated back-to-back on a barrel, facing opposite ways. What could be a better symbol of Ireland's civil strife? At another moment in the play, the "camera eye" picks up a detail that foreshadows the ending. When the Sergeant hides the Ragged Man's hat and wig behind his back, we know that his answer to "Did anyone come this way?" will be "No one."

Once the reader begins to *see*, everything comes into focus. Inge's description early in the play of Bobolink's physical appearance must be kept in view throughout; it completely explains her "spirit." In Gore Vidal's *Visit to a Small Planet,* Kreton's gesture in Spelding's study—his twirling of the globe of the world—is the clue to his visit. And Rattigan's telling us that while Millie is scolding her husband for not standing up to the headmaster (in *The Browning Version*), her husband is turning the pages of *Agamemnon* and not looking at her, is deeply revealing about the nature of their relationship.

Sometimes the close-up is of a detail in the setting. In *Riders to the Sea* there are the white boards and the bundle of clothes hidden in the turf-loft before Maurya enters: both create suspense in a play which has little action but great tension. (And speaking of tension, if the reader sees Cathleen suddenly stopping her wheel and listening when Michael's name is mentioned, or Cathleen and Nora starting when the door is blown open, how alive the play becomes!)

A "pan shot" can help one see many faces, many characters. In *Thunder on Sycamore Street,* at the very end, when the crowd begins to drift away, try to see the groupings. The exit of each family—the Morrisons, the Blakes, the Hayeses—is physically, psychologically meaningful.

We re-create the stage picture. We ask not only "What does the line mean?" but "What is the effect now?" If we pick up the clues to sight and sound, no play is static. Every line, every stage direction, leads up to a moment of emotion or suspense.

Character and Conflict

In the short play, as in any other play, to understand what moves the characters is to understand everything. Molière said that for the theater all he needed was a platform and a passion or two; Galsworthy said that the man makes the plot.

The brevity of form, of course, dictates certain necessities. There are resemblances between the short play and the short story. Both deal with a single significant incident; both introduce only a few characters; both involve the audience immediately and strive for a maximum effect in a minimum time. In neither is there time to develop human beings in all their dimensions (as they are shown in novels or long plays). In both there is concentration, compression, suggestion—and often the limitation makes for greater force. Sometimes the short play is even more concentrated than the short story.

What engages the main character in a play is conflict— between himself and others, between two sides of his own self, between himself and natural forces. And conflict is what engages the reader. Nobody walks away from a fight; we want to know how it comes out.

The more conflicts in a play, the more absorbing we find it. In Chayefsky's *The Mother,* we take a ringside seat for Mother versus Daughter, Daughter versus Self, Boss versus Son-in-Law—and possibly Reader versus Chayefsky, if we don't agree with his "neopsychoanalysis." Even in a play which seems to have neither conflict nor incident, *Riders to the Sea,* we are gripped. Maurya's final words, "No man at all can be living for ever, and we must be satisfied," with which she accepts the loss of her last two sons, are part of a very long conflict between man and the sea. Maurya's story makes but one moment.

If we use the word "crisis" instead of "conflict," we can see how plays are built. The dramatist leads up to a crisis in the life of the main character (leads up very swiftly, in a short play); in the crisis, the character makes an important discovery about himself or others which changes the way he thinks or feels. This discovery alters his direction. The reader is still in suspense: which way will he go?

Tone and Style

To understand the people in a play, and to enjoy them, we must pick up more than the outlines of conflict and crisis. It helps if we catch the inflections of mood, tone, and style which make all the difference between one person and another.

Three of the comedies in this volume reveal interesting facets of character. In Rostand's *The Romancers,* there is irony in the whole situation. Rostand spins the humor of the plot out of the foibles and conventions of the young lovers and their parents. The style, however, is not realistic but mock-heroic. Straforel's inventory of the varieties of abductions is like Cyrano's inventory of the kinds of noses in *Cyrano de Bergerac,* which was written three years later. Chekhov's farce *A Marriage Proposal,* exaggerating human pretensions and excesses, is not intended to show its characters as wholly ridiculous; they are even a little touching. More realistic than either of these is Thornton Wilder's *The Happy Journey to Trenton and Camden,* even though it has four kitchen chairs representing an automobile and a trip of seventy miles occurring in twenty minutes. The Kirby family is as real, as funny, as sad, and possibly as universal as the families in *Our Town,* which came several years after *The Happy Journey.*

It was Thornton Wilder who said to Richard Goldstone in their *Paris Review* interview that the dramatist is one who believes that any action involving human beings is more arresting than any comment that can be made upon it. On the stage, said Mr. Wilder, it is always *now*. . . .

That is what makes reading a play so absorbing. Right there on the page, somebody is coming in, going out, sitting down, making a choice, refusing an offer, living his life, experiencing the shocks and countershocks of existence. And in reading a play—as in reading any work of literature—there come those moments when we suddenly understand that what we are reading is not about strangers in remote places, but about us. We ourselves, and those whom we know best, are there in the play, acting out our anxieties, our fears, our joys, our hopes and aspirations.

R.H.G.
A.H.L.

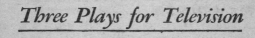

Three Plays for Television

melodrama-

play type
_

an extravagantly
theatrical play, in which
action & plot dominate
over characterization.

The object is to keep
the audience thrilled
by the awakening
of strong feelings:
of pity, or horror, or joy.   Quincy

Morality play-

a kind of poetic drama
of the late middle ages.
The theme is the saving
of mans soul & the central
figure is man.

REGINALD ROSE:

Thunder on Sycamore Street

Reginald Rose (1920–   ) was born in New York City, educated in the New York schools, and attended City College from 1937 to 1938. He served in World War II, attaining the rank of first lieutenant. After the war he devoted himself to writing for television. His two best-known works are *Twelve Angry Men,* which was turned into a distinguished motion picture, and the series *The Defenders.* Mr. Rose is highly respected in television circles for his pioneering script, *Tragedy in a Temporary Town,* as well as for *Thunder on Sycamore Street.*

Thunder on Sycamore Street, like most plays composed for television, is a melodrama. In melodrama the *dramatis personae* lack subtlety because they are necessarily subordinate to the situation in which they find themselves: a confrontation between the force of good and the force of evil. ("Westerns" are invariably melodramas in which we always anticipate the inevitable confrontation between the hero and the villain, with the ultimate triumph of good over evil.) Dialogue in a melodrama is not usually the language of life because it too is subordinate to the situation leading up to the confrontation. Even the plot structure cannot always bear close scrutiny; there are usually flaws in the inherent logic of the development of the story.

These characteristics of melodrama are to be found in *Thunder on Sycamore Street:* What exactly *did* Charlie Denton see in the newspaper? Did he deliberately conceal from his credulous neighbors the full facts surrounding their neighbor's past? Apparently, but why? Is the metamorphosis of Arthur Hayes credible? Why do we or why do we not believe it? Is it likely that a community of gen-

23

teel and respectable suburbanites—on so flimsy a basis—would transform itself into a band of hoodlums and vigilantes?

Basically, what Mr. Rose is offering is not intended to be a realistic reflection of suburban life. Rather he has composed a parable, a morality play for the times . . . a morality play dealing with the sins of conformity, of stiff-necked pride, of arrogance. *Thunder on Sycamore Street* was written and produced in the 1950's, when "McCarthyism" was at its height and when good Americans were in a state of spiritual torpor. Much of the television drama, then as now, was mindless, and few of the television plays manifested the kind of courage which Mr. Rose's plays displayed in championing social and racial minorities.

Few television writers have probed so deeply and sensitively into the complex, subtle, turbulent motives of people in conflict.

Thunder on Sycamore Street

Characters

FRANK MORRISON.
CLARICE MORRISON.
ROGER MORRISON.
CHRISTOPHER MORRISON.
ARTHUR HAYES.
PHYLLIS HAYES.
MR. HARKNESS.
JOSEPH BLAKE.
ANNA BLAKE.
JUDY BLAKE.
MRS. BLAKE.
CHARLIE DENTON.
MRS. CARSON.

ACT I

(*Fade in on a long shot of Sycamore Street in the pleasant and tidy village of Eastmont. It is 6:40 P.M. and just getting dark. We see three houses, modest but attractive, side by side, each an exact replica of the other. Each has a tiny front lawn and a tree or two in front of it. Each has been lived in and cared for by people who take pride in their own hard-won respectability. The street is quiet. Walking toward the houses now we see* ARTHUR HAYES, *a quiet, bespectacled man between thirty-five and thirty-eight years of age. He lives in the second of the three houses. He walks slowly, carrying a newspaper under his arm and smoking a pipe. He stops in front of his house and, almost in a daze, knocks the dottle out of his pipe against his heel. As he is doing this, we see* FRANK MORRISON *enter, also carrying a newspaper. He is a heavy man, forceful and aggressive, with a loud voice and a hearty laugh. He is about forty years of age.* FRANK MORRISON *lives right next door to* ARTHUR *in the first of the three houses. He sees* ARTHUR *and waves.*)

FRANK (*jovially*): Hey, Artie. How ya doin'?

(ARTHUR *is preoccupied. He doesn't register at first. He looks blankly at* FRANK.)

FRANK (*laughing*): Hey . . . wake up, boy. It's almost time for supper.

(ARTHUR *snaps out of it and forces a smile.*)

ARTHUR (*quietly*): Oh . . . hello, Frank. Sorry, I didn't see you.

FRANK: Didn't see me? Hey, wait till I tell Clarice. That diet she's got me on must be working. You have to look twice to see me! (*Laughing hard,* FRANK *reaches for his keys.*) That's a hot one!

(ARTHUR *smiles weakly.*)

FRANK: Say . . . isn't this late for you to be getting home?

ARTHUR: No, I don't think so. (*He looks at his watch.*) It's twenty to seven. I always get home about this time.

FRANK: Yeah. Well I wouldn't want you to be late tonight. You know what tonight is, don't you?

ARTHUR (*slowly*): Yes, I know what tonight is.

FRANK (*a little hard*): Good.

(*We hear footsteps and see a man walk by them. He is* JOSEPH BLAKE, *a man in his late thirties, a big, powerful, but quiet man.* JOSEPH BLAKE *lives in the third house on the street. As he walks by them, they both look at him silently.* ARTHUR *turns away then, but* FRANK *continues to stare at him. Camera moves in on* FRANK *as he stares coldly at* JOSEPH BLAKE. *His face is hard, full of hatred. The footsteps recede.*)

FRANK (*low*): See you later, Artie.

(FRANK *turns and fits the key into the lock. There is utter silence. He fumbles with the lock, then silently swings the door open. He walks into the small foyer. The living room ahead is brightly lighted, but we see no one.* FRANK *walks slowly, silently into the living room. As he enters it, we hear a dozen pistol shots.* FRANK *stiffens, clutches himself and falls to the floor as if dead. Then we hear a chorus of shrill screams and two small boys wearing cowboy hats and carrying pistols fling themselves upon* FRANK'S *body.* FRANK *doesn't move as they clamber over him. One is* ROGER, *age ten; the other is* CHRISTOPHER, *age six.* CHRISTOPHER *wears "Dr. Dentons."*)

CHRISTOPHER (*screaming*): I got him! I got him first.

ROGER: You did not!

CHRISTOPHER: I did so! Get offa him. I got him first. (*Calling*) Hey, Mom . . .

ROGER (*superior*): Boy, are you stupid! I got him three times before you even pulled the trigger.

CHRISTOPHER (*squeaking*): What d'ya mean? I got him before you even—(ROGER *tries to push* CHRISTOPHER *off* FRANK'S *still motionless body.*) Before you even—(CHRISTOPHER *grunts and fights back.*) Cut it out! Hey, Mom . . .

(CLARICE, FRANK'S *wife, a pleasant-looking woman in her early thirties, comes to living-room door from kitchen. She wears an apron. She calls out before she sees them.*)

CLARICE: Now you boys stop that noise. (*She sees* ROGER *pushing* CHRISTOPHER.) Roger!

CHRISTOPHER: Cut it out, willya. I got him—

CLARICE: Roger! Stop that pushing. . . .

CHRISTOPHER: I'm gonna sock you. . . .

CLARICE (*angrily*): Christopher, don't you dare! Frank! Will you do something . . . please!

ROGER: Go ahead. Sock me. You couldn't hurt a flea!

CHRISTOPHER (*winding up*): Who says so?

ROGER: Boy, you must be deaf. I said so!

CLARICE: Frank!

(*As* CHRISTOPHER *swings at* ROGER, FRANK *suddenly comes to life with a tremendous roar. He rolls over, toppling both boys to the floor and with lightning swiftness he grabs both of their cap pistols. He stands up grinning. They both look at him, startled.*)

FRANK (*barking*): Get up! (*They both do, slowly.*) Get your hands up! (*They look at each other.*) Make it snappy if you don't want to draw lead. (CHRISTOPHER *shrugs and raises his hands.*) (*To* ROGER) You too, hombre!

ROGER: Aaaah, Dad . . .

FRANK: Last warning.

ROGER (*disgusted*): Come on . . . (FRANK *shoots him with the cap pistol.*) What are you so serious about?

(*He walks away.* FRANK *watches him, still not giving up the cowboy pose.*)

CLARICE: All right. Now that's enough gunplay. All three of you can just settle down. (*To* FRANK) Hand 'em over.

(*He grins and gives her the guns. Then he bends over and kisses her.*)

FRANK: Hello, honey.

(*She kisses him dutifully, then speaks to* ROGER, *handing him the guns.*)

CLARICE: Put these in your room and come back with your hands washed. We're sitting down to supper right now.

ROGER (*desperately*): Right now? I gotta watch "Rangebusters."

CLARICE: Not tonight. I told you we were eating early.

ROGER: Ah, Mom . . . please . . .

CLARICE: Absolutely not. Come on, now. Inside . . .

(ROGER *slumps off*. CLARICE *turns to* CHRISTOPHER *as* FRANK *begins to take off his coat.*)

CLARICE: And you're going to bed, mister.

CHRISTOPHER: No! I can't go to bed!

CLARICE: Christopher!

CHRISTOPHER (*backing away*): I'm not tired yet. Honest!

(FRANK *is hanging his coat up in the foyer.* CLARICE *advances toward* CHRIS, *who looks for means of escape.*)

CLARICE: I'm not going to argue with you.

CHRISTOPHER: Mom, fifteen minutes. Come on. Please . . .

CLARICE: I'm going to start counting. One, two—

CHRISTOPHER (*fast*): Three four five six seven eight nine ten.

(*He runs away from her, but right into the arms of* FRANK, *who picks him up.*)

FRANK: Trapped! Let's go, pal.

CHRISTOPHER: Aaah . . .

(FRANK *carries him past* CLARICE, *who kisses him on the way by. As they reach the door which leads into bedroom,* ROGER *comes out.* CHRISTOPHER, *in his father's arms, raps* ROGER *on the head with his knuckle.*)

ROGER: Hey!
CHRISTOPHER (*grinning*): Good night, Rog.
ROGER: Stupid!
FRANK: All right, now. That's enough out of both of you. I don't want to hear another peep.

(FRANK *takes* CHRISTOPHER *into bedroom. Camera follows* ROGER *over to a dining table set at one end of living room near a picture window. This would probably be an L-shaped living room-dining room set-up and would be exactly the same in all three houses. The only difference in the three interior sets will be the way in which they are decorated. There are dishes on the table, glassware, etc.* ROGER *slumps into his chair and takes a piece of bread. He munches on it as* CLARICE *comes in from kitchen carrying a steaming bowl of stew. She sets it down and sits down.*)

CLARICE (*calling*): Frank!
FRANK (*off*): Okay. I'll be right there.
ROGER: Hey, Mom, what are we eating so early for?
CLARICE (*serving*): Don't say "Hey, Mom."
ROGER: Well, what are we eating so early for?
CLARICE: Because we feel like eating early. (*Calling.*) Frank!

(FRANK *walks in, loosening his tie.*)

FRANK: What's for supper?
CLARICE: Beef stew.
ROGER: Look, if I could see the first five minutes of "Rangebusters"—

(CLARICE *ladles out the stew as* FRANK *sits at the table.*)

CLARICE: Roger, I'm not going to tell you again.
ROGER (*anguished*): But, Mom, you don't know what's happening. There's this sneaky guy—
FRANK: Come on, boy, dig into your dinner.

(ROGER *makes a face and gives up the battle.*)

FRANK (*to* CLARICE): What time is the sitter coming?

CLARICE: Ten after seven. Do you know that's the third time today you've asked me.

FRANK: Just want to be sure.

CLARICE: I don't see why they have to make it so early anyway.

(FRANK *has a mouthful of food, so he shrugs.*)

ROGER: Make what so early, Dad?

CLARICE: Nothing. Eat your dinner.

FRANK: Good stew.

CLARICE: There's plenty more.

FRANK (*chewing*): Mmmm. Hmmmm. Do anything special today, Rog?

ROGER: Nope. Just kinda hung around.

FRANK: Well, I don't know why you don't get out and do something. A boy your age . . .

ROGER: Some of the kids dumped garbage on the Blakes' lawn again.

FRANK (*casually*): That so? What about you?

ROGER: Ah, what fun is that after you do it a couple of times?

FRANK (*chewing*): Mmmm. Hey, how about eating your stew.

ROGER: I'm not hungry.

CLARICE: Frank, I wish you'd do something about that boy's eating. He's beginning to look like a scarecrow.

FRANK: He'll be all right. What time is it?

CLARICE (*looking at watch*): Five of seven.

FRANK: We'd better snap it up.

CLARICE: Plenty of time. I'm leaving the dishes till later.

FRANK: Y'know, Clarry, this really ought to be something tonight.

(ROGER *starts to get up, but stops.*)

ROGER: What ought to be something?

CLARICE: You just sit down and pay attention to your dinner. There's a glass of milk to be finished before you get up.

ROGER (*grudgingly*): Okay. (*He sips the milk for a moment.*) Where you going tonight, Dad?

FRANK: We're going for a little walk.

ROGER: Well, what d'ya have to go out so early for?

FRANK: Just like that.

ROGER (*aggressively*): Well, what the heck is the big secret, that's what I'd like to know. Everybody's acting so mysterious.

FRANK (*sharply*): That's enough. Now I don't want to hear any more questions out of you. Your mother and I have some business to attend to, and that's it. You mind yours.

(ROGER, *stunned, looks at his father, then down at his plate. There is an awkward silence.* FRANK *eats stolidly. They watch him.*)

FRANK (*to* CLARICE): Where's that sitter?

CLARICE: It's not time yet. Take it easy, Frank.

(FRANK *gets up from the table, goes over to a box of cigars on top of the TV set and lights one.* CLARICE *and* ROGER *watch him silently.*)

CLARICE: Aren't you going to have some dessert, Frank? There's some cherry pie left.

FRANK: I'll have it later.

(*He puffs on the cigar.*)

ROGER (*low*): I'm sorry, Dad.

FRANK (*turning*): Well, it's about time you learned some respect, d'you hear me? If I want you to know something I'll tell it to you.

ROGER (*softly*): Okay . . .

CLARICE (*quickly*): Have some pie, honey. I heated it special.

(FRANK *goes to the table and sits down. He puts the cigar down and* CLARICE *begins to cut him some pie.*)

CLARICE: How late do you think we'll be, Frank?

FRANK: I don't know.

CLARICE: Do you think I ought to pack a thermos of hot coffee? It's going to be chilly.

FRANK: Might not be a bad idea.

(FRANK *now begins to show the first signs of being excited about the evening. He speaks, almost to himself.*)

FRANK: Boy, I can't wait till I see his face. The nerve of him. The absolute nerve. (*Grinning.*) What d'you think he'll do when we all—

CLARICE (*looking at* ROGER): Frank . . .

FRANK (*as* ROGER *stares*): Oh. Yeah, go ahead, Rog. You can turn on your program.

ROGER: Gee thanks, Dad.

(*He jumps up, goes to the TV set and turns it on.* FRANK *and* CLARICE *watch him get settled in front of TV set. We hear dialogue from set faintly.* ROGER *watches in background, enraptured.*)

FRANK (*quietly*): What are they saying on the block?

CLARICE: I didn't speak to anyone. I was ironing all day.

FRANK: Charlie Denton called me at the office. I was right in the middle of taking an order from Martin Brothers for three A-81 tractors.

CLARICE: Three? Frank, that's *wonderful!*

FRANK: Not bad. Anyway, I made Mr. Martin wait while I spoke to Charlie. Charlie says it's gonna be one hundred percent. Every family on the block. He just called to tell me that.

CLARICE: Well, that's good. Everyone should be in on this.

FRANK (*eating*): Clarry, I'm telling you this is going to be a job well done. It's how you have to do these things. Everybody getting together first . . . and boom, it's over. I can't wait till it's started. It's been long enough.

CLARICE: I saw her out the window today, hanging clothes in her yard like nothing was wrong. She didn't even look this way.

FRANK: What time is it?

CLARICE: Now you just asked me two minutes ago. It's about three minutes to seven. What's the matter with you? You'll be getting yourself an ulcer over this thing. Relax, Frank. Here, have some more pie.

FRANK: No. No more.

(*He gets up and walks around nervously, slapping his fist into his palm.* ROGER *is looking at him now. He is tense, excited, completely caught up in the impending event.*)

FRANK: This is something big, you know that, Clarry? We're getting action without pussyfooting for once. That's it. That's the big part. There's too much pussyfooting going on all the time. Can't hurt anyone's feelings. Every time you turn around you're hurting some idiot's feelings. Well that's tough, I say. . . .

CLARICE (*indicating* ROGER): Frank . . .

FRANK: He can hear! He's old enough. You want something bad, you gotta go out and get it! That's how this world is. Boy, I like this, Clarry. You know what it makes me feel like? It makes me feel like a man!

(*He stalks up and down the room for a few moments as they watch him. Then he goes to the window and stands there looking out.*)

CLARICE (*quietly*): I think I'll just stack the dishes.

(*She starts to do it. The doorbell rings.* ROGER *jumps up.*)

ROGER: I'll get it.

(*He goes to the door and opens it.* ARTHUR HAYES *stands there a bit apologetically. He wears no overcoat, having just come from next door. He looks extremely upset.*)

ARTHUR: Rog, is your dad in?
ROGER: Sure. Come on in, Mr. Hayes.

(ARTHUR *walks in slowly.* FRANK *turns around, still excited. He goes over to* ARTHUR.)

FRANK (*loud*): Hey, Artie. Come on in.
ARTHUR: Hello, Frank . . .
FRANK (*laughing*): What can I do for you? (ARTHUR *looks hesitatingly at* ROGER.) Oh, sure. Rog, go help your mother.
ROGER (*annoyed*): Okay . . .

(*He walks off to dining table.*)

FRANK (*chuckling*): That's some kid, isn't he, Artie?
How old is yours now?

ARTHUR: Twenty-one months.

FRANK: Yeah. Well that's still nothing but a crying machine. Wait a couple years. He'll kill you.

ARTHUR: I guess so.

FRANK: And how! Sit down for a minute, Artie. What's on your mind?

ARTHUR (*sitting. Hesitantly*): Well, I don't know . . .
I just . . . well . . . I just wanted . . . to talk.

FRANK: No kidding. Say, y'know you look a little green around the gills? What's the matter?

(ARTHUR HAYES *takes off his eyeglasses and begins to polish them, a nervous habit in which he indulges when upset.*)

ARTHUR: Nothing. I've had an upset stomach for a couple of days. Maybe that's it.

FRANK (*nodding*): Yeah, that'll get you down all right.
Probably a virus.

(ARTHUR *nods and they look at each other awkwardly for a moment.*)

FRANK: Well, what did you want to talk to me about?

(ARTHUR *looks at the floor, trying to frame his answer carefully, afraid to offend. Finally he blurts it out.*)

ARTHUR: What do you think about this thing tonight?

FRANK (*surprised*): What do you mean what do I think about it?

ARTHUR: Well, I've been kind of going over it all day,
Frank. I talked with Phyllis before.

FRANK (*a little hard*): And . . .

ARTHUR: Well, it was just talk. We were just talking it over to get clear on it, you know.

FRANK: Go ahead.

ARTHUR: And . . . well, look, Frank, it's a pretty hard thing. Supposing it were you?

FRANK: It's not.

ARTHUR: Well, I know that, but supposing it were?

(FRANK *stands up and goes over to* ARTHUR.)

FRANK: Your glasses are clean. You wear 'em out, you have to buy a new pair. (ARTHUR *looks down at his glasses, then puts them on nervously.*) Now what about it, Artie? What if I was the guy?

ARTHUR: Well, you know . . . how would you feel?

FRANK: How would I feel, huh? Now that's a good question, Artie. I'll answer it for you. It doesn't make any difference how I'd feel. Now let me ask you a question. Is he a lifelong buddy of yours?

ARTHUR: Well, now, you know he's not, Frank.

FRANK: Do you know him to say hello to?

ARTHUR: That's not the idea. He's—

FRANK: Artie . . . you don't even know the guy. What are you getting yourself all hot and bothered about? We all agreed, didn't we?

ARTHUR: Yes . . . everybody agreed.

FRANK: You. Me. The Dentons. The McAllisters. The Fredericks. The Schofields. Every family on Sycamore Street for that matter. We all agreed. That's how it is. The majority. Right?

ARTHUR: Well . . . I think we all ought to talk it over, maybe. Let it wait a few days.

(*He takes off his glasses again and begins to wipe them.*)

FRANK: Artie . . . we talked it over. (FRANK *takes the handkerchief out of* ARTHUR's *hand and tucks it into his pocket.*) In about ten minutes we're starting. We expect to have a solid front, you know what I mean? Everybody. You included. You're my next door neighbor, boy. I don't want to hear people saying Artie Hayes wasn't there.

ARTHUR (*hesitantly*): Well, I don't know, Frank. I thought—

(*The phone rings.* FRANK *goes toward it.*)

FRANK: Go home, Artie. Don't worry about it. I'll see you in a few minutes. (FRANK *goes to the phone and picks it up.* ARTHUR *stares at him.*) Hello . . . (ARTHUR *turns away and walks slowly to door.*) Speaking.

(ARTHUR *goes out, dazed and frightened.* CLARICE *comes into living room and stands waiting as* FRANK *listens to phone.*)

FRANK (*angry*): What do you mean you can't get here? (*Pause.*) Well, this is a great time to call! (*Pause.*) I know. Yeah. (*He slams the phone down. To* CLARICE.) Our sitter can't get here. How d'you like that?

CLARICE: What's wrong with her?

FRANK: I don't know. She's got a cold, or something. Nice dependable girl you pick.

CLARICE (*snapping*): Well, I didn't exactly arrange for her to get a cold, you know.

FRANK: Look, Clarry, we're going to this thing no matter what.

CLARICE: Well, I'm not leaving Chris with Roger. They'll claw each other to pieces.

FRANK: Then we'll take them with us.

CLARICE: You wouldn't . . .

FRANK: Who wouldn't? We're doing it for them as much as anyone else, aren't we? Well, they might as well see it.

CLARICE: Maybe I'd better stay home with them.

FRANK: No, sir. You've been in on this from the beginning. You're going. Come on, get Chris dressed. We haven't got much time.

CLARICE: Well . . . whatever you think, Frank . . .

FRANK: I'm telling you it's all right. Won't hurt 'em a bit. (*To* ROGER) What d'you say, son? Want to come along?

ROGER (*eagerly*): Oh, boy! Really? (FRANK *nods and grins.* ROGER *leaps happily.*) Gee, Dad, you're the greatest guy in all the whole world.

(*He runs over and hugs* FRANK.)

FRANK (*grinning*): Go on, Clarry. Make it snappy.

(CLARICE *goes into the bedroom. Doorbell rings.*)

ROGER: I'll get it, Dad.

(He runs to the door and opens it. CHARLIE DENTON, *forty years old and eager as a child, stands there. He comes in fast, excited.)*

CHARLIE: Hiya, Rog. Frank, you all set?

FRANK: Hello, Charlie. Another minute or two. How's it look?

CHARLIE: Great. I'm checking house to house. Everybody's ready.

FRANK: Good. Any changes?

CHARLIE: Nope. It's gonna be fast and quiet. What time you got?

FRANK *(calling)*: Clarry, what time is it?

CLARICE *(calling)*: Twelve after.

CHARLIE *(looking at watch)*: Make it thirteen. At fifteen we go.

FRANK: Right. Hey listen, you better look in on Artie Hayes next door. He's been acting a little peculiar.

CHARLIE: I spoke to him a little while ago on the street. I think he was coming over to see you. Don't worry about a thing. I'll be watching him. See you, Frank. Let's make this good.

FRANK: You bet we will. It looks like a beaut. Take off. *(CHARLIE goes out fast.)* Get on your coat, Rog. *(Calling.)* Clarry!

(ROGER goes to closet and begins to get his coat. FRANK *stalks nervously up and down.)*

CLARICE *(calling)*: In a minute . . .

(FRANK goes to the window and looks out. He watches and waits. We can see the excitement building within him. ROGER, *hat and coat on, joins him at window.* FRANK *puts his arm on* ROGER's *shoulder and talks, half to himself.)*

FRANK *(low)*: How do you like that Artie Hayes? Maybe we ought to think it over! I could've belted him one. How do you like that guy!

ROGER: What do you mean, Dad?

FRANK *(calling)*: Clarry!

CLARICE *(calling)*: Here I am. Come on, Chris.

(CLARICE *walks into living room followed by a very sleepy* CHRISTOPHER. *He is in his hat and coat. He wanders over to* FRANK.)

FRANK: What time is it?
CLARICE: Almost fourteen after.
FRANK: Almost fifteen. Put on your coat.

(CLARICE *goes to the closet and does so.* FRANK *follows her and gets his. He puts it on.* CLARICE *picks up a large thermos from the foyer table.*)

CLARICE (*low*): Frank . . . I'm busting with excitement.
FRANK (*low*): Yeah. So'm I, honey. (*Louder.*) Come over here, boys. (*The two boys walk over to them.*) Stand here.

(*They wait now behind the closed front door, all four of them tense, quiet, hardly able to stand the suspense. They wait for several seconds, and then, in the street, we begin to hear the heavy tread of marching feet.*)

CHRISTOPHER: Hey, Daddy . . . where we going?
FRANK: Ssh. Be quiet, son.

(*He bends over and picks* CHRISTOPHER *up. The sound of marching feet grows louder and stronger. They wait till it reaches a crescendo.* FRANK *speaks quietly now.*)

FRANK: Let's go.

(*He opens the front door and they walk into a mob of grimly advancing men and women. They join the mob and walk with them quietly, and the only sound we hear is the frightening noise of the tramping feet. Fade out.*)

ACT II

(*Fade in on long shot of Sycamore Street. It is once again 6:40 P.M., the same night. We have gone backward in time and we now duplicate exactly the scene which opened Act I.* ARTHUR HAYES *walks on, stops in front of his house, knocks his pipe against his heel.* FRANK MORRISON *enters. Each of the movements they make, the attitudes they strike and the inflections they use must be exact imitations of the Act I business. The audience must feel that this scene is a clip of film which we are rerunning.*)

FRANK (*jovially*): Hey, Artie. How ya doin'?

(ARTHUR *is preoccupied. He doesn't register at first. He looks blankly at* FRANK.)

FRANK (*laughing*): Hey . . . wake up, boy. It's almost time for supper.

(ARTHUR *snaps out of it and forces a smile.*)

ARTHUR (*quietly*): Oh . . . hello, Frank. Sorry. I didn't see you.

FRANK: Didn't see me? Hey, wait till I tell Clarice. That diet she's got me on must be working. You have to look twice to see me! (*Laughing hard,* FRANK *reaches for his keys.*) That's a hot one! (ARTHUR *smiles weakly.*) Say . . . isn't this late for you to be getting home?

ARTHUR: No, I don't think so. (*He looks at his watch.*) It's twenty to seven. I always get home about this time.

FRANK: Yeah. Well, I wouldn't want you to be late tonight. You know what tonight is, don't you?

ARTHUR (*slowly*): Yes, I know what tonight is.

FRANK (*a little hard*): Good.

(*We hear footsteps and see a man walk by them. He is* JOSEPH BLAKE, *a man in his late thirties, a big, powerful, but quiet man.* JOSEPH BLAKE *lives in the third house on the street. As he walks by them they both look at him silently. And now, for the first time, this scene moves in a different direction than did the scene at the beginning of Act I. Instead of coming in close on* FRANK, *the camera comes in close on* ARTHUR HAYES *as he stands nervously in front of his door, afraid to look at either* JOSEPH BLAKE *or* FRANK MORRISON. *We hear* JOSEPH'S *footsteps fade out.* ARTHUR *reaches for his keys.*)

FRANK (*low, off*): See you later, Artie.

(ARTHUR *winces at this. We hear* FRANK'S *door open-ing and closing softly.* ARTHUR *turns now and looks off at* JOSEPH BLAKE'S *house for a moment. Then he turns and opens his door. As he enters his foyer we hear dance music playing softly. The living room is lighted, and look-ing in from the foyer, we can see* MR. HARKNESS, ARTHUR'S *father-in-law, seated in an armchair, reading the news-paper. He is perhaps sixty-five years old, and usually does nothing more than sit reading the newspapers. He looks up as* ARTHUR *comes in.*)

MR. HARKNESS: Hello, Arthur. (*Calling off.*) Here he is, Phyllis. (*To* ARTHUR) Little bit late, aren't you?

(ARTHUR *is hanging up his coat. He is obviously wor-ried. His face shows concern. His entire manner is sub-dued. He speaks quietly, even for* ARTHUR.)

ARTHUR: No. Usual time.

(MR. HARKNESS *takes out a pocket watch, looks at it, shakes it.*)

MR. HARKNESS: Mmm. Must be fast.

(*He goes back to his newspaper.* ARTHUR *walks into the living room tiredly.*)

ARTHUR (*not caring*): How's your cough?

MR. HARKNESS (*reading*): Still got it. I guess I must've swigged enough cough syrup to float a rowboat today. Waste of time and money!

(PHYLLIS *enters from kitchen as* ARTHUR *goes over to phonograph from which the dance music is blasting. He is just ready to turn it off as she enters.*)

MR. HARKNESS: Cough'll go away by itself like it always does.

PHYLLIS (*brightly*): Hello, darling. Ah . . . don't turn it off.

(*He turns as she walks over to him. She kisses him pos-sessively and leads him away from the phonograph. The music continues.*)

PHYLLIS: How did it go today, dear?
ARTHUR: All right. Nothing special.
PHYLLIS: What about the Franklin closing?
ARTHUR: It's called off till tomorrow.
PHYLLIS: How come?
ARTHUR: I didn't ask them.
PHYLLIS: Well, you'd think they'd at least give you a reason. You should've asked. I don't like it when people push you around like that.

(ARTHUR *goes over to a chair without answering. A pipe is on an end table next to the chair. He begins to fill it.* PHYLLIS *goes to a small bar on which is a cocktail shaker and one glass. She picks up the shaker.*)

ARTHUR: What's that?
PHYLLIS: I made you a drink.
ARTHUR: No. No thanks. I don't want a drink now.
PHYLLIS: Oh, Artie! I made it specially for you. You look tired. Come on, it'll do you good. (*She begins to pour the drink.*) Sit down, dear. I'll bring it over to you.

(ARTHUR *sits down.* PHYLLIS *finishes pouring the drink and brings it to him. He takes it. She waits, smiling, for him to drink it.*)

ARTHUR: How come you made me a drink tonight?
PHYLLIS: Just for luck. Taste it. (*She sits on the arm of the chair. He tastes it slowly. She puts her arm around him.*) Good?
ARTHUR (*slowly*): It's good.
PHYLLIS: I thought you'd like it.
ARTHUR: Where's Billy?
PHYLLIS: Asleep.
ARTHUR: Isn't it kind of early?
PHYLLIS: He didn't get much of a nap today. The poor baby couldn't keep his eyes open. Artie, he's getting to be such a devil. You should've seen him this afternoon. He got into my bag and took my lipstick. If I only could've taken a picture of his face. He walked into the kitchen and I swear I almost screamed. You never saw anything so red in your life. Drink your drink, darling. It took me ten minutes to scrub it off.

(*Obediently,* ARTHUR *sips his drink.*)

ARTHUR (*mildly*): I'd like to have seen him before he went to bed.

PHYLLIS: Now you know I had to get finished early tonight, Artie. (*She gets up and goes toward the kitchen.*) We're eating in a few minutes. I'm just making melted cheese sandwiches. We can have a snack later if you're hungry.

ARTHUR: Later?

PHYLLIS (*looking at him oddly*): Yes, later. When we get back.

(ARTHUR *puts his drink down. All of his movements are slow, almost mechanical, as if he has that day aged twenty years.* PHYLLIS *goes into the kitchen. He takes off his glasses and begins polishing them.*)

MR. HARKNESS: Melted cheese sandwiches.

ARTHUR (*not hearing*): What?

MR. HARKNESS: I said melted cheese sandwiches. That gluey cheese. Do you like it?

ARTHUR: No.

MR. HARKNESS: Me neither. Never did.

(*He goes back to his paper.* ARTHUR *gets up and goes to phonograph. He stands over it, listening.* PHYLLIS *comes in carrying a tray on which are three glasses of tomato juice. She gives it to* ARTHUR.)

PHYLLIS: Put these on the table like a good boy. (*He takes it and looks at her strangely.*) What's the matter with you, Artie? You've hardly said a word since you got home . . . and you keep looking at me. Are you sick, or something?

ARTHUR: No. I'm not sick.

PHYLLIS: Here, let me feel your head. (*She does so.*) No, you feel all right. What is it?

ARTHUR: Nothing. I'm just tired, I guess.

PHYLLIS: Well, I hope you perk up a little.

(*She goes off into kitchen.* ARTHUR *goes slowly to dining table, which is set in the same spot as the Morrison dining table. He puts the glasses on it, and sets the tray on the end table. He takes a sip of his drink.* PHYLLIS *comes in from the kitchen carrying a platter of melted cheese sandwiches. She goes to the table, puts it down.*)

PHYLLIS: Dinner. Come on, Dad, while they're hot. Artie . . .

ARTHUR: You go ahead. I'm not hungry.

PHYLLIS: Oh, now, let's not start that. You have to eat. Try one. They're nice and runny.

ARTHUR: Really, I'm not hungry.

PHYLLIS: Well, you can at least sit with us. I haven't seen you since half-past eight this morning.

(ARTHUR *goes slowly over to the table and sits down.* MR. HARKNESS *ambles over.*)

MR. HARKNESS: Well, I'm good and hungry. Tell you that. Got any pickles?

PHYLLIS: No pickles. You know they give you heartburn.

MR. HARKNESS: Haven't had heartburn in a long time. Wouldn't mind a slight case if it came from pickles.

(*They are all seated now,* PHYLLIS *facing the window.* ARTHUR *sits quietly.* MR. HARKNESS *busies himself drinking water while* PHYLLIS *serves the sandwiches, potato salad, etc.*)

PHYLLIS: Artie . . . potato salad?

ARTHUR: No. Look, Phyllis . . .

PHYLLIS: Just a little.

(*She puts a spoonful on a heavily loaded plate and passes it to him. He takes it. Now she serves her father.*)

PHYLLIS: Potato salad, Dad?

MR. HARKNESS: I'll help myself.

(*She puts the bowl down and helps herself as does* MR. HARKNESS.)

PHYLLIS (*brightly*): What happened at the office, dear? Anything new?

ARTHUR: No. It was quiet.

PHYLLIS: Did you hear about the Walkers wanting to sell their house?

ARTHUR: No.

PHYLLIS: You know, for a real-estate man you hear less about real estate than anyone I ever saw. I spoke to Margie Walker this morning. I just got to her in time. You're going to handle the sale. She told me she hadn't even thought of you till I called. Why is that, dear?

ARTHUR: I don't know why it is.

PHYLLIS: Well, anyway, she's expecting you to call her tomorrow. It ought to be a very nice sale for you, dear.

(ARTHUR *nods and looks down at his plate. There is silence for a moment.*)

MR. HARKNESS (*chewing*): This stuff gets under my teeth.

PHYLLIS: Dad!

MR. HARKNESS: Well, I can't help it, can I?

(*They eat for a moment and then* PHYLLIS, *looking out the window, sees movement in the house next door, the Blake house. She can no longer hold back the topic she's been trying not to discuss in front of* ARTHUR.)

PHYLLIS: Look at them. Every shade in the house is down. (*She looks at her watch.*) There isn't much more time. I wonder if they know. Do you think they do, Artie?

ARTHUR (*tired*): I don't know.

PHYLLIS: They must. You can't keep a thing like this secret. I wonder how they feel. (*She looks at* ARTHUR.) Artie, aren't you going to eat your dinner?

ARTHUR (*slowly*): How can you talk about them and my dinner in the same breath?

PHYLLIS: For Heaven's sakes . . . I don't know what's the matter with you tonight.

ARTHUR (*quietly*): You don't, do you?

(*He gets up from the table and walks over to the phonograph. He stands there holding it with both hands, listening to the slick dance music. Then abruptly, he turns it off.* PHYLLIS *looks as if she is about to protest, but then decides not to.*)

MR. HARKNESS: What d'you suppose is gonna happen over there? Boy, wouldn't I like to go along tonight.

PHYLLIS (*looking at* ARTHUR): Dad, will you please stop.

MR. HARKNESS: Well, I would! How do you think it feels to be sixty-two years old and baby-sitting when there's real action going on right under your nose? Something a man wants to get into.

ARTHUR (*turning*): Be quiet!

MR. HARKNESS: Now listen here—

ARTHUR: I said be quiet!

(*He takes off his glasses and walks over to the table.*)

PHYLLIS: Artie, stop it! There's no need for you to raise your voice like that.

(ARTHUR *speaks more quietly now, feeling perhaps that he has gone too far.*)

ARTHUR: Then tell your father to keep his ideas to himself!

MR. HARKNESS (*angrily*): Wait a minute!

(PHYLLIS, *in the ensuing argument, is quiet, calm, convincing, never losing her temper, always trying to soothe* ARTHUR, *to sweeten the ugly things she says by saying them gently.*)

PHYLLIS: Dad, be quiet. Listen, Artie, I know you're tired, darling, but there's something we might as well face. In about fifteen or twenty minutes you and I and a group of our friends and neighbors are going to be marching on that house next door. Maybe it's not such a pleasant thing to look forward to, but something has to be done. You know that, Artie. You agreed to it with all the others.

ARTHUR: I didn't agree to anything. You agreed for the Hayes household. Remember?

PHYLLIS: All right, I agreed. I didn't hear you disagreeing. Oh, what's the difference, darling? You've been acting like there's a ten-ton weight on your back ever since you heard about it. And there's no point to it. It's all decided.

ARTHUR: All decided. What right have we got to decide?

PHYLLIS: It's not a question of right, Artie. Don't you see? It's something we have to do, right or wrong. Do you want them to live next door to you? Do you really want them?

ARTHUR: I always thought a man was supposed to be able to live anywhere he chooses no matter what anyone else wants.

PHYLLIS: But, dear, this isn't anywhere. This is Sycamore Street. It's not some back alley in a slum! This is a respectable neighborhood. Artie, let's be realistic. That's one of the few things we can really say we have. We're respectable. Do you remember how hard we worked to get that way?

ARTHUR: Respectable! Phyllis, for Heaven's sakes. We're talking about throwing a man out of his own home. What is the man? He's not a monster. He's a quiet guy who minds his own business. How does that destroy our respectability?

PHYLLIS (*hard*): He got out of prison two months ago. He's a common hoodlum.

ARTHUR: We don't know for sure.

PHYLLIS: We know. Charlie Denton doesn't lie. He saw the man's picture in the Rockville papers just fifty miles from here the day he got out. Tell me, what does he do for a living? Where did he get the money to buy that house?

ARTHUR: I don't think that's any of your business.

PHYLLIS: But, Artie, the man was in jail for four years. That's our business! How do you know what he did? How do you know he won't do it again?

ARTHUR: We have police.

PHYLLIS: Police! Will the police stop his child from playing with Billy? What kind of a child must that be? Think about it. Her father is an ex-convict. That's a lovely thing to tell our friends. Why yes . . . you know Billy's little friend Judy. Of course you do. Her father spent a great deal of time in prison. Charming people. It's beautiful for the neighborhood, isn't it, Artie? It makes real-estate prices just skyrocket up. Tell me, who do you think'll be moving in next . . . and where'll we go?

(ARTHUR *doesn't answer. He sits down in a chair,*

troubled, trying to find an argument. PHYLLIS *watches him closely.*)

MR. HARKNESS: Listen, Artie—

(*But* PHYLLIS *puts her hand on his arm to shut him up.* ARTHUR *is thinking and she wants to see if her argument has worked.*)

ARTHUR: Look, Phyllis, this is a mob we're getting together. We're going to order this man out of his house . . . or we're going to throw him out. What right have we got to do it? Maybe most of us'd rather not have him as a neighbor, but, Phyllis, the man is a human being, not an old dog. This is an ugly thing we're doing. . . .

PHYLLIS: We've got to do something to keep our homes decent. There's no other way. Somebody's always got to lose, Artie. Why should it be all of us when there's only one of him?

ARTHUR: I . . . I don't know.

(ARTHUR *suddenly gets up and goes toward the front door as if going out. He buttons his jacket.* PHYLLIS *gets up, concerned.*)

PHYLLIS: Where are you going?

ARTHUR: I'm going to talk to Frank Morrison.

PHYLLIS: All right. Maybe Frank'll make sense to you. (*Calling.*) Wear your coat.

(*But* ARTHUR *has opened the door and intends to go out without it.* PHYLLIS *looks at her watch.*)

PHYLLIS: Arthur, it's freezing out! (*He is outside the door now.*) You'll catch cold. (*The door closes. She stands watching after him, obviously upset. Her father resumes his eating. She looks at the door for a long time. Then, without looking around*) Dad . . .

MR. HARKNESS: Mmmm?

PHYLLIS: What do you think he'll do?

MR. HARKNESS: Well . . . I don't know. You got any more of these cheese businesses? I'm hungry.

PHYLLIS: No.

(*She goes to the window and looks out.*)

MR. HARKNESS: Why don't you sit down, Phyl? He'll be all right.

PHYLLIS: What do you mean all right? Look at him. He's standing in front of Frank's house afraid to ring the bell.

MR. HARKNESS: He'll calm down. Come away from that window and sit down. Have some coffee.

(*She moves away from window and sits at table.*)

PHYLLIS: I've never seen him like this before.

MR. HARKNESS: Well, what are you worried about? Tell you what. I'll go along with you. Boy, wouldn't I like to be in on a thing like this once. Let Artie stay home and mind the baby if that's how he feels.

(PHYLLIS *turns to her father violently and for the first time we see how much* ARTHUR'S *decision means to her.*)

PHYLLIS (*fiercely*): He's got to go! Don't you understand?

MR. HARKNESS: What the dickens is eating you? No, I don't understand. (PHYLLIS *gets up and goes to the window. She looks out tensely.*) Would you mind telling me what you're talking about?

PHYLLIS (*startled*): Oh no!

(*She turns and runs to the front door. She starts to open it and run out. As she gets it half open we hear a low voice calling,* CHARLIE DENTON'S *voice.*)

CHARLIE (*low*): Artie! Hey, Artie!

(*She closes the door silently and stands against it, frightened. Cut to street in front of* FRANK'S *house.* ARTHUR *stands there, having just been hailed by* CHARLIE. *He turns, and then we see* CHARLIE *hurrying down the street toward him.* CHARLIE *gets to him, takes him by the arm.*)

CHARLIE (*low*): What are you doing out here now?

ARTHUR (*guiltily*): Nothing. I was . . . well, I was getting some air, that's all.

CHARLIE: Look, boy, this thing has got to be timed on

the button. Everybody's supposed to be in his house right now. Nobody's supposed to be wandering around the streets. What time've you got?

ARTHUR (*with an effort*): Listen, Charlie, I want to talk to you about tonight.

CHARLIE: I haven't got time to talk.

ARTHUR: Please. It's important.

CHARLIE (*tough*): What the heck's the matter with you?

ARTHUR: Nothing. Nothing, Charlie . . .

CHARLIE: What time've you got? (*He grabs* ARTHUR'S *wrist and holds it up to the light. He holds his own wrist next to it and compares the watches.*) You're three minutes *slow.*

ARTHUR: I know. This watch . . . it runs slow, Charlie . . .

CHARLIE: Well, fix it, will ya? The timing's the most important part.

ARTHUR: I will. Look, about this thing tonight . . .

CHARLIE: Listen, if you're gonna start in with me about the plan, take it up with the committee, will ya, please? All of a sudden everybody's an expert on how to run the show. If you want the organizing job I'll be glad to give it to you.

ARTHUR: No, it's not that. It's organized very well. There's something else.

CHARLIE: Are you gonna fix that watch?

ARTHUR: I will. I've been meaning to set it all day. Listen . . . these people . . . the Blakes. They've got a kid . . .

CHARLIE: So has my mother. Here, gimme this. (*He grabs* ARTHUR'S *wrist and sets his watch.*) There. At seven-fifteen on the nose we go. Now get back into your house.

(*He walks off fast.*)

ARTHUR: Charlie . . .

(*But* CHARLIE *keeps going.* ARTHUR *watches him. Then he goes up to* FRANK MORRISON'S *front door and rings the bell. From inside we hear* ROGER *calling.*)

ROGER (*off*): I'll get it.

(ROGER *opens the front door, and now again,* ROGER'S *and* ARTHUR'S *movements must be exactly as they were in the first act, except that now the camera catches them from outside the house.*)

ARTHUR: Rog, is your Dad in?

ROGER: Sure. Come on in, Mr. Hayes.

(ARTHUR *walks in slowly. The door closes.*)

(*Fade out.*)

(*Fade in on the living room of* ARTHUR'S *house.* PHYLLIS *sits tensely waiting for him. The dining table is cleared.* MR. HARKNESS *is back in his easy chair reading the papers. We hear a key in the lock, the door opens and* ARTHUR *enters. He walks slowly, despising himself for not having been stronger with* FRANK *or* CHARLIE. PHYLLIS *gets up as he comes in. He doesn't look at her but walks over to the window and stands there. She comes up behind him. He doesn't turn around.*)

PHYLLIS: Artie . . . Artie, are you all right?

(*He turns around slowly, speaks heavily.*)

ARTHUR: Yeah, I'm fine.

PHYLLIS: What happened? What'd you say to them?

ARTHUR: I said nothing.

PHYLLIS (*hopefully*): Well, what do you mean you said nothing. Didn't you talk about it?

ARTHUR: No, I didn't talk about it. I didn't talk about anything. Will you leave me alone?

(*She backs away, alarmed. Then she looks at her watch.*)

PHYLLIS (*softly*): We only have a couple of minutes, dear.

ARTHUR: I'm not going out there.

PHYLLIS: I'd better get our coats.

ARTHUR: Did you hear what I just said?

PHYLLIS: We'll have to bundle up. It's only about twenty degrees out. Did you know that?

ARTHUR: I said I'm not going.

(PHYLLIS *backs away from him. He turns to the window. We can see that she is hugely upset, almost desperate. She looks at him fiercely.* MR. HARKNESS *gets up quietly with his paper and goes into the next room. We hear the door close.* ARTHUR *doesn't move.*)

PHYLLIS (*strongly*): I want to tell you something. I'm going to get our coats now, and we're going to put them on, and we're going to stand in the doorway of our house until it's seven-fifteen.

ARTHUR (*turning*): Stop it.

PHYLLIS: And then we're going to walk out into the gutter, you and me, the Hayes family, and we're going to be just like everybody else on Sycamore Street!

ARTHUR (*shouting*): Phyllis! I've told you . . . I'm not going to be a part of this thing!

(PHYLLIS *studies him for a long moment.*)

PHYLLIS: Listen to me, Artie. Listen to me good. I didn't think you needed to hear this before. But you're going to hear it now. We're going out there. Do you want to know why? Because we're not going to be next!

ARTHUR: You're out of your mind!

PHYLLIS (*roaring*): Sure I am! I'm out of my mind all right. I'm crazy with fear because I don't want to be different. I don't want my neighbors looking at us and wondering why we're not like them.

ARTHUR (*amazed*): Phyllis . . . you're making this up! They won't think that.

PHYLLIS: They will think that! We'll be the only ones, the odd ones who wanted to let an ex-convict live with us. They'll look the other way when we walk the streets. They'll become cold and nasty . . . and all of a sudden we won't have any neighbors. (*Pointing at the Blake house.*) We'll be like them!

(ARTHUR *stands looking at her and it begins to sink in. She knows it and goes after him.*)

PHYLLIS: We can't be different! We can't afford it! We live on the good will of these people. Your business is in this town. Your neighbors buy us the bread we eat! Do you want them to stop?

ARTHUR: I don't know . . . Phyllis . . . I don't know what to think . . . I . . . can't throw a stone at this man.

PHYLLIS (*strong*): You can! You've got to, or we're finished here.

(*He stares at her, not knowing what to say next. She has almost won and knows it. She looks at her watch.*)

PHYLLIS: Now just . . . wait . . . just stand there. . . .

(*She runs to the closet and takes out their overcoats. She throws hers on and brings his to him, holds it for him.*)

PHYLLIS: Put it on!

ARTHUR: I . . . can't. They're people. It's their home.

PHYLLIS (*shouting*): We're people too! I don't care what happens to them. I care what happens to us. We belong here. We've got to live here. Artie, for the love of God, we don't even know them. What's the difference what happens to them? What about us?

(*He has no answer. She begins to put his coat on. He stands there, beaten, wrecked, moving his arms automatically, no longer knowing the woman who is putting on his coat. She talks as she helps him.*)

PHYLLIS: There. It won't be long. I promise you. It won't be long. That's my Artie. That's my darling. Let's button up, dear. It's cold. We'll be back in an hour, and it'll be over. There. Now put on your gloves, darling.

(*She takes him by the arm and he stands there letting her do as she will. He puts on his gloves without knowing he is doing it, and they wait together, there in the doorway. She looks at him, trying to read him, as we begin to hear the cold and chilling sound of the tramping feet. MR. HARKNESS comes out of the bedroom and stands there looking at them. PHYLLIS looks at her watch. The tramping grows louder. They wait in silence. Then she opens the door. We see the crowd, grimly marching, and the MORRISONS are at the head of it. No one looks at the*

HAYESES. *The dull thud of the tramping feet is sickening to hear.* ARTHUR *closes his eyes. Slowly now* PHYLLIS *pushes him forward. He steps out of the house and moves ahead to join the others, as if in a dream.* PHYLLIS *follows, catches up, and takes his arm as they join the marching mob. Fade out.*)

ACT III

(*Fade in on a long shot of Sycamore Street. It is once again 6:40 P.M., same night. We have gone backward in time, and again we duplicate the scene which opened Acts I and II.* ARTHUR HAYES *walks on, stops in front of his house, knocks his pipe against his heel.* FRANK MORRISON *enters. Again, each of the movements must be exact imitations of the movements in Acts I and II. It is as if we are starting the play again.*)

FRANK (*jovially*): Hey, Artie. How ya doin'?

(ARTHUR *is preoccupied. He doesn't register at first. He looks blankly at* FRANK.)

FRANK (*laughing*): Hey . . . wake up, boy. It's almost time for supper.

(ARTHUR *snaps out of it and forces a smile.*)

ARTHUR (*quietly*): Oh . . . hello, Frank. Sorry. I didn't see you.

FRANK: Didn't see me? Hey, wait till I tell Clarice. That diet she's got me on must be working. You have to look twice to see me! (*Laughing hard,* FRANK *reaches for his keys.*) That's a hot one! (ARTHUR *smiles weakly.*) Say . . . isn't this late for you to be getting home?

ARTHUR: No, I don't think so. (*He looks at his watch.*) It's twenty to seven. I always get home about this time.

FRANK: Yeah. Well, I wouldn't want you to be late tonight. You know what tonight is, don't you?

ARTHUR (*slowly*): Yes, I know what tonight is.
FRANK (*a little hard*): Good.

(*We hear footsteps and see a man walk by them. He is* JOSEPH BLAKE. *They both look at him silently. Camera now follows him as he walks silently toward his house, the third of the three houses we see. As he walks, we hear faintly in background:*)

FRANK (*off*): See you later, Artie.

(*We hear* FRANK'S *door open and close. Then we hear* ARTHUR'S *door open, and for an instant, we hear the same dance music coming from* ARTHUR'S *house that we heard in Act II. Then* ARTHUR'S *door closes. By this time* JOSEPH BLAKE *is in front of his door. He looks off silently at the other two houses. Then he opens his front door and enters his house. As he closes the door we hear running feet, and then we see* JUDY, JOE'S *six-year-old daughter, in a bathrobe and slippers, running at him.*)

JUDY (*calling*): Daddy Daddy Daddy Daddy.

(*She runs into his arms. He lifts her up and hugs her.*)

JOE: Mmm. You smell sweet.
JUDY (*excited*): I had a hairwash with Mommy's special shampoo. It smells like gar . . . gar . . .
JOE: Gardenias. Did anyone ever tell you you smelled like gardenias even without Mommy's shampoo?
JUDY (*grinning*): You're silly.

(*He tickles her and she giggles.*)

ANNA (*calling*): Judy!
JUDY (*importantly*): We've got company.
JOE: Oh? Who is it, darling?
ANNA (*calling*): Judy!
JUDY: A lady.

(JOE *puts her down. She runs inside.* JOE *takes off his coat, puts it into the closet, and walks into the living room.* JOE'S *wife,* ANNA, *stands near a chair.* ANNA, *in her early thirties, is a quiet, small woman who has obviously*

*been through a great deal of suffering in the past five
years. She looks extremely nervous and upset now. Seated
at the far end of the room in a rocking chair is* JOE'S
mother, MRS. BLAKE. *She is quite old, quite spry for her
years, and inclined to be snappish. Also seated in the
room is a middle-aged woman, a neighborhood busybody
named* MRS. CARSON. *She wears an odd, old-fashioned hat
and sits stiffly, not at home, quite uncomfortable, but determined to do what she has come to do. The living room
again is an exact duplicate of the Morrison and Hayes
living rooms. It is furnished sparsely and not well. It is
obvious that the Blakes have not been living there long.
As* JOE *gets into the room,* ANNA *comes toward him.)*

ANNA: Joe, this is Mrs. Carson.
JOE (*politely*): Mrs. Carson.

(*He turns to her for a moment. She nods curtly. Then
he turns back to* ANNA *and kisses her gently.*)

JOE: Hello, darling.
ANNA: Joe . . .

(*But he walks away from her and goes to his mother.
He bends over and kisses her on the forehead.*)

MRS. BLAKE: Your face is cold.
JOE (*smiling*): It's freezing out. How do you feel?
MRS. BLAKE: Just fine, Joe.

(*He pats her cheek and turns to find* JUDY *behind him,
holding a piece of drawing paper and a crayon. On the
paper is a childish scribble that looks vaguely like a boat.*
ANNA, *a tortured expression on her face, wants to say
something, but* JOE *looks at the drawing, grinning.*)

JUDY: Daddy . . .
JOE: The *Queen Mary!* Now that is what I call beautiful.
JUDY: It is not! It's just s'posed to be a sailboat. How
do you draw a sail?
ANNA (*shakily*): Joe . . . Mrs. Carson . . .
JOE: Well, let's see. . . . (*He takes the crayon and
paper and studies it.*) I suppose you think it's easy to
draw a sail.

JUDY (*serious*): No. I don't.

ANNA (*sharply*): Joe. (*She comes over and snatches the paper away from him. He looks at her.*) Judy, go into your room.

JOE: Wait a minute, Anna. Take it easy.

ANNA (*near tears*): Judy, did you hear me?

JOE: Darling, what's the matter with you?

ANNA: Joe . . .

JUDY: Mommy, do I have to?

JOE (*gently*): Maybe you'd better go inside for a few minutes, baby.

(JUDY *unhappily goes into her room.* ANNA *waits till we hear the door close.* JOE *puts his arms around her.*)

JOE: Tell me. What's wrong, Anna?

ANNA (*almost sobbing*): Joe! I don't understand it! Mrs. Carson says . . . She . . .

JOE (*gently*): Mrs. Carson says what?

ANNA (*breaking down*): She says . . . Joe . . . they're going to throw us out of our house. Tonight! Right now! What are we going to do?

JOE (*softly*): Well, I don't know. Who's going to throw us out of our house?

(*But* ANNA *can't answer.* JOE *grips her tightly, then releases her and walks to* MRS. CARSON, *who sits stolidly, waiting.*)

JOE: Who's going to throw us out, Mrs. Carson? Do you know?

MRS. CARSON: Well, like I told Mrs. Blake there, I suppose it's none of my business, but I'm just not the kind that thinks a thing like this ought to happen to people without them getting at least a . . . well, a warning. Know what I mean?

JOE: No, I don't know what you mean, Mrs. Carson. Did someone send you here?

MRS. CARSON (*indignantly*): Well, I should say not! If my husband knew I was here he'd drag me out by the hair. No, I sneaked in here, if you please, Mr. Blake. I felt it was my Christian duty. A man ought to have the right to run away, I say.

JOE: What do you mean run away, Mrs. Carson?

MRS. CARSON: Well, you know what I mean.

JOE: Who's going to throw us out?

MRS. CARSON: Well, everybody. The people on Syca-more Street. You know. They don't feel you ought to live here, because . . . Now I don't suppose I have to go into that.

JOE (*understanding*): I see.

ANNA (*breaking in*): Joe, I've been waiting and wait-ing for you to come home. I've been sitting here . . . and waiting. Listen . . .

JOE (*quietly*): Hold it, Anna. (*To* MRS. CARSON) What time are they coming, Mrs. Carson?

MRS. CARSON: Quarter after seven. That's the plan. (*She looks at her watch and gets up.*) It's near seven now. They're very angry people, Mr. Blake. I don't think it'd be right for anyone to get hurt. That's why I'm here. If you take my advice, you'll just put some stuff together in a hurry and get out. I don't think there's any point in your calling the police either. There's only two of 'em in Eastmont and I don't think they'd do much good against a crowd like this.

JOE: Thank you, Mrs. Carson.

MRS. CARSON: Oh, don't thank me. It's like I said. I don't know you people, but there's no need for anyone getting hurt long as you move out like everybody wants. No sir. I don't want no part nor parcel to any violence where it's not necessary. Know what I mean?

JOE: Yes, I know what you mean.

MRS. CARSON: I don't know why a thing like this has to start up anyway. It's none of my business, but a man like you ought to know better than to come pushing in here . . . a fine old neighborhood like this! After all, right is right.

JOE (*controlled*): Get out, Mrs. Carson.

MRS. CARSON: What? Well I never! You don't seem to know what I've done for you, Mr. Blake.

ANNA: Joe . . .

JOE: Get out of this house.

(*He goes to a chair in which lies* MRS. CARSON'S *coat. He picks it up and thrusts it at her. She takes it, indignant and a bit frightened.* JOE *turns from her. She begins to put her coat on.*)

MRS. CARSON: Well, I should think you'd at least have the decency to thank me. I might've expected this though. People like you!

ANNA: Mrs. Carson, please . . .

JOE: Anna, stop it!

(*He strides to the door and holds it open.* MRS. CARSON *walks out.*)

MRS. CARSON: I think maybe you'll be getting what you deserve, Mr. Blake. Good night.

(*She goes out.* JOE *slams the door.*)

ANNA: It's true. I can't believe it! Joe! Did you hear what she said? (*She goes to* JOE, *who still stands at the door, shocked.*) Well, what are you standing there for?

JOE (*amazed*): I don't know.

ANNA: Joe, I'm scared. I'm so scared, I'm sick to my stomach. What are we going to do?

(JOE *puts his arms around her as she begins to sob. He holds her close till she quiets down. Then he walks her slowly over to his mother.*)

JOE (*to his mother*): Will you read to Judy for a few minutes, Mother? It's time for her story. (MRS. BLAKE *starts to get up.*) Winnie the Pooh. She'll tell you what page.

(MRS. BLAKE *nods and gets up and goes into* JUDY'S *room.*)

ANNA: What are you doing, Joe? We've only got fifteen minutes. . . . Don't you understand?

JOE (*quietly*): What do you want me to do? I can't stop them from coming here.

(*She goes to him and looks up at him, pleading now.*)

ANNA (*whispering*): Joe. Let's get out. We've got time. We can throw some things into the car. . . .

JOE: Isn't it a remarkable thing? A quiet street like this and people with thunder in their hearts.

ANNA: Listen to me, Joe—please. We can get most of our clothes in the car. We can stop at a motel. I don't care where we go. Anywhere. Joe, you're not listening. (*Loud.*) What's the matter with you?

JOE: We're staying.

ANNA (*frightened*): No!

JOE: Anna, this is our home and we're staying in it. No one can make us get out of our home. No one. That's a guarantee I happen to have since I'm born.

ANNA (*sobbing*): Joe, you can't! Do you know what a mob is like? Do you know what they're capable of doing?

JOE: It's something I've never thought of before . . . a mob. I guess they're capable of doing ugly things.

ANNA: Joe, you're talking and talking and the clock is ticking so fast. Please . . . please . . . Joe. We can run. We can go somewhere else to live. It's not so hard.

JOE: It's very hard, Anna, when it's not your own choice.

ANNA (*sobbing*): What are you talking about? What else've we got to do? Stand here and fight them? We're not an army. We're one man and one woman and an old lady and a baby.

JOE: And the floor we stand on belongs to us. Not to anyone else.

ANNA: They don't care about things like that. Joe, listen to me, please. You're not making sense. Listen . . . Judy's inside. She's six years old now and she's only really known you for a few weeks. We waited four years for you, and she didn't remember you when you picked her up and kissed her hello, but, Joe, she was so happy. What are you gonna tell her when they set fire to her new house?

JOE: I'm gonna tell her that her father fought like a tiger to stop them.

ANNA (*crying*): Oh, no! No! No! What good will that do? Joe . . . please . . . please . . .

JOE (*thundering*): Stop it! (ANNA *turns away from him and covers her face. After a long pause, quietly.*) It's this way, Anna. We have a few things we own. We have this house we've just bought with money left from before . . .

money you could have used many times. We have a mortgage and a very old car and a few pieces of furniture. We have my job.

ANNA (*bitterly*): Selling pots and pans at kitchen doors.

JOE (*patiently*): We have my job. And we have each other and that's what we have. Except there's one more thing. We have the right to live where we please and how we please. We're keeping all of those things, Anna. They belong to us.

(*He comes up behind her and puts his hands on her shoulders. She sinks down in a chair, turned away from him, and sobs. He stands over her. She continues to sob. He holds her and tries to quiet her. The bedroom door opens and* JUDY *bounces into the room.* JOE *gets up and goes to her as* ANNA *tries to dry her tears.*)

JUDY: Grandma says I'm supposed to go to bed now. Do I have to, Daddy?

JOE (*smiling*): It's time, honey.

JUDY (*disappointed*): Gee whiz. Some night, I'm gonna stay up until four o'clock in the morning!

JOE: Some night, you can. (*He kisses her.*) Good night, baby. Give Mommy a kiss.

(JUDY *goes to* ANNA *and speaks as she is kissing her.*)

JUDY: Really? I really can stay up till four o'clock?
JOE: Really.
JUDY: Night, Mommy.
ANNA: Good night, darling.

(JUDY *runs off gleefully to the bedroom.*)

JUDY: Oh boy! (*Calling*) Grandma . . .

(*The door closes.* ANNA *gets up and goes to window. She is still terrified, but a bit calmer now. She looks out and then turns to* JOE. *He watches her.*)

ANNA: What've we done to hurt them? What've we done? I don't understand.

JOE (*softly*): Well, I guess maybe they think we've destroyed the dignity of their neighborhood, darling. That's why they've thrown garbage on our lawn.

ANNA: Dignity! Throwing garbage. Getting together a mob. Those are dignified things to do. Joe, how can you want to stay? How can you want to live on the same street with them? Don't you see what they are?

JOE: They're people, Anna. And I guess they're afraid, just like we are. That's why they've become a mob. It's why people always do.

(*The bedroom door opens and* JOE'S *mother enters. She goes to her rocker and sits in it and begins to rock.*)

ANNA: What are they afraid of?

JOE: Living next door to someone they think is beneath them. An ex-convict. Me.

(ANNA *runs to* JOE *and grips him excitedly.*)

ANNA: What do they think you did? They must think you're a thief or a murderer.

JOE: Maybe they do.

ANNA: Well, they can't. You'll tell them. You'll tell them, Joe.

JOE: Anna, listen . . .

ANNA: It could've happened to any one of them. Tell them you're not a common criminal. You were in an accident, and that's all it was. An accident. Joe, they'll listen. I know they will.

JOE: No, Anna . . .

ANNA (*eagerly*): All you have to do is tell them and they'll go away. It's not like you committed a crime or anything. You were speeding. Everybody speeds. You hit an old man, and he died. He walked right in front—

JOE: They're not asking what I did, Anna.

ANNA (*pleading*): Joe, please. Look at me. I'm so frightened. . . . You have to tell them.

JOE: Anna, we have our freedom. If we beg for it, then it's gone. Don't you see that?

ANNA (*shouting*): No!

(*He comes to her and grips her, and speaks to her with his face inches from hers.*)

JOE: How can I tell it to you? Listen, Anna, we're only little people, but we have certain rights. Judy's gonna learn about them in school in a couple of years . . . and they'll tell her that no one can take them away from her. She's got to be able to believe that. They include the right to be different. Well, a group of our neighbors have decided that we have to get out of here because they think we're different. They think we're not nice. (*Strongly.*) Do we have to smile in their faces and tell them we are nice? We don't have to win the right to be free! It's the same as running away, Anna. It's staying on their terms, and if we can't stay here on our terms, then there are no more places to stay anywhere. For you—for me—for Judy—for anyone, Anna.

(*She sees it now and she almost smiles, but the tears are running down her cheeks and it's difficult to smile.* JOE *kisses her forehead.*)

JOE (*quietly*): Now we'll wait for them.

(ANNA *goes slowly to a chair and sits in it.* MRS. BLAKE *rocks rhythmically on her rocking chair.* JOE *stands firm at one side of the room and they wait in silence. Suddenly the ticking of the clock on the mantelpiece thunders in our ears and the monotonous beat of it is all we hear. They wait.* ANNA *looks at* JOE *and then speaks softly.*)

ANNA: Joe. My hands are shaking. I don't want them to shake.

(JOE *walks over to her, stands over her strongly and clasps both her hands together. Then he holds them in his till they are still. The clock ticks on, and now we cut to it. It reads ten after seven. Dissolve to a duplicate of the clock which now reads quarter after seven. Cut to long shot of room as we begin to hear the tramping of the feet down the street. They wait. The rocker rocks. The clock ticks. The tramping grows louder.* JOE *stands in the center of the room, hard and firm. Then he turns to his mother and speaks gently and softly.*)

JOE: Go inside, Mother.
MRS. BLAKE (*slowly*): No, Joe. I'm staying here. I want to watch you. I want to hear you. I want to be proud.

(*She continues to rock and now the tramping noise reaches a crescendo and then stops. For a moment there is silence, absolute silence, and then we hear a single angry voice.*)

CHARLIE DENTON (*shouting*): Joseph Blake! (*There is a chorus of shouts and a swelling of noise.*) Joseph Blake . . . come out here!

(*The noise from outside grows in volume. Inside only the rocking chair moves.*)

FIRST MAN (*shouting*): Come out of that house!

(*The noise, the yelling of the crowd, continues to grow. Inside the room no one gives a signal that they have heard.*)

SECOND MAN (*shouting*): We want you, Joseph Blake!

FRANK MORRISON (*shouting*): Come out—or we'll drag you out!

(*The yelling continues, grows louder. Still the BLAKES do not move. Then suddenly a rock smashes through the window. Glass sprays to the floor. The pitch of the noise outside rises even more. JOE begins to walk firmly to the door.*)

ANNA (*softly*): Joe . . .

(*But he doesn't hear her. He gets to the door and flings it open violently and steps outside. As he does, the shouting, which has reached its highest pitch, stops instantly and from deafening noise we plunge into absolute silence, broken only by the steady creaking of the rocking chair inside. JOE stands there in front of his house like a rock. Now for the first time we see the crowd. The camera plays over the silent faces watching him—the faces of the men and women and children. The MORRISONS are directly in front, CHARLIE DENTON is further back. MRS. CARSON is there. And far to the rear we see ARTHUR HAYES and PHYLLIS. Still the silence holds. Then, little by little, the people begin to speak. At first we only hear single voices from different parts of the crowd.*)

FIRST MAN (*shouting*): Look at him, standing there like he owns the block!

(*There is a chorus of ad-lib approvals.*)

SECOND MAN (*shouting*): Who do you think you are busting in where decent people live?

(*Another chorus of approvals.* JOE *stands like a fierce and powerful statue.*)

FIRST WOMAN (*shouting*): Why don't you go live with your own kind . . . in a gutter somewhere?

(*Another chorus of approvals. The camera moves about catching the eagerness, the mounting temper of the crowd, then the shame and anguish of* ARTHUR HAYES, *then the giant strength of* JOE.)

FIRST MAN (*shouting*): Your limousine is waiting, Mr. Blake. You're taking a one-way trip!

(*There are a few laughs at this, and now the crowd, although not moving forward, is a shouting mass again.* JOE *still waits quietly.*)

CHARLIE DENTON (*shouting*): Well, what are we waiting for? Let's get him!

(*The intensity of the noise grows and the mob begins to move forward. Then, with a tremendous roar,* FRANK MORRISON *stops them.*)

FRANK (*roaring*): Quiet! Everybody shut up.

(*The noise dies down gradually.*)

FRANK (*to crowd*): Now listen to me! This thing is gonna be handled the way we planned at the meeting.

(ROGER, *standing next to* FRANK, *looks at him adoringly.* CHRIS *holds* CLARICE'S *hand and looks around calmly.*)

CLARICE (*loud*): That's right! It's what we agreed on.

FRANK (*shouting*): This man here is gonna be asked politely and quietly to pack his things and get his family out of here. We don't have to tell him why. He knows that. He's gonna be given a chance to leave right now. If he's got any brains in his head he'll be out in one hour—and nobody'll touch him or his house. If he hasn't—

(*There is a low-throated, ominous murmur from the crowd.*)

FRANK: Right! This thing is gonna be done fair and square. (*Turning to* JOE) What d'ya say, Mr. Blake?

(JOE *looks at him for a long time. The crowd waits silently.* ARTHUR HAYES *lowers his head and clenches his fists, and looks as if he wants to be sick. The crowd waits. When* JOE *speaks, it is with a controlled fury that these people have never heard before. He speaks directly to* FRANK.)

JOE: I spit on your fairness! (*The crowd gasps.* JOE *waits, then he thunders out.*) I own this house and God gave me the right to live in it. The man who tries to take it away from me is going to have to climb over a pile of bones to do it. You good people of Sycamore Street are going to have to kill me tonight! Are you ready, Mr. Morrison? Don't bother to be fair. You're the head man here. Be first!

(*The crowd, rocked back on its heels, doesn't know what to do. Behind* JOE, *in the house, we see framed in the doorway the rocking chair moving steadily, and* ANNA *standing next to it.* FRANK *is stunned by this outburst. He calls for action. But not with the force he displayed earlier.*)

FRANK: You heard him, everybody. . . . Let's get him.
JOE: I asked for you first, Mr. Morrison!
FRANK (*shouting*): Listen to me! Let's go, men!

(*But the crowd is no longer moving as a whole. Some of them are still strongly with* FRANK, *including* CHARLIE, *the first man, the second man, and several of the others. But others are not so sure of themselves now.*)

CHARLIE (*roaring*): Don't let him throw you, Frank! He asked for it. Let's give it to him!

(JOE *looks only at* FRANK. *Waits calmly for him.*)

FRANK (*roaring*): Come on!

(*He takes a step forward, but the people behind him don't follow. He turns to them.*)

FRANK: What's the matter with you people?
JOE: They're waiting for you, Mr. Morrison.

(FRANK *whirls and faces him and they look long and hard at each other. Cut to* CHARLIE DENTON *at rear of crowd. He has a stone in his hand.*)

CHARLIE (*shouting*): Let's start it off, Frankie boy.

(*He flings the stone. We hear it hit and drop to the ground. The crowd gasps. Cut to* JOE. *There is blood running down the side of his head. He stands there firmly. Cut to* ARTHUR HAYES. *He looks up in horror, and then a transformation comes over him. He seems to grow taller and broader. His face sets strongly and he begins to stride forward, elbowing people aside.* PHYLLIS *knows. She clings to him to pull him back.*)

PHYLLIS (*screaming*): Artie . . . Artie . . . don't . . .

(*But he breaks loose from her and pushes forward. Whoever is in his way is knocked aside, and finally he reaches* JOE. *He looks up at* JOE. *Then he turns and stands next to him. He takes off his eyeglasses and flings them into the crowd.*)

ARTHUR (*strong*): Throw the next stone at me, neighbors. I live here too!

(*Now the crowd is uncertain as the two men stand together and the blood runs down* JOE'S *face.* FRANK *tries to rally them. During his next lines we shoot through the open door into the living room.* MRS. BLAKE *gets up from her rocking chair and takes* ANNA'S *hand. Together they*

*walk to the front door, come outside, and stand proudly
behind* JOE *and* ARTHUR.)

FRANK: Listen to me! Pay attention, you people. Let's
remember what we came here to do . . . and why! This
man is garbage! He's cluttering up our street. He's wreck-
ing our neighborhood. We don't want him here. We
agreed, every last man and woman of us . . . we agreed to
throw him out! Are we gonna let him stop us? If we do—
you know what'll happen.

(MRS. BLAKE *and* ANNA *are out of the house now. They
wait, along with* JOE *and* ARTHUR. *The crowd listens.*
FRANK *shouts on, running from person to person as the
crowd begins ashamedly to drift away.* CHRISTOPHER
clings to FRANK'S *jacket, and begins to sob.*)

FRANK: You know what Sycamore Street'll be like. I
don't have to tell you. How do we know who we'll be
rubbing elbows with next? Listen, where are you going?
We're all together in this! What about our kids? Listen to
me, people. Our kids'll be playing and going to school
with his. How do you like that, neighbors? Makes you a
little sick, doesn't it? Come back here! I'm telling you
we've got to do this! Come back here!

(*But the crowd continues to drift away. Finally only the*
MORRISONS *and* PHYLLIS HAYES *are left in the street.* JOE
and his family, and ARTHUR, *watch them, proudly.* ROGER
*looks at his bewildered father and then he turns away,
takes* CLARICE'S *hand, and his father is no longer the
greatest guy in the world.* FRANK *looks down at the sobbing* CHRISTOPHER, *and picks him up and walks slowly off.*
CLARICE *and* ROGER *follow. The* BLAKES *turn and go into
their house, leaving* ARTHUR *on the porch. And standing
alone, starkly in the middle of the street, is* PHYLLIS. AR-
THUR *looks at her as she stands, heartbreakingly alone,
for a long time.*)

ARTHUR (*sadly*): Well, what are you standing there
for? My neighbor's head is bleeding!

(*And then, slowly, knowing that* ARTHUR *is no longer a grown-up child,* PHYLLIS *moves forward into* JOSEPH BLAKE'S *house.*)

(*Fade out.*)

GORE VIDAL:

Visit to a Small Planet

Gore Vidal (1925–   ) achieved both his majority and recognition as a writer at the same time. He was only twenty-one when his first successful novel, *Williwaw*—based on his World War II experiences—was published. His second novel, *The City and the Pillar* (1948), won him even wider recognition. After working for a time in Hollywood, Mr. Vidal turned to writing plays for television. Some of those plays have been published in *Visit to a Small Planet and Other Television Plays* (1957). Enlarged and rewritten for Broadway, *Small Planet* had a successful career on the stage (1957). Another play, *The Best Man* (1960), is Mr. Vidal's other well-known stage work.

The appeal of *Visit to a Small Planet* lies principally in the way it links two of our principal contemporary preoccupations: our fear of global war and our curiosity about the mysteries of outer space. The play is, of course, a fantasy, employing the familiar devices of "science-fiction." One of the fascinating aspects of these fantastic devices arises from the notion that "it might really have happened" or that "it may yet happen"—just as Mr. Vidal describes it.

It would be unfair to the play, however, if we were to regard it merely in terms of fantasy, or in terms of the possibilities of earth receiving visitors from outer space. The playwright's concerns are much more serious and immediate. We know that in the 1930's and 40's a single individual, Adolf Hitler, did in fact attempt to gain control of the entire planet and came perilously close to succeeding. If Hitler had had additional technological assistance—control of the atom, for example—he could have achieved his final goal: *Heute, haben wir Europa; morgen, die ganze Welt*. (Today, we have Europe; tomorrow, the whole world.) Only a madman could have such aspirations; but just such madmen achieve great power. It is in such frighteningly contemporary terms that Gore Vidal conceived his play.

Note some of the interesting ironies both in the title of the play and in the name of the visitor from outer space: there are implications in Kreton's referring to his journey through space as "simply a visit to your small planet." Why does Mr. Vidal name so urbane a man, *Kreton?* Why does Kreton seem throughout virtually the entire play to be an attractive and likable person? (In a later version the ingenue nearly falls in love with him.) Although *Visit to a Small Planet* was written over a decade ago, it still strikes us with undiminished force.

Visit to a Small Planet

Characters

KRETON.
ROGER SPELDING.
ELLEN SPELDING.
MRS. SPELDING.
TWO TECHNICIANS.
JOHN RANDOLPH.
GENERAL POWERS.
AIDE.
PAUL LAURENT.
SECOND VISITOR.
PRESIDENT OF PARAGUAY.

ACT I

(*Stock Shot: The night sky, stars. Then slowly a luminous object arcs into view. As it is almost upon us, dissolve to the living room of the Spelding house in Maryland.*
Superimpose card: "The Time: The Day After Tomorrow."

The room is comfortably balanced between the expensively decorated and the homely. ROGER SPELDING *is concluding his TV broadcast. He is middle-aged, unctuous, resonant. His wife, bored and vague, knits passively while he talks at his desk. Two technicians are on hand, operating the equipment. His daughter,* ELLEN, *a lively girl of twenty, fidgets as she listens.*)

SPELDING (*into microphone*): . . . and so, according to General Powers . . . who should know if anyone does . . . the flying object which has given rise to so much irresponsible conjecture is nothing more than a meteor passing through the earth's orbit. It is not, as many believe, a secret weapon of this country. Nor is it a space ship as certain lunatic elements have suggested. General Powers has assured me that it is highly doubtful there is any form of life on other planets capable of building a space ship. "If any traveling is to be done in space, we will do it first." And those are his exact words. . . . Which winds up another week of news. (*Crosses to pose with wife and daughter.*) This is Roger Spelding, saying good night to Mother and Father America, from my old homestead in Silver Glen, Maryland, close to the warm pulse-beat of the nation.

TECHNICIAN: Good show tonight, Mr. Spelding.

SPELDING: Thank you.

TECHNICIAN: Yes sir, you were right on time.

(SPELDING *nods wearily, his mechanical smile and heartiness suddenly gone.*)

✳ MRS. SPELDING: Very nice, dear. Very nice.

TECHNICIAN: See you next week, Mr. Spelding.

SPELDING: Thank you, boys.

(*Technicians go.*)

SPELDING: Did you like the broadcast, Ellen?

ELLEN: Of course I did, Daddy.

SPELDING: Then what did I say?

ELLEN: Oh, that's not fair.

SPELDING: It's not very flattering when one's own daughter won't listen to what one says while millions of people . . .

ELLEN: I always listen, Daddy, you know that.

✳ MRS. SPELDING: We love your broadcasts, dear. I don't know what we'd do without them.

SPELDING: Starve.

ELLEN: I wonder what's keeping John?

SPELDING: Certainly not work.

ELLEN: Oh, Daddy, stop it! John works very hard and you know it.

✳ MRS. SPELDING: Yes, he's a perfectly nice boy, Roger. I like him.

SPELDING: I know. I know: he has every virtue except the most important one: he has no get-up-and-go.

ELLEN (*precisely*): He doesn't want to get up and he doesn't want to go because he's already where he wants to be on his own farm which is exactly where *I'm* going to be when we're married.

SPELDING: More thankless than a serpent's tooth is an ungrateful child.

ELLEN: I don't think that's right. Isn't it "more deadly . . ."

SPELDING: Whatever the exact quotation is, I stand by the sentiment.

✻ MRS. SPELDING: Please don't quarrel. It always gives me a headache.

SPELDING: I never quarrel. I merely reason, in my simple way, with Miss Know-it-all here.

ELLEN: Oh, Daddy! Next you'll tell me I should marry for money.

SPELDING: There is nothing wrong with marrying a wealthy man. The horror of it has always eluded me. However, my only wish is that you marry someone hardworking, ambitious, a man who'll make his mark in the world. Not a boy who plans to sit on a farm all his life, growing peanuts.

ELLEN: English walnuts.

SPELDING: Will you stop correcting me?

ELLEN: But, Daddy, John grows walnuts . . .

(JOHN *enters, breathlessly.*)

JOHN: Come out! Quickly. It's coming this way. It's going to land right here!

SPELDING: *What's* going to land?

JOHN: The space ship. Look!

SPELDING: Apparently you didn't hear my broadcast. The flying object in question is a meteor, not a space ship.

(JOHN *has gone out with* ELLEN. SPELDING *and* MRS. SPELDING *follow.*)

✻ MRS. SPELDING: Oh, my! Look! Something *is* falling! Roger, you don't think it's going to hit the house, do you?

SPELDING: The odds against being hit by a falling object that size are, I should say, roughly, ten million to one.

JOHN: Ten million to one or not it's going to land right here and it's *not* falling.

SPELDING: I'm sure it's a meteor.

✻ MRS. SPELDING: Shouldn't we go down to the cellar?

SPELDING: If it's not a meteor, it's an optical illusion . . . mass hysteria.

ELLEN: Daddy, it's a real space ship. I'm sure it is.

SPELDING: Or maybe a weather balloon. Yes, that's what it is. General Powers said only yesterday . . .

JOHN: It's landing!

SPELDING: I'm going to call the police . . . the army!

(*Bolts inside.*)

ELLEN: Oh look how it shines!

JOHN: Here it comes!

✷ MRS. SPELDING: Right in my rose garden!

ELLEN: Maybe it's a balloon.

JOHN: No, it's a space ship and right in your own back-yard.

ELLEN: What makes it shine so?

JOHN: I don't know but I'm going to find out.

(*Runs off toward the light.*)

ELLEN: Oh, darling, don't! John, please! John, John, come back!

(SPELDING, *wide-eyed, returns.*)

✷ MRS. SPELDING: Roger, it's landed right in my rose garden.

SPELDING: I got General Powers. He's coming over. He said they've been watching this thing. They . . . they don't know what it is.

ELLEN: You mean it's nothing of ours?

SPELDING: They believe it . . . (*Swallows hard.*) . . . it's from outer space.

ELLEN: And John's down there! Daddy, get a gun or something.

SPELDING: Perhaps we'd better leave the house until the army gets here.

ELLEN: We can't leave John.

SPELDING: I can. (*Peers nearsightedly.*) Why, it's not much larger than a car. I'm sure it's some kind of meteor.

ELLEN: Meteors are blazing hot.

SPELDING: This is a cold one . . .

ELLEN: It's opening . . . the whole side's opening! (*Shouts.*) John! Come back! Quick. . . .

✷ MRS. SPELDING: Why, there's a man getting out of it! (*Sighs.*) I feel much better already. I'm sure if we ask him, he'll move that thing for us. Roger, you ask him.

SPELDING (*ominously*): If it's really a man?

ELLEN: John's shaking hands with him. (*Calls.*) John darling, come on up here . . .

✱. MRS. SPELDING: And bring your friend . . .

SPELDING: There's something wrong with the way that creature looks . . . if it is a man and not a . . . not a monster.

✱ MRS. SPELDING: He looks perfectly nice to me.

✗ (JOHN *and the* VISITOR *appear. The* VISITOR *is in his forties, a mild, pleasant-looking man with side-whiskers and dressed in the fashion of 1860. He pauses when he sees the three people, in silence for a moment. They stare back at him, equally interested.*)

VISITOR: I seem to've made a mistake. I *am* sorry. I'd better go back and start over again.

SPELDING: My dear sir, you've only just arrived. Come in, come in. I don't need to tell you what a pleasure this is . . . Mister . . . Mister . . .

VISITOR: Kreton . . . This *is* the wrong costume, isn't it?

SPELDING: Wrong for what?

KRETON: For the country, and the time.

SPELDING: Well, it's a trifle old-fashioned.

✱ MRS. SPELDING: But really awfully handsome.

KRETON: Thank you.

✱ MRS. SPELDING (*to husband*): Ask him about moving that thing off my rose bed.

(SPELDING *leads them all into living room.*)

SPELDING: Come on in and sit down. You must be tired after your trip.

KRETON: Yes, I am a little. (*Looks around delightedly.*) Oh, it's better than I'd hoped!

SPELDING: Better? What's better?

KRETON: The house . . . that's what you call it? Or this an apartment?

SPELDING: This is a house in the State of Maryland, U.S.A.

KRETON: In the late twentieth century! To think this is really the twentieth century. I must sit down a moment and collect myself. The *real* thing! (*He sits down.*)

ELLEN: You . . . you're not an American, are you?

KRETON: What a nice thought! No, I'm not.

JOHN: You sound more English.

KRETON: Do I? Is my accent very bad?

JOHN: No, it's quite good.

SPELDING: Where *are* you from, Mr. Kreton?

KRETON (*evasively*): Another place.

SPELDING: On this earth of course.

KRETON: No, not on this planet.

ELLEN: Are you from Mars?

KRETON: Oh dear no, not Mars. There's nobody on Mars . . . at least no one I know.

ELLEN: I'm sure you're testing us and this is all some kind of publicity stunt.

KRETON: No, I really am from another place.

SPELDING: I don't suppose you'd consent to my interviewing you on television?

KRETON: I don't think your authorities will like that. They are terribly upset as it is.

SPELDING: How do you know?

KRETON: Well, I . . . pick up things. For instance, I know that in a few minutes a number of people from your Army will be here to question me and they . . . like you . . . are torn by doubt.

SPELDING: How extraordinary!

ELLEN: Why did you come here?

KRETON: Simply a visit to your small planet. I've been studying it for years. In fact, one might say, you people are my hobby. Especially this period of your development.

JOHN: Are you the first person from your . . . your planet to travel in space like this?

KRETON: Oh my no! Everyone travels who wants to. It's just that no one wants to visit you. I can't think why. *I* always have. You'd be surprised what a thorough study I've made. (*Recites.*) The planet, Earth, is divided into five continents with a number of large islands. It is mostly water. There is one moon. Civilization is only just beginning. . . .

SPELDING: Just beginning! My dear sir, we have had. . . .

KRETON (*blandly*): You are only in the initial stages,

the most fascinating stage as far as I'm concerned . . . I do hope I don't sound patronizing.

ELLEN: Well, we are very proud.

KRETON: I know and that's one of your most endearing, primitive traits. Oh, I can't believe I'm here at last!

(GENERAL POWERS, *a vigorous product of the National Guard, and his* AIDE *enter.*)

POWERS: All right folks. The place is surrounded by troops. Where is the monster?

KRETON: I, my dear General, am the monster.

POWERS: What are you dressed up for, a fancy-dress party?

KRETON: I'd hoped to be in the costume of the period. As you see I am about a hundred years too late.

POWERS: Roger, who is this joker?

SPELDING: This is Mr. Kreton . . . General Powers. Mr. Kreton arrived in that thing outside. He is from another planet.

POWERS: I don't believe it.

ELLEN: It's true. We saw him get out of the flying saucer.

POWERS (*to* AIDE): Captain, go down and look at that ship. But be careful. Don't touch anything. And don't let anybody else near it. (AIDE *goes.*) So you're from another planet.

KRETON: Yes. My, that's a very smart uniform but I prefer the ones made of metal, the ones you used to wear, you know: with the feathers on top.

POWERS: That was five hundred years ago . . . Are you *sure* you're not from the Earth?

KRETON: Yes.

POWERS: Well, I'm not. You've got some pretty tall explaining to do.

KRETON: Anything to oblige.

POWERS: All right, which planet?

KRETON: None that you have ever heard of.

POWERS: Where is it?

KRETON: You wouldn't know.

POWERS: This solar system?

KRETON: No.

POWERS: Another system?

KRETON: Yes.

POWERS: Look, Buster, I don't want to play games: I just want to know where you're from. The law requires it.

KRETON: It's possible that I could explain it to a mathematician but I'm afraid I couldn't explain it to you, not for another five hundred years and by then of course *you'd* be dead because you people do die, don't you?

POWERS: What?

KRETON: Poor fragile butterflies, such brief little moments in the sun. . . . You see *we* don't die.

POWERS: You'll die all right if it turns out you're a spy or a hostile alien.

KRETON: I'm sure you wouldn't be so cruel.

(AIDE *returns; he looks disturbed.*)

POWERS: What did you find?

AIDE: I'm not sure, General.

POWERS (*heavily*): Then do your best to describe what the object is like.

AIDE: Well, it's elliptical, with a fourteen-foot diameter. And it's made of an unknown metal which shines and inside there isn't anything.

POWERS: Isn't anything?

AIDE: There's nothing inside the ship: No instruments, no food, nothing.

POWERS (*to* KRETON): What did you do with your instrument board?

KRETON: With my what? Oh, I don't have one.

POWERS: How does the thing travel?

KRETON: I don't know.

POWERS: You don't know. Now look, Mister, you're in pretty serious trouble. I suggest you do a bit of cooperating. You claim you traveled here from outer space in a machine with no instruments . . .

KRETON: Well, these cars are rather common in my world and I suppose, once upon a time, I must've known the theory on which they operate but I've long since forgotten. After all, General, we're not mechanics, you and I.

POWERS: Roger, do you mind if we use your study?

SPELDING: Not at all. Not at all, General.

✗ POWERS: Mr. Kreton and I are going to have a chat. (*To* AIDE) Put in a call to the Chief of Staff.

AIDE: Yes, General.

(SPELDING *rises, leads* KRETON *and* POWERS *into next room, a handsomely furnished study, many books, and a globe of the world.*)

SPELDING: This way, gentlemen.

(KRETON *sits down comfortably beside the globe which he twirls thoughtfully. At the door,* SPELDING *speaks in a low voice to* POWERS.)

I hope I'll be the one to get the story first, Tom.

POWERS: There isn't any story. Complete censorship. I'm sorry but this house is under martial law. I've a hunch we're in trouble.

(*He shuts the door.* SPELDING *turns and rejoins his family.*)

ELLEN: I think he's wonderful, whoever he is.

✶ MRS. SPELDING: I wonder how much damage he did to my rose garden . . .

JOHN: It's sure hard to believe he's really from outer space. No instruments, no nothing . . . boy, they must be advanced scientifically.

✶ MRS. SPELDING: Is he spending the night, dear?

SPELDING: What?

✶ MRS. SPELDING: Is he spending the night?

SPELDING: Oh yes, yes, I suppose he will be.

✶ MRS. SPELDING: Then I'd better go make up the bedroom. He seems perfectly nice to me. I like his whiskers. They're so very . . . comforting. Like Grandfather Spelding's.

(*She goes.*)

SPELDING (*bitterly*): I *know* this story will leak out before I can interview him. I just know it.

ELLEN: What does it mean, we're under martial law?

SPELDING: It means we have to do what General Powers tells us to do. (*He goes to the window as a soldier passes by.*) See?

JOHN: I wish I'd taken a closer look at that ship when I had the chance.

ELLEN: Perhaps he'll give us a ride in it.

JOHN: Traveling in space! Just like those stories. You know: intergalactic drive stuff.

SPELDING: *If* he's not an impostor.

ELLEN: I have a feeling he isn't.

JOHN: Well, I better call the family and tell them I'm all right.

(*He crosses to telephone by the door which leads into hall.*)

AIDE: I'm sorry, sir, but you can't use the phone.

SPELDING: He certainly can. This is my house . . .

AIDE (*mechanically*): This house is a military reservation until the crisis is over: Order General Powers. I'm sorry.

JOHN: How am I to call home to say where I am?

AIDE: Only General Powers can help you. You're also forbidden to leave this house without permission.

SPELDING: You can't do this!

AIDE: I'm afraid, sir, we've done it.

ELLEN: Isn't it exciting!

(*Cut to study.*)

POWERS: Are you deliberately trying to confuse me?

KRETON: Not deliberately, no.

POWERS: We have gone over and over this for two hours now and all that you've told me is that you're from another planet in another solar system . . .

KRETON: In another dimension. I think that's the word you use.

POWERS: In another dimension and you have come here as a tourist.

KRETON: Up to a point, yes. What did you expect?

POWERS: It is my job to guard the security of this country.

KRETON: I'm sure that must be very interesting work.

POWERS: For all I know, you are a spy, sent here by an alien race to study us, preparatory to invasion.

KRETON: Oh, none of my people would *dream* of invading you.

POWERS: How do I know that's true?

KRETON: You don't, so I suggest you believe me. I should also warn you: I can tell what's inside.

POWERS: What's inside?

KRETON: What's inside your mind.

POWERS: You're a mind reader?

KRETON: I don't really read it. I hear it.

POWERS: What am I thinking?

KRETON: That I am either a lunatic from the Earth or a spy from another world.

POWERS: Correct. But then you could've guessed that. (*Frowns.*) What am I thinking now?

KRETON: You're making a picture. Three silver stars. You're pinning them on your shoulder, instead of the two stars you now wear.

POWERS (*startled*): That's right. I was thinking of my promotion.

KRETON: If there's anything I can do to hurry it along, just let me know.

POWERS: You can. Tell me why you're here.

KRETON: Well, we don't travel much, my people. We used to but since we see everything through special monitors and recreators, there is no particular need to travel. However, *I* am a hobbyist. I love to gad about.

POWERS (*taking notes*): Are you the first to visit us?

KRETON: Oh, no! We started visiting you long before there were people on the planet. However, we are seldom noticed on our trips. I'm sorry to say I slipped up, coming in the way I did . . . but then this visit was all rather impromptu. (*Laughs.*) I am a creature of impulse, I fear.

(AIDE *looks in.*)

AIDE: Chief of Staff on the telephone, General.

POWERS (*picks up phone*): Hello, yes, sir. Powers speaking. I'm talking to him now. No, sir. No, sir. No, we can't determine what method of power was used. He won't talk. Yes, sir. I'll hold him there. I've put the house under martial law . . . belongs to a friend of mine, Roger Spelding, the TV commentator. Roger Spelding, the TV

. . . What? Oh, no, I'm sure he won't say anything. Who . . . oh, yes, sir. Yes, I realize the importance of it. Yes, I will. Good-by. (*Hangs up.*) The President of the United States wants to know all about you.

KRETON: How nice of him! And I want to know all about him. But I do wish you'd let me rest a bit first. Your language is still not familiar to me. I had to learn them all, quite exhausting.

POWERS: You speak *all* our languages?

KRETON: Yes, all of them. But then it's easier than you might think since I can see what's inside.

POWERS: Speaking of what's inside, we're going to take your ship apart.

KRETON: Oh, I wish you wouldn't.

POWERS: Security demands it.

KRETON: In that case *my* security demands you leave it alone.

POWERS: You plan to stop us?

KRETON: I already have . . . Listen.

(*Far-off shouting.* AIDE *rushes into the study.*)

AIDE: Something's happened to the ship, General. The door's shut and there's some kind of wall around it, an invisible wall. We can't get near it.

KRETON (*to camera*): I hope there was no one inside.

POWERS (*to* KRETON): How did you do that?

KRETON: I couldn't begin to explain. Now if you don't mind, I think we should go in and see our hosts.

(*He rises, goes into living room.* POWERS *and* AIDE *look at each other.*)

POWERS: Don't let him out of your sight.

(*Cut to living room as* POWERS *picks up phone.* KRETON *is with* JOHN *and* ELLEN.)

KRETON: I don't mind curiosity but I really can't permit them to wreck my poor ship.

ELLEN: What do you plan to do, now you're here?

KRETON: Oh, keep busy. I have a project or two . . . (*Sighs.*) I can't believe you're real!

JOHN: Then we're all in the same boat.

KRETON: Boat? Oh, yes! Well, I should have come ages ago but I . . . I couldn't get away until yesterday.

JOHN: Yesterday? It took you a *day* to get here?

KRETON: One of *my* days, not yours. But then you don't know about time yet.

JOHN: Oh, you mean relativity.

KRETON: No, it's much more involved than that. You won't know about time until . . . now let me see if I remember . . . no, I don't, but it's about two thousand years.

JOHN: What do we do between now and then?

KRETON: You simply go on the way you are, living your exciting primitive lives . . . you have no idea how much fun you're having now.

ELLEN: I hope you'll stay with us while you're here.

KRETON: That's very nice of you. Perhaps I will. Though I'm sure you'll get tired of having a visitor underfoot all the time.

ELLEN: Certainly not. And Daddy will be deliriously happy. He can interview you by the hour.

JOHN: What's it like in outer space?

KRETON: Dull.

ELLEN: I should think it would be divine!

(POWERS *enters*.)

KRETON: No, General, it won't work.

POWERS: What won't work?

KRETON: Trying to blow up my little force field. You'll just plough up Mrs. Spelding's garden.

(POWERS *snarls and goes into study.*)

ELLEN: Can you tell what we're *all* thinking?

KRETON: Yes. As a matter of fact, it makes me a bit giddy. Your minds are not at all like ours. You see, we control our thoughts while you . . . well, it's extraordinary the things you think about!

ELLEN: Oh, how awful! You can tell *everything* we think?

KRETON: Everything! It's one of the reasons I'm here, to intoxicate myself with your primitive minds . . . with the wonderful rawness of your emotions! You have no idea how it excites me! You simply seethe with unlikely emotions.

ELLEN: I've never felt so sordid.

JOHN: From now on I'm going to think about agriculture.

SPELDING (*entering*): You would.

ELLEN: Daddy!

KRETON: No, no. You must go right on thinking about Ellen. Such wonderfully *purple* thoughts!

SPELDING: Now see here, Powers, you're carrying this martial law thing too far . . .

POWERS: Unfortunately, until I have received word from Washington as to the final disposition of this problem, you must obey my orders: no telephone calls, no communication with the outside.

SPELDING: This is unsupportable.

KRETON: Poor Mr. Spelding! If you like, I shall go. That would solve everything, wouldn't it?

POWERS: You're not going anywhere, Mr. Kreton, until I've had my instructions.

KRETON: I sincerely doubt if you could stop me. However, I put it up to Mr. Spelding. Shall I go?

SPELDING: Yes! (POWERS *gestures a warning.*) Do stay, I mean, we want you to get a good impression of us . . .

KRETON: And of course you still want to be the first journalist to interview me. Fair enough. All right, I'll stay on for a while.

POWERS: Thank you.

KRETON: Don't mention it.

SPELDING: General, may I ask our guest a few questions?

POWERS: Go right ahead, Roger. I hope you'll do better than I did.

SPELDING: Since you read our minds, you probably already know what our fears are.

KRETON: I do, yes.

SPELDING: We are afraid that you represent a hostile race.

KRETON: And I have assured General Powers that my people are not remotely hostile. Except for me, no one is interested in this planet's present stage.

SPELDING: Does this mean you might be interested in a *later* stage?

KRETON: I'm not permitted to discuss your future. Of course my friends think me perverse to be interested in a primitive society but there's no accounting for tastes, is there? You are my hobby. I love you. And that's all there is to it.

POWERS: So you're just here to look around . . . sort of going native.

KRETON: What a nice expression! That's it exactly. I am going native.

POWERS (*grimly*): Well, it is my view that you have been sent here by another civilization for the express purpose of reconnoitering prior to invasion.

KRETON: That *would* be your view! The wonderfully primitive assumption that all strangers are hostile. You're almost too good to be true, General.

POWERS: You deny your people intend to make trouble for us?

KRETON: I deny it.

POWERS: Then are they interested in establishing communication with us? Trade? That kind of thing?

KRETON: We have always had communication with you. As for trade, well, we do not trade . . . that is something peculiar only to your social level. (*Quickly.*) Which I'm not criticizing! As you know, I approve of everything you do.

POWERS: I give up.

SPELDING: You have no interest then in . . . well, trying to dominate the Earth.

KRETON: Oh, yes!

POWERS: I thought you just said your people weren't interested in us.

KRETON: *They're* not, but *I* am.

POWERS: You!

KRETON: Me . . . I mean I. You see I've come here to take charge.

POWERS: Of the United States?

KRETON: No, of the whole world. I'm sure you'll be much happier and it will be great fun for me. You'll get used to it in no time.

POWERS: This is ridiculous. How can one man take over the world?

KRETON (*gaily*): Wait and see!

POWERS (*to* AIDE): Grab him!

(POWERS *and* AIDE *rush* KRETON *but within a foot of him, they stop, stunned.*)

KRETON: You can't touch me. That's part of the game. (*He yawns.*) Now, if you don't mind, I shall go up to my room for a little lie-down.

SPELDING: I'll show you the way.

KRETON: That's all right, I know the way. (*Touches his brow.*) Such savage thoughts! My head is vibrating like a drum. I feel guite giddy, all of you thinking away. (*He starts to the door; he pauses beside* MRS. SPELDING.) No, it's not a dream, dear lady. I shall be here in the morning when you wake up. And now, good night, dear, wicked children. . . .

(*He goes as we fade out.*)

ACT II

(*Fade in on* KRETON'S *bedroom next morning. He lies fully clothed on bed with cat on his lap.*)

KRETON: Poor cat! Of course I sympathize with you. Dogs *are* distasteful. What? Oh, I can well believe they do: yes, yes, how disgusting. They don't ever groom their fur! But you do *constantly*, such a fine coat. No, no, I'm not just saying that. I really mean it: exquisite texture. Of course, I wouldn't say it was *nicer* than skin but even so. . . . What? Oh, no! They *chase* you! Dogs chase you for no reason at all except pure malice? You poor creature. Ah, but you *do* fight back! That's right! Give it to them: slash, bite, scratch! Don't let them get away with a trick.

. . . No! Do dogs really do that? Well, I'm sure *you* don't. What . . . oh, well, yes I completely agree about mice. They *are* delicious! (Ugh!) Pounce, snap and there is a heavenly dinner. No, I don't know any mice yet . . . they're not very amusing? But after all think how you must terrify them because you are so bold, so cunning, so beautifully predatory!

(*Knock at door.*)

Come in.

ELLEN (*enters*): Good morning. I brought you your breakfast.

KRETON: How thoughtful! (*Examines bacon.*) Delicious, but I'm afraid my stomach is not like yours, if you'll pardon me. I don't eat. (*Removes pill from his pocket and swallows it.*) This is all I need for the day. (*Indicates cat.*) Unlike this creature, who would eat her own weight every hour, given a chance.

ELLEN: How do you know?

KRETON: We've had a talk.

ELLEN: You can *speak* to the cat?

KRETON: Not speak exactly but we communicate. I look inside and the cat cooperates. Bright red thoughts, very exciting, though rather on one level.

ELLEN: Does kitty like us?

KRETON: No, I wouldn't say she did. But then she has very few thoughts not connected with food. Have you, my quadruped criminal? (*He strokes the cat, which jumps to the floor.*)

ELLEN: You know you've really upset everyone.

KRETON: I supposed that I would.

ELLEN: Can you really take over the world, just like that?

KRETON: Oh, yes.

ELLEN: What do you plan to do when you *have* taken over?

KRETON: Ah, that is my secret.

ELLEN: Well, I think you'll be a very nice President, *if* they let you, of course.

KRETON: What a sweet girl you are! Marry him right away.

ELLEN: Marry John?

KRETON: Yes. I see it in your head *and* in his. He wants you very much.

ELLEN: Well, we plan to get married this summer, if father doesn't fuss too much.

KRETON: Do it before then. I shall arrange it all if you like.

ELLEN: How?

KRETON: I can convince your father.

ELLEN: That sounds awfully ominous. I think you'd better leave poor Daddy alone.

KRETON: Whatever you say. (*Sighs.*) Oh, I love it so! When I woke up this morning I had to pinch myself to prove I was really here.

ELLEN: We were all doing a bit of pinching too. Ever since dawn we've had nothing but visitors and phone calls and troops outside in the garden. No one has the faintest idea what to do about you.

KRETON: Well, I don't think they'll be confused much longer.

ELLEN: How do you plan to conquer the world?

KRETON: I confess I'm not sure. I suppose I must make some demonstration of strength, some colorful trick that will frighten everyone . . . though I much prefer taking charge quietly. That's why I've sent for the President.

ELLEN: The President? *Our* President?

KRETON: Yes, he'll be along any minute now.

ELLEN: But the President just doesn't go around visiting people.

KRETON: He'll visit me. (*Chuckles.*) It may come as a surprise to him, but he'll be in this house in a very few minutes. I think we'd better go downstairs now. (*To cat.*) No, I will not give you a mouse. You must get your own. Be self-reliant. Beast!

(*Dissolve to the study.* POWERS *is reading book entitled* The Atom and You. *Muffled explosions off stage.*)

AIDE (*entering*): Sir, nothing seems to be working. Do we have the General's permission to try a fission bomb on the force field?

POWERS: No . . . no. We'd better give it up.

AIDE: The men are beginning to talk.

POWERS (*thundering*): Well, keep them quiet! (*Contritely.*) I'm sorry, Captain. I'm on edge. Fortunately, the whole business will soon be in the hands of the World Council.

AIDE: What will the World Council do?

POWERS: It will be interesting to observe them.

AIDE: You don't think this Kreton can really take over the world, do you?

POWERS: Of course not. Nobody can.

(*Dissolve to living room.* MRS. SPELDING *and* SPELDING *are alone.*)

MRS. SPELDING: You still haven't asked Mr. Kreton about moving that thing, have you?

SPELDING: There are too many important things to ask him.

MRS. SPELDING: I hate to be a nag, but you know the trouble I have had getting anything to grow in that part of the garden . . .

JOHN (*enters*): Good morning.

MRS. SPELDING: Good morning, John.

JOHN: Any sign of your guest?

MRS. SPELDING: Ellen took his breakfast up to him a few minutes ago.

JOHN: They don't seem to be having much luck, do they? (*To* SPELDING.) I sure hope you don't mind my staying here like this.

(SPELDING *glowers.*)

MRS. SPELDING: Why, we love having you! I just hope your family aren't too anxious.

JOHN: One of the G.I.'s finally called them, said I was staying here for the week end.

SPELDING: The rest of our lives, if something isn't done soon.

JOHN: Just how long do you think that'll be, Dad?

SPELDING: Who knows?

(KRETON *and* ELLEN *enter.*)

KRETON: Ah, how wonderful to see you again! Let me catch my breath. . . . Oh, your minds! It's not easy for me, you know: so many crude thoughts blazing away! Yes, Mrs. Spelding, I will move the ship off your roses.

MRS. SPELDING: That's awfully sweet of you.

KRETON: Mr. Spelding, if any interviews are to be granted, you will be the first, I promise you.

SPELDING: That's very considerate, I'm sure.

KRETON: So you can stop thinking *those* particular thoughts. And now where is the President?

SPELDING: The President?

KRETON: Yes, I sent for him. He should be here. (*Goes to terrace window.*) Ah, that must be he.

(*A swarthy man in uniform with a sash across his chest is standing, bewildered, on the terrace.* KRETON *opens the glass doors.*)

KRETON: Come in, sir! Come in, Your Excellency. Good of you to come on such short notice.

(*Man enters.*)

MAN (*in Spanish accent*): Where am I?

KRETON: You *are* the President, aren't you?

MAN: Of course I am the President. What am I doing here? I was dedicating a bridge and I find myself . . .

KRETON (*aware of his mistake*): Oh, dear! Where was the bridge?

MAN: Where do you think, you idiot, in Paraguay!

KRETON (*to others*): I seem to've made a mistake. Wrong President. (*Gestures and the man disappears.*) Seemed rather upset, didn't he?

JOHN: You can make people come and go just like that?

KRETON: Just like that.

(POWERS *looks into the room from the study.*)

POWERS: Good morning, Mr. Kreton. Could I see you for a moment?

KRETON: By all means.

(*He crosses to the study.*)

SPELDING: I believe I am going mad.

(*Cut to study. The* AIDE *stands at attention while* POWERS *addresses* KRETON.)

POWERS: . . . and so we feel, the government of the United States feels, that this problem is too big for any one country. Therefore, we have turned the whole affair over to Paul Laurent, the Secretary-General of the World Council.

KRETON: Very sensible. I should've thought of that myself.

POWERS: Mr. Laurent is on his way here now. And may I add, Mr. Kreton, you've made me look singularly ridiculous.

KRETON: I'm awfully sorry. (*Pause.*) No, you can't kill me.

POWERS: You were reading my mind again.

KRETON: I can't really help it, you know. And such *black* thoughts today, but intense, very intense.

POWERS: I regard you as a menace.

KRETON: I know you do and I think it's awfully unkind. I do mean well.

POWERS: Then go back where you came from and leave us alone.

KRETON: No, I'm afraid I can't do that just yet . . .

(*Telephone rings;* AIDE *answers it.*)

AIDE: He's outside? Sure, let him through. (*To* POWERS) The Secretary-General of the World Council is here, sir.

POWERS (*to* KRETON): I hope you'll listen to *him.*

KRETON: Oh, I shall, of course. I love listening.

✳ *(The door opens and* PAUL LAURENT, *middle-aged and serene, enters.* POWERS *and his* AIDE *stand to attention.* KRETON *goes forward to shake hands.)*

LAURENT: Mr. Kreton?

KRETON: At your service, Mr. Laurent.

LAURENT: I welcome you to this planet in the name of the World Council.

KRETON: Thank you, sir, thank you.

LAURENT: Could you leave us alone for a moment, General?

✳ POWERS: Yes, sir.

*(*POWERS *and* AIDE *go.* LAURENT *smiles at* KRETON.)*

LAURENT: Shall we sit down?

KRETON: Yes, yes I love sitting down. I'm afraid my manners are not quite suitable, yet.

(They sit down.)

LAURENT: Now, Mr. Kreton, in violation of all the rules of diplomacy, may I come to the point?

KRETON: You may.

LAURENT: Why are you here?

KRETON: Curiosity. Pleasure.

LAURENT: You are a tourist then in this time and place?

KRETON *(nods)*: Yes. Very well put.

LAURENT: We have been informed that you have extraordinary powers.

KRETON: By your standards, yes, they must seem extraordinary.

LAURENT: We have also been informed that it is your intention to . . . to take charge of this world.

KRETON: That is correct. . . . What a remarkable mind you have! I have difficulty looking inside it.

LAURENT *(laughs)*: Practice. I've attended so many conferences. . . . May I say that your conquest of our world puts your status of tourist in a rather curious light?

KRETON: Oh, I said nothing about *conquest.*

LAURENT: Then how else do you intend to govern? The people won't allow you to direct their lives without a struggle.

KRETON: But I'm sure they will if I ask them to.

LAURENT: You believe you can do all this without, well, without violence?

KRETON: Of course I can. One or two demonstrations and I'm sure they'll do as I ask. (*Smiles.*) Watch this.

(*Pause. Then shouting.* POWERS *bursts into room.*)

POWERS: Now what've you done?

KRETON: Look out the window, Your Excellency.

(LAURENT *goes to window. A rifle floats by, followed by an alarmed soldier.*)

Nice, isn't it? I confess I worked out a number of rather melodramatic tricks last night. Incidentally, all the rifles of all the soldiers in all the world are now floating in the air. (*Gestures.*) Now they have them back.

POWERS (*to* LAURENT): You see, sir, I didn't exaggerate in my report.

LAURENT (*awed*): No, no, you certainly didn't.

KRETON: You were skeptical, weren't you?

LAURENT: Naturally. But now I . . . now I think it's possible.

POWERS: That this . . . this gentleman is going to run everything?

LAURENT: Yes, yes I do. And it might be wonderful.

KRETON: You *are* more clever than the others. You begin to see that I mean only good.

LAURENT: Yes, only good. General, do you realize what this means? We can have one government . . .

KRETON: With innumerable bureaus, and intrigue. . . .

LAURENT (*excited*): And the world could be incredibly prosperous, especially if he'd help us with his superior knowledge.

KRETON (*delighted*): I will, I will. I'll teach you to look into one another's minds. You'll find it devastating but enlightening: all that self-interest, those *lurid* emotions . . .

LAURENT: No more countries. No more wars . . .

KRETON (*startled*): What? Oh, but I like a lot of countries. Besides, at this stage of your development you're supposed to have lots of countries and lots of wars . . . innumerable wars . . .

LAURENT: But you can help us change all that.

KRETON: *Change* all that! My dear sir, I am your friend.

LAURENT: What do you mean?

KRETON: Why, your deepest pleasure is violence. How can you deny that? It is the whole point to you, the whole point to my hobby . . . and you are my hobby, all mine.

LAURENT: But our lives are devoted to *controlling* violence, and not creating it.

KRETON: Now, don't take me for an utter fool. After all, I can see into your minds. My dear fellow, don't you *know* what you are?

LAURENT: What are we?

KRETON: You are savages. I have returned to the dark ages of an insignificant planet simply because I want the glorious excitement of being among you and reveling in your savagery! There is murder in all your hearts and I love it! It intoxicates me!

LAURENT (*slowly*): You hardly flatter us.

KRETON: I didn't mean to be rude but you did ask me why I am here and I've told you.

LAURENT: You have no wish then to . . . to help us poor savages.

KRETON: I couldn't even if I wanted to. You won't be civilized for at least two thousand years and you won't reach the level of my people for about a million years.

LAURENT (*sadly*): Then you have come here only to . . . to observe?

KRETON: No, more than that. I mean to regulate your pastimes. But don't worry: I won't upset things too much. I've decided I don't want to be known to the people. You will go right on with your countries, your squabbles, the way you always have, while I will *secretly* regulate things through you.

LAURENT: The World Council does not govern. We only advise.

KRETON: Well, I shall advise you and you will advise

the governments and we shall have a lovely time.

LAURENT: I don't know what to say. You obviously have the power to do as you please.

KRETON: I'm glad you realize that. Poor General Powers is now wondering if a hydrogen bomb might destroy me. It won't, General.

✗ POWERS: Too bad.

KRETON: Now, Your Excellency, I shall stay in this house until you have laid the groundwork for my first project.

LAURENT: And what is that to be?

KRETON: A war! I want one of your really splendid wars, with all the trimmings, all the noise and the fire . . .

LAURENT: A war! You're joking. Why at this moment we are working as hard as we know how *not* to have a war.

KRETON: But secretly you want one. After all, it's the one thing your little race does well. You'd hardly want me to deprive you of your simple pleasures, now would you?

LAURENT: I think you must be mad.

KRETON: Not mad, simply a philanthropist. Of course I myself shall get a great deal of pleasure out of a war (the vibrations must be incredible!) but I'm doing it mostly for you. So, if you don't mind, I want you to arrange a few incidents, so we can get one started spontaneously.

LAURENT: I refuse.

KRETON: In that event, I shall select someone else to head the World Council. Someone who *will* start a war. I suppose there exist a few people here who might like the idea.

LAURENT: How can you do such a horrible thing to us? Can't you see that we don't want to be savages?

KRETON: But you have no choice. Anyway, you're just pulling my leg! I'm sure you want a war as much as the rest of them do and that's what you're going to get: the biggest war you've ever had!

LAURENT (*stunned*): Heaven help us!

KRETON (*exuberant*): Heaven won't! Oh, what fun it will be! I can hardly wait! (*He strikes the globe of the world a happy blow as we fade out.*)

ACT III

(*Fade in on the study, two weeks later.* KRETON *is sitting at desk on which a map is spread out. He has a pair of dividers, some models of jet aircraft. Occasionally he pretends to dive-bomb, imitating the sound of a bomb going off.* POWERS *enters.*)

POWERS: You wanted me, sir?

KRETON: Yes, I wanted those figures on radioactive fallout.

POWERS: They're being made up now, sir. Anything else?

KRETON: Oh, my dear fellow, why do you dislike me so?

POWERS: I am your military aide, sir: I don't have to answer that question. It is outside the sphere of my duties.

KRETON: Aren't you at least happy about your promotion?

POWERS: Under the circumstances, no, sir.

KRETON: I find your attitude baffling.

POWERS: Is that all, sir?

KRETON: You have never once said what you thought of my war plans. Not once have I got a single word of encouragement from you, a single compliment . . . only black thoughts.

POWERS: Since you read my mind, sir, you know what I think.

KRETON: True, but I can't help but feel that deep down inside of you there is just a twinge of professional jealousy. You don't like the idea of an outsider playing your game better than you do. Now confess!

POWERS: I am acting as your aide only under duress.

KRETON (*sadly*): Bitter, bitter . . . and to think I chose you especially as my aide. Think of all the other generals who would give anything to have your job.

POWERS: Fortunately, they know nothing about my job.

KRETON: Yes, I do think it wise not to advertise my presence, don't you?

POWERS: I can't see that it makes much difference, since you seem bent on destroying our world.

KRETON: I'm not going to destroy it. A few dozen cities, that's all, and not very nice cities either. Think of the fun you'll have building new ones when it's over.

POWERS: How many millions of people do you plan to kill?

KRETON: Well, quite a few, but they love this sort of thing. You can't convince me they don't. Oh, I know what Laurent says. But he's a misfit, out of step with this time. Fortunately, my new World Council is more reasonable.

POWERS: Paralyzed is the word, sir.

KRETON: You don't think they like me either?

POWERS: You *know* they hate you, sir.

KRETON: But love and hate are so confused in your savage minds and the vibrations of the one are so very like those of the other that I can't always distinguish. You see, we neither love nor hate in my world. We simply have hobbies. (*He strokes the globe of the world tenderly.*) But now to work. Tonight's the big night: first, the sneak attack, then: boom! (*He claps his hands gleefully.*)

(*Dissolve to the living room, to* JOHN *and* ELLEN.)

ELLEN: I've never felt so helpless in my life.

JOHN: Here we all stand around doing nothing while he plans to blow up the world.

ELLEN: Suppose we went to the newspapers.

JOHN: He controls the press. When Laurent resigned they didn't even print his speech.

(*A gloomy pause.*)

ELLEN: What are you thinking about, John?
JOHN: Walnuts.

(*They embrace.*)

ELLEN: Can't we do anything?

JOHN: No, I guess there's nothing.

ELLEN (*vehemently*): Oh! I could kill him!

(KRETON *and* POWERS *enter.*)

KRETON: Very good, Ellen, *very* good! I've never felt you so violent.

ELLEN: You heard what I said to John?

KRETON: Not in words, but you were absolutely bathed in malevolence.

POWERS: I'll get the papers you wanted, sir.

(POWERS *exits.*)

KRETON: I don't think he likes me very much but your father does. Only this morning he offered to handle my public relations and I said I'd let him. Wasn't that nice of him?

JOHN: I think I'll go get some fresh air.

(*He goes out through the terrace door.*)

KRETON: Oh, dear! (*Sighs.*) Only your father is really entering the spirit of the game. He's a much better sport than you, my dear.

ELLEN (*exploding*): Sport! That's it! You think we're sport. You think we're animals to be played with: well, we're not. We're people and we don't want to be destroyed.

KRETON (*patiently*): But *I* am not destroying you. You will be destroying one another of your own free will, as you have always done. I am simply a . . . a kibitzer.

ELLEN: No, you are a vampire!

KRETON: A vampire? You mean I drink blood? Ugh!

ELLEN: No, you drink emotions, our emotions. You'll sacrifice us all for the sake of your . . . your vibrations!

KRETON: Touché. Yet what harm am I really doing? It's true I'll enjoy the war more than anybody; but it will be *your* destructiveness after all, not mine.

ELLEN: You could stop it.

KRETON: So could you.

ELLEN: I?

KRETON: Your race. They could stop altogether but they won't. And I can hardly intervene in their natural development. The most I can do is help out in small, practical ways.

ELLEN: We are not what you think. We're not so . . . so primitive.

KRETON: My dear girl, just take this one household: your mother dislikes your father but she is too tired to do anything about it so she knits and she gardens and she tries not to think about him. Your father, on the other hand, is bored with all of you. Don't look shocked: he doesn't like you any more than you like him. . . .

ELLEN: Don't say that!

KRETON: I am only telling you the truth. Your father wants you to marry someone important; therefore he objects to John while you, my girl . . .

ELLEN (*with a fierce cry, grabs vase to throw*): You devil! (*Vase breaks in her hand.*)

KRETON: You see? That proves my point perfectly. (*Gently.*) Poor savage, I cannot help what you are. (*Briskly.*) Anyway, you will soon be distracted from your personal problems. Tonight is the night. If you're a good girl, I'll let you watch the bombing.

✤ (*Dissolve to study: Eleven forty-five.* POWERS *and the* AIDE *gloomily await the war.*)

AIDE: General, isn't there anything we can do?

POWERS: It's out of our hands.

(KRETON, *dressed as a Hussar with shako, enters.*)

KRETON: Everything on schedule?

✕ POWERS: Yes, sir. Planes left for their targets at twenty-two hundred.

KRETON: Good . . . good. I myself shall take off shortly after midnight to observe the attack firsthand.

POWERS: Yes, sir.

✗ (KRETON *goes into the living room, where the family is gloomily assembled.*)

KRETON (*enters from study*): And now the magic hour approaches! I hope you're all as thrilled as I am.

SPELDING: You still won't tell us who's attacking whom?

KRETON: You'll know in exactly . . . fourteen minutes.

ELLEN (*bitterly*): Are we going to be killed too?

KRETON: Certainly not! You're quite safe, at least in the early stages of the war.

ELLEN: Thank you.

✳ MRS. SPELDING: I suppose this will mean rationing again.

SPELDING: Will . . . will we see anything from here?

KRETON: No, but there should be a good picture on the monitor in the study. Powers is tuning in right now.

JOHN (*at window*): Hey look, up there! Coming this way!

(ELLEN *joins him.*)

ELLEN: What is it?

JOHN: Why . . . it's *another* one! And it's going to land.

KRETON (*surprised*): I'm sure you're mistaken. No one would dream of coming here.

(*He has gone to the window, too.*)

ELLEN: It's landing!

SPELDING: Is it a friend of yours, Mr. Kreton?

KRETON (*slowly*): No, no, not a friend . . .

✗ (KRETON *retreats to the study; he inadvertently drops a lace handkerchief beside the sofa.*)

JOHN: Here he comes.

ELLEN (*suddenly bitter*): Now we have two of them.

✳ MRS. SPELDING: My poor roses.

✗ (*The new* VISITOR *enters in a gleam of light from his ship. He is wearing a most futuristic costume. Without a word, he walks past the awed family into the study.*

KRETON *is cowering behind the globe.* POWERS *and the* AIDE *stare, bewildered, as the* VISITOR *gestures sternly and* KRETON *reluctantly removes shako and sword. They communicate by odd sounds.*)

VISITOR (*to* POWERS): Please leave us alone.

(*Cut to living room as* POWERS *and the* AIDE *enter from the study.*)

POWERS (*to* ELLEN): Who on earth was that?

ELLEN: It's another one, another visitor.

POWERS: Now we're done for.

ELLEN: I'm going in there.

MRS. SPELDING: Ellen, don't you dare!

ELLEN: I'm going to talk to them.

(*Starts to door.*)

JOHN: I'm coming, too.

ELLEN (*grimly*): No, alone. I know what I want to say.

(*Cut to interior of the study, to* KRETON *and the other* VISITOR *as* ELLEN *enters.*)

ELLEN: I want you both to listen to me . . .

VISITOR: You don't need to speak. I know what you will say.

ELLEN: That you have no right here? That you mustn't . . .

VISITOR: I agree. Kreton has no right here. He is well aware that it is forbidden to interfere with the past.

ELLEN: The past?

VISITOR (*nods*): You are the past, the dark ages: we are from the future. In fact, we are *your* descendants on another planet. We visit you from time to time but we never interfere because it would change *us* if we did. Fortunately, I have arrived in time.

ELLEN: There won't be a war?

VISITOR: There will be no war. And there will be no memory of any of this. When we leave here you will forget Kreton and me. Time will turn back to the moment before his arrival.

ELLEN: Why did you want to hurt us?

KRETON (*heart-broken*): Oh, but I didn't! I only wanted to have . . . well, to have a little fun, to indulge my hobby . . . against the rules of course.

VISITOR (*to* ELLEN): Kreton is a rarity among us. Mentally and morally he is retarded. He is a child and he regards your period as his toy.

KRETON: A child, now really!

VISITOR: He escaped from his nursery and came back in time to you. . . .

KRETON: And *every*thing went wrong, everything! I wanted to visit 1860 . . . that's my *real* period but then something happened to the car and I ended up here, not that I don't find you nearly as interesting but . . .

VISITOR: We must go, Kreton.

KRETON (*to* ELLEN): You did like me just a bit, didn't you?

ELLEN: Yes, yes I did, until you let your hobby get out of hand. (*To* VISITOR) What is the future like?

VISITOR: Very serene, very different . . .

KRETON: Don't believe him: it is dull, dull, dull beyond belief! One simply floats through eternity: no wars, no excitement . . .

VISITOR: It is forbidden to discuss these matters.

KRETON: I can't see what difference it makes since she's going to forget all about us anyway.

ELLEN: Oh, how I'd love to see the future . . .

VISITOR: It is against . . .

KRETON: Against the rules: how tiresome, you are. (*To* ELLEN) But, alas, you can never pay us a call because you aren't born yet! I mean where we are you are not. Oh, Ellen, dear, think kindly of me, until you forget.

ELLEN: I will.

VISITOR: Come. Time has begun to turn back. Time is bending.

(*He starts to door.* KRETON *turns conspiratorially to* ELLEN.)

KRETON: Don't be sad, my girl. I shall be back one bright day, but a bright day in 1860. I dote on the Civil War, so exciting . . .

VISITOR: Kreton!

KRETON: Only next time I think it'll be more fun if the *South* wins! (*He hurries after the* VISITOR.)

(*Cut to clock as the hands spin backwards. Dissolve to the living room, exactly the same as the first scene:* SPELDING, MRS. SPELDING, ELLEN.)

SPELDING: There is nothing wrong with marrying a wealthy man. The horror of it has always eluded me. However, my only wish is that you marry someone hard-working, ambitious, a man who'll make his mark in the world. Not a boy who is content to sit on a farm all his life, growing peanuts . . .

ELLEN: English walnuts! And he won't just sit there.

SPELDING: Will you stop contradicting me?

ELLEN: But, Daddy, John grows walnuts . . .

(JOHN *enters.*)

JOHN: Hello, everybody.

✱ MRS. SPELDING: Good evening, John.

ELLEN: What kept you, darling? You missed Daddy's broadcast.

JOHN: I saw it before I left home. Wonderful broadcast, sir.

SPELDING: Thank you, John.

(JOHN *crosses to window.*)

JOHN: That meteor you were talking about, well, for a while it looked almost like a space ship or something. You can just barely see it now.

(ELLEN *joins him at window. They watch, arms about one another.*)

SPELDING: Space ship! Nonsense! Remarkable what some people will believe, *want* to believe. Besides, as I said in the broadcast: if there's any traveling to be done in space we'll do it first.

(He notices KRETON'S handkerchief on sofa and picks it up. They all look at it, puzzled, as we cut to stock shot of the starry night against which two space ships vanish in the distance, one serene in its course, the other erratic, as we fade out.)

PADDY CHAYEFSKY:

The Mother

Paddy Chayefsky (1923–   ), a native of New York
City, received his education in the New York City public
schools and at City College. During World War II, while
serving overseas, he was hospitalized and began writing
his first plays. Mr. Chayefsky's first dramatic success was
the television play *Marty*, which was subsequently made
into a successful motion picture. His two most notable
plays for the legitimate theater are *Middle of the Night*
and *The Tenth Man*.

The work of Mr. Chayefsky communicates so intense
an impression of reality that it often causes us to feel as
though we were accidentally eavesdropping on our neighbors, our friends, or members of our own family. In *The
Mother*, a television play, we look through windows into
rooms where we see unmade beds and women in their
nightclothes; we listen to painfully explicit telephone con-
versations. "Painful" is an accurate description of the
feelings engendered by much of Mr. Chayefsky's work, a
pain which is softened by his up-beat, vaguely optimistic
endings.

But painful as *The Mother* is (and what, after all, is
more universally heartbreaking than the sight of a good
mother waging a losing battle against the attritional forces
of time?), the play is not merely a dramatized case history. Mr. Chayefsky is a capable craftsman, possessed of
a faultless ear for the characteristic, flavorful speech of
lower-middle-class New Yorkers. While his work may lack
the poetry of an O'Casey or a Tennessee Williams (that
is to say, it fails to liberate our imagination or evoke a
wide range of emotions), Mr. Chayefsky's plays, at their

best, enlist our deep sympathies, our abiding interest, and our admiration for the courage and the good will of the thoroughly believable and essentially decent human beings who people his plays.

In *The Mother,* Mr. Chayefsky successfully isolates and defines the life patterns, the attitudes, the ideals, and the aspirations of the urban lower-middle class. What specifically, among those ideals and attitudes, comes into focus as we read the play? And how do they differ from those of people who populate the villages and towns, who are of different social-economic backgrounds? To what extent can we conclude that Mr. Chayefsky has illuminated life as it is lived in America?

The Mother

Characters

OLD LADY.
DAUGHTER.
BOSS.
SON-IN-LAW.
NEGRO WOMAN.
SISTER.
MRS. GEEGAN.
MRS. KLINE.
BOOKKEEPER.
PUERTO RICAN GIRL.

ACT I

(Fade in: Film—a quick group of shots showing New York in a real thunderstorm—rain whipping through the streets—real miserable weather.

Dissolve to close-up of an old woman, aged sixty-six, with a shock of gray-white hair, standing by a window in her apartment, looking out, apparently deeply disturbed by the rain slashing against the pane.

We pull back to see that the old woman is wearing an old kimono, under which there is evidence of an old white batiste nightgown. Her gray-white hair hangs loosely down over her shoulders. It is early morning, and she has apparently just gotten out of bed. This is the bedroom of her two-and-a-half-room apartment in a lower-middle-class neighborhood in the Bronx. The bed is still unmade and looks just slept in. The furniture is old and worn. On the chest of drawers there is a galaxy of photographs and portrait pictures, evidently of her various children and grandchildren. She stands looking out the window, troubled, disturbed.

Suddenly the alarm, perched on the little bed table, rings. Camera moves in for close-up of the alarm clock. It reads half past six. The OLD LADY'S *hand comes down and shuts the alarm off.*

Cut to close-up of another alarm clock, ringing in another apartment. It also reads half past six; but it is obviously a different clock, on a much more modern bed table. This one buzzes instead of clangs. A young woman's hand reaches over and turns it off.

Camera pulls back to show that we are in the bedroom of a young couple. The young woman who has turned the clock off is a rather plain girl of thirty. She slowly sits up in bed, assembling herself for the day. On the other half of the bed, her husband turns and tries to go back to sleep.)

SON-IN-LAW *(from under the blankets)*: What time is it?

DAUGHTER *(still seated heavily on the edge of the bed)*: It's half past six.

SON-IN-LAW *(from under the blankets)*: What did you set it so early for?

DAUGHTER: I wanna call my mother. *(She looks out at the window, the rain driving fiercely against it.)* For heaven's sake, listen to that rain! She's not going down today, I'll tell you that, if I have to go over there and chain her in her bed. . . . *(She stands, crosses to the window, studies the rain.)* Boy, look at it rain.

SON-IN-LAW *(still under the covers)*: What?

DAUGHTER: I said, it's raining.

(She makes her way, still heavy with sleep, out of the bedroom into the foyer of the apartment. She pads in her bare feet and pajamas down the foyer to the telephone table, sits on the little chair, trying to clear her head of sleep. A baby's cry is suddenly heard in an off room. The young woman absently goes "Sshh." The baby's cry stops. The young woman picks up the receiver of the phone and dials. She waits. Then. . . .)

DAUGHTER: Ma? This is Annie. Did I wake you up? . . . I figured you'd be up by now. . . . Ma, you're not going downtown today, and I don't wanna hear no arguments. . . . Ma, have you looked out the window? It's raining like . . . Ma, I'm not gonna let you go downtown today, do you hear me? . . . I don't care, Ma . . . Ma, I don't care . . . Ma, I'm coming over. You stay there till . . . Ma, stay there till I come over. I'm getting dressed right now. I'll drive over in the car. It won't take me ten minutes. . . . Ma, you're not going out in this rain. It's not enough that you almost fainted in the subway yesterday . . . Ma, I'm

hanging up, and I'm coming over right now. Stay there
. . . all right, I'm hanging up. . . .

(*She hangs up, sits for a minute, then rises and shuffles
back up the foyer and back into her bedroom. She disappears into the bathroom, unbuttoning the blouse of her
pajamas. She leaves the bathroom door open, and a shaft
of light suddenly shoots out into the dark bedroom.*)

SON-IN-LAW (*awake now, his head visible over the
covers*): Did you talk to her?

DAUGHTER (*off in bathroom*): Yeah, she was all practically ready to leave.

SON-IN-LAW: Look, Annie, I don't wanna tell you how
to treat your own mother, but why don't you leave her
alone? It's obviously very important to her to get a job
for herself. She wants to support herself. She doesn't want
to be a burden on her children. I respect her for that. An
old lady, sixty-six years old, going out and looking for
work. I think that shows a lot of guts.

(*The* DAUGHTER *comes out of the bathroom. She has a
blouse on now and a half-slip.*)

DAUGHTER (*crossing to the closet*): George, please, you
don't know what you're talking about, so do me a favor,
and don't argue with me. I'm not in a good mood. (*She
opens the closet, studies the crowded rack of clothes.*) I'm
turning on the light, so get your eyes ready. (*She turns on
the light. The room is suddenly bright. She blinks and
pokes in the closet for a skirt, which she finally extracts.*)
My mother worked like a dog all her life, and she's not
gonna spend the rest of her life bent over a sewing machine. (*She slips into the skirt.*) She had one of her attacks in the subway yesterday. I was never so scared in my
life when that cop called yesterday. (*She's standing in
front of her mirror now, hastily arranging her hair.*) My
mother worked like a dog to raise me and my brother and
my sister. She worked in my old man's grocery store till
twelve o'clock at night. We owe her a little peace of mind,
my brother and my sister and me. She sacrificed plenty
for us in her time. (*She's back at the closet, fishing for
her topcoat.*) And I want her to move out of that apart-

ment. I don't want her living alone. I want her to come live here with us, George, and I don't want any more arguments about that either. We can move Tommy in with the baby, and she can have Tommy's room. And that reminds me—the baby cried for a minute there. If she cries again, give her her milk because she went to sleep without her milk last night. (*She has her topcoat on now and is already at the door to the foyer.*) All right, I'll probably be back in time to make your breakfast. Have you got the keys to the car? . . . (*She nervously pats the pocket of her coat.*) No, I got them. All right, I'll see you. Good-bye, George . . . (*She goes out into the foyer.*)

SON-IN-LAW: Good-bye, Annie . . .

(*Off in some other room, the baby begins to cry again, a little more insistently. The husband raises his eyebrows and listens for a moment. When it becomes apparent that the baby isn't going to stop, he sighs and begins to get out of bed.*

Dissolve to the OLD LADY *standing by the window again. She is fully dressed now, however, even to the black coat and hat. The coat is unbuttoned. For the first time, we may be aware of a black silk mourning band that the* OLD LADY *has about the sleeve of her coat. Outside, the rain has abated considerably. It is drizzling lightly now. The* OLD LADY *turns to her* DAUGHTER, *standing at the other end of the bedroom, brushing the rain from her coat. When the* OLD LADY *speaks, it is with a mild, but distinct, Irish flavor.*)

OLD LADY: It's letting up a bit.

DAUGHTER (*brushing off her coat*): It isn't letting up at all. It's gonna stop and start all day long.

(*The* OLD LADY *starts out of her bedroom, past her* DAUGHTER, *into her living room.*)

OLD LADY: I'm going to make a bit of coffee for myself and some Rice Krispies. Would you like a cup?

(*The* DAUGHTER *turns and starts into the living room ahead of her mother.*)

DAUGHTER: I'll make it for you.

OLD LADY: You won't make it for me. I'll make it myself.

(*She crowds past the* DAUGHTER *and goes to the kitchen. At the kitchen doorway, she turns and surveys her* DAUGHTER.)

OLD LADY: Annie, you know, you can drive somebody crazy, do you know that?

DAUGHTER: I can drive somebody crazy! *You're* the one who can drive somebody crazy.

OLD LADY: Will you stop hovering over me like I was a cripple in a wheel chair. I can make my own coffee, believe me. Why did you come over here? You've got a husband and two kids to take care of. Go make coffee for them, for heaven's sakes.

(*She turns and goes into the kitchen, muttering away. She opens a cupboard and extracts a jar of instant coffee.*)

OLD LADY: I've taken to making instant coffee, would you like a cup?

(*The* DAUGHTER *is standing on the threshold of the kitchen now, leaning against the doorjamb.*)

DAUGHTER: All right, make me a cup, Ma.

(*The* OLD LADY *takes two cups and saucers out and begins carefully to level out a teaspoonful of the instant coffee into each. The* DAUGHTER *moves into the kitchen, reaches up for something in the cupboard.*)

DAUGHTER: Where do you keep your saccharin, Ma?

(*The* OLD LADY *wheels and slaps the* DAUGHTER'S *outstretched arms down.*)

OLD LADY: Annie, I'll get it myself! (*She points a finger into the living room.*) Go in there and sit down, will you? I'll bring the cup in to you!

(*The* DAUGHTER *leans back against the doorjamb, a little exasperated with the* OLD LADY'S *petulant independence. The* OLD LADY *now takes an old teapot and sets it on the stove and lights a flame under it.*)

OLD LADY: You can drive me to the subway if you want to do something for me.

DAUGHTER: Ma, you're not going downtown today.

OLD LADY: I want to get down there extra early today on the off-chance that they haven't given the job to some-one else. What did I do with that card from the New York State Employment Service? . . .

(*She shuffles out of the kitchen, the* DAUGHTER *moving out of the doorway to give her passage. The* OLD LADY *goes to the table in the living room on which sits her battered black purse. She opens it and takes out a card.*)

OLD LADY: I don't want to lose that. (*She puts the white card back into her purse.*) I'm pretty sure I could have held onto this job, because the chap at the Employment Service called up the boss, you see, over the phone, and he explained to the man that I hadn't worked in quite a number of years. . . .

DAUGHTER (*muttering*): Quite a number of years . . .

OLD LADY: . . . and that I'd need a day or so to get used to the machines again.

DAUGHTER: Did the chap at the Employment Service explain to the boss that it's forty years that you haven't worked?

OLD LADY (*crossing back to the kitchen*): . . . and the boss understood this, you see, so he would have been a little lenient with me. But then, of course, I had to go and faint in the subway, because I was in such a hurry to get down there, you know, I didn't even stop to eat my lunch. I had brought along some sandwiches, you see, cheese and tomatoes. Oh, I hope he hasn't given the job to anyone else. . . .

(*The* OLD LADY *reaches into the cupboard again for a bowl of sugar, an opened box of Rice Krispies, and a bowl. The* DAUGHTER *watches her as she turns to the refrigerator to get out a container of milk.*)

DAUGHTER: Ma, when are you gonna give up?

(*The* OLD LADY *frowns.*)

OLD LADY: Annie, please . . .

(*She pours some Rice Krispies into the bowl.*)

DAUGHTER: Ma, you been trying for three weeks now. If you get a job, you get fired before the day is over. You're too old, Ma, and they don't want to hire old people. . . .

OLD LADY: It's not the age. . . .

DAUGHTER: They don't want to hire white-haired old ladies.

OLD LADY: It's not the age at all! I've seen plenty old people with white hair and all, sitting at those machines. The shop where I almost had that job and he fired me the other day, there was a woman there, eighty years old if she was a day, an old crone of a woman, sitting there all bent over, her machine humming away. The chap at the Employment Service said there's a lot of elderly people working in the needle trades. The young people nowadays don't want to work for thirty-five dollars a week, and there's a lot of old people working in the needle trades.

DAUGHTER: Well, whatever it is, Ma . . .

OLD LADY (*leaning to her* DAUGHTER): It's my fingers. I'm not sure of them any more. When you get old, y'know, you lose the sureness in your fingers. My eyes are all right, but my fingers tremble a lot. I get excited, y'know, when I go in for a tryout, y'know. And I'll go in, y'know, and the boss'll say: "Sit down, let's see what you can do." And I get so excited. And my heart begins thumping so that I can hardly see to thread the needle. And they stand right over you, y'know, while you're working. They give you a packet of sleeves or a shirt or something to put a hem on. Or a seam or something, y'know. It's simple work, really. Single-needle machine. Nothing fancy. And it seems to me I do it all right, but they fire me all the time. They say: "You're too slow." And I'm working as fast as I can. I think, perhaps, I've lost the ability in my fingers. And that's what scares me the most. It's not the age. I've seen plenty of old women working in the shops.

(*She has begun to pour some milk into her bowl of*

*cereal; but she stops now and just stands, staring bleakly
down at the worn oilcloth on her cupboard.)*

DAUGHTER (*gently*): Ma, you worked all your life. Why
don't you take it easy?

OLD LADY: I don't want to take it easy. Now that your
father's dead and in the grave I don't know what to do
with myself.

DAUGHTER: Why don't you go out, sit in the park, get
a little sun like the other old women?

OLD LADY: I sit around here sometimes, going crazy.
We had a lot of fights in our time, your father and I, but
I must admit I miss him badly. You can't live with someone forty-one years and not miss him when he's dead. I'm
glad that he died for his own sake—it may sound hard of
me to say that—but I am glad. He was in nothing but pain
the last few months, and he was a man who could never
stand pain. But I do miss him.

DAUGHTER (*gently*): Ma, why don't you come live with
George and me?

OLD LADY: No, no, Annie, you're a good daughter. . . .

DAUGHTER: We'll move Tommy into the baby's room,
and you can have Tommy's room. It's the nicest room in
the apartment. It gets all the sun. . . .

OLD LADY: I have wonderful children. I thank God
every night for that. I . . .

DAUGHTER: Ma, I don't like you living here alone. . . .

OLD LADY: Annie, I been living in this house for eight
years, and I know all the neighbors and the store people,
and if I lived with you, I'd be a stranger.

DAUGHTER: There's plenty of old people in my neighborhood. You'll make friends.

OLD LADY: Annie, you're a good daughter, but I want
to keep my own home. I want to pay my own rent. I don't
want to be some old lady living with her children. If I can't
take care of myself, I just as soon be in the grave with
your father. I don't want to be a burden on my children. . . .

DAUGHTER: Ma, for heaven's sakes . . .

OLD LADY: More than anything else, I don't want to be
a burden on my children. I pray to God every night to let

me keep my health and my strength so that I won't have to be a burden on my children. . . . (*The teapot suddenly hisses. The* OLD LADY *looks up.*) Annie, the pot is boiling. Would you pour the water in the cups?

(*The* DAUGHTER *moves to the stove. The* OLD LADY, *much of her ginger seemingly sapped out of her, shuffles into the living room. She perches on the edge of one of the wooden chairs.*)

OLD LADY: I been getting some pains in my shoulder the last week or so. I had the electric heating pad on practically the whole night. . . . (*She looks up toward the windows again.*) It's starting to rain a little harder again. Maybe I won't go downtown today after all. Maybe, if it clears up a bit, I'll go out and sit in the park and get some sun.

(*In the kitchen, the* DAUGHTER *pours the boiling water into each cup, stirs.*)

DAUGHTER (*to her mother, off in the living room*): Is this all you're eating for breakfast, Ma? Let me make you something else . . .

(*Dissolve to a park bench. The* OLD LADY *and two other old ladies are seated, all bundled up in their cheap cloth coats with the worn fur collars. The second old lady is also Irish. Her name is* MRS. GEEGAN. *The third old lady is possibly Jewish, certainly a New Yorker by intonation. Her name is* MRS. KLINE. *The rain has stopped; it is a clear, bright, sunny March morning.*)

OLD LADY: . . . Well, it's nice and clear now, isn't it? It was raining something fierce around seven o'clock this morning.

MRS. GEEGAN (*grimacing*): It's too ruddy cold for me. I'd go home except my daughter-in-law's cleaning the house, and I don't want to get in her way.

MRS. KLINE: My daughter-in-law should drop dead tomorrow.

MRS. GEEGAN: My daughter-in-law gets into an awful black temper when she's cleaning.

MRS. KLINE: My daughter-in-law should grow rich and own a hotel with a thousand rooms and be found dead in every one of them.

MRS. GEEGAN (*to the* OLD LADY): I think I'll go over and visit Missus Halley in a little while, would you like to go? She fell down the stairs and broke her hip, and they're suing the owners of the building. I saw her son yesterday, and he says she's awful weak. When you break a hip at that age, you're as good as in the coffin. I don't like to visit Missus Halley. She's always so gloomy about things. But it's a way of killing off an hour or so to lunch. A little later this afternoon, I thought I'd go to confession. It's so warm and solemn in the church. Do you go to Saint John's? I think it's ever so much prettier than Our Lady of Visitation. Why don't you come to Missus Halley's with me, Missus Fanning? Her son's a sweet man, and there's always a bit of fruit they offer you.

OLD LADY: I don't believe I know a Missus Halley.

MRS. GEEGAN: Missus Halley, the one that fell down the stairs last week and dislocated her hip. They're suing the owners of the building for forty thousand dollars.

MRS. KLINE: They'll settle for a hundred, believe me.

MRS. GEEGAN: Oh, it's chilly this morning. I'd go home, but my daughter-in-law is cleaning the house, and she doesn't like me to be about when she's cleaning. I'd like a bottle of beer, that's what I'd like. Oh, my mouth is fairly watering for it. I'm not allowed to have beer, you know. I'm a diabetic. You don't happen to have a quarter on you, Missus Fanning? We could buy a bottle and split it between us. I'd ask my son for it, but they always want to know what I want the money for.

OLD LADY (*looking sharply at* MRS. GEEGAN): Do you have to ask your children for money?

MRS. GEEGAN: Oh, they're generous. They always give me whenever I ask. But I'm not allowed to have beer, you see, and they wouldn't give me the twenty-five cents for that. What do I need money for anyway? Go to the movies? I haven't been to the movies in more than a year, I think. I just like a dollar every now and then for an offering at mass. Do you go to seven o'clock novena,

Missus Fanning? It's a good way to spend an hour, I think.

OLD LADY: Is that what you do with your day, Missus Geegan? Visit dying old ladies and go to confession?

MRS. GEEGAN: Well, I like to stay in the house a lot, watching television in the afternoons, with the kiddie shows and a lot of dancing and Kate Smith and shows like that. But my daughter-in-law's cleaning up today, and she doesn't like me around the house when she's cleaning, so I came out a bit early to sit in the park.

(*The* OLD LADY *regards* MRS. GEEGAN *for a long moment.*)

MRS. KLINE: My daughter-in-law, she should invest all her money in General Motors stock, and they should go bankrupt.

(*A pause settles over the three old ladies. They just sit, huddled, their cheeks pressed into the fur of their collars. After a moment, the* OLD LADY *shivers noticeably.*)

OLD LADY: It's a bit chilly. I think I'll go home. (*She rises.*) Good-bye, Missus Geegan . . . Good-bye, Missus . . .

(*The other two old ladies nod their goodbyes. The* OLD LADY *moves off screen. We hold for a moment on the remaining two old ladies, sitting, shoulders hunched against the morning chill, faces pressed under their collars, staring bleakly ahead.*

Dissolve to door of the old lady's apartment. It opens, and the OLD LADY *comes in. She closes the door behind her, goes up the small foyer to the living room. She unbuttons her coat and walks aimlessly around the room, into the bedroom and out again, across the living room and into the kitchen, and then out of the kitchen. She is frowning as she walks and rubs her hands continually as if she is quite cold. Suddenly she goes to the telephone, picks it up, dials a number, waits.*)

OLD LADY (*snappishly*): Is this Mister McCleod? This is Missus Fanning in Apartment 3F! The place is a refrigerator up here! It's freezing! I want some steam! I want

it right now! That's all there is to it! I want some steam
right now!

(*She hangs up sharply, turns—scowling—and sits heavily down on the edge of a soft chair, scowling, nervous,
rocking a little back and forth. Then abruptly she rises,
crosses the living room to the television set, clicks it on.
She stands in front of it, waiting for a picture to show. At
last the picture comes on. It is the WPIX station signal,
accompanied by the steady high-pitched drone that indicates there are no programs on yet. She turns the set off
almost angrily.*

*She is beginning to breathe heavily now. She turns
nervously and looks at the large ornamental clock on the
sideboard. It reads ten minutes after eleven. She goes to
the small dining table and sits down on one of the hard-
back chairs. Her black purse is still on the table, as it was
during the scene with her daughter. Her eyes rest on it for
a moment; then she reaches over, opens the purse, and
takes out the white employment card. She looks at it briefly,
expressionlessly. Then she returns it to the purse and re-
clasps the purse. Again she sits for a moment, rigid, ex-
pressionless. Then suddenly she stands, grabs the purse,
and starts out the living room, down the foyer, to the front
door of her apartment—buttoning her coat as she goes.
She opens the door, goes out.*

*Camera stays on door as it is closed. There is the noise
of a key being inserted into the lock. A moment later the
bolts on the lock shift into locked position. Hold.*)

(*Fade out.*)

ACT II

(*Fade in: Film—lunchtime in the needle-trade district
of New York—a quick montage of shots of the streets,
jammed with traffic, trucks, and working people hurrying
to the dense little luncheonettes for their lunch.*

Dissolve to interior of the Tiny Tots Sportswear Co., Inc., 137 West Twenty-seventh Street, on the eighth floor. It is lunchtime. We dissolve in on some of the women operators at their lunch. They are seated at their machines, of which there are twenty—in two rows of ten, facing each other. Not all of the operators eat their lunch in: about half go downstairs to join the teeming noontime crowds in the oily little restaurants of the vicinity. The ten-or-so women whom we see—munching their sandwiches and sipping their containers of coffee and chattering shrilly to one another—all wear worn house dresses. A good proportion of the operators are Negro and Puerto Rican. Not a few of them are gray-haired, or at least unmistakably middle-aged.

The rest of the shop seems to consist of endless rows of pipe racks on which hang finished children's dresses, waiting to be shipped. In the middle of these racks is a pressing machine and sorting table at which two of the three men who work in the shop eat their lunch. At the far end of the loft—in a corner so dark that a light must always be on over it—is an old, battered roll-top desk at which sits the BOOKKEEPER, *an angular woman of thirty-five, differentiated from the hand workers in that she wears a clean dress.*

Nearby is the BOSS, *a man in his thirties. He is bent over a machine, working on it with a screw driver. The* BOSS *is really a pleasant man; he works under the illusion, however, that gruffness is a requisite quality of an executive.*

Somehow, a tortured passageway has been worked out between the racks leading to the elevator doors; it is the only visible exit and entrance to the loft.

As we look at these doors, there is a growing whirring and clanging announcing the arrival of the elevator. The doors slide reluctantly open, and the OLD LADY *enters the shop. The elevator doors slide closed behind her. She stands surrounded by pipe racks, a little apprehensive. The arrival of the elevator has caused some of the people to look up briefly. The* OLD LADY *goes to the presser, a Puerto Rican.)*

OLD LADY: Excuse me, I'm looking for the boss.

(*The presser indicates with his hand the spot where the* BOSS *is standing, working on the machine. The* OLD LADY *picks her way through the cluttered pipe racks to the* BOOKKEEPER, *who looks up at her approach. The* BOSS *also looks up briefly at her approach, but goes back to his work. The* OLD LADY *opens her purse, takes out the white card, and proffers it to the* BOOKKEEPER. *She mutters something.*)

BOOKKEEPER: Excuse me, I can't hear what you said.

OLD LADY: I said, I was supposed to be here yesterday, but I was sick in the subway I—fainted, you see and . . .

(*The* BOSS *now turns to the* OLD LADY.)

BOSS: What? . . . What? . . .

OLD LADY: I was sent down from the . . .

BOSS: What?

OLD LADY (*louder*): I was sent down from the New York State Employment Service. I was supposed to be here yesterday.

BOSS: Yes, so what happened?

OLD LADY: I was sick, I fainted in the subway.

BOSS: What?

OLD LADY (*louder*): I was sick. The subway was so hot there, you see—there was a big crush at a Hundred and Forty-ninth Street . . .

BOSS: You was supposed to be here yesterday.

OLD LADY: I had a little trouble. They had my daughter down there and everything. By the time I got down here, it was half past five, and the fellow on the elevator—not the one that was here this morning—another fellow entirely. An old man it was. He said there was nobody up here. So I was going to come down early this morning, but I figured you probably had the job filled anyway. That's why I didn't come down till now.

BOSS: What kind of work do you do?

OLD LADY: Well, I used to do all sections except joining and zippers, but I think the fellow at the Employment

Service explained to you that it's been a number of years since I actually worked in a shop.

BOSS: What do you mean, a number of years?

OLD LADY (*mumbling*): Well, I did a lot of sewing for the Red Cross during the war, y'know, but I haven't actually worked in a shop since nineteen sixteen.

BOSS (*who didn't quite hear her mumbled words*): What?

OLD LADY (*louder*): Nineteen sixteen. October.

BOSS: Nineteen sixteen.

OLD LADY: I'm sure if I could work a little bit, I would be fine. I used to be a very fast worker.

BOSS: Can you thread a machine?

(*The* OLD LADY *nods.*
He starts off through the maze of pipe racks to the two rows of machines. The OLD LADY *follows him, clutching her purse and the white card, her hat still sitting on her head, her coat still buttoned. As they go up the rows of sewing machines, the other operators look up to catch covert glimpses of the new applicant. The* BOSS *indicates one of the open machines.*)

BOSS: All right. Siddown. Show me how you thread a machine.

(*The* OLD LADY *sets her purse down nervously and takes the seat behind the machine. The other operators have all paused in their eating to watch the test. The* OLD LADY *reaches to her side, where there are several spools of thread.*)

OLD LADY: What kind of thread, white or black? . . .

BOSS: White! White!

(*She fumblingly fetches a spool of white thread and, despite the fact she is obviously trembling, she contrives to thread the machine—a process which takes about half a minute. The* BOSS *stands towering over her.*)

BOSS: Can you sleeve?

(*The* OLD LADY *nods, desperately trying to get the*

thread through the eye of the needle and over the proper holes.)

BOSS: It's a simple business. One seam.

(*He reaches into the bin belonging to the machine next to the one the* OLD LADY *is working on and extracts a neatly tied bundle of sleeve material. He drops it on the table beside the* OLD LADY.)

BOSS: All right, make a sleeve. Let's see how you make a sleeve.

(*He breaks the string and gives her a piece of sleeve material. She takes it, but is so nervous it falls to the floor. She hurriedly bends to pick it up, inserts the sleeve into the machine, and hunches into her work—her face screwed tight with intense concentration. She has still not unbuttoned her coat, and beads of sweat begin to appear on her brow. With painstaking laboriousness, she slowly moves the sleeve material into the machine. The* BOSS *stands, impatient and scowling.*)

BOSS: Mama, what are you weaving there, a carpet? It's a lousy sleeve, for Pete's sake.

OLD LADY: I'm a little unsure. My fingers are a little unsure . . .

BOSS: You gotta be fast, Mama. This is week work. It's not piecework. I'm paying you by the hour. I got twenny dozen cottons here, gotta be out by six o'clock. The truck-man isn't gonna wait, you know . . . Mama, Mama, watch what you're doing there. . . . (*He leans quickly forward and reguides the material.*) A straight seam, for heaven's sake! You're making it crooked . . . Watch it! Watch it! Watch what you're doing there, Mama. . . . All right, sew. Don't let me make you nervous. Sew . . . Mama, wadda you sewing there, an appendicitis operation? It's a lousy sleeve. How long you gonna take? I want operators here, not surgeons. . . .

(*Through all this, the terrified* OLD LADY *tremblingly pushes the material through the machine. Finally she's finished. She looks up at the* BOSS, *her eyes wide with appre-*

hension, ready to pick up her purse and dash out to the street. The BOSS *picks up the sleeve, studies it, then drops it on the table, mutters.*)

BOSS: All right, we'll try you out for a while. . . .

(*He turns abruptly and goes back through the pipe racks to the desk. The* OLD LADY *sits, trembling, a little slumped, her coat still buttoned to the collar. A middle-aged* NEGRO WOMAN, *sitting at the next machine over her lunch, leans over to the* OLD LADY.)

NEGRO WOMAN (*gently*): Mama, what are you sitting there in your hat and coat for? Hang them up, honey. You go through that door over there.

(*She points to a door leading into a built-in room. The* OLD LADY *looks up slowly at this genuine sympathy.*)

NEGRO WOMAN: Don't let him get you nervous, Mama. He likes to yell a lot, but he's okay.

(*The tension within the* OLD LADY *suddenly bursts out in the form of a soft, staccato series of sighs. She quickly masters herself.*)

OLD LADY (*smiling at the* NEGRO WOMAN): I'm a little unsure of myself. My fingers are a little unsure.

(*Cut to the* BOSS, *standing by the desk. He leans down to mutter to the* BOOKKEEPER.)

BOSS (*muttering*): How could I say no, will you tell me? How could I say no? . . .
BOOKKEEPER: Nobody says you should say no.
BOSS: She was so nervous, did you see how nervous she was? I bet you she's seventy years old. How could I say no? (*The telephone suddenly rings.*) Answer . . .

(*The* BOOKKEEPER *picks up the receiver.*)

BOOKKEEPER (*on the phone*): Tiny Tots Sportswear . . .
BOSS (*in a low voice*): Who is it?
BOOKKEEPER (*on phone*): He's somewhere on the floor, Mister Raymond. I'll see if I can find him. . . .
BOSS (*frowning*): Which Raymond is it, the younger one or the older one?

BOOKKEEPER: The younger one.

BOSS: You can't find me.

(*The* BOOKKEEPER *starts to relay this message, but the* BOSS *changes his mind. He takes the receiver.*)

BOSS: Hello, Jerry? This is Sam . . . Jerry, for heaven's sake, the twenty dozen just came at half past nine this morning . . . Jerry, I told you six o'clock; it'll be ready six o'clock. . . .(*Suddenly lowers his voice, turns away from the* BOOKKEEPER, *embarrassed at the pleading he's going to have to go through now.*) Jerry, how about that fifty dozen faille sports suits? . . . Have a heart, Jerry, I need the work. I haven't got enough work to keep my girls. Two of them left yesterday . . . Jerry, please, what kind of living can I make on these cheap cottons? Give me a fancier garment. . . . It's such small lots, Jerry. At least give me big lots. . . . (*Lowering his voice even more.*) Jerry, I hate to appeal to you on this level, but I'm your brother-in-law, you know. . . . Things are pretty rough with me right now, Jerry. Have a heart. Send me over the fifty dozen failles you got in yesterday. I'll make a rush job for you . . . please, Jerry, why do you have to make me crawl? All right, I'll have this one for you five o'clock . . . I'll call up the freight man now. How about the failles? . . . Okay, Jerry, thank you, you're a good fellow . . . All right, five o'clock. I'll call the freight man right now . . . Okay . . .

(*He hangs up, stands a moment, sick at his own loss of dignity. He turns to the* BOOKKEEPER, *head bowed.*)

BOSS: My own brother-in-law . . .

(*He shuffles away, looks up. The* OLD LADY, *who had gone into the dressing room to hang up her coat and hat, comes out of the dressing room now. The* BOSS *wheels on her.*)

BOSS: Watsa matter with you? I left you a bundle of sleeves there! You're not even in the shop five minutes, and you walk around like you own the place! (*He wheels to the other operators.*) All right! Come on! Come on! What are you sitting there? Rush job! Rush job! Let's go!

Five o'clock the freight man's coming! Let's go! Let's go!

(*Cut to the bedroom of the* DAUGHTER'S *and* SON-IN-LAW'S *apartment. The bed has been made, the room cleaned up. The blinds have been drawn open, and the room is nice and bright. The* SON-IN-LAW *sits on one of the straight-back chairs, slumped a little, surly, scowling. The* DAUGHTER *sits erectly on the bed, her back to her husband, likewise scowling. Apparently, angry words have passed between them. The doorbell buzzes off. Neither of them moves for a moment. Then the* DAUGHTER *rises. At her move, the* SON-IN-LAW *begins to gather himself together.*)

SON-IN-LAW: I'll get it.

(*The* DAUGHTER *moves—in sullen, quick silence—past him and out into the foyer. The* SON-IN-LAW, *who has started to rise, sits down again.*
In the hallway, the DAUGHTER *pads down to the front door of the apartment. She is wearing a house dress now and house slippers. She opens the door. Waiting at the door is an attractive young woman in her early thirties, in coat and hat.*)

DAUGHTER: Hello, Marie, what are you doing here?
SISTER: Nothing. I just came by for a couple of minutes, that's all. I just brought the kids back to school. I thought I'd drop in for a minute, that's all. How's George?

(*She comes into the apartment. The* DAUGHTER *closes the door after her. The* SISTER *starts down the hallway.*)

DAUGHTER: You came in right in the middle of an argument.

(*The* SON-IN-LAW *is now standing in the bedroom doorway.*)

SON-IN-LAW (*to the* SISTER): Your sister drives me crazy.
SISTER: Watsa matter now?
DAUGHTER (*following her* SISTER *up the foyer*): Nothing's the matter. How's Jack? The kids?

(*The two women go into the bedroom, the* SON-IN-LAW *stepping back to let them in.*)

SISTER: They're fine. Jack's got a little cold, nothing important. I just took the kids back to school, and I thought I'd drop in, see if you feel like going up to Fordham Road, do a little shopping for a couple of hours. (*To the* SON-IN-LAW) What are you doing home?

SON-IN-LAW: It's my vacation. We were gonna leave the kids with my sister, drive downna Virginia, North Carolina, get some warm climate. But your crazy sister don't wanna go. She don't wanna leave your mother. . . . (*Turning to his wife.*) Your mother can take care of herself better than we can. She's a tough old woman. . . . How many vacations you think I get a year? I don't wanna sit in New York for two weeks, watching it rain.

SISTER: Go ahead, Annie. Me and Frank will see that Mom's all right.

DAUGHTER: Sure, you and Frank. Look, Marie, I was over to see Mom this morning . . .

SON-IN-LAW: Half past six she got up this morning, go over to see your mother.

DAUGHTER: After what happened yesterday, I decided to put my foot down. Because Mom got no business at her age riding up and down in the subways. You know how packed they are. Anyway, I called Mom on the phone, and she gave me the usual arguments. You know Mom. So anyway, I went over to see her, and she was very depressed. We talked for about an hour, and she told me she's been feeling very depressed lately. It's no good Mom living there alone, and you know it, Marie. Anyway, I think I finally convinced her to move out of there and come and live over here.

SON-IN-LAW: You didn't convince me.

DAUGHTER: George, please . . .

SON-IN-LAW: Look, Annie, I like your mother. We get along fine. We go over visit her once, twice a week, fine. What I like about her is that she doesn't hang all over you like my mother does.

DAUGHTER: This is the only thing I ever asked you in our whole marriage . . .

SON-IN-LAW: This is just begging for trouble. You know that in the bottom of your heart . . .

DAUGHTER: I don't wanna argue any more about it . . .

SISTER: Look, Annie, I think George is right, I think . . .

(*The* DAUGHTER *suddenly wheels on her* SISTER, *a long-repressed fury trembling out of her.*)

DAUGHTER (*literally screaming*): You keep outta this! You hear me? You never cared about Mom in your whole life! How many times you been over there this week? How many times? I go over every day! Every day! And I go over in the evenings too sometimes!

(*The* SISTER *turns away, not a little shaken by this fierce onslaught. The* DAUGHTER *sits down on the bed again, her back to both her husband and sister, herself confused by the ferocity of her outburst. The* SON-IN-LAW *looks down, embarrassed, at the floor. A moment of sick silence fills the room. Then without turning, but in a much lower voice, the* DAUGHTER *goes on.*)

DAUGHTER: George, I been a good wife to you. Did I ever ask you for mink coats or anything? Anything you want has always been good with me. This is the only thing I ever ask of you. I want my mother to live here with me where I can take care of her.

(*The* SON-IN-LAW *looks up briefly at his wife's unrelenting back and then back to the floor again.*)

SON-IN-LAW: All right, Annie. I won't argue any more with you about it.

SISTER: I guess I better go because I want to get back in the house before three o'clock when the kids come home from school.

(*Nobody says anything, so she starts for the door. The* SON-IN-LAW, *from his sitting position, looks up briefly at her as she passes, but she avoids his eyes. He stands, follows her out into the foyer. They proceed silently down the foyer to the doorway. Here they pause a minute. The scene is conducted in low, intense whispers.*)

SON-IN-LAW: She don't mean nothing, Marie. You know that.

SISTER: I know, I know . . .

SON-IN-LAW: She's a wonderful person. She'd get up at three o'clock in the morning for you. There's nothing she wouldn't do for her family.

SISTER: I know, George. I know Annie better than you know her. When she's sweet, she can be the sweetest person in the world. She's my kid sister but many's the time I came to her to do a little crying. But she's gonna kill my mother with all her sacrifices. She's trying to take away my mother's independence. My mother's been on her own all her life. That's the only way she knows how to live. I went over to see my mother yesterday. She was depressed. It broke my heart because I told Jack; I said: "I think my mother's beginning to give up." My mother used to be so sure of herself all the time, and yesterday she was talking there about how maybe she thinks she is getting a little old to work. It depressed me for the rest of the day. . . .

SON-IN-LAW: Marie, you know that I really like your mother. If I thought it would work out at all, I would have no objection to her coming to live here. But the walls in this place are made out of paper. You can hear everything that goes on in the next room, and . . .

SISTER: It's a big mistake if she comes here. She'll just dry up into bones inside a year.

SON-IN-LAW: Tell that to Annie. Would you do that for me, please?

SISTER: You can't tell Annie nothing. Annie was born at a wrong time. The doctor told my mother she was gonna die if she had Annie, and my mother has been scared of Annie ever since. And if Annie thinks she's gonna get my mother to love her with all these sacrifices, she's crazy. My mother's favorite was always our big brother, Frank, and Annie's been jealous of him as long as I know. I remember one time when we were in Saint John's school on Daly Avenue—I think Annie was about ten years old, and . . . oh, well, look, I better go. I'm not mad at Annie. She's been like this as long as I know her. (*She opens the door.*)

She's doing the worst thing for my mother, absolutely the worst thing. I'll see you, George.

SON-IN-LAW: I'll see you.

(*The* SISTER *goes out, closing the door after her. The* SON-IN-LAW *stands a moment. Then, frowning, he moves back up the foyer to the bedroom. His wife is still seated as we last saw her, her back to the door, her hands in her lap—slumped a little, but with an air of rigid stubbornness about her. The* SON-IN-LAW *regards her for a moment. Then he moves around the bed and sits down beside his wife. He puts his arm around her and pulls her to him. She rests her head on his chest. They sit silently for a moment.*

Dissolve to interior, the shop. The full complement of working operators are there, all hunched over their machines, and the place is a picture of industry. The women chatter shrilly with each other as they work. A radio plays in the background. Occasionally, one of the operators lifts her head and bellows out: "Work! Work! Jessica! Gimme some work!" . . . *The* BOOKKEEPER, *Jessica, scurries back and forth from her desk to the sorting table—where she picks up small cartons of materials, bringing them to the operators—and back to her desk.*

Dissolve to the OLD LADY *and her immediate neighbor, the* NEGRO WOMAN, *both bent over their machines, sewing away. The motors hum. The two women move their materials under the plunging needles. The* OLD LADY *hunches, intense and painfully concentrated, over her work. They sew in silent industry for a moment. Then* . . .)

OLD LADY (*without daring to look up from her work*): I'm getting the feel back, you know?

NEGRO WOMAN (*likewise without looking up*): Sure, you're gonna be all right, Mama.

OLD LADY: I used to be considered a very fast operator. I used to work on the lower East Side in those sweatshops, y'know. Six dollars a week. But I quit in October, 1916, because I got married and, in those days, y'know, it was a terrible disgrace for a married woman to work. So I quit. Not that we had the money. My husband was a house painter when we got married, which is seasonal work at best, and he had to borrow money to go to Atlantic City for three days. That was our honeymoon.

(*They lapse into silence. A woman's shrill voice from farther down the row of machines calls out: "Work! Hey, Jessica! Bring me some work!" The two women sew silently. Then* . . .)

OLD LADY: I got a feeling he's going to keep me on here. The boss, I mean. He seems like a nice enough man.

NEGRO WOMAN: He's nervous, but he's all right.

OLD LADY: I've been looking for almost four weeks now, y'know. My husband died a little more than a month ago.

NEGRO WOMAN: My husband died eighteen years ago.

OLD LADY: He was a very sick man all his life—lead poisoning you know, from the paints. He had to quit the trade after a while, went into the retail grocery business. He was sixty-seven when he died, and I wonder he lived this long. In his last years, the circulation of the blood in his legs was so bad he could hardly walk to the corner.

NEGRO WOMAN: My big trouble is arthritis. I get terrible pains in my arms and in my shoulders sometimes.

OLD LADY: Oh, I been getting a lot of pains in my back, in between my shoulder blades.

NEGRO WOMAN: That's gall bladder.

OLD LADY: Is that what it is?

NEGRO WOMAN: I had that. When you get to our age, Missus Fanning, you gotta expect the bones to rebel.

OLD LADY: Well, now, you're not such an old woman.

NEGRO WOMAN: How old do you think I am?

OLD LADY: I don't know. Maybe forty, fifty.

NEGRO WOMAN: I'm sixty-eight years old.

(*For the first time, the* OLD LADY *looks up. She pauses in her work.*)

OLD LADY: I wouldn't believe you were sixty-eight.

NEGRO WOMAN: I'm sixty-eight. I got more white hair than you have. But I dye it. You oughtta dye your hair too. Just go in the five-and-ten, pick up some kind of hair dye. Because most people don't like to hire old people with white hair. My children don't want me to work no more, but I'm gonna work until I die. How old do you think that old Greek woman over there is?

OLD LADY: How old?

NEGRO WOMAN: She's sixty-nine. She got a son who's a big doctor. She won't quit working either. I like working here. I come in here in the morning, punch the clock. I'm friends with all these women. You see that little Jewish lady down there? That's the funniest little woman I ever met. You get her to tell you some of her jokes during lunch sometime. She gets me laughing sometimes I can hardly stop. What do I wanna sit around my dirty old room for when I got that little Jewish woman there to tell me jokes all day? That's what I tell my children.

(*The* OLD LADY *turns back to her sewing.*)

OLD LADY: Oh, I'd like to hear a couple of jokes.

(*At this moment there is a small burst of high-pitched laughter from farther down the rows of machines. Camera cuts to long shot of the rows of operators, singling out a group of three Puerto Rican girls in their twenties. One of them has apparently just said something that made the other two laugh. A fourth Puerto Rican girl, across the table and up from them, calls to them in Spanish: "What happened? What was so funny?" The Puerto Rican girl who made the others laugh answers in a quick patter of high-pitched Spanish. A sudden gust of laughter sweeps all the Puerto Rican girls at the machines. Another woman calls out: "What she say?" One of the Puerto Rican girls answers in broken English.*)

PUERTO RICAN GIRL: She say, t'ree week ago, she make a mistake, sewed the belts onna dress backward. Nobody found out. Yesterday, she went in to buy her little girl a dress inna store. They tried to sell her one-a these dresses. . . . (*A wave of laughter rolls up and down the two rows of operators.*) She say, the label onna dress say: "Made in California."

(*They absolutely roar at this.*)

(*Close-up: The* OLD LADY *joining in the general laughter. She finishes the sleeve she has been working on. It is apparently the last of the bunch. She gathers together in front of her the two dozen other sleeves she has just finished and begins to tie them up with a black ribbon. She lifts her head up and—with magnificent professionalism—calls out.*)

OLD LADY: Work! Work!

(*Camera closes down on the bundle of sleeves she has tied together with the black ribbon.*
Dissolve to the same bundle of sleeves. We pull back and see it is now being held by the BOSS. *He is frowning down at them. At his elbow is standing one of the Puerto Rican girls. She is muttering in broken English.*)

PUERTO RICAN GIRL: So what I do? The whole bunch, same way . . .

BOSS (*scowling*): All right, all right. Cut them open, resew the whole bunch . . .

PUERTO RICAN GIRL: Cut! I didn't do! I can't cut, sew, five o'clock the truckman . . . I gotta sew them on the blouse. Take two hours . . .

BOSS: All right, all right, cut them open, sew them up again. . . .

(*The girl takes the bundle of sleeves and shuffles away. The* BOSS *turns, suddenly deeply weary. He goes to the desk.*)

BOSS (*to the* BOOKKEEPER): The old lady come in today, she sewed all the sleeves for the left hand. She didn't make any rights. All lefts . . .

BOOKKEEPER: So what are you gonna do? It's half past four.

BOSS: Call up Raymond for me.

(*The* BOOKKEEPER *picks up the phone receiver, dials. The* BOSS *looks up and through the pipe racks at the* OLD LADY, *sitting hunched and intense over her machine, working with concentrated meticulousness. The* BOSS's *attention is called back to the phone by the* BOOKKEEPER. *He takes the phone from her.*)

BOSS (*in a low voice*): Jerry? This is Sam. Listen. I can't give you the whole twenty dozen at five o'clock. . . . All right, wait a minute, lemme . . . All right, wait a minute. I got fifteen dozen on the racks now . . . Jerry, please. I just got a new operator in today. She sewed five dozen sleeves all left-handed. We're gonna have to cut the seams open, and resew them . . . Look, Jerry, I'm sorry, what do you want from me? I can get it for you by six . . . Jerry, I'll pay the extra freight fee myself . . . Jerry . . . Listen, Jerry, how about those fifty dozen faille sport suits? This doesn't change your mind, does it . . . Jerry, it's an accident. It could happen to anyone . . . (*A fury begins to take hold of the* BOSS.) Look, Jerry, you promised me the fifty dozen fai . . . Look, Jerry, you know what you can do with those fifty dozen failles? You think I'm gonna crawl on my knees to you? (*He's shouting now. Every head in the shop begins to look up.*) You're a miserable human being, you hear that? I'd rather go bankrupt than ask you for another order! And don't come over to my house no more! You hear? I ain't gonna crawl to you! You hear me? I ain't gonna crawl to you! . . .

(*He slams the receiver down, stands, his chest heaving, his face flushed. He looks down at the* BOOKKEEPER, *his fury still high.*)

BOSS: Fire her! Fire her! Fire her!

(*He stands, the years of accumulated humiliation and resentment flooding out of him.*)

(*Fade out.*)

ACT III

(*Fade in: Interior of a subway car heading north to the Bronx during the rush hour—absolutely jam-packed. The camera manages to work its way through the dense crowd to settle on the* OLD LADY, *seated in her black coat and hat, her hands folded in her lap, her old purse dangling from her wrist. She is staring bleakly straight ahead of herself, as if in another world. The train hurtles on.*

Dissolve to interior of the OLD LADY'S *apartment—dark —empty. Night has fallen outside. The sound of a key being inserted into the lock. The bolts unlatch, and the door is pushed open. The* OLD LADY *enters. She closes the door after herself, bolts it. She stands a moment in the dark foyer, then shuffles up the foyer to the living room. She unbuttons her coat, sits down by the table, places her purse on the table. For a moment she sits. Then she rises, goes into the kitchen, turns on the light.*

It takes her a moment to remember what she came into the kitchen for. Then, collecting herself, she opens the refrigerator door, extracts a carton of milk, sets it on the cupboard shelf. She opens the cupboard door, reaches in, extracts the box of Rice Krispies and a bowl. She sets the bowl down, begins to open the box of cereal. It falls out of her hands to the floor, a number of the pebbles of cereal rolling out to the floor. She starts to bend to pick the box up, then suddenly straightens and stands breathing heavily, nervously wetting her lips. She moves out of the kitchen quickly now, goes to the table, sits down again, picks up the phone, and dials. There is an edge of desperation in her movements. She waits. Then . . .)

OLD LADY: Frank? Who's this, Lillian? Lillian, dear, this is your mother-in-law, and I . . . oh, I'm sorry, what? . . . Oh, I'm sorry. . . . Who's this, the baby sitter? . . . This is Missus Fanning, dear—Mister Fanning's mother, is he in? . . . Is Missus Fanning in? . . . Well, do you expect them in? I mean, it's half past six. Did they eat their dinner already? . . . Oh, I see. Well, when do you . . . Oh, I see . . . No, dear, this is Mister Fanning's mother. Just tell him I called. It's not important.

(She hangs up, leaving her hand still on the phone. Then she lifts the receiver again and dials another number. She places a smile on her face and waits. Then . . .)

OLD LADY: Oh, Marie, dear, how are you . . . this is

Mother. . . . Oh, I'm glad to hear your voice. . . . Oh, I'm fine . . . fine. How's Jack and the kids? . . . Well, I hope it's nothing serious. . . . Oh, that's good. . . . (*She is mustering up all the good humor she has in her.*) Oh my, what a day I had. Oh, wait'll I tell you. Listen, I haven't taken you away from your dinner or anything? . . . Oh, I went down to look for a job again. . . . Yes, that's right, Annie was here this morning . . . how did you know? . . . Oh, is that right? Well, it cleared up, you know, and I didn't want to just sit around, so I went down to this job, and I got fired again. . . . The stupidest thing, I sewed all left sleeves. . . . Well, you know you have to sew sleeves for the right as well as the left unless your customers are one-armed people. . . . (*She is beginning to laugh nervously.*) Yes, it's comical, isn't it? . . . Yes, all left-handed . . . (*She bursts into a short, almost hysterical laugh. Her lip begins to twitch, and she catches her laughter in its middle and breathes deeply to regain control of herself.*) Well, how's Jack and the kids? . . . Well, that's fine. . . . What are you doing with yourself tonight? . . . (*A deep weariness seems to have taken hold of her. She rests her head in the palm of her free hand. Her eyes are closed.*) Oh, do you have a baby sitter? . . . Well, have a nice time, give my regards to your mother-in-law. . . . No, no, I'm fine . . . No, I was just asking . . . No, no, listen, dear, I'm absolutely fine. I just come in the house, and I'm going to make myself some Rice Krispies, and I've got some rolls somewhere, and I think I've got a piece of fish in the refrigerator, and I'm going to make myself dinner and take a hot tub, and then I think I'll watch some television. What's tonight, Thursday? . . . Well, Groucho Marx is on tonight. . . . No, no, I just called to ask how everything was. How's Jack and the kids? . . . That's fine, have a nice time. . . . Good-bye, dear. . . .

(*She hangs up, sits erectly in the chair now. Her face wears an expression of the most profound weariness. She rises now and shuffles with no purpose into the center of the dark room, her coat flapping loosely around her. Then she goes to the television set, turns it on. In a moment a jumble of lines appear, and the sound comes up. The lines clear up into Faye and Skitch Henderson engaging each other in very clever chitchat. The* OLD LADY *goes back to a television-viewing chair, sits down stiffly—her hands resting on the armrests—and expressionlessly watches the show. Camera comes in for a close-up of the* OLD LADY, *staring wide-eyed right through the television set, not hearing a word of the chitchat. She is breathing with some difficulty. Suddenly she rises and almost lurches back to the table. She takes the phone, dials with obvious trembling, waits . . .)*

OLD LADY: Annie? Annie, I wonder if I could spend the night at your house? I don't want to be alone. . . . I'd appreciate that very much. . . . All right, I'll wait here. . . .

(Dissolve to interior of the OLD LADY'S *bedroom. The* SON-IN-LAW, *in his hat and jacket, is snapping the clasps of an old valise together. Having closed the valise, he picks it off the bed and goes into the living room. The* OLD LADY *is there. She is seated in one of the straight-back chairs by the table, still in her coat and hat, and she is talking to the* DAUGHTER—*who can be seen through the kitchen doorway, reaching up into the pantry for some of her mother's personal groceries.)*

OLD LADY: . . . Well, the truth is, I'm getting old, and there's no point in saying it isn't true. *(To her* SON-IN-LAW *as he sets the valise down beside her)* Thank you, dear. I always have so much trouble with the clasp. . . . Did you hear the stupid thing I did today? I sewed all left-handed sleeves. That's the mark of a wandering mind, a sure sign of age. I'm sorry, George, to put you to all this inconvenience . . .

SON-IN-LAW: Don't be silly, Ma. Always glad to have you.

OLD LADY: Annie dear, what are you looking for?

DAUGHTER *(in the kitchen)*: Your saccharin.

OLD LADY: It's on the lower shelf, dear. . . . This isn't going to be permanent, George. I'll just stay with you a little while till I get a room somewheres with some other old woman. . . .

DAUGHTER *(in the kitchen doorway)*: Ma, you're gonna

stay with us, so, for heaven's sakes, let's not have no more arguments.

OLD LADY: What'll we do with all my furniture? Annie, don't you want the china closet?

DAUGHTER: No, Ma, we haven't got any room for it . . .

OLD LADY: It's such a good-looking piece. What we have to do is to get Jack and Marie and Frank and Lillian and all of us together, and we'll divide among the three of you whatever you want. I've got that fine set of silver—well, it's not the best, of course, silver plate, y'know—it's older than you are, Annie. (*To her* SON-IN-LAW) It was a gift of the girls in my shop when I got married. It's an inexpensive set, but I've shined it every year and it sparkles. (*To her* DAUGHTER *in the kitchen*) Yes, that's what we'll have to do. We'll have to get all of us together one night and I'll apportion out whatever I've got. And whatever you don't want, well, we'll call a furniture dealer . . . (*To her* SON-IN-LAW) . . . although what would he pay for these old things here? . . . (*To her* DAUGHTER) Annie, take the china closet . . . It's such a fine piece . . .

DAUGHTER: Ma, where would we put it?

OLD LADY: Well, take that soft chair there. You always liked that chair . . .

DAUGHTER: Ma . . .

OLD LADY: There's nothing wrong with it. It's not torn or anything. The upholstery's fine. Your father swore by that chair. He said it was the only chair he could sit in.

DAUGHTER: Ma, let's not worry about it now. We'll get together sometime next week with Marie and Lillian.

OLD LADY: I want you to have the chair. . . .

DAUGHTER: Ma, we got all modern furniture in our house . . .

OLD LADY: It's not an old chair. We just bought it about six years ago. No, seven . . .

DAUGHTER: Ma, what do we need the . . .

OLD LADY: Annie, I don't want to sell it to a dealer! It's my home. I don't want it to go piece by piece into a second-hand shop.

DAUGHTER: Ma . . .

SON-IN-LAW: Annie! we'll take the chair!

DAUGHTER: All right, Ma, the chair is ours.

OLD LADY: I know that Lillian likes those lace linens I've got in the cedar chest. And the carpets. Now these are good carpets, Annie. There's no sense just throwing them out. They're good broadloom. The first good money your father was making we bought them. When we almost bought that house in Passaic, New Jersey. You ought to remember that, Annie, you were about seven then. But we bought the grocery store instead. Oh, how we scraped in that store. In the heart of the depression. We used to sell bread for six cents a loaf. I remember my husband said: "Let's buy a grocery store. At least we'll always have food in the house." It seems to me my whole life has been hand-to-mouth. Did we ever not worry about the rent? I remember as a girl in Cork, eating boiled potatoes every day. I don't know what it all means, I really don't. . . . (*She stares rather abstractedly at her* SON-IN-LAW.) I'm sixty-six years old, and I don't know what the purpose of it all was.

SON-IN-LAW: Missus Fanning . . .

OLD LADY: An endless, endless struggle. And for what? For what? (*She is beginning to cry now.*) Is this what it all comes to? An old woman parceling out the old furniture in her house . . . ?

(*She bows her head and stands, thirty years of repressed tears tortuously working their way through her body in racking shudders.*)

DAUGHTER: Ma . . .

(*The* OLD LADY *stands, her shoulders slumped, her head bowed, crying with a violent agony.*)

OLD LADY (*the words tumbling out between her sobs*): Oh, I don't care . . . I don't care . . .

(*Hold on the* OLD LADY *standing, crying.*)

(*Dissolve to film—rain whipping through the streets of New York at night—same film we opened the show with —a frightening thunderstorm.*

Dissolve to the OLD LADY'S *valise, now open, lying on a narrow single bed. We pull back to see the* OLD LADY—*in a dress, but with her coat off—rummaging in the valise for something. The room she is in is obviously a little boy's room. There are a child's paintings and drawings and cut-outs Scotch-taped to the wall, and toys and things on the floor. It is dark outside, and the rain whacks against the window panes. The* OLD LADY *finally extracts from out of the valise a long woolen nightgown and, holding it in both arms, she shuffles to the one chair in the room and sits down. She sets the nightgown in her lap and bends to remove her shoes. This is something of an effort and costs her a few moments of quick breathing. She sits, ex-pressionless, catching her breath, the white nightgown on her lap, her hands folded on it. Even after she regains her breath, she sits this way, now staring fixedly at the floor at her feet.*

Hold.

Dissolve to the window of the child's bedroom. It is daylight now, and the rain has stopped. The cold morning sun shines thinly through the white chintz curtains. The camera pulls slowly back and finally comes to rest on the OLD LADY *sitting just as we saw her last, unmoving, wrapped in thought, the white nightgown on her lap, her hands folded. From some room off, the thin voice of a baby suddenly rises and abruptly falls. The* OLD LADY *looks slowly up.*

Then she bends and puts her shoes on. She rises, sets the nightgown on the chair from which she has just risen, moves with a slight edge of purpose down the room to the closet, opens the door, reaches in, and takes out her coat. She puts it on, stands a moment, looking about the room for something. She finds her hat and purse sitting on the chest of drawers. She picks them up. Then she turns to the door of the room and carefully opens it. She looks out onto the hallway. Across from her, the door to her daugh-ter's and son-in-law's bedroom stands slightly ajar. She crosses to the door, looks in. Her DAUGHTER *and* SON-IN-LAW *make two large bundles under their blankets. For a moment she stands and surveys them. Then the* DAUGHTER *turns in her bed so that she faces her mother. Her eyes are open; she has not been asleep. At the sight of her mother in the doorway, she leans upon one elbow.)*

OLD LADY (*in an intense whisper*): Annie, it just wasn't

comfortable, you know? I just can't sleep anywheres but in my own bed, and that's the truth. I'm sorry, Annie, honest. You're a fine daughter, and it warms me to know that I'm welcome here. But what'll I do with myself, Annie, what'll I do? . . .

(*The* DAUGHTER *regards her mother for a moment.*)

DAUGHTER: Where are you going, Ma, with your coat on?

OLD LADY: I'm going out and look for a job. And, Annie, please don't tell me that everything's against me. I know it. Well, I'll see you, dear. I didn't mean to wake you up. . . .

(*She turns and disappears from the doorway. The* DAUGHTER *starts quickly from the bed.*)

DAUGHTER: Ma . . .

(*She moves quickly across the room to the door of the hallway. She is in her pajamas. She looks down the hallway, which is fairly dark. Her mother is already at the front door, at the other end.*)

DAUGHTER: Ma . . .

OLD LADY: I'm leaving the valise with all my things. I'll pick them up tonight. And please don't start an argument with me, Annie, because I won't listen to you. I'm a woman of respect. I can take care of myself. I always have. And don't tell me it's raining because it stopped about an hour ago. And don't say you'll drive me home because I can get the bus two blocks away. Work is the meaning of my life. It's all I know what to do. I can't change my ways at this late time.

(*For a long moment the mother and* DAUGHTER *regard each other. Then the* DAUGHTER *pads quietly down to the* OLD LADY.)

DAUGHTER (*quietly*): When I'm your age, Ma, I hope I'm like you.

(*For a moment the two women stand in the dark hallway. Then they quickly embrace and release each other.*

The OLD LADY *unbolts the door and disappears outside, closing the door after her. The* DAUGHTER *bolts it shut with a click. She turns and goes back up the dark foyer to her own bedroom. She goes in, shuffles to the bed, gets back under the covers. For a moment she just lies there. Then she nudges her sleeping husband, who grunts.)*

DAUGHTER: George, let's drop the kids at your sister's for a week or ten days and drive down to Virginia. You don't want to spend your one vacation a year sitting in New York, watching it rain.

(The SON-IN-LAW, *who hasn't heard a word, grunts once or twice more. The* DAUGHTER *pulls the blankets up over her shoulders, turns on her side, and closes her eyes.)*

(Fade out.)

Three Realistic Dramas

LADY AUGUSTA GREGORY:

The Rising of the Moon

Lady Isabella Augusta Gregory (1859–1932) is the un-
common example of a woman who becomes well known
as a writer late in life. Lady Gregory led the conventional
existence of a gentlewoman until her fortieth year, when
her husband, Sir William, died. It was then that her interest in the literature and history of Ireland began to
develop and to play a dominant role in her life. By 1898,
when she met William Butler Yeats, she was ready to be
influenced by him. The most important result of their association was their close involvement with Dublin's Abbey
Theater, of which Lady Gregory became a principal director and for which she wrote a large number of one-act
plays.

Just as the American Civil War remained a focus of
experience for three generations of American writers, so
was Ireland's struggle for liberation from British rule, for
most of the writers of the Irish renaissance, the center of
a passionate concern. No one loves his country more than
when he is convinced that it is threatened. And so it is
that patriotism as a major theme in the work of Yeats,
Lady Gregory, and Sean O'Casey has grown out of the
bloody and unhappy history of the Irish people.

The Rising of the Moon, produced at the Abbey Theater in 1907, is related to the struggle between the Irish
revolutionaries and the forces loyal to the British government, a conflict which literally set brother against brother
for decades on end. It is interesting to note that Lady
Gregory, in her play, never explicitly states that the es-
capee is a revolutionary; yet the audience is almost im-

mediately aware that the wanted man is not a criminal but a patriot.

What *The Rising of the Moon* dramatizes, of course, is the ambivalence existing among the Irish people themselves. The three policemen—though we are not told so—are presumably Irishmen, but loyal to British sovereignty, for among the comfortable middle class and the office-holders there was no strong impulse to separate or work for independence from Great Britain.

What fascinates us in this play, apart from its adroit manipulation of the technique of suspense, is the manner and the means by which a mature and responsible man is weaned away from what he thinks he believes and desires to what he at last sees he must do. The whole sense of a vital moment in history is revealed in one dramatic thrust.

The Rising of the Moon

Characters

SERGEANT.
POLICEMAN X.
POLICEMAN B.
A RAGGED MAN.

(SCENE: *Side of a wharf in a seaport town. Some posts and chains. A large barrel. Enter three* POLICEMEN. *Moonlight.*

SERGEANT, *who is older than the others, crosses the stage to right and looks down steps. The others put down a pastepot and unroll a bundle of placards.*)

POLICEMAN B: I think this would be a good place to put up a notice.

(*He points to barrel.*)

POLICEMAN X: Better ask him. (*Calls to* SERGEANT.) Will this be a good place for a placard?

(*No answer.*)

POLICEMAN B: Will we put up a notice on the barrel?

(*No answer.*)

SERGEANT: There's a flight of steps here that leads to the water. This is a place that should be minded well. If he got down here, his friends might have a boat to meet him; they might send it in here from outside.

POLICEMAN B: Would the barrel be a good place to put up a notice?

SERGEANT: It might; you can put it there.

(*They paste the notice up.*)

SERGEANT (*reading it*): Dark hair—dark eyes, smooth

The Rising of the Moon is reprinted by permission of Lady Gregory and Putnam & Company Ltd. (Publishers).

face, height, five feet five—there's not much to take hold of in that—It's a pity I had no chance of seeing him before he broke out of jail. They say he's a wonder, that it's he makes all the plans for the whole organization. There isn't another man in Ireland would have broken jail the way he did. He must have some friends among the jailers.

POLICEMAN B: A hundred pounds is little enough for the Government to offer for him. You may be sure any man in the force that takes him will get promotion.

SERGEANT: I'll mind this place myself. I wouldn't wonder at all if he came this way. He might come slipping along there (*points to side of wharf*), and his friends might be waiting for him there (*points down steps*), and once he got away it's little chance we'd have of finding him; it's maybe under a load of kelp he'd be in a fishing boat, and not one to help a married man that wants it to the reward.

POLICEMAN X: And if we get him itself, nothing but abuse on our heads for it from the people, and maybe from our own relations.

SERGEANT: Well, we have to do our duty in the force. Haven't we the whole country depending on us to keep law and order? It's those that are down would be up and those that are up would be down, if it wasn't for us. Well, hurry on, you have plenty of other places to placard yet, and come back here then to me. You can take the lantern. Don't be too long now. It's very lonesome here with nothing but the moon.

POLICEMAN B: It's a pity we can't stop with you. The Government should have brought more police into the town, with *him* in jail, and at assize time too. Well, good luck to your watch.

(*They go out.*)

SERGEANT (*walks up and down once or twice and looks at placard*): A hundred pounds and promotion sure. There must be a great deal of spending in a hundred pounds. It's a pity some honest man not to be the better of that.

(A RAGGED MAN *appears at left and tries to slip past.*
SERGEANT *suddenly turns.*)

SERGEANT: Where are you going?

MAN: I'm a poor ballad-singer, your honor. I thought
to sell some of these (*holds out bundle of ballads*) to the
sailors.

(*He goes on.*)

SERGEANT: Stop! Didn't I tell you to stop? You can't
go on there.

MAN: Oh, very well. It's a hard thing to be poor. All
the world's against the poor.

SERGEANT: Who are you?

MAN: You'd be as wise as myself if I told you, but I
don't mind. I'm one Jimmy Walsh, a ballad-singer.

SERGEANT: Jimmy Walsh? I don't know that name.

MAN: Ah, sure, they know it well enough in Ennis.
Were you ever in Ennis, sergeant?

SERGEANT: What brought you here?

MAN: Sure, it's to the assizes I came, thinking I might
make a few shillings here or there. It's in the one train
with the judges I came.

SERGEANT: Well, if you came so far, you may as well
go farther, for you'll walk out of this.

MAN: I will, I will; I'll just go on where I was going.

(*Goes toward steps.*)

SERGEANT: Come back from those steps; no one has
leave to pass down them tonight.

MAN: I'll just sit on the top of the steps till I see will
some sailor buy a ballad off me that would give me my
supper. They do be late going back to the ship. It's often
I saw them in Cork carried down the wharf in a hand-
cart.

SERGEANT: Move on, I tell you. I won't have anyone
lingering about the wharf tonight.

MAN: Well, I'll go. It's the poor have the hard life!
Maybe yourself might like one, sergeant. Here's the good
sheet now. (*Turns one over.*) "Content and a pipe"—

that's not much. "The Peeler and the Goat"—you wouldn't like that. "Johnny Hart"—that's a lovely song.

SERGEANT: Move on.

MAN: Ah, wait till you hear it.

(*Sings.*)

There was a rich farmer's daughter lived near the town of Ross;
She courted a Highland soldier, his name was Johnny Hart;
Says the mother to her daughter, "I'll go distracted mad
If you marry that Highland soldier dressed up in Highland plaid."

SERGEANT: Where are you going?

MAN: Sure you told me to be going, and I am going.

SERGEANT: Don't be a fool. I didn't tell you to go that way; I told you to go back to the town.

MAN: Back to the town, is it?

SERGEANT (*taking him by the shoulder and shoving him before him*): Here, I'll show you the way. Be off with you. What are you stopping for?

MAN (*who has been keeping his eye on the notice, points to it*): I think I know what you're waiting for, sergeant.

SERGEANT: What's that to you?

MAN: And I knew well the man you're waiting for—I know him well—I'll be going.

(*He shuffles on.*)

SERGEANT: You know him? Come back here. What sort is he?

MAN: Come back is it, sergeant? Do you want to have me killed?

SERGEANT: Why do you say that?

MAN: Never mind. I'm going. I wouldn't be in your shoes if the reward was ten times as much. (*Goes off stage to left.*) Not if it was ten times as much.

SERGEANT (*rushing after him*): Come back here, come back. (*Drags him back.*) What sort is he? Where did you see him?

MAN: I saw him in my own place, in the County Clare. I tell you you wouldn't like to be looking at him. You'd be afraid to be in the one place with him. There isn't a weapon he doesn't know the use of, and as to strength, his muscles are as hard as that board.

(*Slaps barrel.*)

SERGEANT: Is he as bad as that?

MAN: He is then.

SERGEANT: Do you tell me so?

MAN: There was a poor man in our place, a sergeant from Ballyvaughan.—It was with a lump of stone he did it.

SERGEANT: I never heard of that.

MAN: And you wouldn't, sergeant. It's not everything that happens gets into the papers. And there was a policeman in plain clothes, too . . . It is in Limerick he was . . . It was after the time of the attack on the police barrack at Kilmallock . . . Moonlight . . . just like this . . . waterside . . . Nothing was known for certain.

SERGEANT: Do you say so? It's a terrible country to belong to.

MAN: That's so, indeed! You might be standing there, looking out that way, thinking you saw him coming up this side of the wharf (*points*), and he might be coming up this other side (*points*), and he'd be on you before you knew where you were.

SERGEANT: It's a whole troop of police they ought to put here to stop a man like that.

MAN: But if you'd like me to stop with you, I could be looking down this side. I could be sitting up here on this barrel.

SERGEANT: And you know him well, too?

MAN: I'd know him a mile off, sergeant.

SERGEANT: But you wouldn't want to share the reward?

MAN: Is it a poor man like me, that has to be going the roads and singing in fairs, to have the name on him that he took a reward? But you don't want me. I'll be safer in the town.

SERGEANT: Well, you can stop.

MAN (*getting up on barrel*): All right, sergeant. I wonder, now, you're not tired out, sergeant, walking up and down the way you are.

SERGEANT: If I'm tired I'm used to it.

MAN: You might have hard work before you tonight yet. Take it easy while you can. There's plenty of room up here on the barrel, and you can see farther when you're higher up.

SERGEANT: May be so. (*Gets up beside him on barrel, facing right. They sit back to back, looking different ways.*) You made me feel a bit queer with the way you talked.

MAN: Give me a match, sergeant. (*He gives it, and* MAN *lights pipe.*) Take a draw yourself? It'll quiet you. Wait now till I give you a light, but you needn't turn round. Don't take your eye off the wharf for the life of you.

SERGEANT: Never fear, I won't. (*Lights pipe. They both smoke.*) Indeed, it's a hard thing to be in the force, out at night and no thanks for it, for all the danger we're in. And it's little we get but abuse from the people, and no choice but to obey our orders, and never asked when a man is sent into danger, if you are a married man with a family.

MAN (*sings*):

As through the hills I walked to view the hills and
shamrock plain,
I stood awhile where nature smiles to view the rocks
and streams,
On a matron fair I fixed my eyes beneath a fertile vale,
As she sang her song it was on the wrong of poor old
Granuaile.

SERGEANT: Stop that; that's no song to be singing in these times.

MAN: Ah, sergeant, I was only singing to keep my heart up. It sinks when I think of him. To think of us two sitting here, and he creeping up the wharf, maybe, to get to us.

SERGEANT: Are you keeping a good lookout?

MAN: I am; and for no reward too. Amn't I the foolish man? But when I saw a man in trouble, I never could help trying to get him out of it. What's that? Did something hit me?

SERGEANT (*patting him on the shoulder*): You will get your reward in heaven.

MAN: I know that, I know that, sergeant, but life is precious.

SERGEANT: Well, you can sing if it gives you more courage.

MAN (*sings*):

Her head was bare, her hands and feet with iron bands were bound,
Her pensive strain and plaintive wail mingled with the evening gale,
And the song she sang with mournful air, I am old Granuaile.
Her lips so sweet that monarchs kissed . . .

SERGEANT: That's not it . . . "Her gown she wore was stained with gore." . . . That's it—you missed that.

MAN: You're right, sergeant, so it is; I missed it. (*Repeats the line.*) But to think a man like you knowing a song like that.

SERGEANT: There's many a thing a man might know and might not have any wish for.

MAN: Now, I daresay, sergeant, in your youth, you used to be sitting up on a wall, the way you are sitting up on this barrel now, and the other lads beside you, and you singing "Granuaile"?

SERGEANT: I did then.

MAN: And the "Shan Bhean Bhocht"?

SERGEANT: I did then.

MAN: And the "Green on the Cape?"

SERGEANT: That was one of them.

MAN: And maybe the man you are watching for tonight used to be sitting on the wall, when he was young, and singing those same songs. . . . It's a queer world. . . .

SERGEANT: Whisht! . . . I think I see something coming. . . . It's only a dog.

MAN: And isn't it a queer world? . . . Maybe it's one of the boys you used to be singing with that time you will be arresting today or tomorrow, and sending into the dock. . . .

SERGEANT: That's true indeed.

MAN: And maybe one night, after you had been singing, if the other boys had told you some plan they had, some plan to free the country, you might have joined them . . . and maybe it is you might be in trouble now.

SERGEANT: Well, who knows but I might? I had great spirit in those days.

MAN: It's a queer world, sergeant, and it's a little any mother knows when she sees her child creeping on the floor what might happen to it before it has gone through its life, or who will be who in the end.

SERGEANT: That's a queer thought now, and a true thought. Wait now till I think it out. . . . If it wasn't for the sense I have, and for my wife and family, and for me joining the force the time I did, it might be myself now would be after breaking jail and hiding in the dark, and it might be him that's hiding in the dark and that got out of jail would be sitting up where I am on this barrel. . . . And it might be myself would be creeping up trying to make my escape from himself, and it might be himself would be keeping the law, and myself would be breaking it, and myself would be trying maybe to put a bullet in his head, or to take up a lump of stone the way you said he did . . . no, that myself did. . . . Oh! (*Gasps. After a pause.*) What's that?

(*Grasps* MAN'S *arm.*)

MAN (*jumps off barrel and listens, looking out over water*): It's nothing, sergeant.

SERGEANT: I thought it might be a boat. I had a notion there might be friends of his coming about the wharfs with a boat.

MAN: Sergeant, I am thinking it was with the people you were, and not with the law you were when you were a young man.

SERGEANT: Well, if I was foolish then, that time's gone.

MAN: Maybe, sergeant, it comes into your head sometimes, in spite of your belt and your tunic, that it might have been as well for you to have followed Granuaile.

SERGEANT: It's no business of yours what I think.

MAN: Maybe, sergeant, you'll be on the side of the country yet.

SERGEANT (*gets off barrel*): Don't talk to me like that. I have my duties and I know them. (*Looks round.*) That was a boat; I hear the oars.

(*Goes to the steps and looks down.*)

MAN (*sings*):

> O, then, tell me, Shawn O'Farrell,
>   Where the gathering is to be.
> In the old spot by the river
>   Right well known to you and me!

SERGEANT: Stop that! Stop that, I tell you!

MAN (*sings louder*):

> One word more, for signal token,
>   Whistle up the marching tune,
> With your pike upon your shoulder,
>   At the Rising of the Moon.

SERGEANT: If you don't stop that, I'll arrest you.

(*A whistle from below answers, repeating the air.*)

SERGEANT: That's a signal. (*Stands between him and steps.*) You must not pass this way. . . . Step farther back. . . . Who are you? You are no ballad-singer.

MAN: You needn't ask who I am; that placard will tell you.

(*Points to placard.*)

SERGEANT: You are the man I am looking for.

MAN (*takes off hat and wig.* SERGEANT *seizes them.*): I am. There's a hundred pounds on my head. There is a friend of mine below in a boat. He knows a safe place to bring me to.

SERGEANT (*looking still at hat and wig*): It's a pity! It's a pity. You deceived me. You deceived me well.

MAN: I am a friend of Granuaile. There is a hundred pounds on my head.

SERGEANT: It's a pity, it's a pity!

MAN: Will you let me pass, or must I make you let me?

SERGEANT: I am in the force. I will not let you pass.

MAN: I thought to do it with my tongue. (*Puts hand in breast.*) What is that?

(*Voice of* POLICEMAN X *outside.*) Here, this is where we left him.

SERGEANT: It's my comrades coming.

MAN: You won't betray me . . . the friend of Granuaile.

(*Slips behind barrel.*)

(*Voice of* POLICEMAN B.) That was the last of the placards.

POLICEMAN X (*as they come in*): If he makes his escape it won't be unknown he'll make it.

(SERGEANT *puts hat and wig behind his back.*)

POLICEMAN B: Did anyone come this way?

SERGEANT (*after a pause*): No one.

POLICEMAN B: No one at all?

SERGEANT: No one at all.

POLICEMAN B: We had no orders to go back to the station; we can stop along with you.

SERGEANT: I don't want you. There is nothing for you to do here.

POLICEMAN B: You bade us to come back here and keep watch with you.

SERGEANT: I'd sooner be alone. Would any man come this way and you making all that talk? It is better the place be quiet.

POLICEMAN B: Well, we'll leave you the lantern anyhow.

(*Hands it to him.*)

SERGEANT: I don't want it. Bring it with you.

POLICEMAN B: You might want it. There are clouds coming up and you have the darkness of the night before you yet. I'll leave it over here on the barrel.

(*Goes to barrel.*)

SERGEANT: Bring it with you, I tell you. No more talk.

POLICEMAN B: Well, I thought it might be a comfort

to you. I often think when I have it in my hand and can be flashing it about into every dark corner (*doing so*) that it's the same as being beside the fire at home, and the bits of bogwood blazing up now and again.

(*Flashes it about, now on the barrel, now on* SER-GEANT.)

SERGEANT (*furious*): Be off the two of you, yourselves and your lantern!

(*They go out.* MAN *comes from behind barrel. He and* SERGEANT *stand looking at one another.*)

SERGEANT: What are you waiting for?
MAN: For my hat, of course, and my wig. You wouldn't wish me to get my death of cold?

(SERGEANT *gives them.*)

MAN (*going toward steps*): Well, good-night comrade, and thank you. You did me a good turn tonight, and I'm obliged to you. Maybe I'll be able to do as much for you when the small rise up and the big fall down . . . when we all change places at the Rising (*waves his hand and disappears*) of the Moon.
SERGEANT (*turning his back to audience and reading placard*): A hundred pounds reward! A hundred pounds! (*Turns toward audience.*) I wonder now, am I as great a fool as I think I am?

TERENCE RATTIGAN:

The Browning Version

Terence Rattigan, born in London in 1911, was educated at Harrow and at Trinity College, Oxford. He wrote his first play in 1934 but did not achieve an international reputation until 1946 with *The Winslow Boy*. His other plays include *The Deep Blue Sea* (1952) and *Separate Tables* (1955). Mr. Rattigan was a flight lieutenant in World War II.

The Browning Version, though it is technically a one-act play, is considerably different from most short plays, different certainly from all of the other plays in this collection. The difference lies in its texture. It has the complexity, the density, the interweaving of thematic strands that we generally associate with the full-length play in which time allows for the admixture of tone and color. The tone of *The Browning Version* shifts from farce to satire to melodrama, though it never ceases to be essentially a drawing-room drama. Unlike the usual one-act play whose focus—like that of the short story—is direct, *The Browning Version* deals with several matters. It lays bare the death of a man's youthful hopes and aspirations; it anatomizes an unsuccessful marriage; it explores what constitutes good teaching and who is the good teacher; it examines the respective roles of the humanities, the sciences, and athletics in the great public schools of England and the values which students and administrators assign to each of the three. And running throughout are some interesting implications about the nature of friendship.

For all its complexity and density as a play, however, *The Browning Version,* constructed with consummate craftsmanship, provides us with a dramatic experience which not only totally involves us, but enriches our understanding of life.

Like Taplow, we have intimations of Crocker-Harris's lost greatness; like Frank Hunter, we would like to be able to win Crocker-Harris's friendship. Finally we understand that Crocker-Harris's failure, the death of his career—which is the death of him as an intellectually functioning man—has all the inevitability of a Greek tragedy. The play is, finally, still another version of "what is perhaps the greatest play ever written": the *Agamemnon*.

The Browning Version

Characters

JOHN TAPLOW.
FRANK HUNTER.
MILLIE CROCKER-HARRIS.
ANDREW CROCKER-HARRIS.
DR. FROBISHER.
PETER GILBERT.
MRS. GILBERT.

(SCENE: *The sitting room in the Crocker-Harris's flat in a public school in the south of England. About 6:30 P.M. of a day in July.*

The building in which the flat is situated is large and Victorian, and at some fairly recent time has been converted into flats of varying size for masters, married and unmarried. The Crocker-Harrises have the ground floor and their sitting room is probably the biggest—and gloomiest—room in the house. It boasts, however, access (through a stained-glass door left) to a small garden, and is furnished with chintzy and genteel cheerfulness. Another door, up right, leads into the hall and a third, up center, to the rest of the flat. The hall door is partially concealed by a screen. There is a large bay window in the left wall below the garden door. Near the window is a flat-topped desk with a swivel chair behind it and an upright chair on the other side. The fireplace is down right. Below it is an easy chair and a small table with a telephone. A settee stands in front of the fireplace at right center. There is an oval dining-table with two chairs up center right of the door; up center is a sideboard; and against the wall left of the door up right is a hall stand, in which some walking sticks are kept. A small cupboard stands against the wall down right.

When the curtain rises the room is empty. There are copies of The Times *and the* Tatler *on the settee. We hear the front door opening and closing and immediately after there is a timorous knock on the door up right. After a pause the knock is repeated. The door opens and* JOHN TAPLOW *makes his appearance. He is a plain moon-faced*

166

boy of about sixteen, with glasses. He carries a book and
an exercise book. He is dressed in gray flannels, a dark
blue coat, and white scarf. He stands in doubt at the door
for a moment, then goes back into the hall.)

TAPLOW (*off; calling*): Sir! Sir! (*After a pause he*
comes back into the room, crosses to the garden door up
left and opens it. He calls.) Sir! (*There is no reply.* TAP-
LOW, *standing in the bright sunshine at the door, emits a*
plaintive sigh, then closes it firmly and comes down right
of the desk on which he places the book, the notebook,
and a pen. He sits in the chair right of the desk. He looks
round the room. On a table center is a small box of
chocolates, probably the Crocker-Harris's ration for the
month. TAPLOW *rises, moves above the table and opens*
the box. He counts the number inside, and removes two.
One of these he eats and the other, after a second's strug-
gle, either with his conscience or his judgment of what
he might be able to get away with, virtuously replaces in
the box. He puts back the box on the table, and moves up
right to the hall stand. He selects a walking stick with a
crooked handle, comes down center, and makes a couple
of golf swings, with an air of great concentration. FRANK
HUNTER *enters up right and appears from behind the*
screen covering the door. He is a rugged young man—
not perhaps quite as rugged as his deliberately cultivated
manner of ruthless honesty makes him appear, but
wrapped in all the self-confidence of the popular master.
He watches TAPLOW, *whose back is to the door, making*
his swing.)

FRANK (*coming down behind* TAPLOW): Roll the wrists
away from the ball. Don't break them like that. (*He puts*
his large hands over the abashed TAPLOW'S.) Now swing.
(TAPLOW, *guided by* FRANK'S *evidently expert hands, suc-*
ceeds in hitting the carpet with more effect than before.
He breaks away right of TAPLOW.) Too quick. Slow back
and stiff left arm. It's no good just whacking the ball as if
you were the headmaster and the ball was you. It'll never
go more than fifty yards if you do. Get a rhythm. A good
golf swing is a matter of aesthetics, not of brute strength.

(TAPLOW, *only half listening, is gazing at the carpet.*)

FRANK: What's the matter?

TAPLOW: I think we've made a tear in the carpet, sir.

(FRANK *examines the spot perfunctorily.*)

FRANK (*taking the stick from* TAPLOW): Nonsense. That was there already. (*He crosses up right and puts the stick in the hall stand.*) Do I know you?

(*He comes down left of the settee to right of* TAPLOW.)

TAPLOW: No, sir.

FRANK: What's your name?

TAPLOW: Taplow.

FRANK: Taplow? No, I don't. You're not a scientist, I gather.

TAPLOW: No, sir. I'm still in the lower fifth. I can't specialize until next term—that's to say if I've got my remove all right.

FRANK: Don't you know yet if you've got your remove?

TAPLOW: No, sir. Mr. Crocker-Harris doesn't tell us the results like the other masters.

FRANK: Why not?

TAPLOW: Well, you know what he's like, sir.

FRANK (*moving away to the fireplace*): I believe there *is* a rule that form results should only be announced by the headmaster on the last day of term.

TAPLOW: Yes; but who else pays any attention to it—except Mr. Crocker-Harris?

FRANK: I don't, I admit—but that's no criterion. So you've got to wait until tomorrow to know your fate, have you?

TAPLOW: Yes, sir.

FRANK: Supposing the answer is favorable—what then?

TAPLOW: Oh—science, sir, of course.

FRANK (*sadly*): Yes. We get all the slackers.

TAPLOW (*protestingly*): I'm extremely interested in science, sir.

FRANK: Are you? I'm not. Not at least in the science I have to teach.

TAPLOW (*moving above the desk*): Well, anyway, sir, it's a good deal more exciting than this muck.

(*He indicates the book he put on the desk.*)

FRANK: What is this muck?

TAPLOW: Aeschylus, sir. *The Agamemnon.*

FRANK (*moving to the left end of the couch*): And your considered view is that *The Agamemnon* of Aeschylus is muck, is it?

TAPLOW: Well, no, sir. I don't think the play is muck —exactly. I suppose, in a way, it's rather a good plot, really; a wife murdering her husband and having a lover and all that. I only meant the way it's taught to us—just a lot of Greek words strung together and fifty lines if you get them wrong.

FRANK: You sound a little bitter, Taplow.

TAPLOW: I am rather, sir.

FRANK: Kept in, eh?

TAPLOW: No, sir. Extra work.

FRANK: Extra work—on the last day of school?

TAPLOW: Yes, sir—and I might be playing golf. (*He moves into the window, upstage end.*) You'd think *he'd* have enough to do anyway himself, considering he's leaving tomorrow for good—but oh no. I missed a day last week when I had 'flu—so here I am—and look at the weather, sir.

FRANK: Bad luck. Still there's one consolation. You're pretty well bound to get your remove tomorrow for being a good boy in taking extra work.

TAPLOW (*crossing to center*): Well, I'm not so sure, sir. That would be true of the ordinary masters all right. They just wouldn't dare not give a chap a remove after his taking extra work—it would be such a bad advertisement for them. But those sort of rules don't apply to the Crock —Mr. Crocker-Harris. I asked him yesterday outright if he'd given me a remove and do you know what he said, sir?

FRANK: No, what?

TAPLOW (*mimicking a very gentle, rather throaty voice*): "My dear Taplow, I have given you exactly what you deserve. No less; and certainly no more." Do you know, sir, I think he may have marked me down, rather than up, for taking extra work. I mean, the man's barely human. (*He breaks off quickly.*) Sorry, sir. Have I gone too far?

FRANK (*sitting on the settee, left end, and packing up* The Times): Yes. Much too far.

TAPLOW: Sorry, sir. I got sort of carried away.

FRANK: Evidently. (*He opens* The Times *and reads.* TAPLOW *moves to the chair right of the desk and sits.*) Er—Taplow.

TAPLOW: Yes, sir?

FRANK: What was that Mr. Crocker-Harris said to you? Just—er—repeat it, would you?

TAPLOW (*mimicking*): "My dear Taplow, I have given you exactly what you deserve. No less; and certainly no more."

(FRANK *snorts, then looks stern.*)

FRANK: Not in the least like him. Read your nice Aeschylus and be quiet.

TAPLOW (*with weary disgust*): Aeschylus.

FRANK: Look, what time did Mr. Crocker-Harris tell you to be here?

TAPLOW: Six-thirty, sir.

FRANK: Well, he's ten minutes late. Why don't you cut? You could still get nine holes in before lock-up.

TAPLOW (*genuinely shocked*): Oh, no, I couldn't cut. Cut the Crock—Mr. Crocker-Harris? I shouldn't think it's ever been done in the whole time he's been here. God knows what would happen if I did. He'd probably follow me home, or something.

FRANK: I must admit I envy him the effect he seems to have on you boys in his form. You all seem scared to death of him. What does he do—beat you all or something?

TAPLOW (*rising and moving to the left end of the settee*): Good Lord, no. He's not a sadist, like one or two of the others.

FRANK: I beg your pardon?

TAPLOW: A sadist, sir, is someone who gets pleasure out of giving pain.

FRANK: Indeed? But I think you went on to say that some other masters . . .

TAPLOW: Well, of course they are, sir. I won't mention names, but you know them as well as I do. Of course I know most masters think we boys don't understand a thing—but dash it, sir, you're different. You're young—well comparatively anyway—and you're science and you canvassed for Labour in the last election. You must know what sadism is.

(FRANK *stares for a moment at* TAPLOW, *then turns away.*)

FRANK: Good Lord! What are public schools coming to?

TAPLOW (*crossing to right of the desk, below the chair, and leaning against it*): Anyway, the Crock isn't a sadist. That's what I'm saying. He wouldn't be so frightening if he were—because at least it would show he had some feelings. But he hasn't. He's all shriveled up inside like a nut and he seems to hate people to like him. It's funny, that. I don't know any other master who doesn't like being liked.

FRANK: And I don't know any boy who doesn't trade on that very foible.

TAPLOW: Well, it's natural, sir. But not with the Crock.

FRANK (*making a feeble attempt at reestablishing the correct relationship*): Mr. Crocker-Harris.

TAPLOW: Mr. Crocker-Harris. The funny thing is that in spite of everything, I do rather like him. I can't help it. And sometimes I think he sees it and that seems to shrivel him up even more.

FRANK: I'm sure you're exaggerating.

TAPLOW: No, sir. I'm not. In form the other day he made one of his little classical jokes. Of course nobody laughed because nobody understood it, myself included. Still, I knew he'd meant it as funny, so I laughed. Not out of sucking-up, sir, I swear, but ordinary common politeness, and feeling a bit sorry for him having made a dud joke. (*He moves round below the desk to left of it.*) Now I can't remember what the joke was—but let's say it was—(*mimicking*) Benedictus, benedicatur, benedictine . . . Now, you laugh, sir. (FRANK *laughs formally.*

TAPLOW *looks at him over an imaginary pair of spectacles, and then, very gently crooks his forefinger to him in indication to approach the table.* FRANK *rises. He is genuinely interested in the incident. In a gentle, throaty voice.*) Taplow—you laughed at my little pun, I noticed. I must confess I am flattered at the evident advance your Latinity has made that you should so readily have understood what the rest of the form did not. Perhaps, now, you would be good enough to explain it to them, so that they too can share your pleasure.

(*The door up right is pushed open and* MILLIE CROCKER-HARRIS *enters. She is a thin woman in the late thirties, rather more smartly dressed than the general run of schoolmasters' wives. She is wearing a cape and carries a shopping basket. She closes the door and then stands by the screen watching* TAPLOW *and* FRANK. *It is a few seconds before they notice her.*)

Come along, Taplow. (FRANK *moves slowly above the desk.*) Do not be so selfish as to keep a good joke to yourself. Tell the others . . . (*He breaks off suddenly, noticing* MILLIE.) Oh Lord!

(FRANK *turns quickly, and seems infinitely relieved at seeing* MILLIE.)

FRANK: Oh, hullo.
MILLIE (*without expression*): Hullo.

(*She comes down to the sideboard and puts her basket on it.*)

TAPLOW (*moving up to left of* FRANK; *whispering frantically*): Do you think she heard? (FRANK *shakes his head comfortingly.* MILLIE *takes off her cape and hangs it on the hall stand.*) I think she did. She was standing there quite a time. If she did and she tells him, there goes my remove.
FRANK: Nonsense.

(*He crosses to the fireplace.* MILLIE *takes the basket from the sideboard, moves above the table center and puts the basket on it.*)

MILLIE (*to* TAPLOW): Waiting for my husband?

TAPLOW (*moving down left of the table center*): Er—yes.

MILLIE: He's at the Bursar's and might be there quite a time. If I were you I'd go.

TAPLOW (*doubtfully*): He said most particularly I was to come.

MILLIE: Well, why don't you run away for a quarter of an hour and come back?

(*She unpacks some things from the basket.*)

TAPLOW: Supposing he gets here before me?

MILLIE (*smiling*): I'll take the blame. (*She takes a prescription out of the basket.*) I tell you what—you can do a job for him. Take this prescription to the chemist and get it made up.

TAPLOW: All right, Mrs. Crocker-Harris.

(*He crosses toward the door up right.*)

MILLIE: And while you're there you might as well slip into Stewart's and have an ice. Here. Catch.

(*She takes a shilling from her bag and throws it to him.*)

TAPLOW (*turning and catching it*): Thanks awfully.

(*He signals to* FRANK *not to tell, and moves to the door up right.*)

MILLIE: Oh, Taplow.

(*She crosses to him.*)

TAPLOW (*turning on the step*): Yes, Mrs. Crocker-Harris.

MILLIE: I had a letter from my father today in which he says he once had the pleasure of meeting your mother.

TAPLOW (*uninterested but polite*): Oh, really?

MILLIE: Yes. It was at some fête or other in Bradford. My uncle—that's Sir William Bartop, you know—made a speech and so did your mother. My father met her afterwards at tea.

TAPLOW: Oh really?

MILLIE: He said he found her quite charming.

TAPLOW: Yes, she's jolly good at those sort of functions. (*Becoming aware of his lack of tact.*) I mean—I'm sure she found him charming, too. So long.

(*He goes out up right.*)

MILLIE (*coming down to the left end of the settee*): Thank you for coming round,

FRANK: That's all right.

MILLIE: You're staying for dinner?

FRANK: If I may.

MILLIE: If you may! (*She crosses below the settee to him.*) Give me a cigarette. (FRANK *takes out his case and extends it to her.* MILLIE *takes a cigarette. Indicating the case.*) You haven't given it away yet, I see.

FRANK: Do you think I would?

MILLIE: Frankly, yes. Luckily it's a man's case. I don't suppose any of your girl friends would want it.

FRANK: Don't be silly.

MILLIE: Where have you been all this week?

FRANK (*sitting in the easy chair*): Correcting exam papers—making reports. You know what end of term is like.

MILLIE (*crossing below the settee and moving above the table center*): I do know what end of term is like. But even Andrew has managed this last week to take a few hours off to say good-bye to people.

(*She takes some packages out of the shopping basket.*)

FRANK: I really have been appallingly busy. Besides, I'm coming to stay with you in Bradford.

MILLIE: Not for over a month. Andrew doesn't start his new job until September first. That's one of the things I had to tell you.

FRANK: Oh. I had meant to be in Devonshire in September.

MILLIE (*quickly*): Who with?

FRANK: My family.

MILLIE: Surely you can go earlier, can't you? Go in August.

FRANK: It'll be difficult.

MILLIE: Then you'd better come to me in August.

FRANK: But Andrew will still be there. (*There is a pause.* MILLIE *crosses to left of the desk, opens a drawer, and takes out some scissors.*) I think I can manage September.

MILLIE (*shutting the drawer*): That'd be better—from every point of view. (*She moves below the table center and puts down the scissors.*) Except that it means I shan't see you for six weeks.

FRANK (*lightly*): You'll survive that, all right.

MILLIE: Yes, I'll survive it—(*she moves to the left end of the settee*) but not as easily as you will. (FRANK *says nothing.*) I haven't much pride, have I? (*She crosses to* FRANK *and stands above the easy chair.*) Frank, darling— (*she sits on the arm of the chair and kisses him*) I love you so much. (FRANK *kisses her on the mouth, but a trifle perfunctorily, and then rises and breaks quickly away, as if afraid someone had come into the room. He moves below the settee. She laughs.*) You're very nervous.

FRANK: I'm afraid of that screen arrangement. You can't see people coming in.

MILLIE: Oh yes. (*She rises and stands by the fireplace.*) That reminds me. What were you and Taplow up to when I came in just now? Making fun of my husband?

FRANK: Afraid so. Yes.

MILLIE: It sounded rather a good imitation. I must get him to do it for me sometime. It was very naughty of you to encourage him.

FRANK: I know. It was.

MILLIE (*ironically*): Bad for discipline.

FRANK (*sitting on the settee*): Exactly. Currying favor with the boys, too. My God, how easy it is to be popular. I've only been a master three years, but I've already slipped into an act and a vernacular that I just can't get out of. Why can't anyone ever be natural with the little blighters?

MILLIE: They probably wouldn't like it if you were.

(*She crosses below the settee and moves above the table center. She picks up the scissors and a packet of luggage labels and cuts the latter one by one from the packet.*)

FRANK: I don't see why not. No one seems to have tried it yet, anyway. I suppose the trouble is—we're all too scared of them. Either one gets forced into an attitude of false and hearty and jocular bonhomie like myself, or into the sort of petty, soulless tyranny which your husband uses to protect himself against the lower fifth.

MILLIE (*rather bored with this*): He'd never be popular —whatever he did.

FRANK: Possibly not. He ought never to have become a schoolmaster really. Why did he?

MILLIE: It was his vocation, he said. He was sure he'd make a big success of it, especially when he got his job here first off. (*Bitterly.*) Fine success he's made, hasn't he?

FRANK: You should have stopped him.

MILLIE: How was I to know? He talked about getting a house, then a headmastership.

FRANK (*rising*): The Crock a headmaster! That's a pretty thought.

MILLIE: Yes, it's funny to think of now, all right. Still, he wasn't always the Crock, you know. He had a bit more gumption once. At least I thought he had. Don't let's talk anymore about him—(*she comes right round the table to center*) it's too depressing.

(*She starts to move left.*)

FRANK: I'm sorry for him.

MILLIE (*stopping and turning; indifferently*): He's not sorry for himself, so why should you be? It's me you should be sorry for.

FRANK: I am.

MILLIE (*moving in a few steps toward* FRANK; *smiling*): Then show me.

(*She stretches out her arms to him.* FRANK *moves to her and kisses her again quickly and lightly. She holds him hungrily. He has to free himself almost roughly.*)

FRANK (*crossing to the fireplace*): What have you been doing all day?

MILLIE: Calling on the other masters' wives—saying

fond farewells. I've worked off twelve. I've another seven to do tomorrow.

FRANK: You poor thing! I don't envy you.

MILLIE (*moving above the desk to left of it with some labels*): It's the housemasters' wives that are the worst. (*She picks up a pen and writes on the labels.*) They're all so damn patronizing. You should have heard Betty Carstairs. "My dear—it's such terrible bad luck on you both—that your husband should get this heart trouble just when, if only he'd stayed on, he'd have been bound to get a house. I mean, he's considerably senior to my Arthur as it is, and they simply couldn't have gone on passing him over, could they?"

FRANK: There's a word for Betty Carstairs, my dear, that I would hesitate to employ before a lady.

MILLIE: She's got her eye on you, anyway.

FRANK: Betty Carstairs? What utter rot!

MILLIE: Oh yes, she has. I saw you at that concert. Don't think I didn't notice.

FRANK: Millie, darling! Really! I detest the woman.

MILLIE: Then what were you doing in her box at Lord's?

FRANK: Carstairs invited me. I went there because it was a good place to see the match from.

MILLIE: Yes, I'm sure it was. Much better than the grandstand anyway.

FRANK (*remembering something suddenly*): Oh, my God!

MILLIE (*coming below the desk*): It's all right, my dear. Don't bother to apologize. We gave the seat away, as it happens.

FRANK: I'm most terribly sorry.

MILLIE: It's all right. (*She moves to right of the desk.*) We couldn't afford a box, you see.

FRANK (*moving a few steps toward right*): It wasn't that. You know it wasn't that. It's just that I—well, I clean forgot.

MILLIE: Funny you didn't forget the Carstairs invitation.

FRANK: Millie—don't be a fool.

MILLIE: It's you who are the fool. (*Appealingly.*) Frank—have you never been in love? I know you're not in love with me—but haven't you ever been in love with anyone? Don't you realize what torture you inflict on someone who loves you when you do a thing like that?

FRANK: I've told you I'm sorry—I don't know what more I can say.

MILLIE: Why not the truth?

FRANK: The truth is—I clean forgot.

MILLIE: The truth is—you had something better to do—and why not say it?

FRANK: All right. Believe that if you like. It happens to be a lie, but believe it all the same. Only for God's sake stop this.

(*He turns and moves down right.*)

MILLIE: Then for God's sake show me some pity. Do you think it's any pleasanter for me to believe that you cut me because you forgot? Do you think that doesn't hurt either? (FRANK *turns away. She moves above the up right corner of the desk and faces the door up left.*) Oh damn! I was so determined to be brave and not mention Lord's. Why did I? Frank, just tell me one thing. Just tell me you're not running away from me—that's all I want to hear.

FRANK: I'm coming to Bradford.

MILLIE (*turning to* FRANK): I think, if you don't, I'll kill myself.

FRANK (*turning and taking a few steps in toward* MILLIE): I'm coming to Bradford.

(*The door up right opens.* FRANK *stops at the sound.* MILLIE *recovers herself and crosses above the table center to the sideboard.* ANDREW CROCKER-HARRIS *enters and appears from behind the screen. Despite the summer sun he wears a serge suit and a stiff collar. He carries a mackintosh and a rolled-up timetable and looks, as ever, neat, complacent, and unruffled. He speaks in a very gentle voice which he rarely raises.*)

ANDREW (*hanging his mackintosh on the hallstand*): Is Taplow here?

(FRANK *eases toward the fireplace.*)

MILLIE: I sent him to the chemist to get your prescription made up.

ANDREW: What prescription?

MILLIE: Your heart medicine. Don't you remember? You told me this morning it had run out.

ANDREW: Of course I remember, my dear, but there was no need to send Taplow for it. If you had telephoned the chemist he would have sent it round in plenty of time. He knows the prescription. (*He comes down to the left end of the settee.*) Now Taplow will be late and I am so pressed for time I hardly know how to fit him in. (*He sees* FRANK.) Ah, Hunter! How are you?

(*He moves right to* FRANK.)

FRANK: Very well, thanks.

(*They shake hands.*)

ANDREW: Most kind of you to drop in, but, as Millie should have warned you, I am expecting a pupil for extra work and . . .

MILLIE: He's staying to dinner, Andrew.

ANDREW: Good. Then I shall see something of you. However, when Taplow returns I'm sure you won't mind . . .

FRANK (*making a move*): No, of course not. I'll make myself scarce now, if you'd rather—I mean, if you're busy . . .

(*He turns away and moves center.*)

ANDREW: Oh no. There is no need for that. Sit down, do. Will you smoke? I don't, as you know, but Millie does. (*He crosses below the desk and moves up left of it.*) Millie, give our guest a cigarette.

MILLIE (*moving down to the table center*): I haven't any, I'm afraid. I've had to cadge from him.

(*She takes a copy of the* Tatler *from the basket.* ANDREW *opens the drawer that should contain the scissors.* FRANK *takes out his cigarette case, crosses to right of the table center, and offers it to* MILLIE. *She exchanges a glance with him as she takes a cigarette.*)

ANDREW (*looking for the scissors*): We expected you at Lord's, Hunter.

FRANK: What? Oh yes. I'm most terribly sorry. I . . .

MILLIE (*crossing behind the settee*): He clean forgot, Andrew. Imagine.

ANDREW: Forgot?

MILLIE: Not everyone is blessed with your superhuman memory, you see.

FRANK: I really can't apologize enough.

ANDREW: Please don't bother to mention it. On the second day we managed to sell the seat to a certain Dr. Lambert, who wore, I regret to say, the colors of the opposing faction, but who otherwise seemed a passably agreeable person. (*He moves above the table center.*) You liked him, didn't you, Millie?

MILLIE (*looking at* FRANK): Very much indeed. I thought him quite charming.

ANDREW: A charming old gentleman. (*To* FRANK) You have had tea?

(*He picks up the scissors.*)

FRANK: Yes—thank you.

ANDREW: Is there any other refreshment I can offer you?

FRANK: No, thank you.

ANDREW (*cutting the string round the timetable*): Would it interest you to see the new timetable I have drafted for next term?

FRANK: Yes, very much. (*He moves up right of* AN-DREW. ANDREW *opens out a long roll of paper, made by pasting pieces of foolscap together, and which is entirely covered by his meticulous writing.*) I never knew you drafted our timetables.

ANDREW: Didn't you? I have done so for the last fifteen years. (MILLIE *wanders down right of the settee.*) Of course, they are always issued in mimeograph under the headmaster's signature. Now what form do you take? Upper fifth Science—there you are—that's the general picture; but on the back you will see each form specified under separate headings—there—that's a new idea of mine—Millie, this might interest you.

MILLIE (*sitting in the easy chair; suddenly harsh*): You know it bores me to death.

(FRANK *looks up, surprised and uncomfortable.* ANDREW *does not move his eyes from the timetable.*)

ANDREW: Millie has no head for this sort of work. There you see. Now here you can follow the upper fifth Science throughout every day of the week.

FRANK (*indicating the timetable*): I must say, I think this is a really wonderful job.

ANDREW: Thank you. It has the merit of clarity, I think.

(*He starts to roll up the timetable.*)

FRANK: I don't know what they'll do without you.

ANDREW (*without expression*): They'll find somebody else, I expect.

(*There is a pause.*)

FRANK: What sort of job is this you're going to?

ANDREW (*looking at* MILLIE *for the first time*): Hasn't Millie told you?

FRANK: She said it was a cr— a private school.

ANDREW: A crammer's—for backward boys. It is run by an old Oxford contemporary of mine who lives in Dorset. (*He moves round left of the table center and finishes rolling up the timetable.*) The work will not be so arduous as here and my doctor seems to think I will be able to undertake it without—er danger.

FRANK (*with genuine sympathy*): It's the most rotten bad luck for you. I'm awfully sorry.

ANDREW (*raising his voice a little*): My dear Hunter, there is nothing whatever to be sorry for. I am looking forward to the change. (*There is a knock at the door left.*) Come in. (*He crosses below the table to center.* TAPLOW *enters up right, a trifle breathless and guilty-looking. He carries a medicine bottle wrapped and sealed.*) Ah, Taplow. Good. You have been running, I see.

TAPLOW: Yes, sir.

(*He crosses to the left end of the settee.*)

ANDREW: There was a queue at the chemist's, I suppose?
TAPLOW: Yes, sir.
ANDREW: And doubtless an even longer one at Stewart's?
TAPLOW: Yes, sir—I mean—no, sir—I mean—(*he looks at* MILLIE) yes, sir.

(*He crosses below the settee to* MILLIE *and hands her the medicine.*)

MILLIE: You were late yourself, Andrew.
ANDREW: Exactly. And for that I apologize, Taplow.
TAPLOW: That's all right, sir.
ANDREW (*crossing below the desk and moving left of it*): Luckily we have still a good hour before lock-up, so nothing has been lost.

(*He puts the timetable on the desk.*)

FRANK (*moving to the door up left; to* MILLIE): May I use the short cut? I'm going back to my digs.

(ANDREW *sits at his desk and opens a book.*)

MILLIE (*rising and moving up right of the settee*): Yes. Go ahead. Come back soon. If Andrew hasn't finished we can sit in the garden. (*She crosses above the table center and picks up the shopping basket. She puts the medicine on the sideboard.*) I'd better go and see about dinner.

(*She goes out up center.*)

ANDREW (*to* FRANK): Taplow is desirous of obtaining a remove from my form, Hunter, so that he can spend the rest of his career here playing happily with the crucibles, retorts, and bunsen burners of your science fifth.
FRANK (*turning at the door*): Oh. Has he?
ANDREW: Has he what?
FRANK: Obtained his remove?
ANDREW (*after a pause*): He has obtained exactly

what he deserves. No less; and certainly no more. (TAP-LOW *mutters an explosion of mirth.* FRANK *nods, thoughtfully, and goes out.* ANDREW *has caught sight of* TAPLOW'S *contorted face, but passes no remark on it. He beckons* TAPLOW *across and signs to him to sit in the chair right of the desk.* TAPLOW *sits.* ANDREW *picks up a copy of* The Agamemnon *and* TAPLOW *does the same.*) Line thirteen hundred and ninety-nine. Begin.

(*He leans back.*)

TAPLOW (*reading slowly*): Chorus. We—are surprised at . . .
ANDREW (*automatically*): We marvel at.
TAPLOW: We marvel at—thy tongue—how bold thou art—that you . . .
ANDREW: Thou.

(*His interruptions are automatic. His thoughts are evidently far distant.*)

TAPLOW: Thou—can . . .
ANDREW: Canst.
TAPLOW: Canst—boastfully speak . . .
ANDREW: Utter such a boastful speech.
TAPLOW: Utter such a boastful speech—over—(*in a sudden rush of inspiration*) the bloody corpse of the husband you have slain.

(ANDREW *puts on his glasses and looks down at his text for the first time.* TAPLOW *looks apprehensive.*)

ANDREW (*after a pause*): Taplow—I presume you are using a different text from mine.
TAPLOW: No, sir.
ANDREW: That is strange, for the line as I have it reads: "heetis toiond ep andri compadzise logon." However diligently I search I can discover no "bloody"—no "corpse" —no "you have slain." Simply "husband."
TAPLOW: Yes, sir. That's right.
ANDREW: Then why do you invent words that simply are not there?
TAPLOW: I thought they sounded better, sir. More ex-

citing. After all, she did kill her husband, sir. (*With relish.*) She's just been revealed with his dead body and Cassandra's weltering in gore.

ANDREW: I am delighted at this evidence, Taplow, of your interest in the rather more lurid aspects of dramaturgy, but I feel I must remind you that you are supposed to be construing Greek, not collaborating with Aeschylus.

(*He leans back.*)

TAPLOW (*greatly daring*): Yes, but still, sir, translator's license, sir—I didn't get anything wrong—and after all it *is* a play and not just a bit of Greek construe.

ANDREW (*momentarily at a loss*): I seem to detect a note of end of term in your remarks. I am not denying that *The Agamemnon* is a play. It is perhaps the greatest play ever written.

(*He leans forward.*)

TAPLOW (*quickly*): I wonder how many people in the form think that? (*He pauses; instantly frightened of what he has said.*) Sorry, sir. Shall I go on? (ANDREW *does not answer. He sits motionless, staring at his book.*) Shall I go on, sir?

(*There is another pause.* ANDREW *raises his head slowly from his book.*)

ANDREW (*murmuring gently, not looking at* TAPLOW): When I was a very young man, only two years older than you are now, Taplow, I wrote, for my own pleasure, a translation of *The Agamemnon*—a very free translation— I remember—in rhyming couplets.

TAPLOW: The whole *Agamemnon*—in verse? That must have been hard work, sir.

ANDREW: It was hard work; but I derived great joy from it. The play had so excited and moved me that I wished to communicate, however imperfectly, some of that emotion to others. When I had finished it, I remember, I thought it very beautiful—almost more beautiful than the original.

(*He leans back.*)

TAPLOW: Was it ever published, sir?

ANDREW: No. Yesterday I looked for the manuscript while I was packing my papers. I was unable to find it. I fear it is lost—like so many other things. Lost for good.

TAPLOW: Hard luck, sir. (ANDREW *is silent again.* TAPLOW *steals a timid glance at him.*) Shall I go on, sir?

(ANDREW, *with a slight effort, lowers his eyes again to his text.*)

ANDREW (*leaning forward; raising his voice slightly*): No. Go back and get that last line right.

(TAPLOW, *out of* ANDREW'S *vision, as he thinks, makes a disgusted grimace in his direction.*)

TAPLOW: That—thou canst utter such a boastful speech over thy husband.

ANDREW: Yes. And now, if you would be so kind, you will do the line again, without the facial contortion which you just found necessary to accompany it.

(TAPLOW *is about to begin the line again.* MILLIE *enters up center, hurriedly. She is wearing an apron.* TAPLOW *rises.*)

MILLIE: The headmaster's just coming up the drive. Don't tell him I'm in. The fish pie isn't in the oven yet.

(*She exits up center.*)

TAPLOW (*turning hopefully to* ANDREW): I'd better go, hadn't I, sir? I mean—I don't want to be in the way.

ANDREW: We do not yet know that it is I the headmaster wishes to see. Other people live in this building. (*There is a knock at the door up right.*) Come in.

(DR. FROBISHER *enters up right. He looks more like a distinguished diplomat than a doctor of literature and a classical scholar. He is in the middle fifties and goes to a very good tailor.* ANDREW *rises.*)

FROBISHER: Ah, Crocker-Harris, I've caught you in. I'm

so glad. (*He crosses behind the settee and comes down left of it.*) I hope I'm not disturbing you?

ANDREW: I have been taking a pupil in extra work.

(TAPLOW *eases below the table center.*)

FROBISHER: On the penultimate day of term? That argues either great conscientiousness on your part or considerable backwardness on his.

ANDREW: Perhaps a combination of both.

FROBISHER: Quite so, but as this is my only chance of speaking to you before tomorrow, I think that perhaps your pupil will be good enough to excuse us.

(*He turns politely to* TAPLOW.)

TAPLOW: Oh yes, sir. That's really quite all right.

(*He grabs his books off* ANDREW'S *desk.*)

ANDREW (*crossing to* TAPLOW): I'm extremely sorry, Taplow. You will please explain to your father exactly what occurred over this lost hour and tell him that I shall in due course be writing to him to return the money involved.

(FROBISHER *moves below the settee to the fireplace.*)

TAPLOW (*hurriedly*): Yes, sir. But please don't bother, sir. (*He dashes to the door up right.*) I know it's all right, sir. Thank you, sir. (*He darts out.*)

FROBISHER (*idly picking up an ornament on the mantelpiece*): Have the Gilberts called on you yet?

(*He turns to* ANDREW.)

ANDREW (*moving center*): The Gilberts, sir? Who are they?

FROBISHER: Gilbert is your successor with the lower fifth. He is down here today with his wife, and as they will be taking over this flat I thought perhaps you wouldn't mind if they came in to look it over.

ANDREW: Of course not.

FROBISHER: I've told you about him, I think. He is a very brilliant young man and won exceptionally high honors at Oxford.

ANDREW: So I understand, sir.

FROBISHER: Not, of course, as high as the honors you yourself won there. He didn't, for instance, win the Chancellor's prize for Latin verse or the Gainsford.

ANDREW: He won the Hertford Latin, then?

FROBISHER (*replacing the ornament*): No. (*Mildly surprised.*) Did you win that, too? (ANDREW *nods.*) It's sometimes rather hard to remember that you are perhaps the most brilliant classical scholar we have ever had at the school.

ANDREW: You are very kind.

FROBISHER (*urbanely correcting his gaffe*): Hard to remember, I mean—because of your other activities—your brilliant work on the school timetable, for instance, and also for your heroic battle for so long and against such odds with the soul-destroying lower fifth.

ANDREW: I have not found that my soul has been destroyed by the lower fifth, Headmaster.

FROBISHER: I was joking, of course.

ANDREW: Oh. I see.

FROBISHER: Is your wife in?

ANDREW: Er—no. Not at the moment.

FROBISHER: I shall have a chance of saying good-bye to her tomorrow. (*He moves in a few steps below the settee.*) I am rather glad I have got you to myself. I have a delicate matter—two rather delicate matters—to broach.

ANDREW (*moving in slightly; indicating the settee*): Please sit down.

(*He stands at the left end of the settee.*)

FROBISHER: Thank you. (*He sits.*) Now you have been with us, in all, eighteen years, haven't you? (ANDREW *nods.*) It is extremely unlucky that you should have had to retire at so comparatively early an age and so short a time before you would have been eligible for a pension.

(*He is regarding his nails, as he speaks, studiously avoiding meeting ANDREW'S gaze. ANDREW crosses below the settee to the fireplace and stands facing it.*)

ANDREW (*after a pause*): You have decided, then, not to award me a pension?

FROBISHER: Not I, my dear fellow. It has nothing at all to do with me. It's the governors who, I'm afraid, have been forced to turn down your application. I put your case to them as well as I could—(ANDREW *turns and faces* FROBISHER)—but they decided with great regret, that they couldn't make an exception to the rule.

ANDREW: But I thought—my wife thought, that an exception was made some five years ago . . .

FROBISHER: Ah! In the case of Buller, you mean? True. But the circumstances with Buller were quite remarkable. It was, after all, in playing rugger against the school that he received that injury.

ANDREW: Yes. I remember.

FROBISHER: And then the governors received a petition from boys, old boys and parents, with over five hundred signatures.

ANDREW: I would have signed that petition myself, but through some oversight I was not asked.

FROBISHER: He was a splendid fellow, Buller. Splendid. Doing very well, too, now, I gather.

ANDREW: I'm delighted to hear it.

FROBISHER: Your own case, of course, is equally deserving. If not more so—for Buller was a younger man. Unfortunately—rules are rules—and are not made to be broken every few years; at any rate that is the governors' view.

ANDREW: I quite understand.

FROBISHER: I knew you would. Now might I ask you a rather impertinent question?

ANDREW: Certainly.

FROBISHER: You have, I take it, private means?

ANDREW: My wife has some.

FROBISHER: Ah, yes. Your wife has often told me of her family connections. I understand her father has a business in—Bradford—isn't it?

ANDREW: Yes. He runs a men's clothing shop in the Arcade.

FROBISHER: Indeed? Your wife's remarks had led me to imagine something a little more—extensive.

ANDREW: My father-in-law made a settlement on my wife at the time of our marriage. She has about three hundred a year of her own. I have nothing. Is that the answer to your question, Headmaster?

FROBISHER: Yes. Thank you for your frankness. Now, this private school you are going to . . .

ANDREW: My salary at the crammer's is to be two hundred pounds a year.

FROBISHER: Quite so. With board and lodging, of course?

ANDREW: For eight months of the year.

FROBISHER: Yes, I see. (*He ponders a second.*) Of course, you know, there is the School Benevolent Fund that deals with cases of actual hardship.

ANDREW: There will be no actual hardship, Headmaster.

FROBISHER: No. I am glad you take that view. I must admit, though, I had hoped that your own means had proved a little more ample. Your wife had certainly led me to suppose . . .

ANDREW: I am not denying that a pension would have been very welcome, Headmaster, but I see no reason to quarrel with the governors' decision. What is the other delicate matter you have to discuss?

FROBISHER: Well, it concerns the arrangements at prize-giving tomorrow. You are, of course, prepared to say a few words?

ANDREW: I had assumed you would call on me to do so.

FROBISHER: Of course. It is always done, and I know the boys appreciate the custom.

ANDREW (*crossing to the upstage end of the desk*): I have already made a few notes of what I am going to say. Perhaps you would care . . .

FROBISHER: No, no. That isn't necessary at all. I know I can trust your discretion—not to say your wit. It will be, I know, a very moving moment for you—indeed for us all—but, as I'm sure you realize, it is far better to keep these occasions from becoming too heavy and distressing. You know how little the boys appreciate sentiment.

ANDREW: I do.

FROBISHER: That is why I've planned my own reference to you at the end of my speech to be rather more light and jocular than I would otherwise have made it.

ANDREW: I quite understand. (*He moves to left of the desk, puts on his glasses, and picks up his speech.*) I too have prepared a few little jokes and puns for my speech. One—a play of words on *vale,* farewell and Wally, the Christian name of a backward boy in my class, is, I think, rather happy.

FROBISHER: Yes. (*He laughs belatedly.*) Very neat. That should go down extremely well.

ANDREW: I'm glad you like it.

FROBISHER (*rising and crossing to right of the desk*): Well, now—there is a particular favor I have to ask of you in connection with the ceremony, and I know I shall not have to ask in vain. Fletcher, as you know, is leaving too.

ANDREW: Yes. He is going into the city, they tell me.

FROBISHER: Yes. Now he is, of course, considerably junior to you. He has only been here—let me see—five years. But, as you know, he has done great things for our cricket—positive wonders, when you remember what doldrums we were in before he came.

ANDREW: Our win at Lord's this year was certainly most inspiriting.

FROBISHER: Exactly. (*He moves above the desk.*) Now I'm sure that tomorrow the boys will make the occasion of his farewell speech a tremendous demonstration of gratitude. The applause might go on for minutes—you know what the boys feel about Lord's—and I seriously doubt my ability to cut it short or even, I admit, the propriety of trying to do so. Now, you see the quandary in which I am placed?

ANDREW: Perfectly. You wish to refer to me and for me to make my speech before you come to Fletcher?

FROBISHER: It's extremely awkward, and I feel wretched about asking it of you—but it's more for your own sake than for mine or Fletcher's that I do. After all, a climax is what one must try to work up to on these occasions.

ANDREW: Naturally, Headmaster, I wouldn't wish to provide an anticlimax.

FROBISHER: You really mustn't take it amiss, my dear fellow. The boys, in applauding Fletcher for several minutes and yourself say—for—well, for not quite so long—

won't be making any personal demonstration between you. It will be quite impersonal—I assure you—quite impersonal.

ANDREW: I understand.

FROBISHER (*patting* ANDREW'S *shoulder; warmly*): I knew you would (*he looks at his watch*) and I can hardly tell you how wisely I think you have chosen. Well now— as that is all my business, I think perhaps I had better be getting along. (*He crosses to right of the table.*) This has been a terribly busy day for me—for you too, I imagine.

ANDREW: Yes.

(MILLIE *enters up center. She has taken off her apron and tidied herself up. She comes to left of* FROBISHER.)

MILLIE (*in her social manner*): Ah, Headmaster. How good of you to drop in.

FROBISHER (*more at home with her than with* AN-DREW): Mrs. Crocker-Harris. How are you? (*They shake hands.*) You're looking extremely well, I must say. (*To* ANDREW) Has anyone ever told you, Crocker-Harris, that you have a very attractive wife?

ANDREW: Many people, sir. But then I hardly need to be told.

MILLIE: Can I persuade you to stay a few moments and have a drink, Headmaster? It's so rarely we have the pleasure of seeing you.

FROBISHER: Unfortunately, dear lady, I was just on the point of leaving. I have two frantic parents waiting for me at home. You are dining with us tomorrow—both of you, aren't you?

MILLIE: Yes, indeed—and so looking forward to it.

(FROBISHER *and* MILLIE *move to the door up right.*)

FROBISHER: I'm so glad. We can say our sad farewells then. (*To* ANDREW) Au revoir, Crocker-Harris, and thank you very much.

(*He opens the door.* ANDREW *gives a slight bow.* MILLIE *holds the door open.* FROBISHER *goes out.*)

MILLIE (*to* ANDREW): Don't forget to take your medicine, dear, will you?

(*She goes out.*)

ANDREW: No.

FROBISHER (*off*): Lucky invalid! To have such a very charming nurse.

MILLIE (*off*): I really don't know what to say to all these compliments, Headmaster. I don't believe you mean a word of them.

(ANDREW *turns and looks out of the window.*)

FROBISHER (*off*): Every word. Till tomorrow, then? Good-bye.

(*The outer door is heard to slam.* ANDREW *is staring out of the window.* MILLIE *enters up right.*)

MILLIE: Well? Do we get it?

(*She stands on the step.*)

ANDREW (*turning and moving below the chair left of his desk; absently*): Get what?

MILLIE: The pension, of course. Do we get it?

ANDREW: No.

MILLIE (*crossing above the settee to center*): My God! Why not?

ANDREW (*sitting at his desk*): It's against the rules.

MILLIE: Buller got it, didn't he? Buller got it. What's the idea of giving it to him and not to us?

ANDREW: The governors are afraid of establishing a precedent.

MILLIE: The mean old brutes! My God, what I wouldn't like to say to them! (*She moves above the desk and rounds on* ANDREW.) And what did you say? Just sat there and made a joke in Latin, I suppose?

ANDREW: There wasn't very much I could say, in Latin or any other language.

MILLIE: Oh, wasn't there? I'd have said it all right. I wouldn't just have sat there twiddling my thumbs and taking it from that old phoney of a headmaster. But, then, of course, I'm not a man. (ANDREW *is turning the pages of* The Agamemnon, *not looking at her.*) What do they expect you to do? Live on my money, I suppose.

ANDREW: There has never been any question of that. I shall be perfectly able to support myself.

MILLIE: Yourself? Doesn't the marriage service say something about the husband supporting his wife? (*She leans on the desk.*) Doesn't it? You ought to know.

ANDREW: Yes, it does.

MILLIE: And how do you think you're going to do that on two hundred a year?

ANDREW: I shall do my utmost to save some of it. You're welcome to it, if I can.

MILLIE: Thank you for precisely nothing. (ANDREW *underlines a word in the text he is reading.*) What else did the old fool have to say?

(*She moves to right of the chair, right of the desk.*)

ANDREW: The headmaster? He wants me to make my speech tomorrow before instead of after Fletcher.

MILLIE (*sitting right of the desk*): Yes. I knew he was going to ask that.

ANDREW (*without surprise*): You knew?

MILLIE: Yes. He asked my advice about it a week ago. I told him to go ahead. I knew you wouldn't mind, and as there isn't a Mrs. Fletcher to make *me* look a fool, I didn't give two hoots. (*There is a knock on the door up right.*) Come in.

(MR. *and* MRS. GILBERT *enter up right. He is about twenty-two, and his wife a year or so younger.* MILLIE *rises and stands at the downstage corner of the desk.*)

GILBERT: Mr. Crocker-Harris?

ANDREW: Yes. (*He rises.*) Is it Mr. and Mrs. Gilbert? The headmaster told me you might look in.

MRS. GILBERT (*crossing above the settee to center*): I do hope we're not disturbing you.

(GILBERT *follows* MRS. GILBERT *and stands down stage of, and slightly behind, her.*)

ANDREW: Not at all. This is my wife.

MRS. GILBERT: How do you do?

ANDREW: Mr. and Mrs. Gilbert are our successors to this flat, my dear.

MILLIE: Oh yes. (*She moves to left of* MRS. GILBERT.) How nice to meet you both.

GILBERT: How do you do? We really won't keep you more than a second—my wife thought as we were here you wouldn't mind us taking a squint at our future home.

MRS. GILBERT (*unnecessarily*): This is the drawing room, I suppose?

(GILBERT *crosses to the fireplace. He looks for a moment at the picture above the mantelpiece, then turns and watches the others.*)

MILLIE: Well, it's really a living room. Andrew uses it as a study.

MRS. GILBERT: How charmingly you've done it!

MILLIE: Oh, do you think so? I'm afraid it isn't nearly as nice as I'd like to make it—but a schoolmaster's wife has to think of so many other things besides curtains and covers. Boys with dirty books and a husband with leaky fountain pens, for instance.

MRS. GILBERT: Yes, I suppose so. Of course, I haven't been a schoolmaster's wife for very long, you know.

GILBERT: Don't swank, darling. You haven't been a schoolmaster's wife at all yet.

MRS. GILBERT: Oh yes, I have—for two months. You were a schoolmaster when I married you.

GILBERT: Prep school doesn't count.

MILLIE: Have you only been married two months?

MRS. GILBERT: Two months and sixteen days.

GILBERT: Seventeen.

MILLIE (*sentimentally*): Andrew, did you hear? They've only been married two months.

ANDREW: Indeed? Is that all?

MRS. GILBERT (*crossing above* MILLIE *to the window*): Oh, look, darling. They've got a garden. It is yours, isn't it?

MILLIE: Oh, yes. It's only a pocket handkerchief, I'm afraid, but it's very useful to Andrew. He often works out there, don't you, dear?

ANDREW: Yes, indeed. I find it very agreeable.

MILLIE (*moving to the door up center*): Shall I show you the rest of the flat? It's a bit untidy, I'm afraid, but you must forgive that.

(*She opens the door.*)

MRS. GILBERT (*moving up to left of* MILLIE): Oh, of course.

MILLIE: And the kitchen is in a terrible mess. I'm in the middle of cooking dinner.

MRS. GILBERT (*breathlessly*): Oh, do you cook?

MILLIE: Oh, yes. I have to. We haven't had a maid for five years.

MRS. GILBERT: Oh! I do think that's wonderful of you. I'm scared stiff of having to do it for Peter—I know the first dinner I have to cook for him will wreck our married life.

GILBERT: Highly probable.

(MRS. GILBERT *exits up center.*)

MILLIE (*following* MRS. GILBERT): Well, these days we've all got to try and do things we weren't really brought up to do.

(*She goes out, closing the door.*)

ANDREW (*to* GILBERT): Don't you want to see the rest of the flat?

GILBERT (*crossing to center*): No. I leave all that sort of thing to my wife. She's the boss. I thought perhaps you could tell me something about the lower fifth.

ANDREW: What would you like to know?

GILBERT: Well, sir, quite frankly, I'm petrified.

ANDREW: I don't think you need to be. May I give you some sherry?

(*He comes down left to the cupboard.*)

GILBERT: Thank you.

ANDREW: They are mostly boys of about fifteen or sixteen. They are not very difficult to handle.

(*He takes out a bottle and a glass.*)

GILBERT: The headmaster said you ruled them with a rod of iron. He called you "the Himmler of the lower fifth."

ANDREW (*turning, bottle and glass in hand*): Did he? "The Himmler of the lower fifth." I think he exaggerated. I hope he exaggerated. "The Himmler of the lower fifth."

(*He puts the bottle on the desk, then fills the glass.*)

GILBERT (*puzzled*): He only meant that you kept the most wonderful discipline. I must say I do admire you for that. I couldn't even manage that with eleven-year-olds, so what I'll be like with fifteens and sixteens I shudder to think.

(*He moves below the chair right of the desk.*)

ANDREW: It is not so difficult. (*He hands* GILBERT *the glass.*) They aren't bad boys. Sometimes a little wild and unfeeling, perhaps—but not bad. "The Himmler of the lower fifth." Dear me!

(*He turns to the cabinet with the bottle.*)

GILBERT: Perhaps I shouldn't have said that. I've been tactless, I'm afraid.

ANDREW: Oh no. (*He puts the bottle in the cupboard.*) Please sit down.

(*He stands by the downstage end of the desk.*)

GILBERT: Thank you, sir.

(*He sits right of the desk.*)

ANDREW: From the very beginning I realized that I didn't possess the knack of making myself liked—a knack that you will find you do possess.

GILBERT: Do you think so?

ANDREW: Oh yes. I am quite sure of it. (*He moves up left of the desk.*) It is not a quality of great importance to a schoolmaster though, for too much of it, as you may also find, is as great a danger as the total lack of it. Forgive me lecturing, won't you?

GILBERT: I want to learn.

ANDREW: I can only teach you from my own experience. For two or three years I tried very hard to communicate to the boys some of my own joy in the great literature of the past. Of course I failed, as you will fail, nine hundred and ninety-nine times out of a thousand. But a single success can atone, and more than atone, for all the failure in the world. And sometimes—very rarely, it is true—but sometimes I had that success. That was in the early years.

GILBERT (*eagerly listening*): Please go on, sir.

ANDREW: In early years too, I discovered an easy substitute for popularity. (*He picks up his speech.*) I had of course acquired—we all do—many little mannerisms and tricks of speech, and I found that the boys were beginning to laugh at me. I was very happy at that, and encouraged the boys' laughter by playing up to it. It made our relationship so very much easier. They didn't like me as a man, but they found me funny as a character, and you can teach more things by laughter than by earnestness—for I never did have much sense of humor. So, for a time, you see, I was quite a success as a schoolmaster . . . (*He stops.*) I fear this is all very personal and embarrassing to you. Forgive me. You need have no fears about the lower fifth.

(*He puts the speech into his pocket and turns to the window.* GILBERT *rises and moves above the desk.*)

GILBERT (*after a pause*): I'm afraid I said something that hurt you very much. It's myself you must forgive, sir. Believe me, I'm desperately sorry.

ANDREW (*turning down stage and leaning slightly on the back of the swivel chair*): There's no need. You were merely telling me what I should have known for myself. Perhaps I did in my heart, and hadn't the courage to acknowledge it. I knew, of course, that I was not only not liked, but now positively disliked. I had realized too that the boys—for many long years now—had ceased to laugh at me. I don't know why they no longer found me a joke. Perhaps it was my illness. No, I don't think it was that. Something deeper than that. Not a sickness of the body, but a sickness of the soul. At all events it didn't take much discernment on my part to realize I had become an utter failure as a schoolmaster. Still, stupidly enough, I hadn't realized that I was also feared. "The Himmler of the lower fifth." I suppose that will become my epitaph. (GILBERT *is now deeply embarrassed and rather upset, but he remains silent. He sits on the upstage end of the window seat. With a mild laugh.*) I cannot for the life of me imagine why I should choose to unburden myself to you—a total stranger—when I have been silent to others for so long. Perhaps it is because my very unworthy mantle is about to fall on your shoulders. If that is so I shall take a prophet's privilege and foretell that you will have a very great success with the lower fifth.

GILBERT: Thank you, sir. I shall do my best.

ANDREW: I can't offer you a cigarette, I'm afraid. I don't smoke.

GILBERT: That's all right, sir. Nor do I.

MRS. GILBERT (*off*): Thank you so much for showing me round.

(MILLIE *and* MRS. GILBERT *enter up center.* ANDREW *rises.* MILLIE *comes down right of the table center, picks up the papers on the settee, and puts them on the fender down right.* MRS. GILBERT *comes down left of the table center to right of* GILBERT.)

ANDREW: I trust your wife has found no major snags in your new flat.

MR. GILBERT: No. None at all.

MRS. GILBERT: Just imagine, Peter, Mr. and Mrs. Crocker-Harris first met each other on a holiday in the Lake District. Isn't that a coincidence?

GILBERT (*a little distrait*): Yes. Yes, it certainly is. On a walking tour, too?

(ANDREW *turns and looks out of the window.*)

MILLIE: Andrew was on a walking tour. No walking for me. I can't abide it. I was staying with my uncle—that's Sir William Bartop, you know—you may have heard of him. (GILBERT *and* MRS. GILBERT *try to look as though they had heard of him constantly. She moves below the settee.*) He'd taken a house near Windermere—quite a mansion it was really—rather silly for an old gentleman living alone—and Andrew knocked on our front door one day and asked the footman for a glass of water. So my uncle invited him in to tea.

MRS. GILBERT (*moving center*): Our meeting wasn't quite as romantic as that.

GILBERT: I knocked her flat on her face.

(*He moves behind* MRS. GILBERT *and puts his hands on her shoulders.*)

MRS. GILBERT: Not with love at first sight. With the swing doors of our hotel bar. So of course then he apologized and . . .

(ANDREW *turns and faces into the room.*)

GILBERT (*briskly*): Darling. The Crocker-Harrises, I'm sure, have far more important things to do than to listen to your detailed but inaccurate account of our very sordid little encounter. Why not just say I married you for your money and leave it at that? Come on, we must go.

MRS. GILBERT (*moving above the settee; to* MILLIE): Isn't he awful to me?

MILLIE (*moving round the right end of the settee to the door up right*): Men have no souls, my dear. My husband is just as bad.

MRS. GILBERT: Good-bye, Mr. Crocker-Harris.

ANDREW (*with a slight bow*): Good-bye.

MRS. GILBERT (*moving to the door up right; to* MIL-LIE): I think your idea about the dining room is awfully good—if only I can get the permit . . .

(MILLIE *and* MRS. GILBERT *go out.* GILBERT *has dallied to say good-bye alone to* ANDREW.)

GILBERT: Good-bye, sir.

ANDREW (*crossing center to left of* GILBERT): Er—you will, I know, respect the confidences I have just made to you.

GILBERT: I should hate you to think I wouldn't.

ANDREW: I am sorry to have embarrassed you. I don't know what came over me. I have not been very well, you know. Good-bye, my dear fellow, and my best wishes.

GILBERT: Thank you. The very best of good luck to you too, sir, in your future career.

ANDREW: My future career? Yes. Thank you.

GILBERT: Well, good-bye, sir.

(*He crosses up right and goes out.* ANDREW *moves to the chair right of the desk and sits. He picks up a book and looks at it.* MILLIE *enters up right. She crosses above the table center, picks up the box of chocolates, and eats one as she speaks.*)

MILLIE: Good-looking couple.

ANDREW: Very.

MILLIE: He looks as if he'd got what it takes. I should think he'll be a success all right.

ANDREW: That's what I thought.

MILLIE: I don't think it's much of a career, though—a schoolmaster—for a likely young chap like that.

ANDREW: I know you don't.

MILLIE (*crossing down to the desk and picking up the luggage labels*): Still, I bet when he leaves this place it won't be without a pension. It'll be roses, roses all the way, and tears and cheers and good-bye, Mr. Chips.

ANDREW: I expect so.

MILLIE: What's the matter with you?

ANDREW: Nothing.

MILLIE: You're not going to have another of your attacks, are you? You look dreadful.

ANDREW: I'm perfectly all right.

MILLIE (*indifferently*): You know best. Your medicine's there, anyway, if you want it.

(*She goes out up center.* ANDREW, *left alone, continues for a time staring at the text he has been pretending to read. Then he puts one hand over his eyes. There is a knock at the door up right.*)

ANDREW: Come in. (TAPLOW *enters up right and appears timidly from behind the screen. He is carrying a small book behind his back. Sharply.*) Yes, Taplow? What is it?

TAPLOW: Nothing, sir.

ANDREW: What do you mean, nothing?

TAPLOW (*timidly*): I just came back to say good-bye, sir.

ANDREW: Oh.

(*He puts down the book and rises.*)

TAPLOW (*moving center*): I didn't have a chance with the head here. I rather dashed out, I'm afraid. I thought I'd just come back and—wish you luck, sir.

ANDREW: Thank you, Taplow. That's good of you.

TAPLOW: I—er—thought this might interest you, sir.

(*He quickly thrusts the small book toward* ANDREW.)

ANDREW (*taking out his glasses and putting them on*): What is it?

TAPLOW: Verse translation of *The Agamemnon*, sir. The Browning version. It's not much good. I've been reading it in the Chapel gardens.

ANDREW (*taking the book*): Very interesting, Taplow. (*He seems to have a little difficulty in speaking. He clears his throat and then goes on in his level, gentle voice.*) I know the translation, of course. It has its faults, I agree, but I think you will enjoy it more when you get used to the meter he employs.

(*He hands the book to* TAPLOW.)

TAPLOW (*brusquely thrusting the book back to* ANDREW): It's for you, sir.

ANDREW: For me?

TAPLOW: Yes, sir. I've written in it.

(ANDREW *opens the flyleaf and reads whatever is written there.*)

ANDREW: Did you buy this?

TAPLOW: Yes, sir. It was only second-hand.

ANDREW: You shouldn't have spent your pocket money this way.

TAPLOW: That's all right, sir. It wasn't very much. (*Suddenly appalled.*) The price isn't still inside, is it?

(ANDREW *carefully wipes his glasses and puts them on again.*)

ANDREW (*at length*): No. Just what you've written. Nothing else.

TAPLOW: Good. I'm sorry you've got it already. I thought you probably would have.

ANDREW: I haven't got it already. I may have had it once. I can't remember. But I haven't got it now.

TAPLOW: That's all right, then. (ANDREW *continues to stare at* TAPLOW'S *inscription on the flyleaf. Suspiciously.*) What's the matter, sir? Have I got the accent wrong on "eumenose"?

ANDREW: No. The perispomenon is perfectly correct. (*His hands are shaking. He lowers the book and turns away above the chair right of the desk.*) Taplow, would you be good enough to take that bottle of medicine, which you so kindly brought in, and pour me out one dose in a glass which you will find in the bathroom?

TAPLOW (*seeing something is wrong*): Yes, sir.

(*He moves up to the sideboard and picks up the bottle.*)

ANDREW: The doses are clearly marked on the bottle. I usually put a little water with it.

TAPLOW: Yes, sir.

(*He darts out up center.* ANDREW, *the moment he is gone, breaks down and begins to sob uncontrollably. He sits in the chair left of the desk and makes a desperate attempt, after a moment, to control himself, but when* TAPLOW *comes back his emotion is still apparent.* TAPLOW *re-enters with the bottle and a glass, comes to the upstage end of the desk, and holds out the glass.*)

ANDREW (*taking the glass*): Thank you. (*He drinks, turning his back on* TAPLOW *as he does so.*) You must forgive this exhibition of weakness, Taplow. The truth is I have been going through rather a strain lately.

TAPLOW (*putting the bottle on the desk*): Of course, sir. I quite understand.

(*He eases toward center. There is a knock on the door upper left.*)

FRANK: Oh, sorry. I thought you'd be finished by now.

(*He moves to left of* TAPLOW.)

ANDREW: Come in, Hunter, do. It's perfectly all right. Our lesson was over some time ago, but Taplow most kindly came back to say good-bye.

(FRANK, *taking in* TAPLOW'S *rather startled face and* ANDREW'S *obvious emotion, looks a little puzzled.*)

FRANK: Are you sure I'm not intruding?
ANDREW: No, no. I want you to see this book that Taplow has given me, Hunter. Look. A translation of *The Agamemnon*, by Robert Browning. (*He rises.*) Do you see the inscription he has put into it?

(*He hands the book open to* FRANK *across the desk.*)

FRANK (*glancing at the book*): Yes, but it's no use to me, I'm afraid. I never learned Greek.
ANDREW: Then we'll have to translate it for him, won't we, Taplow? (*He recites by heart.*) "*ton kratownta malthecose theos prosothen eumenose prosdirkati.*" That means—in a rough translation: "God from afar looks graciously upon a gentle master." It comes from a speech of Agamemnon's to Clytaemnestra.
FRANK: I see. Very pleasant and very apt.

(*He hands the book back to* ANDREW.)

ANDREW: Very pleasant. But perhaps not, after all, so very apt.

(*He turns quickly away from both of them as emotion once more seems about to overcome him.* FRANK *brusquely jerks his head to the bewildered* TAPLOW *to get out.* TAPLOW *nods.*)

TAPLOW: Good-bye, sir, and the best of luck.
ANDREW: Good-bye, Taplow, and thank you very much.

(TAPLOW *flees quickly up right and goes out.* FRANK *watches* ANDREW'S *back with a mixture of embarrassment and sympathy.*)

ANDREW (*turning at length, slightly recovered*): Dear me, what a fool I made of myself in front of that boy. And in front of you, Hunter. (*He moves in to the desk.*) I can't imagine what you must think of me.

FRANK: Nonsense.

ANDREW: I am not a very emotional person, as you know, but there was something so very touching and kindly about his action, and coming as it did just after . . . (*He stops, then glances at the book in his hand.*) This is a very delightful thing to have, don't you think?

FRANK: Delightful.

ANDREW: The quotation, of course, he didn't find entirely by himself. I happened to make some little joke about the line in form the other day. But he must have remembered it all the same to have found it so readily—and perhaps he means it.

FRANK: I'm sure he does, or he wouldn't have written it.

(MILLIE *enters up center with a tray of supper things. She puts the tray on the sideboard. She puts table napkins, mats, and bread on the table.* ANDREW *turns and looks out of the window.*)

MILLIE: Hullo, Frank. I'm glad you're in time. Lend me a cigarette. I've been gasping for one for an hour.

(FRANK *moves up left of the table center and once more extends his case.* MILLIE *takes a cigarette.*)

FRANK: Your husband has just had a very nice present.

MILLIE: Oh? Who from?

FRANK: Taplow.

(*He comes down left of the table.*)

MILLIE (*coming down right of the table; smiling*): Oh, Taplow.

(FRANK *lights* MILLIE'S *cigarette.*)

ANDREW (*moving above the desk to the chair right of it*): He bought it with his own pocket money, Millie, and wrote a very charming inscription inside.

FRANK: "God looks kindly upon a gracious master."

ANDREW: No—not gracious—gentle, I think. *"ton kra-townta malthecose"*—yes, I think gentle is the better translation. I would rather have had this present, I think, than almost anything I can think of.

(*There is a pause.* MILLIE *laughs suddenly.*)

MILLIE (*holding out her hand*): Let's see it. The artful little beast.

(ANDREW *hands the book across to* MILLIE. MILLIE *opens it.*)

FRANK (*urgently*): Millie.

(MILLIE *looks at* ANDREW.)

ANDREW: Artful? (MILLIE *looks at* FRANK). Why artful? (FRANK *stares meaningly at* MILLIE. MILLIE *looks at* ANDREW.) Why artful, Millie?

(MILLIE *laughs again, quite lightly.*)

MILLIE: My dear, because I came into this room this afternoon to find him giving an imitation of you to Frank here. Obviously he was scared stiff I was going to tell you, and you'd ditch his remove or something. I don't blame him for trying a few bobs' worth of appeasement.

(*She gives the book to* ANDREW, *then moves up right of the table to the sideboard, where she stubs out her cigarette, picks up some cutlery, and starts to lay the table.* ANDREW *stands quite still, looking down at the book.*)

ANDREW (*after a pause; nodding*): I see.

(*He puts the book gently on the desk, picks up the bottle of medicine, and moves up left of the table to the door up center.*)

MILLIE: Where are you going, dear? Dinner's nearly ready.

ANDREW (*opening the door*): Only to my room for a moment. I won't be long.

MILLIE: You've just had a dose of that, dear. I shouldn't have another, if I were you.

ANDREW: I am allowed two at a time.

MILLIE: Well, see it is two and no more, won't you?

(ANDREW *meets her eye for a moment, then goes out quietly.* MILLIE *moves to left of the table and lays the last knife and fork. She looks at* FRANK *with an expression half defiant and half ashamed.*)

FRANK (*with a note of real repulsion in his voice*): Millie! My God! How could you?

MILLIE: Well, why not? (*She crosses above the table and comes down left of the settee.*) Why should he be allowed his comforting little illusions? I'm not.

FRANK (*advancing on her*): Listen. You're to go to his room now and tell him that was a lie.

MILLIE: Certainly not. It wasn't a lie.

FRANK: If you don't, I will.

MILLIE: I shouldn't, if I were you. It'll only make things worse. He won't believe you.

FRANK (*moving up right of the table center*): We'll see about that.

MILLIE: Go ahead. See what happens. He knows I don't lie to him. He knows what I told him was the truth, and he won't like your sympathy. He'll think you're making fun of him, like Taplow.

(FRANK *hesitates, then comes slowly down center again.* MILLIE *watches him, a little frightened.*)

FRANK (*after a pause*): We're finished, Millie—you and I.

MILLIE (*laughing*): Frank, really! Don't be hysterical.

FRANK: I'm not. I mean it.

MILLIE (*lightly*): Oh yes, you mean it. Of course you mean it. Now just sit down, dear, and relax, and forget all about artful little boys and their five-bob presents, and talk to me.

(*She pulls at his coat.*)

FRANK (*pulling away*): Forget? If I live to be a hundred I shall never forget that little glimpse you've just given me of yourself.

MILLIE: Frank—you're making a frightening mountain out of an absurd little molehill.

FRANK: Of course, but the mountain I'm making in my imagination is so frightening that I'd rather try to forget both it and the repulsive little molehill that gave it birth. But as I know I never can, I tell you, Millie—from this moment you and I are finished.

MILLIE (*quietly*): You can't scare me, Frank. (*She turns away toward the fireplace.*) I know that's what you're trying to do, but you can't do it.

FRANK (*quietly*): I'm not trying to scare you, Millie. I'm telling you the simple truth. I'm not coming to Bradford.

(*There is a pause.*)

MILLIE (*turning to face* FRANK; *with an attempt at bravado*): All right, my dear, if that's the way you feel about it. Don't come to Bradford.

FRANK: Right. Now I think you ought to go to your room and look after Andrew. (*He crosses toward the door up left.*) I'm leaving.

MILLIE (*following* FRANK): What is this? Frank, I don't understand, really I don't. What have I done?

FRANK: I think you know what you've done, Millie. Go and look after Andrew.

MILLIE (*moving to the left end of the settee*): Andrew? Why this sudden concern for Andrew?

FRANK: Because I think he's just been about as badly hurt as a human being can be; and as he's a sick man and in a rather hysterical state it might be a good plan to go and see how he is.

MILLIE (*scornfully*): Hurt? Andrew hurt? You can't hurt Andrew. He's dead.

FRANK (*moving to right of* MILLIE): Why do you hate him so much, Millie?

MILLIE: Because he keeps me from you.

FRANK: That isn't true.

MILLIE: Because he's not a man at all.

FRANK: He's a human being.

MILLIE: You've got a fine right to be so noble about him, after deceiving him for six months.

FRANK: Twice in six months—at your urgent invitation. (MILLIE *slaps his face, in a violent paroxysm of rage.*) Thank you for that. I deserved it. (*He crosses to the chair right of the desk.*) I deserve a lot worse than that, too.

MILLIE (*running to him*): Frank, forgive me—I didn't mean it.

FRANK (*quietly*): You'd better have the truth, Millie, it had to come some time. (*He turns to face* MILLIE.) I've never loved you. I've never told you I loved you.

MILLIE: I know, Frank, I know. (*She backs away slightly.*) I've always accepted that.

FRANK: You asked me just now if I was running away from you. Well, I was.

MILLIE: I knew that, too.

FRANK: But I was coming to Bradford. It was going to be the very last time I was ever going to see you and at Bradford I would have told you that.

MILLIE: You wouldn't. You wouldn't. You've tried to tell me that so often before—(*she crosses to the fireplace*) and I've always stopped you somehow—somehow. I would have stopped you again.

FRANK (*quietly*): I don't think so, Millie. Not this time.

MILLIE (*crossing to right of the table center*): Frank, I don't care what humiliations you heap on me. I know you don't give two hoots for me as a person. I've always known that. I've never minded so long as you cared for me as a woman. And you do, Frank. You do. You do, don't you? (FRANK *is silent. He crosses slowly to the fireplace.*) It'll be all right at Bradford, you see. It'll be all right there.

FRANK: I'm not coming to Bradford, Millie.

(*The door up center opens slowly and* ANDREW *enters. He is carrying the bottle of medicine. He hands it to* MILLIE *and passes on crossing down left below the desk.* MILLIE *holds the bottle up to the light.*)

ANDREW (*gently*): You should know me well enough by now, my dear, to realize how unlikely it is that I should ever take an overdose.

(MILLIE, *without a word, puts the bottle on the side-board and goes out up center.* ANDREW *goes to the cup-board down left and takes out the sherry and one glass.*)

FRANK: I'm not staying to dinner, I'm afraid.

ANDREW: Indeed? I'm sorry to hear that. You'll have a glass of sherry?

FRANK: No, thank you.

ANDREW: You will forgive me if I do.

FRANK: Of course. Perhaps I'll change my mind. (*He crosses to center.* ANDREW *takes out a second glass and fills both of them.*) About Taplow . . .

ANDREW: Oh yes?

FRANK: It *is* perfectly true that he was imitating you. I, of course, was mostly to blame in that, and I'm very sorry.

ANDREW: That is perfectly all right. Was it a good imitation?

FRANK: No.

ANDREW: I expect it was. Boys are often very clever mimics.

FRANK: We talked about you, of course, before that. (*He moves in to right of the desk.*) He said—you probably won't believe this, but I thought I ought to tell you—he said he liked you very much.

(ANDREW *smiles slightly.*)

ANDREW: Indeed?

(*He drinks.*)

FRANK: I can remember very clearly his exact words. He said: "He doesn't seem to like people to like him—but in spite of that, I do—very much." (*Lightly.*) So you see it looks after all as if the book might not have been a mere question of—appeasement.

ANDREW: The book? (*He picks it up.*) Dear me! What a lot of fuss about a little book—and a not very good little book at that.

(*He drops it on the desk.*)

FRANK: I would like you to believe me.

ANDREW: Possibly you would, my dear Hunter; but I

can assure you I am not particularly concerned about Taplow's views of my character: or about yours either, if it comes to that.

FRANK (*hopelessly*): I think you should keep that book all the same. You may find it'll mean something to you after all.

ANDREW (*turning to the cupboard and pouring himself another sherry*): Exactly. It will mean a perpetual reminder to myself of the story with which Taplow is at this very moment regaling his friends in the House. "I gave the Crock a book, to buy him off, and he blubbed. The Crock blubbed. I tell you I was there. I saw it. The Crock blubbed." My mimicry is not as good as his, I fear. Forgive me. (*He moves up left of the desk.*) And now let us leave this idiotic subject and talk of more pleasant things. Do you like this sherry? I got it on my last visit to London.

FRANK: If Taplow ever breathes a word of that story to anyone at all, I'll murder him. But he won't. And if you think I will you greatly underestimate my character as well as his. (*He drains his glass and puts it on the desk. He moves to the door up left.* ANDREW *comes down left, puts his glass on the cupboard, and stands facing down stage.*) Good-bye.

ANDREW: Are you leaving so soon? Good-bye, my dear fellow.

(FRANK *stops. He takes out his cigarette case and places it on the left end of the table center.*)

FRANK: As this is the last time I shall probably ever see you, I'm going to offer you a word of advice.

ANDREW (*politely*): I shall be glad to listen to it.

FRANK: Leave your wife.

(*There is a pause.* ANDREW *looks out of the window.*)

ANDREW: So that you may the more easily carry on your intrigue with her?

FRANK (*moving in to the upstage end of the desk*): How long have you known that?

ANDREW: Since it first began.

FRANK: How did you find out?

ANDREW: By information.

FRANK: By whose information?

ANDREW: By someone's whose word I could hardly discredit.

(*There is a pause.*)

FRANK (*slowly, with repulsion*): No! That's too horrible to think of.

ANDREW (*turning to* FRANK): Nothing is ever too horrible to think of, Hunter. It is simply a question of facing facts.

FRANK: She might have told you a lie. Have you faced that fact?

ANDREW: She never tells me a lie. In twenty years she has never told me a lie. Only the truth.

FRANK: That was a lie.

ANDREW (*moving up left of* FRANK): No, my dear Hunter. Do you wish me to quote you dates?

FRANK (*still unable to believe it*): And she told you six months ago?

ANDREW (*moving down left*): Isn't it seven?

FRANK (*savagely*): Then why have you allowed me inside your home? Why haven't you done something—reported me to the governors—anything—made a scene, knocked me down?

ANDREW: Knocked you down?

FRANK: You didn't have to invite me to dinner.

ANDREW: My dear Hunter, if, over the last twenty years, I had allowed such petty considerations to influence my choice of dinner guests I would have found it increasingly hard to remember which master to invite and which to refuse. You see, Hunter, you mustn't flatter yourself you are the first. My information is a good deal better than yours, you understand. It's authentic.

(*There is a pause.*)

FRANK: She's evil.

ANDREW: That's hardly a kindly epithet to apply to a lady whom, I gather, you have asked to marry.

FRANK: Did she tell you that?

ANDREW: She's a dutiful wife. She tells me everything.

FRANK: That, at least, was a lie.

ANDREW: She never lies.

FRANK (*leaning on the desk*): That was a lie. Do you want the truth? Can you bear the truth?

ANDREW: I can bear anything.

(*He crosses to the fireplace.*)

FRANK (*turning to face* ANDREW): What I did I did coldbloodedly out of weakness and ignorance and crass stupidity. I'm bitterly, bitterly ashamed of myself, but, in a sense, I'm glad you know (*he moves center*) though I'd rather a thousand times that you'd heard it from me than from your wife. I won't ask you to forgive me. I can only tell you, with complete truth, that the only emotion she has ever succeeded in arousing in me she aroused in me for the first time ten minutes ago—an intense and passionate disgust.

ANDREW: What a delightfully chivalrous statement.

FRANK (*moving below the settee*): Forget chivalry, Crock, for God's sake. Forget all your fine mosaic scruples. You must leave her—it's your only chance.

ANDREW: She's my wife, Hunter. You seem to forget that. As long as she wishes to remain my wife, she may.

FRANK: She's out to kill you.

ANDREW: My dear Hunter, if that was indeed her purpose, you should know by now that she fulfilled it long ago.

FRANK: Why won't you leave her?

ANDREW: Because I wouldn't wish to add another grave wrong to one I have already done her.

FRANK: What wrong have you done her?

ANDREW: To marry her. (*There is a pause.* FRANK *stares at him in silence.*) You see, my dear Hunter, she is really quite as much to be pitied as I. We are both of us interesting subjects for your microscope. (*He sits on the fender.*) Both of us needing from the other something that would make life supportable for us, and neither of us able to give it. Two kinds of love. Hers and mine. Worlds apart as I know now, though when I married her I didn't think they were incompatible. In those days I hadn't thought that her kind of love—the love she requires and which I was unable to give her—was so important that its absence would drive out the other kind of love—the kind of love that I require and which I thought, in my folly, was by far the greater part of love. (*He rises.*) I may have been, you see, Hunter, a brilliant classical scholar, but I was woefully ignorant of the facts of life. I know better now, of course. I know that in both of us, the love that we should have borne each other has turned to bitter hatred. That's all the problem is. Not a very unusual one, I venture to think—nor nearly as tragic as you seem to imagine. Merely the problem of an unsatisfied wife and a henpecked husband. You'll find it all over the world. It is usually, I believe, a subject for farce. (*He turns to the mantelpiece and adjusts the hands of the clock.*) And now, if you have to leave us, my dear fellow, please don't let me detain you any longer.

(FRANK *makes no move to go.*)

FRANK: Don't go to Bradford. Stay here, until you take up your new job.

ANDREW: I think I've already told you I'm not interested in your advice.

FRANK: Leave her. It's the only way.

ANDREW (*violently*): Will you please go!

FRANK: All right. I'd just like you to say good-bye to me properly, though. Will you? I shan't see you again. I know you don't want my pity, but I would like to be of some help.

(ANDREW *turns and faces* FRANK.)

ANDREW: If you think, by this expression of kindness, Hunter, that you can get me to repeat the shameful exhibition of emotion I made to Taplow a moment ago, I must tell you that you have no chance. My hysteria over that book just now was no more than a sort of reflex action of the spirit. The muscular twitchings of a corpse. It can never happen again.

FRANK: A corpse can be revived.

ANDREW: I don't believe in miracles.

FRANK: Don't you? Funnily enough, as a scientist, I do.

ANDREW (*turning to the fireplace*): Your faith would be touching, if I were capable of being touched by it.

FRANK: You are, I think. (*He moves behind* ANDREW. *After a pause.*) I'd like to come and visit you at this crammer's.

ANDREW: That is an absurd suggestion.

FRANK: I suppose it is rather, but all the same I'd like to do it. May I?

ANDREW: Of course not.

FRANK (*sitting on the settee*): Your term begins on the first day of September, doesn't it?

(*He takes out a pocket diary.*)

ANDREW: I tell you the idea is quite childish.

FRANK: I could come about the second week.

ANDREW: You would be bored to death. So, probably, would I.

FRANK (*glancing at his diary*): Let's say Monday the twelfth then.

ANDREW (*turning to face* FRANK, *his hands beginning to tremble*): Say anything you like, only please go, Hunter.

FRANK (*writing in his book and not looking at* ANDREW): That's fixed, then. Monday, September the twelfth. Will you remember that?

ANDREW (*after a pause; with difficulty*): I suppose I'm at least as likely to remember it as you are.

FRANK: That's fixed, then. (*He rises, slips the book into his pocket, and puts out his hand.*) Good-bye, until then.

(*He moves in to* ANDREW. ANDREW *hesitates, then shakes his hand.*)

ANDREW: Good-bye.

FRANK: May I go out through your garden?

(*He crosses to center.*)

ANDREW (*nodding*): Of course.

FRANK: I'm off to have a quick word with Taplow. By the way, may I take him a message from you?

ANDREW: What message?

FRANK: Has he or has he not got his remove?

ANDREW: He has.

FRANK: May I tell him?

ANDREW: It is highly irregular. Yes, you may.

FRANK: Good. (*He turns to go, then turns back.*) Oh, by the way, I'd better have the address of that crammer's.

(*He moves below the settee, takes out his diary, and points his pencil, ready to write.* MILLIE *enters up center. She carries a casserole on three plates.*)

MILLIE (*coming above the table center*): Dinner's ready. You're staying, Frank, aren't you?

(*She puts the casserole and plates on the table.*)

FRANK (*politely*): No. I'm afraid not. (*To* ANDREW) What's that address?

ANDREW (*after great hesitation*): The Old Deanery, Malcombe, Dorset.

FRANK: I'll write to you and you can let me know about trains. Good-bye. (*To* MILLIE) Good-bye.

(*He crosses to the door up left and goes out.* MILLIE *is silent for a moment. Then she laughs.*)

MILLIE: That's a laugh, I must say.

ANDREW: What's a laugh, my dear?

MILLIE: You inviting him to stay with you.

ANDREW: I didn't. He suggested it.

MILLIE (*moving to the left end of the settee*): He's coming to Bradford.

ANDREW: Yes. I remember your telling me so.

MILLIE: He's coming to Bradford. He's not going to you.

ANDREW: The likeliest contingency is, that he's not going to either of us.

MILLIE: He's coming to Bradford.

ANDREW: I expect so. Oh, by the way, I'm not. I shall be staying here until I go to Dorset.

MILLIE (*indifferently*): Suit yourself. What makes you think I'll join you there?

ANDREW: I don't.

MILLIE: You needn't expect me.

ANDREW: I don't think either of us has the right to expect anything further from the other. (*The telephone rings.*) Excuse me. (*He moves to the table down right and lifts the receiver.*) Hullo . . . (*While he is speaking* MILLIE *crosses to left of the table center. About to sit, she sees the cigarette case. She picks it up, fingers it for a moment, and finally drops it into her pocket.*) Yes, Headmaster . . . The timetable? . . . It's perfectly simple. The middle fourth B division will take a ten-minute break on Tuesdays and a fifteen-minute break on alternate Wednesdays; while exactly the reverse procedure will apply to the lower Shell, C division. I thought I had sufficiently explained that on my chart . . . Oh, I see . . . Thank you, that is very good of you . . . Yes. I think you will find it will work out quite satisfactorily . . . Oh by the way, Headmaster. I have changed my mind about the prize-giving ceremony. I intend to speak after, instead of before, Fletcher, as is my privilege . . . Yes, I quite understand, but I am now seeing the matter in a different light . . . I know, but I am of opinion that occasionally an anti-climax can be surprisingly effective. Good-bye. (*He replaces the receiver, crosses to right of the table center, and sits.*) Come along, my dear. We mustn't let our dinner get cold.

(*He unrolls his table napkin.* MILLIE *sits left of the table and unrolls her table napkin.* ANDREW *offers her the bread. She ignores it. He takes a piece. She removes the lid of the casserole as—*

CURTAIN

TENNESSEE WILLIAMS:

Lord Byron's Love Letter

Tennessee Williams (christened Thomas Lanier Williams) was born in Columbus, Mississippi, in 1911. His first produced play, *You Touched Me* (1942), based on a short story by D. H. Lawrence, was written in collaboration with Donald Windham. But he achieved his first real success with *The Glass Menagerie* in 1945. In addition to the several plays which constitute the main body of his work, Mr. Williams has published two volumes of short stories and books of poems.

Lord Byron's Love Letter, an early play of Mr. Williams, in theme and in execution anticipates the plays of his great creative period (1945–60). What we are principally faced with in this short play are two irreconcilable worlds: the tawdry world of noise and excitement, and a world whose denizens pursue dreams and fancies, who are incapable or unwilling to come to terms with reality, with the necessary concerns of ordinary day-to-day living. This confrontation between two worlds, which Mr. Williams used again and again—in *The Glass Menagerie,* in *A Streetcar Named Desire,* in *Summer and Smoke,* and more recently in *The Milk Train Doesn't Stop Here Anymore*—provokes an interestingly ambivalent attitude in the audience and in the reader: we empathize with the spinster and the grandmother; we accept their shabby gentility and their transparent pretensions. And yet we cannot help asking ourselves if somehow the two pathetic women—one sadly middle-aged, the other desperately old—are not practicing a gross deception upon the random visitors whose contributions the two women solicit.

A love letter from Lord Byron would be a symbol of something very precious, for it would be an object embodying everything we associate with the word "romance." When the play begins, we—like the Milwaukee matron—hope for a glimpse of that magic scrap of paper. We hope that somehow a touch of its magic will rub off on us, that we may become a link in the chain between the prosaic present and the romantic past.

And so the Milwaukee lady and we in the audience are caught up in the spell which the two women in the play cast upon us. We believe that we are actually in the presence of someone who was held in the arms of England's most romantic poet-hero. Then the spell is broken and we ask ourselves, Was it all a fraud? In the cold light of reality, perhaps it was. But our confrontation with beautiful words and with the passionate feeling of the old woman, speaking the lines of her own poem, was not a fraud. In the end it is the two women who are cheated of what is their due—not the couple from Milwaukee, not we, the audience-reader. The artist always gives more than he receives.

Lord Byron's Love Letter

Characters

THE SPINSTER.
THE OLD WOMAN.
THE MATRON.
THE HUSBAND.

(SCENE: *The parlor of a faded old residence in the French Quarter of New Orleans in the late nineteenth century.*

The shuttered doors of the room open directly upon the sidewalk and the noise of the Mardi Gras festivities can be faintly distinguished. The interior is very dusky. Beside a rose-shaded lamp, the SPINSTER, *a woman of forty, is sewing. In the opposite corner, completely motionless, the* OLD WOMAN *sits in a black silk dress. The doorbell tinkles.*)

SPINSTER (*rising*): It's probably someone coming to look at the letter.

OLD WOMAN (*rising on her cane*): Give me time to get out.

From Tennessee Williams, *27 Wagons Full of Cotton.* Copyright 1945 by Tennessee Williams. All rights reserved. Reprinted by permission of New Directions Publishing Corporation and of Ashley Famous Agency, Inc.

(She withdraws gradually behind the curtains. One of her claw-like hands remains visible, holding a curtain slightly open so that she can watch the visitors. The SPINSTER *opens the door and the* MATRON, *a middle-aged woman, walks into the room.)*

SPINSTER: Won't you come in?

MATRON: Thank you.

SPINSTER: You're from out of town?

MATRON: Oh, yes, we're all the way from Milwaukee. We've come for Mardi Gras, my husband and I. *(She suddenly notices a stuffed canary in its tiny pink and ivory cage.)* Oh, this poor little bird in such a tiny cage! It's much too small to keep a canary in!

SPINSTER: It isn't a live canary.

OLD WOMAN *(from behind the curtain)*: No. It's stuffed.

MATRON: Oh. *(She self-consciously touches a stuffed bird on her hat.)* Winston is out there dilly-dallying on the street, afraid he'll miss the parade. The parade comes by here, don't it?

SPINSTER: Yes, unfortunately it does.

MATRON: I noticed your sign at the door. Is it true that you have one of Lord Byron's love letters?

SPINSTER: Yes.

MATRON: How very interesting! How did you get it?

SPINSTER: It was written to my grandmother, Irénée Marguerite de Poitevent.

MATRON: How very interesting! Where did she meet Lord Byron?

SPINSTER: On the steps of the Acropolis in Athens.

MATRON: How very, *very* interesting! I didn't know that Lord Byron was ever in Greece.

SPINSTER: Lord Byron spent the final years of his turbulent life in Greece.

OLD WOMAN *(still behind the curtains)*: He was exiled from England!

SPINSTER: Yes, he went into voluntary exile from England.

OLD WOMAN: Because of scandalous gossip in the Regent's court.

SPINSTER: Yes, involving his half-sister!

OLD WOMAN: It was false—completely.

SPINSTER: It was never confirmed.

OLD WOMAN: He was a passionate man but not an evil man.

SPINSTER: Morals are such ambiguous matters, I think.

MATRON: Won't the lady behind the curtains come in?

SPINSTER: You'll have to excuse her. She prefers to stay out.

MATRON (*stiffly*): Oh, I see. What was Lord Byron doing in Greece, may I ask?

OLD WOMAN (*proudly*): *Fighting for Freedom!*

SPINSTER: Yes, Lord Byron went to Greece to join the force that fought against the infidels.

OLD WOMAN: He gave his life in defense of the universal cause of freedom!

MATRON: What was that, did she say?

SPINSTER (*repeating automatically*): He gave his life in defense of the universal cause of freedom.

MATRON: Oh, how very interesting!

OLD WOMAN: Also he swam the Hellespont.

SPINSTER: Yes.

OLD WOMAN: And burned the body of the poet Shelley who was drowned in a storm on the Mediterranean with a volume of Keats in his pocket!

MATRON (*incredulously*): Pardon?

SPINSTER (*repeating*): And burned the body of the poet Shelley who was drowned in a storm on the Mediterranean with a volume of Keats in his pocket.

MATRON: Oh. How very, very interesting! Indeed, I'd like so much to have my husband hear it. Do you mind if I just step out for a moment to call him in?

SPINSTER: Please do.

(*The* MATRON *steps out quickly, calling, "Winston! Winston!"*)

OLD WOMAN (*poking her head out for a moment*): Watch them carefully! Keep a sharp eye on them!

SPINSTER: Yes. Be still.

(*The* MATRON *returns with her* HUSBAND *who has been drinking and wears a paper cap sprinkled with confetti.*)

MATRON: Winston, remove that cap. Sit down on the sofa. These ladies are going to show us Lord Byron's love letter.

SPINSTER: Shall I proceed?

MATRON: Oh, yes. This—uh—is my husband—Mr. Tutwiler.

SPINSTER (*coldly*): How do you do.

MATRON: I am *Mrs.* Tutwiler.

SPINSTER: Of course. Please keep your seat.

MATRON (*nervously*): He's been—celebrating a little.

OLD WOMAN (*shaking the curtain that conceals her*): Ask him please to be careful with his cigar.

SPINSTER: Oh, that's all right, you may use this bowl for your ashes.

OLD WOMAN: Smoking is such an unnecessary habit!

HUSBAND: Uh!

MATRON: This lady was telling us how her grandmother happened to meet Lord Byron. In Italy, wasn't it?

SPINSTER: No.

OLD WOMAN (*firmly*): In Greece, in Athens, on the steps of the Acropolis! We've mentioned that *twice,* I believe. Ariadne, you may read them a passage from the journal first.

SPINSTER: Yes.

OLD WOMAN: But please be careful what you choose to read!

(*The* SPINSTER *has removed from the secretary a volume wrapped in tissue and tied with ribbon.*)

SPINSTER: Like many other young American girls of that day and this, my grandmother went to Europe.

OLD WOMAN: The year before she was going to be presented to society!

MATRON: How old was she?

OLD WOMAN: Sixteen! Barely sixteen! She was very beautiful too! Please show her the picture, show these people the picture! It's in the front of the journal.

(*The* SPINSTER *removes the picture from the book and hands it to the* MATRON.)

MATRON (*taking a look*): What a lovely young girl. (*Passing it to her* HUSBAND.) Don't you think it resembles Agnes a little?

HUSBAND: Uh!

OLD WOMAN: Watch out! Ariadne, you'll have to *watch* the man. I believe he's been drinking. I *do* believe that he's been——

HUSBAND (*truculently*): Yeah? What is she saying back there?

MATRON (*touching his arm warningly*): Winston! Be *quiet*.

HUSBAND: Uh.

SPINSTER (*quickly*): Near the end of her tour, my grandmother and her aunt went to Greece, to study the classic remains of the oldest civilization.

OLD WOMAN (*correcting*): The oldest *European* civilization.

SPINSTER: It was an early morning in April of the year eighteen hundred and——

OLD WOMAN: Twenty-seven!

SPINSTER: Yes. In my grandmother's journal she mentions——

OLD WOMAN: Read it, read it, *read* it.

MATRON: Yes, *please* read it to us.

SPINSTER: I'm trying to find the place, if you'll just be patient.

MATRON: Certainly, excuse me. (*She punches her* HUSBAND *who is nodding.*) Winston!

SPINSTER: Ah, here it is.

OLD WOMAN: Be *careful!* Remember where to *stop* at, Ariadne!

SPINSTER: Shhh! (*She adjusts her glasses and seats herself by the lamp.*) "We set out early that morning to inspect the ruins of the Acropolis. I know I shall never forget how extraordinarily pure the atmosphere was that morning. It seemed as though the world were not very old, but very, very young, almost as though the world had been newly created. There was a taste of earliness in the air, a feeling of freshness, exhilarating my senses, exalting my spirit. How shall I tell you, dear Diary, the way the sky looked? It was almost as though I had moistened the tip of my pen in a shallow bowl full of milk, so delicate was the blue in the dome of the heavens. The sun was barely up yet, a tentative breeze disturbed the ends of my scarf, the plumes of the marvelous hat which I had bought in Paris and thrilled me with pride whenever I saw them reflected! The papers that morning, we read them over our coffee before we left the hotel, had spoken of possible war, but it seemed unlikely, unreal: nothing was real, indeed, but the spell of golden antiquity and rose-colored romance that breathed from this fabulous city."

OLD WOMAN: Skip that part! Get on to where she meets him!

SPINSTER: Yes . . . (*She turns several pages and continues.*) "Out of the tongues of ancients, the lyrical voices of many long-ago poets who dreamed of the world of ideals, who had in their hearts the pure and absolute image——"

OLD WOMAN: *Skip* that part! Slip down to where——

SPINSTER: Yes! *Here! Do* let us manage without any more *interruptions!* "The carriage came to a halt at the foot of the hill and my aunt, not being too well——"

OLD WOMAN: She had a sore throat that morning.

SPINSTER: "——preferred to remain with the driver while I undertook the rather steep climb on foot. As I ascended the long and crumbling flight of old stone steps——"

OLD WOMAN: Yes, yes, that's the place! (*The* SPINSTER *looks up in annoyance. The* OLD WOMAN'S *cane taps impatiently behind the curtains.*) Go *on,* Ariadne!

SPINSTER: "I could not help observing continually above me a man who walked with a barely perceptible limp——"

OLD WOMAN (*in hushed wonder*): Yes—Lord Byron!

SPINSTER: "——and as he turned now and then to observe beneath him the lovely panorama——"

OLD WOMAN: Actually he was watching the girl behind him.

SPINSTER (*sharply*): Will you *please* let me finish! (*There is no answer from behind the curtains, and she continues to read.*) "I was irresistibly impressed by the unusual nobility and refinement of his features!"

(*She turns a page.*)

OLD WOMAN: The handsomest man that ever walked the earth!

(*She emphasizes the speech with three slow but loud taps of her cane.*)

SPINSTER (*flurriedly*): "The strength and grace of his throat, like that of a statue, the classic outlines of his profile, the sensitive lips and the slightly dilated nostrils, the dark lock of hair that fell down over his forehead in such a way that——"

OLD WOMAN (*tapping her cane rapidly*): Skip that, it goes on for pages!

SPINSTER: ". . . When he had reached the very summit of the Acropolis he spread out his arms in a great, magnificent gesture like a young god. Now, thought I to myself, Apollo has come to earth in modern dress."

OLD WOMAN: Go on, skip that, get on to where she *meets* him!

SPINSTER: "Fearing to interrupt his poetic trance, I slackened my pace and pretended to watch the view. I kept my look thus carefully averted until the narrowness of the steps compelled me to move close by him."

OLD WOMAN: Of course he pretended not to see she was coming!

SPINSTER: "Then finally I faced him."

OLD WOMAN: Yes!

SPINSTER: "Our eyes came together!"

OLD WOMAN: Yes! Yes! That's the part!

SPINSTER: "A thing which I don't understand had occurred between us, a flush as of recognition swept through my whole being! Suffused my——"

OLD WOMAN: Yes . . . Yes, that's the part!

SPINSTER: " 'Pardon me,' he exclaimed, 'you have dropped your glove!' And indeed to my surprise I found that I had, and as he returned it to me, his fingers ever so lightly pressed the cups of my palm."

OLD WOMAN (*hoarsely*): *Yes!*

(*Her bony fingers clutch higher up on the curtain, the*

other hand also appears, slightly widening the aperture.)

SPINSTER: "Believe me, dear Diary, I became quite faint and breathless, I almost wondered if I could continue my lonely walk through the ruins. Perhaps I stumbled, perhaps I swayed a little. I leaned for a moment against the side of a column. The sun seemed terribly brilliant, it hurt my eyes. Close behind me I heard that voice again, almost it seemed I could feel his breath on my——"

OLD WOMAN: Stop *there!* That will be quite enough!

(*The* SPINSTER *closes the journal.*)

MATRON: Oh, is that all?

OLD WOMAN: There's a great deal more that's not to be read to people.

MATRON: Oh.

SPINSTER: I'm sorry. I'll show you the letter.

MATRON: How nice! I'm dying to see it! Winston? *Do* sit *up!*

(*He has nearly fallen asleep. The* SPINSTER *produces from the cabinet another small packet which she unfolds. It contains the letter. She hands it to the* MATRON, *who starts to open it.*)

OLD WOMAN: Watch out, watch *out*, that woman can't *open* the letter!

SPINSTER: No, no, please, you mustn't. The contents of the letter are strictly private. I'll hold it over here at a little distance so you can see the writing.

OLD WOMAN: Not too close, she's holding up her glasses!

(*The* MATRON *quickly lowers her lorgnette.*)

SPINSTER: Only a short while later Byron was killed.

MATRON: How did he die?

OLD WOMAN: He was killed in action, defending the cause of freedom!

(*This is uttered so strongly the* HUSBAND *starts.*)

SPINSTER: When my grandmother received the news of Lord Byron's death in battle, she retired from the world and remained in complete seclusion for the rest of her life.

MATRON: Tch-tch-tch! How dreadful! I think that was foolish of her.

(*The cane taps furiously behind the curtains.*)

SPINSTER: You don't understand. When a life is completed, it ought to be put away. It's like a sonnet. When you've written the final couplet, why go on any further? You only destroy the part that's already written!

OLD WOMAN: Read them the poem, the sonnet your grandmother wrote to the memory of Lord Byron.

SPINSTER: Would you be interested?

MATRON: We'd adore it—truly!

SPINSTER: It's called "Enchantment."

MATRON (*she assumes a rapt expression*): *Aahhh!*

SPINSTER (*reciting*):

Un saison enchanté! I mused, Beguiled
Seemed Time herself, her erstwhile errant ways
Briefly forgotten, she stayed here and smiled,
Caught in a net of blue and golden days.

OLD WOMAN: Not blue and golden—gold and *azure* days!

SPINSTER:

Caught in a net—of gold and azure days!

But I lacked wit to see how lightly shoon
Were Time and you, to vagrancy so used——

(*The* OLD WOMAN *begins to accompany in a hoarse undertone. Faint band music can be heard.*)

That by the touch of one October moon
From summer's tranquil spell you might be loosed!

OLD WOMAN (*rising stridently with intense feeling above the* SPINSTER'S *voice*):

Think you love is writ on my soul with chalk,
To be washed off by a few parting tears?

Then you know not with what slow step I walk
The barren way of those hibernal years—

My life a vanished interlude, a shell
Whose walls are your first kiss—and last farewell!

(*The band, leading the parade, has started down the
street, growing rapidly louder. It passes by like the heed-
less, turbulent years. The* HUSBAND, *roused from his
stupor, lunges to the door.*)

MATRON: What's that, what's that? The *parade?*

(*The* HUSBAND *slaps the paper cap on his head and
rushes for the door.*)

HUSBAND (*at the door*): Come on, Mama, you'll miss it!
SPINSTER (*quickly*): We usually accept—you understand?—a small sum of money, just anything that you
happen to think you can spare.
OLD WOMAN: Stop him! He's gone outside!

(*The* HUSBAND *has escaped to the street. The band
blares through the door.*)

SPINSTER (*extending her hand*): Please—a dollar . . .
OLD WOMAN: *Fifty cents!*
SPINSTER: Or a *quarter!*
MATRON (*paying no attention to them*): Oh, my good-
ness—*Winston!* He's *disappeared* in the crowd! Winston—
Winston! Excuse me! (*She rushes out onto the door sill.*)
Winston! Oh, my goodness gracious, he's off again!
SPINSTER (*quickly*): We usually accept a little money
for the display of the letter. Whatever you feel that you
are able to give. As a matter of fact it's all that we have
to *live* on!
OLD WOMAN (*loudly*): One dollar!
SPINSTER: Fifty cents—or a quarter!
MATRON (*oblivious, at the door*): Winston! *Winston!*
Heavenly days. *Good-bye!*

(*She rushes out on the street. The* SPINSTER *follows to
the door and shields her eyes from the light as she looks
after the* MATRON. *A stream of confetti is tossed through*

the doorway into her face. Trumpets blare. She slams the door shut and bolts it.)

SPINSTER: *Canaille! . . . Canaille!*
OLD WOMAN: Gone? Without paying? *Cheated* us?

(*She parts the curtains.*)

SPINSTER: *Yes—the canaille!*

(*She fastidiously plucks the thread of confetti from her shoulder. The* OLD WOMAN *steps from behind the curtain, rigid with anger.*)

OLD WOMAN: Ariadne, my letter! You've dropped my letter! Your grandfather's letter is lying on the floor!

Three Comedies

ANTON CHEKHOV:

A Marriage Proposal

Anton Chekhov (1860–1904) is, of all the playwrights represented in this collection, the greatest literary artist. Not only did he—in a very real sense—redirect the whole mainstream of modern drama, but he also had as great an effect upon the modern short story. A significant number of the best stories and plays of the twentieth century have been more profoundly influenced by Chekhov than by any other single writer. His major dramatic works are *The Sea Gull, Uncle Vanya, The Three Sisters,* and *The Cherry Orchard,* all written after 1890. Earlier he had written a number of short plays which enjoyed enormous success in Russia's little theaters and throughout the world. Of these short plays, the best known in the United States are *On the Harmfulness of Tobacco, Swan Song, The Boor,* and *A Marriage Proposal.* Chekhov was trained as a physician; and though he devoted more of his short life to writing than he did to the practice of medicine, the dispassionate, clear-eyed gaze of the diagnostician is reflected in all of his writing.

Chekhov describes human behavior objectively, without comment, leaving no doubt in our minds about what it is that motivates and disturbs the people of his plays and stories. On the surface, *A Marriage Proposal* is mere farce, a broadly comic play, exaggerating the behavior of its characters and overdrawing their foibles. The play provokes our uninhibited laughter; we know that in such a situation, in real life, the participants would exercise more self-restraint. But given these three people, if they allowed themselves to react wholly in accordance with their true nature, they would be acting and speaking precisely as Chekhov depicted them.

Most adults, Chekhov seems to be saying, retain to some degree an element of their childishness. And when the child in us is given expression—as it is in this play—the contrast between the solemnity of the occasion and the childish behavior of the principals is both comic and appalling. Our laughter is our defense against what basically dismays us.

The two lovers, for example, are past the age when men and women generally choose to marry. Why have they waited so long? Is their decision to wed based on the conventionally stated reasons for getting married? We can anticipate what their married life together will be like. Can they? Such considerations characterize that Chekhovian mixture of laughter and pathos in *A Marriage Proposal* and, to be sure, in all of his plays.

A Marriage Proposal

TRANSLATED BY
JOACHIM NEUGROSCHEL

Characters

STEPÁN STEPÁNOVICH CHOOBOOKÓV, *a landowner.*
NATÁLIA STEPÁNOVNA, *his twenty-five-year-old daughter.*
IVÁN VASSÍLIEVICH LÓMOV, CHOOBOOKÓV'S *neighbor, a
healthy and well-fed, but terribly hypochondriac
landowner.*

The action takes place in the drawing room of CHOO-
BOOKÓV'S *country house.*

Scene I

(CHOOBOOKÓV *and* LÓMOV. *The latter enters, wearing tails and white gloves.*)

CHOOBOOKÓV (*going over to welcome his guest*): Why, of all people! My old friend, Iván Vassílievich! How nice to see you! (*Shakes his hand.*) This really is a surprise, old boy. . . . How *are* you?

LÓMOV: Very well, thank you. And may I ask how *you* are?

CHOOBOOKÓV: Not bad at all, old friend, with the help of your prayers and so on. . . . Please have a seat. . . . Now, really, it's not very nice of you to neglect your neighbors, my dear boy. And what are you all dressed up for? Morning coat, gloves, and so on! Are you off on a visit, old boy?

LÓMOV: No, I'm just calling on you, my esteemed neighbor.

CHOOBOOKÓV: But why the morning coat, old friend? This isn't New Year's Day!

LÓMOV: Well, you see, the fact of the matter is . . . (*Takes his arm.*) I've burst in on you like this, Stepán Stepánovich, my esteemed neighbor, in order to ask a favor of you. I've already had the honor more than once of turning to you for help and you've always, so to speak, uh! . . . But forgive me, my nerves . . . I must have a sip of water, dear Stepán Stepánovich.

Translation copyright © 1969 by Joachim Neugroschel.

(*Drinks some water.*)

CHOOBOOKÓV (*aside*): He's after money. Fat chance! (*To* LÓMOV) What is it, my dear fellow?

LÓMOV: Well, you see, my Stepán dearovich, uh! I mean dear Stepánovich . . . uh! I mean, my nerves are in a terrible condition, which you yourself are so kind as to see. In short, you're the only one who can help me, although, of course, I've done nothing to deserve it and . . . and I don't even have the right to count on your help. . . .

CHOOBOOKÓV: Now, now; don't beat about the bush, old friend. Out with it! . . . Well?

LÓMOV: All right, here you are. The fact of the matter is, I've come to ask for your daughter Natália's hand in marriage.

CHOOBOOKÓV (*overjoyed*): My *dearest* friend! Iván Vassílievich. Could you repeat that—I'm not sure I heard right!

LÓMOV: I have the honor of asking——

CHOOBOOKÓV (*breaking in*): My oldest and dearest friend . . . I'm *so* delighted and so on . . . Yes really, and all that sort of thing. (*Hugging and kissing him.*) I've been yearning for this for ages. It's been my constant desire. (*Sheds a tear.*) And I've always loved you like a son, you wonderful person, you. May God grant you love and guidance and so on, it's been my most fervent wish. . . . But why am I standing here like a blockhead? I'm dumbstruck by the sheer joy of it, completely dumbstruck. Oh, with all my heart and soul . . . I'll go get Natasha, and so on.

LÓMOV (*deeply moved*): Stepán Stepánovich, my esteemed friend, do you think I may count on her accepting me?

CHOOBOOKÓV: A handsome devil like you? How could she possibly resist? She's *mad*ly in love with you, don't worry, *mad*ly, and so on . . . I'll call her right away.

(*Exit.*)

Scene II

LÓMOV (*alone*): It's so cold . . . I'm shaking all over, like before a final exam. The important thing is to make up your mind. If you think about it too long, or waver, talk about it too much, and wait for the ideal woman or for true love, you'll never marry. . . . Brr! It's cold! Natália Stepánovna is an excellent housekeeper, she's not bad-looking, and she's got some education. . . . What more could I ask for? Oh, I'm so nervous, I can hear a buzzing in my ears. (*Drinks some water.*) It would be best for me to get married . . . First of all, I'm thirty-five years old already—and that, as they say, is a critical age. And then, I have to start leading a steady and regular life. . . . I've got a heart condition, with palpitations all the time. . . . I've got an awful temper and I'm always getting terribly wrought up. . . . Even now, my lips are trembling and my right eyelid is twitching. . . . But the worst thing is when I try to sleep. The instant I get to bed and start dropping off, something *stabs* me in my left side—ungh! And it cuts right through my shoulder straight into my head—ungh! I jump like a lunatic, walk about a little, and then I lie down again, but the moment I start to doze off, I feel it in my side again—ungh! And it keeps on and on for at least twenty times. . . .

Scene III

(NATÁLIA STEPÁNOVNA *and* LÓMOV.)

NATÁLIA (*entering*): Ah, it's you. And Papa said a customer had come for the merchandise. How do you do, Iván Vassílievich!

LÓMOV: How do you do, my esteemed Natália Stepánovna!

NATÁLIA: I'm sorry about my apron and not being dressed. . . . We're shelling peas for drying. Where've you been keeping yourself? Have a seat. . . . (*They sit down.*) Would you like a bite of lunch?

LÓMOV: Thank you so much, but I've already eaten.

NATÁLIA: Well, then have a cigarette. . . . The matches are over here. . . . The weather's magnificent today, but yesterday it rained so hard that the men couldn't do a thing all day long. How much hay did *you* get done? Can you imagine, I was so greedy that I had the whole meadow mown, and now I regret it, I'm scared that all my hay may rot. I should have waited. But what's this? I do believe you're wearing a morning coat! How original! Are you going to a ball or something? Incidentally, you're getting quite handsome. . . . But honestly, why are you all dolled up?

LÓMOV (*nervously*): You see, my esteemed Natália Stepánovna . . . the fact is I've made up my mind to ask you to listen to me. . . . Naturally you'll be surprised and even angry, but I . . . (*Aside.*) God, it's cold!

NATÁLIA: What is it? (*Pause.*) Well?

LÓMOV: I'll try to be brief. You are well aware, my esteemed Natália Stepánovna, that for a long time now, in fact since my childhood, I have had the honor of knowing your family. My late aunt and her husband, whose estate as you know I inherited, always held your father and your late mother in utmost esteem. The Lómov family and the Choobookóv family have always maintained extremely friendly, one might even say, intimate relations. Furthermore, as you know, my property borders on yours. Perhaps you will be so kind as to recall that my Ox Meadows run along your birch forest.

NATÁLIA: Excuse me for interrupting you. You said "*my* Ox Meadows" . . . Are they *yours*?

LÓMOV: Of course. . . .

NATÁLIA: Oh, come now! The Ox Meadows belong to us, not you!

LÓMOV: Oh no! They're mine, dear Natália Stepánovna.

NATÁLIA: That's news to me. How did they ever get to be yours?

LÓMOV: What do you mean? I'm talking about the Ox

Meadows that are wedged in between your birch forest and the Burnt Marsh.

NATÁLIA: Exactly. . . . They're ours.

LÓMOV: No, you're mistaken, dear Natália Stepánovna —they're mine.

NATÁLIA: Do be reasonable, Iván Vassílievich! Since when have they been yours?

LÓMOV: Since when? They've always been ours, as far back as I can remember.

NATÁLIA: Excuse me, but this is too much!

LÓMOV: You can look at the documents, dear Natália Stepánovna. At one time, there *were* some quarrels about the Ox Meadows, you're quite right. But now, everyone knows they're mine. Why argue about it? If you will permit me to explain: my aunt's grandmother lent them to your paternal great-grandfather's peasants for an indefinite period and free of charge in return for their firing her bricks. Your great-grandfather's peasants used the Meadows free of charge for some forty years and began thinking of them as their own . . . and then after the Emancipation, when a statute was passed——

NATÁLIA: You've got it all wrong! Both my grandfather and great-grandfather regarded their property as reaching all the way to the Burnt Swamp—which means that the Ox Meadows were ours. What's there to argue about?—I don't understand. How annoying!

LÓMOV: I'll show you the documents, Natália Stepánovna.

NATÁLIA: No; you're joking or trying to tease me. . . . What a surprise! We've owned the land for practically three hundred years and now suddenly we're told it's not ours! I'm sorry, Iván Vassílievich, but I just can't believe my ears. Those Meadows don't mean a thing to me. The whole area probably doesn't come to more than forty acres, it's worth about three hundred rubles; but I'm terribly upset by the injustice of it all. You can say what you like, but I simply can't stand injustice.

LÓMOV: Please listen to me, I beseech you. Your paternal great-grandfather's peasants, as I have already had the honor of telling you, fired bricks for my aunt's grandmother. Now, my aunt's grandmother, wishing to do them a favor in return——

NATÁLIA: Grandfather, grandmother, aunt . . . I don't know *what* you're talking about! The Meadows are *ours,* and that's that.

LÓMOV: They're *mine!*

NATÁLIA: They're ours! You can keep arguing for two days, you can put on fifteen morning coats if you like, but they're ours, ours, ours! . . . I don't desire *your* property, but I don't care to lose mine. . . . Do as you like!

LÓMOV: I don't need the Meadows, Natália Stepánovna, but it's the principle of the thing. If you want, I'll *give* them to you.

NATÁLIA: It would be *my* privilege to give them to *you,* they're mine! . . . All this is rather odd—to put it mildly, Iván Vassílievich. Up till now we've always considered you a good neighbor and friend. Last year we let you borrow our threshing machine, and as a result we couldn't finish our own grain until November, and now you're treating us like Gypsies. You're *giving* me my own land. Excuse me, but that's not a neighborly thing to do! To *my* mind, it's impertinent, if you care to——

LÓMOV: Are you trying to tell me that I'm a land-grabber? Madam, I've never seized anyone else's property, and I won't allow anyone to *say* I have. . . . (*Hurries over to the carafe and drinks some water.*) The Ox Meadows are mine!

NATÁLIA: That's not true, they're ours.

LÓMOV: They're mine.

NATÁLIA: That's not true. I'll prove it to you! I'll send my men over to mow them this afternoon.

LÓMOV: What?!

NATÁLIA: My men will be there this afternoon!

LÓMOV: I'll kick them out!

NATÁLIA: You wouldn't dare!

LÓMOV (*clutching at his heart*): The Ox Meadows are mine! Do you hear! Mine!

NATÁLIA: Stop shouting! Please! You can shout your lungs out in your own place, but I must ask you to control yourself here.

LÓMOV: Madam, if it weren't for these awful, excruciating palpitations and the veins throbbing in my temples, I'd speak to you in a totally different way! (*Shouting.*) The Ox Meadows are mine.

NATÁLIA: Ours!

LÓMOV: Mine!

NATÁLIA: Ours!

LÓMOV: Mine!

SCENE IV

(*Enter* CHOOBOOKÓV.)

CHOOBOOKÓV: What's going on? What's all the shouting about?

NATÁLIA: Papa, please tell this gentleman whom the Ox Meadows belong to. Us or him.

CHOOBOOKÓV (*to* LÓMOV): Why, the Meadows belong to us, old friend.

LÓMOV: But for goodness' sake, Stepán Stepánovich, how can that be? Can't *you* be reasonable at least? My aunt's grandmother lent the Meadows to your grandfather's peasants for temporary use and free of charge. His peasants used the land for forty years and got in the habit of regarding it as their own, but after the Land Settlement——

CHOOBOOKÓV: Excuse me, old boy . . . You're forgetting that our peasants didn't pay your grandmother and so on precisely *because* the Meadows were disputed and what not. . . . But now every child knows that they're ours. I guess you've never looked at the maps.

LÓMOV: I'll *prove* they're mine!

CHOOBOOKÓV: You won't prove a thing, my boy.

LÓMOV: I will *so* prove it!

CHOOBOOKÓV: My dear boy, why carry on like this? You won't prove a thing by shouting. I don't want anything of yours, but I don't intend to let go of what's mine. Why should I? If it comes to that, dear friend, if you mean to dispute my ownership of the Meadows, and so on, I'd sooner let my peasants have them than you. So there!

LÓMOV: I don't understand. What right do you have to give away other people's property?

CHOOBOOKÓV: Allow me to decide whether or not I've got the right. Really, young man, I'm not accustomed to being spoken to in that tone of voice, and what not. I'm old enough to be your father, and I must ask you to calm down when you speak to me, and so forth.

LÓMOV: No! You're treating me like an idiot, and laughing at me. You tell me that *my* property is yours, and then you expect me to remain calm and talk to you in a normal fashion. That's not a very neighborly thing to do, Stepán Stepánovich. You're no neighbor, you're a robber baron.

CHOOBOOKÓV: What?! What did you say, my good man?

NATÁLIA: Papa, have the men mow the Ox Meadows right now!

CHOOBOOKÓV (to LÓMOV): What did you say, sir?

NATÁLIA: The Ox Meadows are our property, and I won't let anyone else have them. I won't, I won't, I won't!

LÓMOV: We'll see about that! I'll prove to you in court that they're mine.

CHOOBOOKÓV: In court? My good man, you can take it to court, and what not. Go right ahead! I know you, you've just been waiting for a chance to litigate, and so on. You're a quibbler from the word go. Your whole family's nothing but a bunch of pettifoggers. All of them!

LÓMOV: I must ask you not to insult my family. The Lómovs have always been law-abiding folk. None of them was ever hauled into court for embezzlement the way your uncle was.

CHOOBOOKÓV: Every last one of them was insane.

NATÁLIA: Every last one of them, every last one!

CHOOBOOKÓV: Your grandfather drank like a fish, and the whole county knows that your youngest aunt, Nastasia, ran off with an architect, and what not——

LÓMOV: And your mother was a hunchback! (*Clutch-*

ing at his heart.) There's a twitching in my side. . . .
My head's throbbing. . . . Oh, God . . . Water!

CHOOBOOKÓV: And your father was a gambler and he
ate like a pig!

NATÁLIA: And no one could beat your aunt at scandal-
mongering.

LÓMOV: My left leg's paralyzed . . . . And you're a
schemer. . . . Oooh! My heart! . . . And it's no secret to
anyone that just before the elections you—— There are
stars bursting before my eyes. . . . Where's my hat?

NATÁLIA: Vermin! Liar! Brute!

CHOOBOOKÓV: You're a spiteful, double-dealing schemer! So there!

LÓMOV: Ah, my hat . . . My heart. Where am I?
Where's the door? Oooh! . . . I think I'm dying. . . .
My foot's totally paralyzed.

(*Drags himself to the door.*)

CHOOBOOKÓV (*calling after him*): And don't ever set
your foot in my home again!

NATÁLIA: Go to court! Sue us! Just wait and see!

(LÓMOV *staggers out.*)

SCENE V

(CHOOBOOKÓV *and* NATÁLIA STEPÁNOVNA.)

CHOOBOOKÓV: He can go straight to hell, damn him!

(*Walks about, all wrought up.*)

NATÁLIA: Isn't he the worst crook? Catch me trusting
a good neighbor after this!

CHOOBOOKÓV: The chiseler! The scarecrow!

NATÁLIA: The monster! He not only grabs other people's property, he calls them names, to boot.

CHOOBOOKÓV: And that clown, that . . . freak had the

colossal nerve to ask me for your hand in marriage, and so on. Can you imagine? He wanted to propose.

NATÁLIA: Propose?

CHOOBOOKÓV: Exactly! That's what he came for. To propose to you.

NATÁLIA: Propose? To me? Why didn't you *say* so?

CHOOBOOKÓV: And he got all dolled up in a morning coat. That pipsqueak. That upstart.

NATÁLIA: Propose? To me? Ohhh! (*Collapses into an armchair and wails.*) Bring him back. Get him. Ohh! Get him!

CHOOBOOKÓV: Get whom?

NATÁLIA: Hurry up, hurry! I feel sick. Bring him back. (*Hysterical.*)

CHOOBOOKÓV: What is it? What's wrong? (*Grabbing his head.*) This is awful! I'll shoot myself. I'll hang myself. They've worn me out.

NATÁLIA: I'm dying! Bring him back!

CHOOBOOKÓV: All right. Stop yelling!

(*Runs out.*)

NATÁLIA (*alone, wailing*): What've we done? Bring him back! Bring him back!

CHOOBOOKÓV (*running in*): He's coming and all that, goddamn him. Ughh! *You* talk to him, alone, I really don't feel like . . .

NATÁLIA (*wailing*): Bring him back!

CHOOBOOKÓV (*shouting*): He's coming, I tell you. Oh God! What did I ever do to deserve a grown-up daughter? I'll cut my throat. I swear, I'll cut my throat. We insulted and abused him, and it's all your fault!

NATÁLIA: My fault? It was yours!

CHOOBOOKÓV: Now *I'm* the culprit!

(LÓMOV *appears at the French doors.* CHOOBOOKÓV *exits.*)

SCENE VI

(NATÁLIA *and* LÓMOV.)

LÓMOV (*entering, exhausted*): What horrible palpitations . . . my foot's gone numb . . . there's a jabbing in my side . . .

NATÁLIA: My apologies, Iván Vassílievich, we got so worked up. . . . I do recall now that the Ox Meadows are actually *your* property.

LÓMOV: My heart's palpitating. . . . The Meadows *are* mine . . . . There are stars bursting in both my eyes.

(*They sit down.*)

NATÁLIA: We were wrong.

LÓMOV: It's the principle of the thing. . . . I don't care about the land, it's the principle of the thing——

NATÁLIA: Exactly, the principle . . . Let's talk about something else.

LÓMOV: Particularly since I have proof. My aunt's grandmother let your paternal great-grandfather's peasants——

NATÁLIA: All right, all right . . . (*Aside.*) I don't know how to go about it. . . . (*To* LÓMOV) Will you start hunting soon?

LÓMOV: Yes, for grouse, Natália Stepánovna. I think I shall begin after the harvest. Oh, have you heard what bad luck I had? My hound Guess—you know the one—he's gone lame.

NATÁLIA: What a pity! How did it happen?

LÓMOV: I don't know. He must have twisted his leg, or else some other dog bit him. . . . (*Sighs.*) My very best hound, not to mention the money! Why, I paid Mirónov a hundred and twenty-five rubles for him.

NATÁLIA: You overpaid him, Iván Vassílievich.

LÓMOV: I don't think so. It was very little for a wonderful dog.

NATÁLIA: Papa bought his dog Leap for eighty-five rubles, and Leap is vastly superior to your Guess.

LÓMOV: Leap superior to Guess? Oh, come now. (*Laughs.*) Leap superior to Guess!

NATÁLIA: Of course he is! I know that Leap is still young, he's not a full-grown hound yet. But for points and action, not even Volchanietsky has a better dog.

LÓMOV: Excuse me, Natália Stepánovna, but you're forgetting that he's pug-jawed, which makes him a poor hunting dog.

NATÁLIA: Pug-jawed? That's news to me.

LÓMOV: I can assure you, his lower jaw is shorter than his upper jaw.

NATÁLIA: Have you measured it?

LÓMOV: Indeed, I have. He'll do for pointing, of course, but when it comes to retrieving, he can hardly hold a cand——

NATÁLIA: First of all, our Leap is a pedigreed greyhound—he's the son of Harness and Chisel, whereas your Guess is so piebald that not even Solomon could figure out his breed. . . . Furthermore, he's as old and ugly as a broken-down nag——

LÓMOV: He may be old, but I wouldn't trade him for five of your Leaps. . . . The very idea! Guess is a real hound, but Leap . . . Why argue? It's ridiculous. . . . Every huntsman's assistant has a dog like your Leap. At twenty-five rubles he'd be overpriced.

NATÁLIA: You seem to be possessed by some demon of contradiction, Iván Vassílievich. First you fancy that the Ox Meadows are yours, then you pretend that Guess is a better hound than Leap. If there's one thing I don't like it's a person who says the opposite of what he thinks. You know perfectly well that Leap is a hundred times better than . . . than that stupid Guess of yours. Why do you insist on denying it?

LÓMOV: You obviously must think, Natália Stepánovna, that I'm either blind or mentally retarded. Can't you see that your Leap has a pug jaw?

NATÁLIA: That's not true.

LÓMOV: A pug jaw.

NATÁLIA (*screaming*): That's not true.

LÓMOV: Why are you screaming, Madam?

NATÁLIA: Why are you talking such rubbish? It's exasperating! Your Guess is just about ready to be put out of his misery, and you compare him to Leap.

LÓMOV: Excuse me, but I can't keep on arguing like this. My heart's palpitating.

NATÁLIA: I've noticed that the sportsmen who argue most don't understand the first thing about hunting.

LÓMOV: Madam, pleeeease, keep quiet . . . My heart's bursting. . . . (*Shouts.*) Keep quiet!

NATÁLIA: I won't keep quiet until you admit that Leap is a hundred times superior to your Guess!

LÓMOV: He's a hundred times *in*ferior. Someone ought to shoot him. My temples . . . my eyes . . . my shoulder . . .

NATÁLIA: No one has to wish that idiotic mutt of yours dead, because he's just skin and bones anyway.

LÓMOV: Keep quiet! I'm having heart failure!

NATÁLIA: I will *not* keep quiet!

SCENE VII

CHOOBOOKÓV (*entering*): What's going on now?

NATÁLIA: Papa, tell me, honestly and sincerely: which is the better dog—our Leap or his Guess?

LÓMOV: Stepán Stepánovich, I beseech you, just tell me one thing: is your Leap pug-jawed or isn't he? Yes or no?

CHOOBOOKÓV: So what! Who cares? He's still the best hound in the country, and what not.

LÓMOV: And my Guess isn't better? Tell the truth.

CHOOBOOKÓV: Don't get all worked up, old boy. . . . Let me explain. . . . Your Guess *does* have a few good qualities. . . . He's pure-bred, he's got solid legs, he's well put together, and what not. But if you must know, my good man, your dog's got two basic faults: he's old, and his muzzle's too short.

LÓMOV: Excuse me, my heart's racing madly. . . . Let's examine the facts. . . . Please don't forget that when we were hunting in the Mapooskin Fields, my Guess ran neck and neck with the count's dog Waggy, while your Leap lagged behind by half a mile.

CHOOBOOKÓV: That was because the Count's assistant struck him with his riding crop.

LÓMOV: Naturally. All the other dogs were chasing the fox, but yours started running after sheep.

CHOOBOOKÓV: That's a lie! My dear boy, I fly off the handle easily, so please let's stop arguing. The man whipped him because people are always envious of everyone else's dogs. Yes, they're all filled with spite! And you, sir, are no exception. Why, the minute you notice that anyone else's dog is better than your Guess, you instantly start up something or other . . . and what not. I've got the memory of an elephant!

LÓMOV: And so do I.

CHOOBOOKÓV (*mimicking him*): "And so do I." . . . And what does your memory tell you?

LÓMOV: My heart's palpitating. . . . My foot's paralyzed. . . . I can't anymore . . .

NATÁLIA (*mimicking*): "My heart's palpitating . . ." What kind of hunter are you anyway? You ought to be home in bed catching cockroaches instead of out hunting foxes. Palpitations! . . .

CHOOBOOKÓV: That's right, what kind of hunter are you? If you've got palpitations, stay home; don't go wobbling around the countryside on horseback. It wouldn't be so bad if you really hunted, but you only tag along in order to start arguments or meddle with other people's dogs, and what not. We'd better stop, I fly off the handle easily. You, sir, are not a hunter, and that's that.

LÓMOV: And you *are*, I suppose. The only reason *you* go hunting is to flatter the count and carry on your backstabbing little intrigues. . . . Oh, my heart! . . . You schemer!

CHOOBOOKÓV: Me, a schemer. (*Shouting.*) Shut up!

LÓMOV: Schemer!

CHOOBOOKÓV: Upstart! Pipsqueak!

LÓMOV: You old fogy! You hypocrite!

CHOOBOOKÓV: Shut up, or I'll blast you with a shot gun like a partridge.

LÓMOV: The whole county knows that—Oh, my heart!
—your late wife used to beat you. . . . My leg . . . my
temples . . . I see stars . . . I'm falling, falling . . .

CHOOBOOKÓV: And your housekeeper henpecks you all
over the place!

LÓMOV: There, you see . . . my heart's burst! My
shoulder's torn off. . . . Where's my shoulder? . . . I'm
dying! (*Collapses into armchair.*) Get a doctor! (*Faints.*)

CHOOBOOKÓV: Pipsqueak. Weakling. Windbag. I feel
sick. (*Drinks some water.*) I feel sick.

NATÁLIA: What kind of hunter are you anyway? You
don't even know how to sit in a saddle! (*To her father*)
Papa! What's the matter with him? Papa! Look, Papa!
(*Screams.*) Iván Vassílievich! He's dead!

CHOOBOOKÓV: I feel sick! . . . I can't breathe! . . . Air!

NATÁLIA: He's dead! (*Tugs at* LÓMOV's *sleeve.*) Iván
Vassílievich! Iván Vassílievich! What've we done? He's
dead. (*Collapses into easy chair.*) Get a doctor. (*She becomes hysterical.*)

CHOOBOOKÓV: Oh! . . . What is it? What's wrong?

NATÁLIA (*moaning*): He's dead . . . he's dead!

CHOOBOOKÓV: Who's dead? (*Glancing at* LÓMOV.) He
really is dead! Oh, my God! Get some water! Get a doctor! (*Holds a glass to* LÓMOV's *mouth.*) Go ahead and
drink! . . . He won't drink. . . . I guess he's dead and so
on. . . . Why does everything have to happen to me? Why
didn't I put a bullet through my head long ago? Why
didn't I cut my throat? What am I waiting for? Give me
a knife! Give me a gun!

(LÓMOV *stirs.*)
He's reviving, I think. . . . Drink some water! . . . That's
right.

LÓMOV: Stars . . . fog . . . where am I?

CHOOBOOKÓV: You two'd better hurry up and get married . . . Dammit! She accepts. . . . (*Joins* LÓMOV's
hand with NATÁLIA's.) She accepts. . . . My blessings and
so forth. . . . Just do me a favor and leave me in peace.

LÓMOV: What? (*Getting up.*) Who?

CHOOBOOKÓV: She accepts. Well? Kiss her and . . . the
two of you can go straight to hell.

NATÁLIA (*moaning*): He's alive. . . . I accept, I accept. . . .

CHOOBOOKÓV: Kiss and make up.

LÓMOV: What? Who? (*Kisses* NATÁLIA.) *Enchanté* . . . Excuse me, but what's going on? Oh yes, I remember. . . . My heart . . . stars . . . I'm very happy, Natália Stepánovna. (*Kisses her hands.*) My leg's paralyzed. . . .

NATÁLIA: I . . . I'm very happy, too. . . .

CHOOBOOKÓV: That's a load off my back. . . . Whew!

NATÁLIA: But . . . all the same, why don't you finally admit that Guess isn't as good as Leap.

LÓMOV: He's much better.

NATÁLIA: He's worse.

CHOOBOOKÓV: The launching of marital bliss! Champagne!

LÓMOV: He's better.

NATÁLIA: Worse! Worse! Worse!

CHOOBOOKÓV (*trying to outshout them*): Champagne! Champagne!

EDMOND ROSTAND:

The Romancers

Edmond Rostand (1868–1918) is best remembered for
his romantic tragicomedy, *Cyrano de Bergerac*. Written in
reaction against the realistic-naturalistic plays of Ibsen and
Zola, *Cyrano* was a return to the romanticism of the early
nineteenth century. It transported its audiences back to the
days of Louis XIII, of guardsmen and musketeers with
their flashing swords and white plumes. Among the actors who have triumphed in this most triumphant play
have been Coquelin, Richard Mansfield, and Walter
Hampden. Rostand's other important works for the stage
were *L'Aiglon* (which starred Sarah Bernhardt), *Chante-
cler* (with Maude Adams), and *Les Romanesques*.

Actually the first act of *Les Romanesques* (*The Romancers*), is most frequently read and performed as a
work complete in itself, probably having so been originally
conceived by Rostand. Written when its author was only
twenty-two years old, *Les Romanesques* received the
Comédie Française prize of 4,000 francs and was produced by the French National Theater.

Although Rostand is thought of as a playwright in the
romantic tradition of Victor Hugo, his romanticism is
tinged with the same deep sense of irony, verging on the
burlesque, which characterizes the writing of another
romantic poet (and sometime playwright)—Lord Byron.
The Romancers, while it is essentially romantic in overall
feeling, satirizes the melodramatic trappings and theatrical
clichés of earlier romantic plays. For example, Straforel,
the hired kidnapper, would have reminded Rostand's audience of Sparafucile in *Rigoletto* (based on Victor Hugo's
Le Roi S'Amuse). The two lovers who think of themselves

as the counterparts of Romeo and Juliet would in all likelihood have recalled to the Parisian audience the two young lovers, Camille and Perdican, in Musset's *On ne Badine pas avec l'Amour* (*You Don't Play Games with Love;* 1834)—a fascinating play to read and to compare with *The Romancers.*

Just as the Parisian theater audiences of the '90's delighted in this early play of Rostand's, New York audiences during the past nine years have broken attendance records at the musical adaptation of *Les Romanesques—The Fantasticks.*

The Romancers

Translated by
Joachim Neugroschel

Characters

SYLVETTE.
PERCINET.
STRAFOREL.
BERGAMIN, *Percinet's father.*
PASQUINOT, *Sylvette's father.*
A WALL, *silent figurant.*
SWORDSMEN, MUSICIANS, MOORS, TORCHBEARERS.

The action can take place anywhere, as long as the costumes are attractive.

(*The stage is cut in half by an old moss-grown wall completely covered with lush vines, creepers, and flowers. At the right, a corner of the Bergamin park, at the left a corner of the Pasquinot park. A bench is placed on each side of the wall. As the curtain goes up,* PERCINET *is sitting atop the wall. He has a book in his lap and is reading to* SYLVETTE, *who listens attentively. She is standing on the bench on the other side and leaning against the wall.*)

SYLVETTE: Oh! Monsieur Percinet, how beautiful!
PERCINET: Yes, isn't it? Listen to Romeo's reply.

(*He reads.*)

It was the lark, the herald of the morn;
No nightingale. Look, love, what envious streaks
Do lace the severing clouds in yonder East.
Night's candles are burnt out, and jocund day
Stands tiptoe on the misty mountaintops.

SYLVETTE (*suddenly straining her ear*): Hush!
PERCINET (*listening for a moment, then*): There's no one coming, Mademoiselle. You mustn't take fright like the sparrow that flutters from a branch at the slightest sound. . . . Listen to the Immortal Lovers speak:

Juliet: Yond light is not daylight; I know it, I,
          It is some meteor that the sun exhales
          To be to thee this night a torchbearer

> And light thee on thy way to Mantua.
> Therefore stay yet; thou need'st not to be gone.

Romeo: Let me be ta'en, let me be put to death.
I am content, so thou wilt have it so. . . .
Come, death, and welcome!

SYLVETTE: Oh no! I don't want him to talk about that! If he does, I'll start crying. . . .

PERCINET: All right, then let's stop there: we'll close our book until tomorrow, and for your sake we'll let gentle Romeo live on. (*He shuts the book and looks around.*) What a wonderful spot, I think it's the perfect place to indulge in the beautiful verses of the Great Bard.

SYLVETTE: Yes, those lines are so beautiful, and the divine murmur of the leaves and the boughs is really a fine accompaniment, and the setting of this green shade is just right. Yes, indeed, Monsieur Percinet, those verses *are* lovely. But what makes their beauty even more poignant is the way you recite them in your melodious voice.

PERCINET: You terrible flatterer, you!

SYLVETTE (*sighing*): Ah! The poor lovers! How cruel their destiny, how wretched the world was to them! (*With a sigh.*) Ah! . . .

PERCINET: What are you thinking about?

SYLVETTE (*sharply*): Nothing!

PERCINET: But all at once, something made you turn crimson.

SYLVETTE (*sharply*): Nothing!

PERCINET: You little liar . . . Your eyes are too transparent! I can see what you're thinking about! (*Lowering his voice.*) Our parents!

SYLVETTE: Perhaps . . .

PERCINET: Your father and mine, and the hatred that divides them!

SYLVETTE: Well, yes, that's what distresses me and often makes me weep in secret. Last month, when I came home from the convent my father showed me your father's park and said, "My dear child, there you see the lair of my old mortal enemy Bergamin. Keep away from that wretch and that son of his; and I'll disown you unless you promise me to regard those people as your everlasting enemies, for since time immemorial their family has execrated ours." I gave him my word. . . . And you see, Monsieur, how I keep it.

PERCINET: And didn't I also promise my father to hate you forever, Sylvette?—And I love you!

SYLVETTE: Oh, goodness me!

PERCINET: And I love you, my darling.

SYLVETTE: How sinful.

PERCINET: Very sinful . . . but who can blame us? The more you're kept from loving someone, the more you *want* to love. Sylvette, kiss me!

SYLVETTE: Never!

(*She jumps off the bench and moves away from the wall.*)

PERCINET: But you *do* love me!

SYLVETTE: What did he say?

PERCINET: My darling, I said something that your heart is still struggling against, but it would be foolish to deny it any longer. I said . . . the very same thing you said. Yes, you, Sylvette, when you compared us to the Lovers of Verona.

SYLVETTE: I never compared——

PERCINET: You did so! You likened my father and yours to those of Romeo and Juliet, my darling! That's why *we* are Romeo and Juliet, and that's why we're so madly in love! And despite all their intense hatred, I'll defy both Pasquinot-Capulet and Bergamin-Montague!

SYLVETTE (*drawing a bit closer to the wall*): So then we're in love? But Monsieur Percinet, how did it happen so quickly?

PERCINET: Love comes when it has to, and no one can say how or why. I would often see you passing by my window . . .

SYLVETTE: And I saw you passing, too. . . .

PERCINET: And our eyes conversed in code.

SYLVETTE: One day, I was here, gathering nuts near the wall, and by chance . . .

PERCINET: I happened to be reading Shakespeare; and see how all things conspired to unite two hearts. . . .

SYLVETTE: Whoosh! The wind blew my ribbon over to you!

PERCINET: I climbed up on the bench to retrieve it . . .

SYLVETTE (*climbing*): I climbed up on the bench . . .

PERCINET: And ever since then, my darling, I've been waiting for you every day, and every day my heart beats faster when—oh, blessed signal—your gentle fledgling laughter rises from behind the wall, and it doesn't stop until your head emerges from the trembling tangle of vines and ivy.

SYLVETTE: Since we're in love, we ought to be engaged.

PERCINET: I was just thinking the very same thing.

SYLVETTE (*solemnly*): I, the last of the Pasquinots, do pledge myself to you, the last of the Bergamins.

PERCINET: What noble folly!

SYLVETTE: They'll speak of us in future ages!

PERCINET: Oh! Tenderhearted children of two callous fathers!

SYLVETTE: But, darling, who knows? Perhaps the time's at hand when Heaven will use us to wipe out their hatred.

PERCINET: I don't think so.

SYLVETTE: Well, I have faith, I can foresee five or six highly possible solutions.

PERCINET: Really? Tell me.

SYLVETTE: Just suppose—I've read of similar things in lots of old romances—just suppose the Reigning Prince were to ride by one day. . . . I would hurry over to him, throw myself at his feet, tell him about our love and the old feud dividing our fathers. . . . After all, a king married Don Rodrigo and Ximene—The Prince will summon our fathers and reconcile them.

PERCINET: And he'll give me your hand!

SYLVETTE: Or else it will happen the same way as in *The Donkey's Skin*. You'll be at the point of death, a stupid doctor will despair of your life . . .

PERCINET: My father, panic-stricken, will ask me, "What do you want?"

SYLVETTE: You'll say, "I want Sylvette!"

PERCINET: And his stubborn pride will be forced to yield!

SYLVETTE: Or else, here's another possibility: an old duke, seeing my portrait, falls in love with me, sends a magnificent equerry to me in his name, and offers to make me a duchess . . .

PERCINET: And you answer, "No!"

SYLVETTE: This infuriates him. One lovely evening, as I wander, lost in dreams, down a dark garden path, strange men seize me! . . . I scream! . . .

PERCINET: And I'm at your side immediately. Trusting in my sword, I fight like a lion, slice up——

SYLVETTE: Three or four men. My father runs up, flings his arms about you. You tell him your name. His heart softens. He gives me to my rescuer. And your father is so proud of your valor that he consents!

PERCINET: And we live happily ever after!

SYLVETTE: And none of this seems the least bit unlikely.

PERCINET (*hearing a noise*): Someone's coming!

SYLVETTE (*losing her head*): Kiss me goodbye!

PERCINET (*kisses her*): And tonight, when the bell rings for mass, will you be here? Tell me.

SYLVETTE: No.

PERCINET: Yes.

SYLVETTE (*vanishing behind the wall*): Your father!

(PERCINET *leaps down from the wall.* SYLVETTE, *having stepped down, can't be seen by* BERGAMIN.)

BERGAMIN: Ah! So I've caught you daydreaming again, all alone in this corner of the park?

PERCINET: Father, I love . . . this part of the park! I love sitting on this bench, sheltered by the overhanging vines on the wall! . . . Isn't the vine graceful? Look at those arabesque festoons. It's so good to breathe pure air in this spot.

BERGAMIN: In front of that wall?

PERCINET: I love this wall.

BERGAMIN: I don't see anything lovable about it.

SYLVETTE (*aside*): How can he?

PERCINET: Why, it's a wonderful old wall, look at its grassy top, look at the scarlet creeper, and the green ivy, and the long flossy clusters of the mauve wisteria, and the honeysuckle and the woodbine over there. This ancient, crumbling wall is studded with tiny flowers and filled with cracks that hang strange red hair into the sunshine. And the moss is so thick and rich that like a velvet backdrop it turns the humble bench into a royal throne!

BERGAMIN: Now, now, you young pup, do you really expect me to believe that you come here just to feast your eyes on the wall?

PERCINET: To feast my eyes on the eyes of the wall! . . . (*Facing the wall.*) Such lovely eyes, fresh azure smiles, gentle blue crannies, deep flowers, limpid eyes, to feast my eyes upon. And if ever any tears dim your hue, I'll kiss them away at once.

BERGAMIN: But the wall hasn't got any eyes.

PERCINET: It's got these morning glories.

(*And quickly breaking one off, he gracefully presents it to* BERGAMIN.)

SYLVETTE: Oh, he's so clever!

BERGAMIN: What a dunce! But I know why you're all wrought up. (PERCINET *and* SYLVETTE *start.*) You come here to read on the sly! (*He takes the book jutting out of* PERCINET'S *pocket and glances at the title.*) Plays! (*He opens it and, horrified, drops it.*) In verse! Verse. That's why your brain's in a whirl. No wonder you roam about dreaming, avoiding other people. No wonder you carry on about wisteria, no wonder you see blue eyes in the wall! Walls don't need to be attractive, they have to be sturdy! I'm going to have all that green junk removed, it may be concealing some open gaps. And for better protection against that insolent neighbor, I'm going to remortar the whole surface and build a fine white wall. Very white, very smooth, and very clean. And there'll be no wisteria. I'll cut notches into the plaster on top for broken bottle ends, a sharp and jagged battalion of them in serried ranks.

PERCINET: Have pity, Father!

BERGAMIN: Never! I hereby issue a decree: up and down and all along the top.

SYLVETTE *and* PERCINET (*aghast*): Ohh!

BERGAMIN (*sitting down on the bench*): Now then, it's time you and I had a chat! (*He gets up again and, as if suspecting something, steps back from the wall.*) Hmmm!

. . . Walls may not have eyes, but they do have ears! (*He is about to mount the bench.* PERCINET *is terror-stricken.* SYLVETTE, *hearing the noise, crouches against the wall. However,* BERGAMIN, *grimacing because of some chronic pain, changes his mind and motions to his son to climb up instead and have a look.*) Just see if anyone's eavesdropping . . .

(PERCINET *hops lithely onto the bench and leans over the wall.* SYLVETTE *stands up and he murmurs to her.*)

PERCINET: Till tonight!

SYLVETTE (*letting him kiss her hand, whispers back*): I'll come before the hour strikes.

PERCINET (*whispering*): I'll be here.

SYLVETTE (*whispering*): I love you.

BERGAMIN (*to* PERCINET): Well?

PERCINET (*jumping back down, says aloud*): Well, nobody there!

BERGAMIN (*feeling reassured, sits down again*): Fine, then let's have our little talk . . . Percinet, I want you to get married.

SYLVETTE: Ohh!

BERGAMIN: What was that?

PERCINET: Nothing.

BERGAMIN: I heard a feeble cry.

PERCINET (*looking up*): Some fledgling must have hurt itself—(SYLVETTE *sighs.*)—in the branches.

BERGAMIN: At any rate, my boy, after careful consideration, I've settled on a wife for you.

(PERCINET *walks upstage, whistling.*)

BERGAMIN (*after choking for an instant, follows him*): I'm a stubborn man, sir, and I'll force you to—

(PERCINET *returns, whistling.*)

BERGAMIN: Will you stop that whistling, you magpie! . . . The woman I've chosen is still young and she's very rich—a gem of a girl.

PERCINET: Who cares about your gem!

BERGAMIN: Just you wait! I'll show you, you scamp. . . .

PERCINET (*pushing back his father's raised cane*):

Spring has filled the bushes with the fluttering of wings,
Father, and near the forest brooks tiny birds swoop down
as loving couples . . .

BERGAMIN: You're indecent!

PERCINET: All creatures are blithely welcoming April.
The butterflies——

BERGAMIN: You rascal!

PERCINET: ——are flocking through the countryside to
marry all the flowers that they love! . . . Love——

BERGAMIN: You villain!

PERCINET: ——is making all hearts blossom. . . . And
you expect me to marry for money!

BERGAMIN: Of course, you little cur!

PERCINET (*in a vibrant voice*): Well, then, no, Father,
no! I swear—by this wall—I hope it can hear me—that
my marriage will be more romantic than the wildest romance in any of the old romances.

(*He dashes away.*)

BERGAMIN (*running after him*): Oh, when I catch him!

(*Exeunt.*)

SYLVETTE (*alone*): Honestly, now I understand why
Daddy hates that nasty old——

PASQUINOT (*entering left*): Well, what are you doing
here, young lady?

SYLVETTE: Nothing. Just strolling about.

PASQUINOT: Here! All by yourself? Why, you silly
thing! . . . Aren't you afraid?

SYLVETTE: I'm not the nervous kind.

PASQUINOT: All by yourself near that wall! . . . Didn't
I order you never to go near it! You foolhardy child, just
take a good look at that park: it's the lair of my old
mortal enemy——

SYLVETTE: I know, Father.

PASQUINOT: And yet you deliberately expose yourself to
insults, or even . . . ? There's no telling what those people
are capable of! If that wretched neighbor of mine or his
son knew that my daughter comes all alone to this arbor
to daydream— Oh! It makes me shiver just to think of it.
Why, I'll cover that wall with armor, I'll bard it, I'll

caparison it, I'll put a row of spikes on top to impale any invader, to disembowel anyone trying to climb over it, to slash anyone who even comes near it!

SYLVETTE: He'll never do it, it would cost too much. Daddy's a bit stingy.

PASQUINOT: Get back in the house—and quickly!

(*She exits; he stares after her angrily.*)

BERGAMIN (*in the wings*): Take this letter to Monsieur Straforel immediately.

PASQUINOT (*dashes over to the wall and climbs up*): Bergamin!

BERGAMIN (*following suit*): Pasquinot!

(*They embrace.*)

PASQUINOT: How *are* you?

BERGAMIN: Not bad.

PASQUINOT: How's your gout?

BERGAMIN: Better. And how's your head cold?

PASQUINOT: The damn thing won't go away!

BERGAMIN: Well, the marriage is settled!

PASQUINOT: What?

BERGAMIN: I was hidden in the foliage and I heard everything. They're madly in love.

PASQUINOT: Wonderful!

BERGAMIN: Now, we've got to bring matters to a head! (*Rubbing his hands.*) Ha! Ha! Both of us widowers, and fathers to boot. My son had a slightly over-romantic mother who named him Percinet.

PASQUINOT: Yes, it does sound grotesque.

BERGAMIN: And your daughter Sylvette is a daydreaming little maid from school, with an ethereal soul. What was our sole aim?

PASQUINOT: To tear down the wall.

BERGAMIN: To live together—

PASQUINOT: And merge our two estates into one.

BERGAMIN: A scheme of old friends—

PASQUINOT: And landowners.

BERGAMIN: How could we do it?

PASQUINOT: If our children married each other.

BERGAMIN: Exactly! But could we have succeeded if

they had so much as suspected our wishes and our agreement? A prearranged marriage is not very enticing for two young poetic canaries. Which is why, taking advantage of their living far away, we hushed up our matrimonial plans. But then, his boarding school and her convent came to an end this year. I thought that if we prevented them from meeting they'd be sure to seek one another out and fall in love surreptitiously and sinfully. And so I concocted this marvelous hatred! . . . Remember, you were worried that such an extraordinary plan might not succeed? Well, now all we have to do is give our consent.

PASQUINOT: Fine! But how? How can we be foxy to say "yes" without arousing their suspicions? After all, I called you a wretch, an idiot—

BERGAMIN: An idiot? "Wretch" would have been enough. Don't say any more than you have to.

PASQUINOT: Yes, but what pretext can we use? . . .

BERGAMIN: Listen! Your daughter herself gave me the idea. As she spoke, my plan for a final strategem took shape. They're meeting here tonight. Percinet is coming first. The moment Sylvette appears, men in black will burst out of hiding and seize her. She'll scream, and my young hero will leap upon the kidnappers and attack them with his sword. They'll pretend to flee, you turn up suddenly, so do I, your daughter and her honor will be safe and sound, you're overjoyed, you shed a few tears and bless the rescuing hero, I relent: tableau and curtain!

PASQUINOT: Why, that's brilliant! . . . That's absolutely brilliant. . . .

BERGAMIN (*modestly*): Well, yes . . . if I do say so myself. Hush! Look who's coming! It's Straforel, the famous bravo. I just dropped him a line about my project. He's the one who's going to stage our kidnapping.

(STRAFOREL, *gorgeously bedizened as a bravo, appears upstage and moves forward majestically.*)

BERGAMIN (*descending from the wall and bowing*): Ahem! First of all, may I introduce my friend Pasquinot . . .

STRAFOREL (*bowing*): Monsieur . . .

(*Upon straightening up, he is astonished not to see* PASQUINOT.)

BERGAMIN (*pointing to* PASQUINOT *astride the wall*): There he is, on the wall.

STRAFOREL (*aside*): An amazing exercise for a man of his years!

BERGAMIN: What do you think of my plan, Straforel?

STRAFOREL: There'll be no problems.

BERGAMIN: Good; you know how to grasp things quickly and act swiftly—

STRAFOREL: And hold my tongue.

BERGAMIN: A make-believe abduction and a sham swordfight, have you got that?

STRAFOREL: It's all clear.

BERGAMIN: Use skillful swordsmen who won't wound my little boy. I love him. He's my only child.

STRAFOREL: I'll attend to the operation personally.

BERGAMIN: Excellent. In that case, I needn't worry. . . .

PASQUINOT (*in a low voice to* BERGAMIN): Listen, ask him how much it's going to cost us.

BERGAMIN: How much do you charge for an abduction, Monsieur Straforel?

STRAFOREL: It all depends on what's involved, Monsieur. And the prices vary accordingly. But I gather that you don't care about the expense. So if I were you, Monsieur, I'd take a—first-class abduction!

BERGAMIN: Oh! You've got more than one class?

STRAFOREL: Why of course, Monsieur! We offer an abduction with two men in black; a commonplace abduction by carriage—it's one of our least popular items. A midnight abduction. A daytime abduction. A pomp-and-circumstance abduction, by royal coach, with powdered and bewigged lackeys—there's an extra charge for the wigs—and with mutes, eunuchs, Moors, sbirri, brigands, musketeers—all included in the price! Then we offer an abduction by post chaise, two horses, or three, four, five —as many as you like. A discreet abduction in a berlin coach—it's a bit somber. Then a humorous abduction, in a sack. A romantic abduction by boat—except we'd need a lake! A Venetian abduction by gondola—but we'd have to have a canal! An abduction by the dark of the moon—moonlight is so much in demand nowadays that the cost is slightly higher! A sinister abduction with flashes of lightning, stamping of feet, screams and shouts, dueling, clash of swords, wide-brimmed hats, and gray cloaks. A brutal abduction. A polite abduction. A torchlight abduction—it's very lovely! A so-called classical abduction in masks. A gallant abduction, to a musical accompaniment. An abduction by sedan chair, the gayest, the most modern, Monsieur, and by far the most distinguished!

BERGAMIN (*scratching his head, to* PASQUINOT): Well, what do you think?

PASQUINOT: Uh . . . I don't know, what do you think?

BERGAMIN: I think we've got to overwhelm their imagination! Money can be no object! . . . We need a bit of everything! . . . Let's have——

STRAFOREL: Everything! Why not?

BERGAMIN: Give us something memorable for our young romancers. A sedan chair, cloaks, torches, music, masks!

STRAFOREL (*jotting down notes in a memo book*): To combine these diverse elements, we'll have a first-class abduction—with all the trimmings.

BERGAMIN: Wonderful!

STRAFOREL: I'll be back soon. (*Pointing to* PASQUINOT.) But he'll have to leave the gate to his park ajar. . . .

BERGAMIN: He will, don't worry.

STRAFOREL (*bowing*): Gentlemen, I wish you the very best! (*Before exiting.*) A first-class abduction with all the paraphernalia.

(*Exit.*)

PASQUINOT: Off he goes, a gentleman and a scholar, with his high-and-mighty manner . . . and he didn't even set the price.

BERGAMIN: Never mind, the whole thing's settled! We're going to knock down the wall and have only one home.

PASQUINOT: And during the winter, only one rent to pay in town.

BERGAMIN: We'll do entrancing things in the park!

PASQUINOT: We'll trim the yew trees!

BERGAMIN: We'll gravel the paths.

PASQUINOT: In the middle of each flower bed, we'll intertwine our monograms in floral calligraphy!

BERGAMIN: And since this greenery is a bit too severe—

PASQUINOT: We'll brighten it up with decorations!

BERGAMIN: We'll have fish in a brand-new pond!

PASQUINOT: We'll have a fountain with a stone egg dancing on the peak of the spray! We'll have a mass of rock! What do you think of that!

BERGAMIN: All our wishes are coming true.

PASQUINOT: We'll grow old together.

BERGAMIN: And your daughter's provided for.

PASQUINOT: And so is your son.

BERGAMIN: Ah, good old Pasquinot!

PASQUINOT: Ah, good old Bergamin!

(SYLVETTE *and* PERCINET *suddenly enter on their respective sides.*)

SYLVETTE (*seeing her father holding* BERGAMIN): Oh!

BERGAMIN (*to* PASQUINOT, *upon noticing* SYLVETTE): Your daughter.

PERCINET (*seeing his father holding* PASQUINOT): Oh!

PASQUINOT (*to* BERGAMIN, *upon noticing* PERCINET): Your son!

BERGAMIN (*sotto voce to* PASQUINOT): Let's fight. (*They turn their hug into a scuffle.*) You blackguard!

PASQUINOT: You wretch!

SYLVETTE (*pulling at her father's coattails*): Daddy! . . .

PERCINET (*pulling at his father's coattails*): Dad! . . .

BERGAMIN: Leave us alone, you little brats.

PASQUINOT: He started it, he insulted me!

BERGAMIN: He hit me!

PASQUINOT: Coward!

SYLVETTE: Daddy.

BERGAMIN: Swindler!

PERCINET: Dad!!

PASQUINOT: Robber!

SYLVETTE: Daddy!!

(*The children manage to separate them.*)

PERCINET (*dragging his father off*): Let's go home, it's getting late.

BERGAMIN (*trying to come back*): I'm in a towering rage!

(PERCINET *takes him away.*)

PASQUINOT (*likewise with* SYLVETTE): I'm boiling!

SYLVETTE: It's getting cool out. Think of your rheumatism!

(*All exeunt.*)

(*Twilight is beginning to set in. The stage is empty for a moment. Then* STRAFOREL *and his* SWORDSMEN, MUSICIANS, *et al., enter the park.*)

STRAFOREL: There's already one star out in the clear sky, the day is dying . . . (*He places his men in their positions.*) You stay there. . . . And you, here. . . . And you, over there. Evening mass will be starting any moment. She'll appear as soon as the bell rings, and then I'll whistle. . . . (*He looks at the moon.*) The moon? . . . Wonderful! We won't omit a single effect tonight! (*Looking at the extravagant cloaks of his bravos.*) The cloaks are excellent! . . . Let them ride up a bit more on the rapiers: bear down on the hilts. (*A sedan chair is brought in.*) Put the chair over here, in the shade. (*Staring at the chairmen.*) Ah! The Moors! Not bad at all! (*Speaking into the wings.*) Don't forget to bring out the torches when I signal. (*The back of the stage is tinged with the dim pink reflections of the torches from behind the trees. The* MUSICIANS *enter.*) The musicians? There, against a background of rosy light. (*He positions them upstage.*) Grace, tenderness! Vary your poses! Will the mandolinist please stand up, and the violinist sit down! Just as in Watteau's *Rustic Concert!* (*In a severe tone, to a bravo*) Masked man, number one: stop slouching! Is that what you call bearing? —Fine. —Instruments, *con sordini!* Please tune up. . . . Very good! Sol, mi, sol.

(He puts on his mask.)

PERCINET *(enters slowly. As he declaims the following lines, the night grows darker and the stars emerge)*: My father's calmed down. . . . I've managed to come here. . . . The twilight is settling. . . . The air is redolent with the heady fragrance of the elder trees. . . . The gray shadows are making the flowers close.

STRAFOREL *(sotto voce to the violins)*: Music!

(The MUSICIANS *play softly until the end of the act.)*

PERCINET: I'm trembling like a reed. What's wrong with me? . . . She'll be here soon!

STRAFOREL *(to the* MUSICIANS*)*: *Amoroso!* . . .

PERCINET: This is my first evening rendezvous. . . . Oh! I feel faint! . . . The breeze is rustling like a silken gown. . . . I can't see the flowers anymore . . . there are tears in my eyes. . . . I can't see the flowers . . . but I can smell their fragrance! Oh! That tall tree with a star on top! . . . But who's playing here? The night has come—

Now old desire doth in his deathbed lie,
    And young affection gapes to be his heir;
That fair for which love groaned for and would die,
    With tender Juliet matched, is now not fair.
Now Romeo is beloved and loves again,
    Alike bewitchèd by the charm of looks;
But to his foe supposed he must complain,
    And she steal love's sweet bait from fearful hooks.
Being held a foe, he may not have access
    To breathe such vows as lovers use to swear,
And she as much in love, her means much less
    To meet her new belovèd anywhere;
But passion lends them power, time means, to meet,
Temp'ring extremities with extreme sweet.

(A bell peals in the distance.)

SYLVETTE *(appearing at the sound of the bell)*: The bell! He must be waiting. *(A whistle.* STRAFOREL *looms up before her, the torches appear.)* Oh! *(The bravos seize her and thrust her into the sedan chair.)* Help!

PERCINET: Good God!

SYLVETTE: Percinet, I'm being abducted!

PERCINET: I'm coming. (*He leaps over the wall, draws his sword, and fences with a few of the bravos.*) Take that . . . and that . . . and that.

STRAFOREL (*to the* MUSICIANS): Tremolo! (*The violins surge up in a dramatic tremolo. The bravos dash off.* STRAFOREL, *in a theatrical voice*) Zounds! That lad's a devil! (*Duel between* STRAFOREL *and* PERCINET. STRAFOREL *clutches his chest.*) That blow . . . is mortal.

(*He falls.*)

PERCINET (*running over to* SYLVETTE): Sylvette!

(*Tableau. She is in the sedan chair, he is kneeling beside her.*)

SYLVETTE: My hero!

PASQUINOT (*appearing*): Bergamin's son a hero? Your rescuer? . . . Let me shake his hand.

SYLVETTE *and* PERCINET: Oh joy!

(BERGAMIN *enters on his side, followed by torch-bearing servants.*)

PASQUINOT (*to* BERGAMIN, *who appears on top of the wall*): Bergamin, your son is a hero! . . . Let's put an end to our feud and make our children happy!

BERGAMIN (*solemnly*): My hatred is allayed.

PERCINET: Sylvette, we must be dreaming. Sylvette, speak low, or else the sound of our voices will awaken us! . . .

BERGAMIN: Hatred always ends in a wedding. Peace is upon us. (*Pointing to the wall*) Down with the Pyrenees!

PERCINET: Who would have dreamt that my father could change?

SYLVETTE (*naïvely*): Didn't I tell you it would all work out in the end?

(*As the lovers go upstage with* PASQUINOT, STRAFOREL, *rises and hands* BERGAMIN *a slip of paper.*)

BERGAMIN (*in a low voice*): What? What's this piece of paper with your signature on it?

STRAFOREL (*bowing*): Monsieur, this is my bill.

(*He drops back to the ground.*)

WILLIAM INGE

To Bobolink, for Her Spirit

William Inge (1913–   ), a native of Independence, Kansas, was an English instructor at Washington University in St. Louis when the New York Theater Guild decided in 1950 to produce his play, *Come Back, Little Sheba*. Having thus been launched as a playwright, Inge successfully wrote a series of widely acclaimed plays about the Kansas-Missouri-Oklahoma region of his youth: *Picnic, Bus Stop, The Dark at the Top of the Stairs,* and *A Loss of Roses.* He has also, in several of his one-act plays and in the full-length plays *Natural Affection* and *Where's Daddy?,* described the urban scene of New York and Chicago. Inge wrote (and produced with Elia Kazan) the film *Splendor in the Grass,* appearing in the role of the minister. He now makes his home in Hollywood, California.

Clusters of celebrity seekers and autograph collectors are a commonplace of the great cities of the world. Composed of harmless and pathetic adolescents for the most part, these groups are regarded by most observers with indifference, distaste, or condescension; these mindless little packs are, after all, peripheral to the urgent business of the great metropolises of London, New York, or Rome. Why, then, does a playwright choose to celebrate their existence in a play in which they play all the parts? The answer to this question lies partly in the fact that of all American playwrights, William Inge has written most perceptively and compassionately about the pains and perplexities of adolescence. In each of his major plays, youth's frustrated aspirations constitute a major or secondary theme. So *Bobolink* represents another facet of

Inge's abiding interest in the alienated or isolated young.

All this is not to say that we can exactly define Inge's attitude toward Bobolink and her little band. For the portrayal of them is objective and dispassionate, as if the playwright were withholding judgment. The responsibility for taking an attitude toward the characters in the play falls upon us, the audience or the reader of the play.

In reading the play we note that the little group falls into two parts: four teen-agers and the two older women. Is it possible that Bobolink and Nellie are searching for something different from that sought by the youngsters? Is it possible that for some, the sight of a celebrity is merely a dramatic moment; while for others, it is a kind of deep fulfillment? Are Gretchen and Annamarie going to become what Bobolink and Nellie already are: members of that sad body of life's irremediable failures? Does the existence of these clusters of adolescents and quasi-adolescents have any implications relating to American cultural values?

Most of us have a few "idols" in our own lives: a statesman; an athlete; an opera star; a ballet dancer; a pop singer; a concert pianist—usually somebody who does supremely well something we would like to be able to do, and can't, and never will. What differentiates our enthusiasms from those of the Bobolinks of this world? Is the difference *merely* one of degree?

To Bobolink, for Her Spirit

Characters

BOBOLINK BOWEN.
NELLIE.
RENALDO.
FRITZ.
GRETCHEN.
ANNAMARIE.
DOORMAN.

(Every day the weather permits, a group of autograph hunters assembles outside the 21 Club in New York. The size of the group varies from day to day and seems to depend upon the number and magnitude of the movie stars reported to be inside. It is an oddly assorted group, most of them teen-agers, but sometimes middle-aged women are included. The ringleader of today's group is BOBOLINK BOWEN, *a woman probably in her early thirties, who is so fat that her body, in silhouette, would form an almost perfect circle.* BOBOLINK *has the fat woman's usual disposition, stolidly complacent and happy. Her lips usually are formed in a grin of guzzling contentment. Her hair is short and kinky; she wears thick-lensed glasses that reduce her eyes to the size of buttonholes, and her clothes by necessity are simple: a man's coat-style sweater, saddle shoes, and bobbysocks, and bare legs that swell at the calves like bowling pins.* NELLIE, *a starved and eager woman in her late twenties, is* BOBOLINK'S *dependable standby.*

The two young boys, RENALDO *and* FRITZ, *are friends; the two young girls,* GRETCHEN *and* ANNAMARIE, *are friends also. They are people without any personal attraction they could possibly lay claim to, and so must find in others attributes they want and lack in themselves.* ANNAMARIE, *in her dress, has tried to emulate one of her favorite film stars; she wears exotic sun glasses, a complicated coiffure, and exciting shoes with straps, bows, and platform soles. The group has been standing around for over an hour. They have learned to handle these periods of waiting like patients in a rest home; they talk idly with one another, move restlessly about in a limited space.* GRETCHEN *knits,* FRITZ *is working a crossword puzzle. Behind them stands the* DOORMAN, *a man of rigid and calculated dignity, dressed in a colorful uniform. He holds his head high and keeps it turned away from the autograph seekers as though to disclaim any association with them.)*

RENALDO: I heard Lana Turner was in this joint last week. Man, wouldn't that be something?

FRITZ: Just imagine walking down the street one day and . . . plop! all of a sudden there's Lana Turner . . . just outa the blue. Man, I'd drop my teeth.

NELLIE (*making a claim that* BOBOLINK *would be too proud to make for herself*): Bobolink here's got Lana Turner's autograph. Haven't you, Bobby?

BOBOLINK: Lana's no better'n anyone else.

FRITZ (*impressed; to* BOBOLINK): No foolin'? You got Lana Turner's autograph?

BOBOLINK (*proving it with her autograph book*): Think I was lying to you?

FRITZ (*to* RENALDO): Look, Ronny, she's got it.

NELLIE: Oh, Bobolink's got 'em all.

BOBOLINK (*she always holds her own*): I got all of 'em that's worth gettin'.

GRETCHEN: My girl friend saw her. My girl friend goes out to California every summer. Her folks are real wealthy. She saw Lana Turner on the beach one day and she just goes up to her and says, "Hi, Lana" . . . just like that. And Lana smiles back and says, "Hi!"

BOBOLINK: Sure, she's not stuck-up. Now Katharine

Hepburn's stuck-up, but Lana Turner's not at all. The best ones never are stuck-up.

FRITZ (*addressing the* DOORMAN, *who stands with rigid dignity*): Hey, mister, how long's Perry Como been inside?

(*The* DOORMAN *does not respond.*)

BOBOLINK (*to* FRITZ): Hey, don't you know anything? Those guys don't pay no attention to movie stars. They see so many of 'em they get sick of 'em. You can't find out anything from him.

FRITZ: Are we sure Perry Como's there?

BOBOLINK (*impatiently*): I told you I seen him, didn't I? Well, what more do you want? I was up there on the corner waitin' for a bus. Nellie here nudges me and says, "Hey, ain't that Perry Como goin' into the 21 Club?" And I looked and sure enough. There was a guy goin' in, had on the same kinda suit Perry Como had on last week over at the Paramount. Looked exactly like him.

FRITZ: But are you sure it was him?

BOBOLINK: Look, boy, you're never sure of anything in this world, don't you know that?

FRITZ: We been waiting here over an hour.

BOBOLINK: No one's asking you to stay. I waited outside the Stork Club three hours one night, three whole hours, and it was snowin'. Someone told me Elizabeth Taylor was inside and I wanted her autograph. It wasn't Elizabeth Taylor at all. Just some college girl trying to make out she was Elizabeth Taylor. I was sore, but what the heck!

NELLIE: Besides, you never know what's going to happen in this racket; like the time we was waitin' outside the St. Regis for Ronald Colman, and shoot! Who cares about Ronald Colman . . .

RENALDO: He's famous.

NELLIE: Not very. Anyway, we was waitin' for his autograph and . . .

BOBOLINK (*taking over*): Oh, yeh, and we'd been waiting for Ronald Colman all night and we was just about to give up and go home and then what do you think happened?

(*She's going to build up suspense by making them guess.*)

NELLIE: That was the best luck we ever had, wasn't it, Bobby?

BOBOLINK: Well, we was just about to give up and go home when a taxi draws up at the curb and Van Johnson and Peter Lawford get out, and we got 'em both, right there on the same spot.

(*This is an impressive story. The others are a little awed.*)

GRETCHEN: No foolin'! You got Van Johnson and Peter Lawford?

BOBOLINK (*she produces her autograph book proudly*): And both at the same time!

NELLIE (*producing her own evidence*): I got 'em, too.

BOBOLINK: See what Peter Lawford wrote? "All my love to Bobolink." I told him that was my name.

NELLIE: And he said the same thing on mine, but my name's Nellie. They're both just as cute in real life as they are in pictures, aren't they, Bobby?

BOBOLINK: Not a bit stuck-up.

(*An elaborately dressed couple appears in the doorway coming out of the restaurant. The woman wears a dress of dramatic cut and an exotic hat. Their manner is ridiculously aloof and they make quite a thing of ignoring the autograph hounds.*)

FRITZ (*nudging* RENALDO): Hey, who's that?

(*They all look.*)

GRETCHEN: Looks like Rosalind Russell, don't it?

BOBOLINK: Naw, that ain't Rosalind Russell. I seen Rosalind Russell. She's real tall.

ANNAMARIE: Isn't she stunning? Don't you just love that dress?

GRETCHEN: I bet that dress cost two or three hundred dollars.

ANNAMARIE: 'Course it did. Probably cost more than that.

(BOBOLINK *is studying the woman, trying to decide who she is. The woman and her escort now stand at the curb waiting for the* DOORMAN *to hail them a cab. The hounds are gaping at them.*)

FRITZ (*approaching the glamorous woman*): Miss, can I have your autograph?

(*The woman is a little surprised. She looks questioningly at her escort, who gives her an indulgent smile. So the woman, a little mystified, signs her name to* FRITZ'S *book. Then she and her escort disappear in a cab.* FRITZ *studies the signature. The others flock around him to see who it is, but* BOBOLINK *is not as quickly curious as the others.*)

ALL: Who is she? Hey, let's see. It's not Rosalind Russell, is it? If I missed Rosalind Russell, I could kill myself. Let's see.

FRITZ: I'm trying to make it out. (*He attempts a pronunciation of the name.*) Irina Nechibidikoff.

BOBOLINK (*emphatically*): Russian!

FRITZ: Hey, she may be someone famous.

BOBOLINK: Whoever heard of Irina Nechibidikoff?

ANNAMARIE: Maybe she's a famous dancer.

BOBOLINK: So what? She's not in the movies, is she? With a name like that.

GRETCHEN: Maybe she's a famous singer.

FRITZ: Anyway, I got her, whoever she is.

BOBOLINK: I'm waitin' here for Perry Como. I come for Perry Como, and I'm gonna stay till I *get* Perry Como.

NELLIE (*to the others*): Bobby always finishes up what she starts out to do.

BOBOLINK: You tell the world I do. And I'm not leavin' here without Perry Como's autograph. I been trailin' him for two years. I got Bing Crosby; I got Frank Sinatra; I got Van Johnson and Peter Lawford and Jimmy Stewart and Tyrone Power . . .

NELLIE: Tell 'em about the time you got Tyrone Power, Bobby.

BOBOLINK: Now I mean to get Perry Como. He's not my favorite or anything, but I want to get his autograph.

NELLIE: Tyrone Power's your real favorite, isn't he, Bobolink?

BOBOLINK (*with modest adoration*): Yeah. Tyrone's a real guy.

NELLIE (*to the others*): Bobby's president of the Tyrone Power Fan Club up in Irvington. (*The others are impressed.*) Go on, Bobby, tell 'em about Tyrone.

BOBOLINK (*this is too sacred to be treated lightly and* BOBOLINK *is capable of dramatizing her modesty*): No, Nellie, I don't think it's right a person should go around boasting about things like that.

NELLIE: Tell 'em, Bobby. If you don't, I will. (BOBOLINK, *after all, can't stop her.*) Bobby's too modest about it, I think. But Tyrone Power shook her hand and told her personally that he was very indebted to her . . .

BOBOLINK: I met him at the train; don't forget that, Nellie.

NELLIE: As president of the Tyrone Power Fan Club in Irvington, she met his train at the Pennsylvania Station when he came in from Hollywood.

BOBOLINK: And I had to fight the man at the gate to let me pass.

NELLIE: That's right. She did. See, it wasn't supposed to be known that Tyrone was on that train, but the Pasadena Fan Club had wired us he was coming, so Bobby and I met him at the train to welcome him to New York, didn't we, Bobby?

BOBOLINK: We didn't want him t'arrive in town all alone.

NELLIE: 'Course not. So we went down to the station together. The man at the gate wouldn't let us through, but Bobby got by him, didn't you, Bobby? I had to stay behind, but Bobby got through and got right on the train, didn't you, Bobby?

BOBOLINK: And I hunted all through them cars till I found him. He was still packing his things and he was in a hurry.

NELLIE: But he wasn't stuck-up, was he, Bobby?

BOBOLINK (*this is sacred to her*): No, he wasn't stuck-up at all. I introduced myself as the president of the

Irvington Fan Club, and told him we had forty-three
members and met once a week to discuss his career.

NELLIE: And he was very pleased, wasn't he, Bobby?

BOBOLINK: Of course he was. And I told him us fans
was awful glad he didn't marry Lana Turner 'cause, although our club don't have anything personal against
Lana Turner, we never did think she was the right sort for
Tyrone. And I told him that in just those words.

NELLIE: And she isn't. I mean, I like Lana Turner and
I think she's awfully pretty and of course she's awful
famous, but she isn't the right sort of girl for Tyrone at
all.

GRETCHEN: And you got his autograph?

BOBOLINK: 'Course I got his autograph, silly. Nellie did,
too. And he gave me lots of his autographs to give to
other club members, but he made me promise not to give
them to anyone else. (*She displays her proudest acquisi-
tion.*) Just club members. Then he told me to call him
Tyrone, and he said he was very indebted to me. See what
he wrote?

FRITZ (*reading the inscription aloud*): "To Bobolink,
for her faithful enthusiasm and spirit." Gee!

BOBOLINK: Then he had his secretary give me a picture
and he autographed it, too. It just says, "With gratitude,
Tyrone." Then he shook my hand and he said he wished
he could come to Irvington to visit the fan club, but he
was going to be terribly busy in New York, he wouldn't
have a minute to spare, and then he had to get back to
Hollywood to make another picture.

ANNAMARIE (*to* NELLIE): Did you meet him?

NELLIE: No, but I saw him. He came hurrying through
the gate with his coat collar turned up so no one would
recognize him. I called out, "Hi, Tyrone! I'm a friend of
Bobolink," but he started running.

BOBOLINK: He didn't want people to know who he was.
Sometimes they get mobbed by fans and get their clothes
ripped off and even get hurt. I wouldn't want anything like
that to happen to Tyrone.

(*Another couple appear in entrance way. The young
man is dapper and handsome and the girl is pretty and*

expensively dressed. The haughty DOORMAN *starts hailing a cab.*)

RENALDO: Hey, who's this?

GRETCHEN: Is this Perry Como?

BOBOLINK (*with a look*): No, that ain't Perry Como.

NELLIE: She looks familiar, don't she? I bet she's in pictures.

BOBOLINK (*after a moment's study*): No, she ain't in pictures.

FRITZ: They might be somebody. They might be somebody we haven't heard about yet. (*The couple stand at the curb now.* FRITZ *approaches them.*) Mister, can I have your autograph?

ANNAMARIE (*to the girl*): Are you in pictures?

(*The girl smiles tolerantly and shakes her head no.*)

GRETCHEN: Go on and sign anyway, will you please?

ANNAMARIE: I bet you're both in pictures and just don't wanta admit it. C'mon and give us your autograph.

(*The young man and the girl smile at each other and sign the books, while the* DOORMAN *hails a cab. But this is small-time stuff for* BOBOLINK. *She has the dignity of her past career to think of. She stays back, leaning against the grill fence surrounding the club, with a look of superior calm on her face.* NELLIE *stays by her side.*)

NELLIE: I don't think they're anyone famous, do you, Bobolink?

BOBOLINK: 'Course not. I can tell the famous ones. I can tell.

NELLIE: Sure you can, Bobby.

(*The couple go off in a cab. The* DOORMAN *returns to his position by the doorway. The young autograph seekers start studying the names that have been inscribed in their books.*)

BOBOLINK: They might be famous *one* day . . . I said they *might* be . . . But I don't have time to waste on people that *might* be famous.

NELLIE: 'Course not.

(*They stand quietly, removed from the others now.*)

FRITZ (*reading his new acquisitions*): Frederick Bischoff and Mary Milton. Who are they?

ANNAMARIE: Yah, who are they?

GRETCHEN: I bet she models. I think I seen her picture once in an ad for hair remover. Yah, that was her. I know it was. It was a picture showed her with one arm stretched over her head so you could see she didn't have no hair under her arm and was smiling real pretty.

ANNAMARIE: He's probably just a model, too. He was kinda cute, though.

BOBOLINK (*personally to* NELLIE, *in appraisal of her colleagues*): These are just kids, Nellie.

NELLIE: Yah.

FRITZ: Isn't anyone famous ever coming outa there?

RENALDO (*to* BOBOLINK): Are you sure you saw Perry Como go inside?

BOBOLINK: I said Perry Como was inside, didn't I? If you don't believe me, you don't have to.

NELLIE: Bobolink knows a lot more about these things than you kids do. She spotted Perry Como two blocks away and Bobolink don't make mistakes.

RENALDO: O.K. O.K. Don't get sore.

NELLIE: You might remember that Bobolink is president of the Tyrone Power Fan Club.

FRITZ: We wasn't doubtin' your word. C'mon, Renaldo. Let's wait.

GRETCHEN: Let's wait a little longer, Annamarie.

ANNAMARIE: I gotta get home for supper, Gretchen.

GRETCHEN: Let's wait.

FRITZ (*to* RENALDO): Let's wait.

(*They resume their positions of patient attendance.*)

A Play for Radio

EDWIN GRANBERRY:

A Trip to Czardis

ADAPTED BY JAMES AND ELIZABETH HART

Edwin Granberry (1897–   ), American novelist and college teacher, was born in Mississippi but moved to Florida while in his teens. Receiving his undergraduate degree from Columbia, Mr. Granberry established himself as a writer of fiction, winning the O. Henry Memorial Prize for the best short story in 1931–32. The next few years found him back in Florida, where he began his long career as teacher of creative writing at Rollins College.

James and Elizabeth Hart began their long and successful careers as radio playwrights with their adaptation of Mr. Granberry's *A Trip to Czardis;* it was first performed on the Columbia Workshop in 1939.

A collection of short plays drawn principally from the literature of the twentieth century would be incomplete if it did not include an example of the radio play. For nearly twenty-five years, radio plays—generally of twenty-five minutes' duration—occupied a considerable proportion of prime radio time. Gifted writers devoted their entire careers to the writing of radio drama. So distinguished a poet as Archibald MacLeish contributed significant work to the medium. The radio play was a potentially new art form, and indeed its influence on the work of the new dramatists, Samuel Beckett and Harold Pinter among them, is unmistakable.

Not a great many of the plays written for radio, however, have survived. Nearly all of them are already forgotten, even those hundreds which were anthologized in play collections. The reason, apart from their generally poor quality, is to be found in the fact that the impact of drama is at least as visual as it is auditory. The radio play focused on sound; its appeal to the imagination was marginal, and the dimensions of time and space were, in radio drama, vastly diminished—partly because most radio playwrights were inadequate to the challenge the new medium presented. The once flourishing radio play is now largely a matter of cultural history. A few have survived, and *A Trip to Czardis* is one of the happy few.

A great many of the best radio plays were adaptations. *A Trip to Czardis* was first written as a short story. It lends itself to radio dramatization because it is so perfectly focused: everything that happens is funneled through the consciousness of two children, so that our growing awareness of the full implications of the events coincides with the older child's awareness.

A Trip to Czardis

Characters

MAMMA.
JIM.
DAN'L.
PAPA.
UNCLE HOLLY.
THE GUARD.
MINISTER.
VENDORS.

(*Music: Opening melody, suggesting morning in country, fading into*
Sound: The subdued sounds of daybreak in the Florida scrub. Now a distant cock crow. Presently the far-off howling of a dog. Close at hand, the sad call of mourning doves, drawn out, repeated, subsiding reluctantly. Pause. Then the sound of weary footfalls mounting steep stairs.)

MAMMA (*a hint of pity in her voice*): Sleepin' and dreamin' . . . still full of their baby concerns. Hit ain't in my heart to waken 'em. Hit ain't in my heart to—oh, Lord, I'm fearful. I don't know iffen I'm actin' right or not, Lord.

(*Sound: The mourning doves call softly at the window.*)

MAMMA: Our Father which art in heaven, Hallowed be thy name. Thy kingdom come. Thy will be done on earth as it is in heaven . . . (*Breaks off sobbing.*)
JIM (*startled from sleep*): Mamma! Mamma!
MAMMA (*reassuringly*): Nothin's wrong, Jim. Don't be scairt.
JIM: Mamma, you ain't cryin'?
MAMMA: No, Jim.
JIM: You're a-prayin'?
MAMMA: Yes, I were prayin'. Hit'll be day soon. You better be risin' up. Your Uncle Holly'll be along directly.
JIM (*with growing excitement*): Hit's really come. The

day. The day we're goin' to Czardis in the wagon to see Papa.

MAMMA (*dully*): Hit's come, all right.

JIM: Seems like I jest cain't believe yet we're goin' . . .

MAMMA (*cutting in*): There ain't time fur talk now, Jim. You best bestir yourself. And waken up Dan'l, too.

(*Sound: Receding footsteps on floor boards.*)

MAMMA (*voice more distant—off mike*): Put on the clean things I washed out fur you so you'll look decent and be a credit to your raisin'.

(*Sound: Footsteps descending stairs, then fade-out.*)

JIM: Wake up, Dan'l. Wake up!

DAN'L (*whimpering in his sleep*): Leave me be. Make 'em leave me be. Jim! . . . Jim!

JIM (*patient, kind*): Don't be feared, Dan'l. Ain't nobody a-botherin' you.

DAN'L: Hit's dark. I cain't see, Jim.

JIM: Ain't e'er a soul here but me and you. See, I got my arm around you. Open up your eyes now.

DAN'L (*wakes, still frightened*): Oh . . . oh, I were dreamin'.

JIM: What dreamin' were you havin'?

DAN'L: Hit's gone right out of my head. But it were fearful, Jim, fearful, what I dreamed.

JIM: The day's come, Dan'l.

DAN'L: What, Jim?

JIM: The day. Hit's here right now. The day we been waitin' fur to come. You'll recollect it all in a minute.

DAN'L: I recollect. (*Full of excitement.*) Hit's the day we're goin' in the wagon to see Papa.

JIM: We're goin' all the way this time, right on to Czardis, where Papa is. I never see sech a place as Czardis. Papa takened me one time he was goin' to market. You were too little then, and he were feared you'd get tuckered. You started up whimperin' jest as we drove off, and Papa jumped outen the wagon and run back and told you, "Don't take on, Dan'l. Soon's you get to be six, I'll bring you, too, and we'll have us a right fine time." (*Fading.*) Hit were terrible long ago that Papa takened

me, but I can see it all plain, just like it was happenin'
now.

(*Music: Fade in merry-go-round music as background.*)

VENDORS (*babble of many voices*): 'Taters! Sweet
'taters! Pick 'em up, gents. Pick 'em up! Grapefruit,
oranges, and lemons! Grapefruit, oranges, and lemons!
Floridy's finest, ladies! Floridy's finest! Fresh, fresh fish!
Fresh, fresh fish! Red snapper! Red snapper! Right out
of the gulf, folks! Right out of the gulf!

JIM (*making himself heard over the tumult*): You
mean I can sure enough ride on 'em?

PAPA: That's jest what I do mean, young 'un. Which
do you favor? How about this red colt? Here, I'll h'ist
you on his back. Mind you holt on tight now.

(*Music: Merry-go-round up loud.*
Sound: Laughter and squeals of children.
Music: Merry-go-round gradually fades out.
Sound: Crowd in background.)

PAPA: Well, son, were it a good ride?

JIM: Papa, hit were like nothin' else in the world,
a-ridin' the horses that make music.

PAPA: I'm happy it pleasured you, son.

JIM: Are they always in Czardis?

PAPA: Only jest on market day. Likely the feller that
owns 'em figgers there'll always be a parcel of young
'uns a-comin' along with their mas and pas, and iffen the
mas and pas ain't downright mean they can spare a nickel
to give the young 'uns a treat.

VENDORS: *Vendors' cries up momentarily, then fade
quickly into background.*

JIM: Oh, look, Papa. Over yonder on top of that big
buildin'. They got a gold ball stickin' up in the air!

PAPA: That's the courthouse. I calculate that ball must
be twenty, twenty-five foot round the middle. Awful
purty, catchin' the sun the way it does.

JIM: Is it bigger round'n our well?

PAPA: Oh, it's a sight bigger'n the well.

VENDOR (*fading in*): Lemonade! Ice-cold lemonade!
Here you are. Ice-cold lemonade!

PAPA: Reckon you could stand wettin' your whistle, eh, Jim? Here, mister, let's have a couple of them lemonades.

VENDOR: Mighty hot day. . . . Here you are.

PAPA: I thank you. . . . Well, how do it go down, son?

JIM: Hit's colder'n the spring water in the hollow. I never knew there could be somethin' so cold. I can feel it a-freezin' my teeth together.

VENDOR: That's the ice makes it so cold.

JIM: I ain't never had ice.

VENDOR: Here, young feller, I'll put a little piece in your glass, so's you can eat it.

(*Sound: Tinkle of ice.*)

JIM: I sure thank you.

(*Sound: Crowd noises and vendor's cries intrude briefly.*)

PAPA: Don't them turkeys look plump 'n' tasty? Now iffen I jest weren't so scarce of money, I'd certain take one home for your mamma. Hit's a long time since I were able to shoot her a wild one.

JIM: I never see so many things to eat in my life! Oh, look, Papa, look comin'. What's all them?

PAPA: Them's balloons.

JIM: Balloons. They're somethin' like a big soap bubble, only with the same color all over. Jest look at 'em a-bobbin' and swayin' like as if they was tryin' to get away.

PAPA: Hit's the gas in 'em makes 'em pull that-a-way.

JIM: Gas?

PAPA: Somethin' in 'em that makes 'em go up in the air iffen you let go the string.

JIM (*wistfully*): I reckon they cost a heap of money.

PAPA (*laughs*): Hit's a good thing you don't come often to town, young squirrel, lessen your papa wouldn't have a cent to his name. I expect we can get you a balloon, though. Hey! you . . .

JIM (*solemnly*): Oh, Papa, I won't forget today all the other days I live, Papa.

(*Sound: Cries of the crowd and vendors grow louder,*

then fade into silence. After a moment a cock crows.)

JIM (*dreamily*): I never see anything like it. You jest can't pitcher it, Dan'l, till you been there.

DAN'L: I recollect the water tower.

JIM: Not in your own right. Hit's by my tellin' it you see it in your mind.

DAN'L: And lemonade with ice in it.... and balloons of every kind and color ...

JIM (*cutting in*): That, too, I seen and told to you.

DAN'L (*incredulous*): Then I never seen any of it at all?

JIM: Hit's me were there. I let you play like, but hit's me went to Czardis. You weren't olden enough.

DAN'L: I'm six now, ain't I, Jim?

JIM: Well ... and you're a-goin' today.

DAN'L: But it's Mamma and Uncle Holly that's takin' me.

JIM: Papa would of done it iffen he'd stayed here. Anyways, hit's much the same. We're goin' to see him.

DAN'L: Do Papa live in Czardis now?

JIM: I don't rightly know. He went there a long time back, but ...

MAMMA (*off-mike, cutting in*): Jim! Dan'l!

JIM: Yes, Mamma?

MAMMA (*off-mike*): Are you a-gettin' your clothes on? Breakfast is 'most fixed.

JIM: Yes, ma'am. (*To* DAN'L) Come on, pile outen that bed.

(*Sound: Bare feet on floor boards.*)

DAN'L (*shiveringly*): Oh-h ... the cold aches me!

JIM: Skin into your britches quick, while I'm a-holdin' 'em. There. Stay still now, and I'll get that shirt over your head. (*Soothingly.*) You won't be shiverin' long, Dan'l. Hit's goin' to be fair. Mournin' doves startin' a'ready. The sun'll bake you warm.

DAN'L: Is it sunshiny in Czardis?

JIM: Hit's past believin', Dan'l. And when it shines on that gold ball that's perched on the courthouse ...

DAN'L: The one that's bigger'n our well?

JIM: Hit's twenty-five foot round the mid—

MAMMA (*off-mike; cuts in*): Come eat now, you young 'uns!

JIM (*calling*): Yes, ma'am, We're a-coming!

(*Sound: Double footsteps gropingly descend a stairway. Continue through next speeches.*)

JIM: Catch a holt of my hand. These stairs is mighty dark.

DAN'L: Mornin', Mamma!

MAMMA: Mornin', boys. (*A pause.*) You look right neat. But your hands could be a mite cleaner. There's a bucket of fresh water yonder and some soap. Look careful you don't drip none on your clothes.

(*Sound: Splashing of water continues through next two speeches.*)

DAN'L: Might I could touch the gold ball, Jim?

JIM: Not lessen you was to get you the tallest ladder in Floridy and climb up to the courthouse roof. Then you'd need you another ladder to . . .

MAMMA: Draw up, boys, and get to eatin'. Dan'l, you look half froze. Best set close to the stove.

(*Sound: Scraping of chairs on floor.*)

MAMMA (*sternly*): Ain't you forgot somethin', Jim?

JIM: Huh? . . . Oh! . . . (*In a rapid singsong.*) We give thanks, Lord, fur the food that Thou hast provided and that we're a-goin' to eat. Amen.

MAMMA: I don't want never again to see you tearin' into your rations before you've said a blessin' for 'em.

JIM (*meekly*): I didn't study to do it, Mamma. It's jest that I was thinkin' about us goin' to see Papa in Czardis till I forgot.

MAMMA: All right; go ahead and eat now, so's you'll be ready when your Uncle Holly comes.

DAN'L (*in a confidential undertone to* JIM): Will Uncle Holly buy us lemonade in Czardis?

JIM: It ain't decided yet. He ain't spoke.

DAN'L (*hopefully*): Mebbe Papa . . .

JIM: Likely Papa will. Mebbe somethin' better'n lemon-ade.

DAN'L: What would it be?

JIM: It might could be ice-cream cones.

DAN'L (*rapturously*): Ice-cream cones? Oh, Jim!

(*Sound: Sound of knock on light door.*)

JIM (*warningly*): Hush! There's Uncle Holly now.

(*Sound: Door opens.*)

MAMMA: Mornin', Holly.

HOLLY: Mornin', Mary. Mornin', young 'uns.

(*Sound: Door slams shut.*)

DAN'L (*with shrill eagerness*): Can I sit up in front with you, Uncle Holly?

HOLLY: I'll have to study about that, Dan'l. (*To* MAMMA, *in a low, disapproving voice*) You fixed on takin' them still?

MAMMA (*quietly*): I am.

HOLLY: I reckon you know, Mary, hit's not my nature to meddle in other folks' doin's, but I can't he'p thinkin' you're dead wrong to take 'em. It'd be different if they were older.

JIM (*breaks in protestingly*): Uncle Holly! I'm ten years now, and Papa takened me when I wasn't hardly older'n Dan'l.

MAMMA: Hush, Jim. (*Still very quiet but with complete finality.*) He asked to see them, Holly. Nobody but God Almighty ought to tell a soul what it can or can't have.

HOLLY: God knows I don't grudge him the sight of 'em. I were only thinkin' iffen they were my sons . . .

MAMMA: They are Jim's sons, Holly. (*Abruptly.*) It's time I were hitchin' the wagon. You can he'p me if you've a mind to. (*Fading.*) Boys, come out soon's you finish. Don't tarry.

(*Sound: Door opens and closes.*)

DAN'L: That were mighty mean of Uncle Holly.

JIM (*slowly*): Uncle Holly ain't got a mean bone to

his body. I cain't figger why he didn't want us, lessen he were feared we'd fret Papa while he's ailin'.

DAN'L: Is Papa ailin'?

JIM: Not bad. But the doctor don't like too many folks a-visitin' him. He must be a sight better now, though, or Mamma wouldn't be takin' us. (*A pause.*) You haven't et your corn pone.

DAN'L: I'm savin' it to take to Papa.

JIM: Papa don't crave e'er ol' corn pone.

DAN'L: Mebbe he would want to have my whistle—the one that were in the Crackerjack box Uncle Holly brung me.

JIM: That ain't a whistle fur a man, Dan'l. Papa'd jest laugh at a puny, squeakin' trick like that.

(*Sound: Chair pushed back.*)

JIM: Iffen you've et enough, we'd best go out. Mamma'll be riled if we keep 'em waitin'.

DAN'L: All right. (*Wistfully.*) Seems like there must be somethin' I could take him.

(*Sound: Opening and shutting of door; then sound of horses stamping near at hand.*)

MAMMA: Jim, where you off to?

JIM (*off-mike, breathlessly*): Jest a minute!

MAMMA: Come back here. You hear me? (*Voice growing fainter as she pursues him.*) Jim! (*Voice comes up stronger again.*) Get down out of there! Are worms gnawin' you that you skin up a pomegranate tree at this hour? Don't I feed you enough?

JIM (*timidly*): I were only . . .

MAMMA (*cuts in, more quietly*): We ain't yet come to the shame of you and Dan'l huntin' your food offen the trees and grass. People passin' on the road and seein' you gnawin' will say that Jim Cameron's sons are starved, foragin' like cattle of the field.

JIM: I were gettin' the pomegranates fur Papa.

MAMMA: Oh. . . . (*Gently.*) I guess we won't take any, Jim. But I'm proud it come to you to take your papa somethin'.

JIM (*a bit reluctantly*): Well . . . hit were Dan'l it come to, Mamma.

MAMMA: It were a fine thought, and I'm right proud . . . though today we won't take anything.

JIM: I guess there's better pomegranates in Czardis anyways.

MAMMA: There's no better pomegranates in all Floridy than what's right above your head. Iffen pomegranates were needed (*a faint tremor in her voice*), we would take him his own.

JIM (*anxiously*): Is Papa feelin' too poorly to relish 'em?

MAMMA (*hesitates*): Yes . . . I reckon he is. . . . You'd best got to know, Jim . . . Papa won't be like you recollect him. He's been right sick . . . sicker'n I've let on to you till now. Dan'l were sech a baby when he seen him last that he won't take any notice likely . . . but you're older, son.

JIM (*troubled*): Mamma . . .

MAMMA (*trying desperately to keep back the tears*): Papa will look pale, and he won't be as bright-mannered as you recollect. So don't labor him with questions. Speak when it behooves you, and let him see you are upright.

JIM: Yes, Mamma. (*With anxious eagerness.*) He's mendin' now, though, ain't he? He's gettin' . . .

HOLLY (*calling off-mike*): Sun's risin', Mary.

MAMMA (*her voice trailing off as she walks away*): Come along. We got to get started.

(*Sound: A horse whinnies. Stomping of horses' hoofs.*)

HOLLY: Climb up in back of your ma, young 'uns. I've bedded it down with straw to spare your bones some.

DAN'L: Ain't you drivin', Uncle Holly?

MAMMA: Uncle Holly's goin' ahead of us in his own wagon. Get in, Dan'l.

JIM: Why do we got to take two wagons? Can't we all ride together in Uncle Holly's?

DAN'L: His horse goes faster'n ours.

HOLLY (*brusquely*): Climb in, you pesky little varmints, before I toss you in.

MAMMA (*off-mike*): What are you doin' back there, Holly?

HOLLY: I were fixin' to put the top up. Could be you'd feel right glad to have it over you when we get to the highway.

MAMMA (*off-mike*): I thank you, but we're all right as we are.

DAN'L: We don't never have the top up lessen rain's fallin'.

HOLLY (*muttering*): There's things a shield'd be needed against more'n rain.

JIM: What things, Uncle Holly?

HOLLY (*embarrassed*): Uh . . . er . . . why the sun, young 'un. Hit's like to be a turrible hot day. You'll be plumb roasted time we get to Czardis.

DAN'L: I like feelin' roasted.

MAMMA: I been ridin' under the open sky all my life. So has the boys. I guess we won't change our ways today.

HOLLY (*resignedly*): Iffen that's the way you feel, Mary, there's no more to be said. I'll go on now.

(*Sound: Receding footsteps on clay road.*)

HOLLY (*off-mike, calling back*): Do I be gettin' too far ahead, give a holler and I'll slow her down. Giddyap.

(*Sound: Horse's hoofs off, jog-trotting briskly away, continuing through next speeches.*)

DAN'L (*excitedly*): Betsy's a-trottin'! Hurry, Mamma, hurry!

(*Sound: A cluck to the horse, more hoofbeats come up; the pace quickens under the pattern of sound.*
Music: Starts softly, grows in volume. The sound of the hoofbeats fades out. Music plays for a long interval. Then it fades into
Sound: Hoofbeats, this time sharper and more staccato, as though falling on asphalt instead of clay. An auto horn sounds faintly in the distance, and the wheezing noise of an ancient car comes up gradually.)

DAN'L (*cutting in and over car noise*): Howdy! Yoo-hoo, Miz Fletcher!

(*Sound: Roar of car passing, fading gradually into clop-clop of hoofbeats, which continue in background.*)

DAN'L: Jim! That were Fletcher's truck went by us!

JIM: Sounded like it.

DAN'L: Miz Fletcher were sittin' up on the front seat, and Clem were drivin' it. (*Disappointedly.*) Wonder why they didn't holler back?

JIM: Likely they didn't hear you. That ol' car makes sech a ruckus you couldn't hardly hear a wildcat was he to howl in your ear.

DAN'L (*wistfully*): It do go fast, though.

JIM: Not so turrible fast. Were we to try, we could give 'em a right good race in the wagon.

DAN'L (*doubtfully*): Mebbe.

JIM: And I bet Uncle Holly could beat the puddin' out of 'em with Betsy.

DAN'L (*sighs*): Jest the same, I'd admire to ride in a truck sometimes.

JIM: Did I ride, I'd pick me somethin' spryer'n Fletcher's ol' car.

(*Sound: "Beep-beep" of a modern motor horn and purr of auto passing at average speed; fades out quickly. Hoofbeats continue in background.*)

JIM: Now there goes somethin' like.

DAN'L: Hit sure were travelin'. And weren't it a purty one!

JIM: You'll see a heap jest as purty when we get to Czardis.

DAN'L: I already seen more'n I ever did before.

JIM: There do seem a plenty goin' our way, a heap of wagons too. Must be market day.

DAN'L (*in high excitement*): Oh, Jim! Then will I get to see the balloon man? And the horses that makes music?

JIM: Iffen hit's market day, they'll be there.

DAN'L: Mamma, is it market day today in Czardis? (*Mamma makes no reply.*) Is it, Mamma?

MAMMA: You and Jim get your mind offen balloons and flyin' horses and sech. We've no business that'll take us to the market today, be they havin' it or not.

DAN'L (*plaintively*): Aw, Mamma!

MAMMA (*sternly*): I don't want to hear you frettin', Dan'l, and I don't want to hear you tormentin' Papa to take you, neither.

JIM (*quickly*): We won't, Mamma. (*In a low tone to* DAN'L.) Don't take on, Dan'l. There's a sight of things in Czardis besides the market.

DAN'L (*in an anxious whisper*): Papa'll buy us the ice-cream cones, won't he?

JIM: You don't want to go askin' him fur 'em.

DAN'L (*whimpering*): But you told me . . .

JIM (*cuts in*): Hush up, and have patience. We'll get somethin' sure. (*In an effort to distract.*) Look! Ain't that old man Bennett a-turnin' at the fork?

DAN'L: Where?

JIM: Right up there ahead of us . . . ridin' on that runty little black horse. We'll be passin' him in a second.

MAMMA (*severely*): Don't neither of you call to him or wave. Sit up tall, and look straight ahead like I do.

(*Sound: Hoofbeats come up and then fade again into the distance.*)

MAMMA: You stay that way now. We're a-comin' into Czardis, and it ain't seemly for you to be lollin' all over the wagon, peerin' and hollerin' at everybody you see.

JIM: But, Mamma, should they call "howdy" to us first?

MAMMA (*bitterly*): There's a small risk of that. You do like I say, anyways. (*Pause.*)

DAN'L: Ain't it mannerly to call "howdy" in Czardis? (MAMMA *does not reply, and* DAN'L *speaks to* JIM *in a worried undertone.*) Is Mamma riled?"

JIM: Not truly, Dan'l. She jest . . . (*He hesitates.*)

DAN'L: Why does she keep rompin' on us fur?

JIM (*his growing bewilderment and apprehension escaping into his voice*): I don't rightly know. There's things this mornin' I jest cain't figger.

DAN'L (*after a pause*): Jim! Why you lookin' scairt?

JIM: Why I ain't! Whatever is there to be scairt of? (*Laughs.*) I never see the like of you fur gettin' notions. Look, Dan'l—rearin' up there against the sky!

DAN'L (*almost shouting*): Hits the water tower!

JIM: That's what it is.

DAN'L: I knowed it right off. Hit's jest like you told, only it goes up higher. Hit's higher'n even the big pine to Palmetto Swamp!

JIM: And yonder's the depot, where the trains come in from Jacksonville and sech.

(*Sound: Small-town street noises: clatter of horses' hoofs, an occasional "whoa," now and then an auto horn, and the hum of voices. All this is heard clearly for a moment, then fades into background.*)

DAN'L: Does all these folks live here, Jim?

JIM: This here's Main Street. All the stores mostly is along here, and the movin' pitcher theayter.

DAN'L (*breathlessly*): Where's that, Jim? Show me.

JIM: It's down the block a piece—(*In dismay.*) Mamma! Why's Uncle Holly turnin' off here?

MAMMA: Because that's the way we're goin'.

JIM: Cain't we keep along Main Street jest a little ways further? Dan'l ain't even . . .

(*Sound: Street noises flare up, then fade. The hoofbeats are now falling on cobblestones.*)

MAMMA (*almost pleadingly*): Please, Jim! Don't fuss.

DAN'L: I didn't get to see the movin' pitcher theayter.

JIM: Mebbe we can see it goin' back.

DAN'L: Jim! The gold ball!

JIM: Why, so 'tis! That must be the courthouse, on'y we're seein' it sideways 'stead of straight on, or mebbe that's the back of it. I've got kind of muddle-minded with all this twistin' and turnin' we're doin'.

DAN'L: What's the other big buildin'? The one with the wall all 'round it? Look, they got a bobbed-wire fence fixed on top of the wall! What's the sense of that? Ain't no bear nor wildcat could jump that high anyways, and they'd have a right hard time climbin' them slippery stones.

JIM: 'Tain't there to keep the beasts out. If I recollect right, this buildin' is . . .

DAN'L (*cuts in*): I never see so many windows! And

every one of 'em with rails acrost it.

JIM: Them ain't rails. Them're bars, made outen iron. This is—(*He breaks off suddenly, then goes on in a shrill voice compounded of horror and incredulity.*) Mamma! Uncle Holly's stopped here! He's hitchin' up Betsy to a tree!

MAMMA (*her voice deep with compassion*): We come to where we were goin', Jim.

(*Sound: Hoofbeats slowing to a walk, then stopping.*)

DAN'L: Can we get out, Mamma?

MAMMA: In a second, son.

DAN'L: Who's that man Uncle Holly's talkin' to at the gate? Is he a soldier? (*No one replies.*) Mamma! Look at all the men peerin' out the windows.

HOLLY (*in a low voice*): Hit's all right, Mary. I talked to him and he'll let us in this way. Like I thought, they's mostly gathered on the other side.

MAMMA: Get out, boys.

HOLLY: Hold your arms out, and I'll lift you down.

DAN'L: Why do they have those things acrost the windows, Uncle Holly? Jim says they're made outen iron.

JIM (*in a high, strained, unnatural voice, close to hysteria*): Hush up, Dan'l! Don't talk. Don't say nothin' more. We're goin' to see Papa now, and he's sick. Talkin' makes him worse. He's turrible sick . . . turrible, turrible sick.

(*Music: Tempestuous and somber. Sustained at length, then fading into*
Sound: Footsteps of five people passing down corridor.)

GUARD: Jest come along this way, Miz Cameron.

(*Sound: Footsteps continue for a second, then halt. A key grating in lock. The clang of a steel door being shut and locked again.*)

GUARD: Right down the hall, ma'am, where the deputy's standin'. He's got the door open for you.

HOLLY: Me'n the boys'll wait here a spell, Mary. You jest call us when you're ready.

JIM (*in a low voice*): Mamma . . .

MAMMA: Wait here with your uncle, now. (*Huskily.*) I'm right proud of you, son. (*A long pause.*) We're here, Jim.

PAPA (*agonized*): Mary! Mary!

MAN: Mornin', Miz Cameron.

MAMMA: Mornin', Reverend.

MAN: I'll be comin' back, Jim. Good-by, ma'am; God bless you and he'p you.

MAMMA: I thank you, Reverend.

(*Sound: Slight creak of hinge. Soft footsteps receding.*)

PAPA: Let me holt you to me, Mary, honey. Let me feel you to me again!

MAMMA (*passionately*): Jim! Jim! I ain't never goin' to let loose of you. Ain't no one can make me. Ain't no one . . . (*Her voice breaks in a hard sob.*)

PAPA (*recovering*): This ain't the way fur me to act—makin' the misery worse fur you.

MAMMA: There's no makin' worse what I'm feelin'.

PAPA (*cuts in*): Young 'uns come?

MAMMA (*controlling herself*): Like you asked. They're waitin' with Holly.

PAPA: I thank you, Mary. I know it were cruel hard on you to bring 'em. Mebbe I shouldn't of asked it. But . . .

MAMMA: Hit's your right to see 'em, Jim.

PAPA: You ain't spoke to them?

MAMMA: Only to tell 'em you were ailin' bad. I'll fetch 'em in now. (*Calls softly.*) Holly! You can come along now.

PAPA (*quickly*): Do they guess more'n you . . .

MAMMA: Dan'l don't. He's too little. But Jim's right sharp and—(*Breaks off.*) Step in, boys, and greet your papa.

(*Sound: Creak of hinge. Brief, shuffling footsteps.*)

PAPA: Mornin', Holly. . . . Jim! Dan'l! Hit's a treat to see you, sons! It's a treat to my heart!

MAMMA (*speaking after a silence*): Have your feet froze to the ground that you cain't do nothin' but stand there gapin'? Seems like you'd want to give your papa a hug after not seein' him fur so long.

DAN'L (*shyly*): Howdy, Papa.

JIM: Oh, Papa . . .

(*Sound: Confused, tremulous laughter and broken endearments as first* JIM, *then* DAN'L *throw themselves into their father's arms.*)

JIM (*his voice catching*): I'm turrible happy to see you, Papa!

PAPA (*jerkily*): Me, too, Jim! Me, too, young 'un! And Dan'l! I'm like to squeeze the breath outen you both, I'm that glad.

DAN'L: We come all the way in the wagon, Papa.

PAPA: That were quite a trip fur you, young feller. You ain't done so much travelin' yet.

DAN'L: I aimed to bring you my whistle, but Jim said it made too puny a sound fur a man.

PAPA: Never mind, Dan'l. The thought you would want to bring it pleasures me more'n the finest whistle in the world.

MAMMA: Jim, here, picked some pomegranates offen the tree to bring you, but I . . .

PAPA: Son, I'm mighty happy you recollected how I used to love them pomegranates. I thank you. I'm right proud of both you and Dan'l.

HOLLY: Jim . . . I hates to say it, and you too, Mary, but this feller outside says there ain't much more'n ten minutes now. Iffen you want to get the young 'uns out, Mary . . .

JIM: Do we got to go?

PAPA: Yes, son.

MAMMA (*uncontrollably*): Oh, Jim!

PAPA (*gently*): Best go now, Mary. I want you should be on the road before . . .

JIM: Can we come back soon, Papa? Might we could come back next week?

PAPA: Come over here, son, and you too, Dan'l. Papa wants to say somethin' fur you to hear.

DAN'L: Papa, will you . . .

MAMMA (*cutting in*): Dan'l! Listen while your papa's speakin'.

PAPA: I want you should both grow up to be upright men. Take care of your mamma, and always do her biddin'.

JIM (*in a stifled voice*): Yes, Papa.

PAPA: Mind against anger catchin' you by the throat and blindin' your eyes. Anger and hate—don't never let them master you and drive you on. (*A pause.*) I'm goin' to give you my watch, Jim. You're the oldest. I want you should keep it till you're a grown man. And, Dan'l, here is the chain. That's fur you.

HOLLY: Come on, young 'uns. Come along with me.

DAN'L: Ain't Mamma . . .

HOLLY: She'll follow after. Come along.

DAN'L (*off, voice receding*): I thank you, Papa.

PAPA (*desperately*): Mary, honey! Mary, honey!

(*Music: Surges up menacingly, then fades under and out.*)

HOLLY: You want I should walk to the wagon with you, Mary? There's a millin' throng out there.

MAMMA (*with still, cold hatred*): Black-hearted trash! May what they've come to peer at rot their eyes in their heads! We'll walk alone, Holly. You wait here.

(*Sound: A door opens. Then rises the muffled roar of a great crowd.*)

DAN'L (*voice high with excitement*): Look yonder at them trees! Every one full of folks, perched up like squirrels!

JIM (*shrill with shock and horror*): Mamma! They're a-peerin' over the wall here! They're . . .

MAMMA (*fiercely*): Put your head up, son. Dan'l, catch a holt of my hand. Come along now, and don't waste one look at that swarm of carrion flies!

(*Sound: Crowd noises up to a roar, long and terrifying. Abruptly they are cut off. A short pause.*

Music: The opening theme holds softly for a time, then fades to the regular clop-clop of horses' hoofs.)

JIM: Mamma?

MAMMA: Yes, Jim.

JIM (*chokingly*): Is Papa . . . comin' home with Uncle Holly?

MAMMA: Yes, son.

JIM: (*Sobs.*)

DAN'L: We never got our ice-cream cones, did we, Jim?

JIM: (*Sobs are louder, more convulsive.*)

DAN'L: Don't take on. We got somethin' better. We got a watch and chain, Jim.

JIM (*through his weeping*): Dan'l . . . he don't know, Mamma.

MAMMA: No, son.

(*Sound: The hoofbeats become more insistent under* JIM'S *sobs.*)

DAN'L (*with slow, happy wonder*): I never see scch a place as Czardis!

Music: Welling up in quick climax.

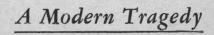

A Modern Tragedy

JOHN MILLINGTON SYNGE:

Riders to the Sea

John Millington Synge was born in Ireland in 1871 and died thirty-eight years later at the height of his powers. He received his education in Ireland and, after his graduation from Dublin's Trinity College, continued his studies on the Continent. In Paris, where he was writing poetry and translating French Symbolist poets, Synge met William Butler Yeats, who urged him to study the language and the culture of their native Ireland. Settling for a time on the Aran Islands, learning the vocabulary and the inflections of Irish peasant speech, Synge—out of this experience—composed five plays, including his masterpiece, *The Playboy of the Western World* (1907), the unfinished *Deirdre of the Sorrows,* and the one-act tragedy, *Riders to the Sea. The Playboy,* in its first performances at the Abbey Theater in 1908, provoked riots (and further outbreaks in subsequent performances in Philadelphia and New York). Synge's hardheaded, realistic portrayal of the Irish, which provided a model for Sean O'Casey, was the major force in establishing the Irish dramatic revival.

Riders to the Sea is nearly always described as a modern tragedy, a term rarely applied to a one-act play. In point of fact, few plays since the seventeenth century have been accepted as true tragedies; Synge's play, compared with *Agamemnon* or *Oedipus Rex* or *Lear* or *Phédre,* seems like a different kind of play. In classical tragedy, the tragic hero is the victim of Fate, suffering from a tribal curse which the gods require that he expiate. The renaissance and seventeenth-century tragedies, products of a Christian culture, magnify the flaw in the tragic hero's nature—a flaw that brings about his misfortunes, which generally enable him to find redemption through death and transfiguration.

If Maurya is the protagonist of *Riders to the Sea* we are given no hint that she is living under a tribal curse or that her misfortunes are due to some weakness that resides within her. Rather than assuming the role of a tragic heroine (like Hecuba in Euripides' *The Trojan Women*) Maurya is more the stoic victim who bows to the unhappy circumstances which have robbed her of all her sons.

Riders to the Sea takes on a tragic dimension if we identify Maurya with Ireland as a mother country losing its sons through war, famine, and disease. But even on its own terms, as a play about a single family, the tragic note is unmistakable. Can we not identify those elements within the play which provide us with the tragic sense of life? Do we not hear in the voice of Maurya the voice of the poor and dispossessed in all countries, in all time— the voice which accepts all the blows that life can rain down upon a human being and yet can say, "We must be satisfied."?

Riders to the Sea

Characters

MAURYA, *an old woman.*
BARTLEY, *her son.*
CATHLEEN, *her daughter.*
NORA, *a younger daughter.*
MEN *and* WOMEN.

Errand Islands

(SCENE: *An island off the coast of Ireland. Cottage kitchen, with nets, oilskins, spinning wheel, some new boards standing by the wall, etc.* CATHLEEN, *a girl of about twenty, finishes kneading cake, and puts it down in the pot oven by the fire; then wipes her hands, and begins to spin at the wheel.* NORA, *a young girl, puts her head in at the door.*)

NORA (*in a low voice*): Where is she?

CATHLEEN: She's lying down, God help her, and maybe sleeping if she's able.

(NORA *comes in softly, and takes a bundle from under her shawl.*)

CATHLEEN (*spinning the wheel rapidly*): What is it you have?

NORA: The young priest is after bringing them. It's a shirt and a plain stocking were got off a drowned man in Donegal.

(CATHLEEN *stops her wheel with a sudden movement, and leans out to listen.*)

NORA: We're to find out if it's Michael's they are; sometime herself will be down looking by the sea.

CATHLEEN: How would they be Michael's, Nora? How would he go the length of that way to the Far North?

NORA: The young priest says he's known the like of it. "If it's Michael's they are," says he, "you can tell herself he's got a clean burial by the grace of God, and if they're not his, let no one say a word about them, for she'll be getting her death," says he, "with crying and lamenting."

(*The door which* NORA *half closed is blown open by a gust of wind.*)

CATHLEEN (*looking out anxiously*): Did you ask him would he stop Bartley going this day with the horses to the Galway fair?

NORA: "I won't stop him," says he, "but let you not be afraid. Herself does be saying prayers half through the night, and the Almighty God won't leave her destitute," says he, "with no son living."

CATHLEEN: Is the sea bad by the white rocks, Nora?

NORA: Middling bad, God help us. There's a great roaring in the west, and it's worse it'll be getting when the tide's turned to the wind. (*She goes over to the table with the bundle.*) Shall I open it now?

CATHLEEN: Maybe she'd wake up on us, and come in before we'd done. (*Coming to the table.*) It's a long time we'll be, and the two of us crying.

NORA (*goes to the inner door and listens*): She's moving about on the bed. She'll be coming in a minute.

CATHLEEN: Give me the ladder, and I'll put them up in the turf loft, the way she won't know of them at all, and maybe when the tide turns she'll be going down to see would he be floating from the east.

(*They put the ladder against the gable of the chimney;* CATHLEEN *goes up a few steps and hides the bundle in the turf loft.* MAURYA *comes from the inner room.*)

MAURYA (*looking up at* CATHLEEN *and speaking querulously*): Isn't it turf enough you have for this day and evening?

CATHLEEN: There's a cake baking at the fire for a short space (*throwing down the turf*) and Bartley will want it when the tide turns if he goes to Connemara.

(NORA *picks up the turf and puts it round the pot oven.*)

MAURYA (*sitting down on a stool at the fire*): He won't

go this day with the wind rising from the south and west. He won't go this day, for the young priest will stop him surely.

NORA: He'll not stop him, Mother, and I heard Eamon Simon and Stephen Pheety and Colum Shawn saying he would go.

MAURYA: Where is he itself?

NORA: He went down to see would there be another boat sailing in the week, and I'm thinking it won't be long till he's here now, for the tide's turning at the green head, and the hooker's tacking from the east.

CATHLEEN: I hear someone passing the big stones.

NORA (*looking out*): He's coming now, and he's in a hurry.

BARTLEY (*comes in and looks round the room; speaking sadly and quietly*): Where is the bit of new rope, Cathleen, was bought in Connemara?

CATHLEEN (*coming down*): Give it to him, Nora; it's on a nail by the white boards. I hung it up this morning, for the pig with the black feet was eating it.

NORA (*giving him a rope*): Is that it, Bartley?

MAURYA: You'd do right to leave that rope, Bartley, hanging by the boards. (BARTLEY *takes the rope.*) It will be wanting in this place, I'm telling you, if Michael is washed up tomorrow morning, or the next morning, or any morning in the week, for it's a deep grave we'll make him by the grace of God.

BARTLEY (*beginning to work with the rope*): I've no halter the way I can ride down on the mare, and I must go now quickly. This is the one boat going for two weeks or beyond it, and the fair will be a good fair for horses, I heard them saying below.

MAURYA: It's a hard thing they'll be saying below if the body is washed up and there's no man in it to make the coffin, and I after giving a big price for the finest white boards you'd find in Connemara.

(*She looks round at the boards.*)

BARTLEY: How would it be washed up, and we after looking each day for nine days, and a strong wind blowing a while back from the west and south?

MAURYA: If it wasn't found itself, that wind is raising the sea, and there was a star up against the moon, and it rising in the night. If it was a hundred horses, or a thousand horses you had itself, what is the price of a thousand horses against a son where there is one son only?

BARTLEY (*working at the halter, to* CATHLEEN): Let you go down each day, and see the sheep aren't jumping in on the rye, and if the jobber comes you can sell the pig with the black feet if there is a good price going.

MAURYA: How would the like of her get a good price for a pig?

BARTLEY (*to* CATHLEEN): If the west wind holds with the last bit of the moon let you and Nora get up weed enough for another cock for the kelp. It's hard set we'll be from this day with no one in it but one man to work.

· MAURYA: It's hard set we'll be surely the day you're drownd'd with the rest. What way will I live and the girls with me, and I an old woman looking for the grave?

(BARTLEY *lays down the halter, takes off his old coat, and puts on a newer one of the same flannel.*)

BARTLEY (*to* NORA): Is she coming to the pier?

NORA (*looking out*): She's passing the green head and letting fall her sails.

BARTLEY (*getting his purse and tobacco*): I'll have half an hour to go down, and you'll see me coming again in two days, or in three days, or maybe in four days if the wind is bad.

MAURYA (*turning round to the fire, and putting her shawl over her head*): Isn't it a hard and cruel man won't hear a word from an old woman, and she holding him from the sea?

CATHLEEN: It's the life of a young man to be going on the sea, and who would listen to an old woman with one thing and she saying it over?

BARTLEY (*taking the halter*): I must go now quickly. I'll ride down on the red mare, and the gray pony'll run behind me. The blessing of God on you.

(*He goes out.*)

MAURYA (*crying out as he is in the door*): He's gone

now, God spare us, and we'll not see him again. He's gone now, and when the black night is falling I'll have no son left me in the world.

CATHLEEN: Why wouldn't you give him your blessing and he looking round in the door? Isn't it sorrow enough is on everyone in this house without your sending him out with an unlucky word behind him, and a hard word in his ear?

(MAURYA *takes up the tongs and begins raking the fire aimlessly without looking round.*)

NORA (*turning toward her*): You're taking away the turf from the cake.

CATHLEEN (*crying out*): The Son of God forgive us, Nora, we're after forgetting his bit of bread.

(*She comes over to the fire.*)

NORA: And it's destroyed he'll be going till dark night, and he after eating nothing since the sun went up.

CATHLEEN (*turning the cake out of the oven*): It's destroyed he'll be, surely. There's no sense left on any person in a house where an old woman will be talking forever.

(MAURYA *sways herself on her stool.*)

CATHLEEN (*cutting off some of the bread and rolling it in a cloth, to* MAURYA): Let you go down now to the spring-well and give him this and he passing. You'll see him then and the dark word will be broken, and you can say, "God speed you," the way he'll be easy in his mind.

MAURYA (*taking the bread*): Will I be in it as soon as himself?

CATHLEEN: If you go now quickly.

MAURYA (*standing up unsteadily*): It's hard set I am to walk.

CATHLEEN (*looking at her anxiously*): Give her the stick, Nora, or maybe she'll slip on the big stones.

NORA: What stick?

CATHLEEN: The stick Michael brought from Connemara.

MAURYA (*taking a stick* NORA *gives her*): In the big

world the old people do be leaving things after them for their sons and children, but in this place it is the young men do be leaving things behind for them that do be old.

(*She goes out slowly.* NORA *goes over to the ladder.*)

CATHLEEN: Wait, Nora, maybe she'd turn back quickly. She's that sorry, God help her, you wouldn't know the thing she'd do.

NORA: Is she gone round by the bush?

CATHLEEN (*looking out*): She's gone now. Throw it down quickly, for the Lord knows when she'll be out of it again.

NORA (*getting the bundle from the loft*): The young priest said he'd be passing tomorrow, and we might go down and speak to him below if it's Michael's they are surely.

CATHLEEN (*taking the bundle*): Did he say what way they were found?

NORA (*coming down*): "There were two men," says he, "and they rowing round with poteen before the cocks crowed, and the oar of one of them caught the body, and they passing the black cliffs of the north."

CATHLEEN (*trying to open the bundle*): Give me a knife, Nora; the string's perished with the salt water, and there's a black knot on it you wouldn't loosen in a week.

NORA (*giving her a knife*): I've heard tell it was a long way to Donegal.

CATHLEEN (*cutting the string*): It is surely. There was a man in here a while ago—the man sold us that knife—and he said if you set off walking from the rocks beyond it, it would be seven days you'd be in Donegal.

NORA: And what time would a man take, and he floating?

(CATHLEEN *opens the bundle and takes out a bit of a stocking. They look at them eagerly.*)

CATHLEEN (*in a low voice*): The Lord spare us, Nora! Isn't it a queer hard thing to say if it's his they are surely?

NORA: I'll get his shirt off the hook the way we can put the one flannel on the other. (*She looks through some clothes hanging in the corner.*) It's not with them, Cathleen, and where will it be?

CATHLEEN: I'm thinking Bartley put it on him in the morning, for his own shirt was heavy with the salt in it. (*Pointing to the corner.*) There's a bit of a sleeve was of the same stuff. Give me that and it will do.

(NORA *brings it to her and they compare the flannel.*)

CATHLEEN: It's the same stuff, Nora; but if it is itself, aren't there great rolls of it in the shops of Galway, and isn't it many another man may have a shirt of it as well as Michael himself?

NORA (*who has taken up the stocking and counted the stitches, crying out*): It's Michael, Cathleen, it's Michael; God spare his soul, and what will herself say when she hears this story, and Bartley on the sea?

CATHLEEN (*taking the stocking*): It's a plain stocking.

NORA: It's the second one of the third pair I knitted, and I put up threescore stitches, and I dropped four of them.

CATHLEEN (*counts the stitches*): It's that number is in it. (*Crying out.*) Ah, Nora, isn't it a bitter thing to think of him floating that way to the Far North, and no one to keen him but the black hags that do be flying on the sea?

NORA (*swinging herself round, and throwing out her arms on the clothes*): And isn't it a pitiful thing when there is nothing left of a man who was a great rower and fisher, but a bit of an old shirt and a plain stocking?

CATHLEEN (*after an instant*): Tell me is herself coming, Nora? I hear a little sound on the path.

NORA (*looking out*): She is, Cathleen. She's coming up to the door.

CATHLEEN: Put these things away before she'll come in. Maybe it's easier she'll be after giving her blessing to Bartley, and we won't let on we've heard anything the time he's on the sea.

NORA (*helping* CATHLEEN *to close the bundle*): We'll put them here in the corner.

(*They put them into a hole in the chimney corner.* CATHLEEN *goes back to the spinning wheel.*)

NORA: Will she see it was crying I was?

CATHLEEN: Keep your back to the door the way the light'll not be on you.

(NORA *sits down at the chimney corner, with her back to the door.* MAURYA *comes in very slowly, without looking at the girls, and goes over to her stool at the other side of the fire. The cloth with the bread is still in her hand. The girls look at each other, and* NORA *points to the bundle of bread.*)

CATHLEEN (*after spinning for a moment*): You didn't give him his bit of bread?

(MAURYA *begins to keen softly, without turning round.*)

CATHLEEN: Did you see him riding down?

(MAURYA *goes on keening.*)

CATHLEEN (*a little impatiently*): God forgive you; isn't it a better thing to raise your voice and tell what you seen, than to be making lamentation for a thing that's done? Did you see Bartley, I'm saying to you.

MAURYA (*with a weak voice*): My heart's broken from this day.

CATHLEEN (*as before*): Did you see Bartley?

MAURYA: I seen the fearfulest thing.

CATHLEEN (*leaves her wheel and looks out*): God forgive you; he's riding the mare now over the green head, and the gray pony behind him.

MAURYA (*starts, so that her shawl falls back from her head and shows her white tossed hair; with a frightened voice*): The gray pony behind him.

CATHLEEN (*coming to the fire*): What is it ails you, at all?

MAURYA (*speaking very slowly*): I've seen the fearfulest thing any person has seen, since the day Bride Dara seen the dead man with a child in his arms.

CATHLEEN and NORA: Uah.

(*They crouch down in front of the old woman at the fire.*)

NORA: Tell us what it is you seen.

MAURYA: I went down to the spring-well, and I stood there saying a prayer to myself. Then Bartley came along, and he riding on the red mare with the gray pony behind him. (*She puts up her hands, as if to hide something from her eyes.*) The Son of God spare us, Nora!

CATHLEEN: What is it you seen?

MAURYA: I seen Michael himself.

CATHLEEN (*speaking softly*): You did not, Mother; it wasn't Michael you seen, for his body is after being found in the Far North, and he's got a clean burial by the grace of God.

MAURYA (*a little defiantly*): I'm after seeing him this day, and he riding and galloping. Bartley came first on the red mare; and I tried to say "God speed you," but something choked the words in my throat. He went by quickly; and, "The blessing of God on you," says he, and I could say nothing. I looked up then, and I crying, at the gray pony, and there was Michael upon it—with fine clothes on him, and new shoes on his feet.

CATHLEEN (*begins to keen*): It's destroyed we are from this day. It's destroyed, surely.

NORA: Didn't the young priest say the Almighty God wouldn't leave her destitute with no son living?

MAURYA (*in a low voice, but clearly*): It's little the like of him knows of the sea. . . . Bartley will be lost now, and let you call in Eamon to make me a good coffin out of the white boards, for I won't live after them. I've had a husband, and a husband's father, and six sons in this house— six fine men, though it was a hard birth I had with every one of them and they coming to the world—and some of them were found and some of them were not found, but they're gone now, the lot of them. . . . There were Stephen, and Shawn, were lost in the great wind, and found after in the Bay of Gregory of the Golden Mouth, and carried up the two of them on the one plank, and in by that door.

(*She pauses for a moment, the girls start as if they heard something through the door that is half open behind them.*)

NORA (*in a whisper*): Did you hear that, Cathleen? Did you hear a noise in the northeast?

CATHLEEN (*in a whisper*): There's someone after crying out by the seashore.

MAURYA (*continues without hearing anything*): There was Sheamus and his father, and his own father again, were lost in a dark night, and not a stick or sign was seen of them when the sun went up. There was Patch after was drowned out of a currach that turned over. I was sitting here with Bartley, and he a baby, lying on my two knees, and I seen two women, and three women, and four women coming in, and they crossing themselves, and not saying a word. I looked out then, and there were men coming after them, and they holding a thing in the half of a red sail, and water dripping out of it—it was a dry day, Nora—and leaving a track to the door.

(*She pauses again with her hand stretched out toward the door. It opens softly and old women begin to come in, crossing themselves on the threshold, and kneeling down in front of the stage with red petticoats over their heads.*)

MAURYA (*half in a dream, to* CATHLEEN): Is it Patch, or Michael, or what is it at all?

CATHLEEN: Michael is after being found in the Far North, and when he is found there how could he be here in this place?

MAURYA: There does be a power of young men floating round in the sea, and what way would they know if it was Michael they had, or another man like him, for when a man is nine days in the sea, and the wind blowing, it's hard set his own mother would be to say what man was it.

CATHLEEN: It's Michael, God spare him, for they're after sending us a bit of his clothes from the Far North.

(*She reaches out and hands* MAURYA *the clothes that belonged to* MICHAEL. MAURYA *stands up slowly, and takes them in her hands.* NORA *looks out.*)

NORA: They're carrying a thing among them and there's

water dripping out of it and leaving a track by the big stones.

CATHLEEN (*in a whisper to the women who have come in*): Is it Bartley it is?

ONE OF THE WOMEN: It is surely, God rest his soul.

(*Two younger women come in and pull out the table. Then men carry in the body of* BARTLEY, *laid on a plank, with a bit of a sail over it, and lay it on the table.*)

CATHLEEN (*to the women, as they are doing so*): What way was he drowned?

ONE OF THE WOMEN: The gray pony knocked him into the sea, and he was washed out where there is a great surf on the white rocks.

(MAURYA *has gone over and knelt down at the head of the table. The women are keening softly and swaying themselves with a slow movement.* CATHLEEN *and* NORA *kneel at the other end of the table. The men kneel near the door.*)

MAURYA (*raising her head and speaking as if she did not see the people around her*): They're all gone now, and there isn't anything more the sea can do to me. . . . I'll have no call now to be up crying and praying when the wind breaks from the south, and you can hear the surf is in the east, and the surf is in the west, making a great stir with the two noises, and they hitting one on the other. I'll have no call now to be going down and getting holy water in the dark nights after Samhain, and I won't care what way the sea is when the other women will be keening. (*To* NORA) Give me the holy water, Nora; there's a small cup still on the dresser.

(NORA *gives it to her.*)

MAURYA (*drops* MICHAEL'S *clothes across* BARTLEY'S *feet, and sprinkles the holy water over him*): It isn't that I haven't prayed for you, Bartley, to the Almighty God. It isn't that I haven't said prayers in the dark night till you wouldn't know what I'd be saying; but it's a great rest I'll have now, and it's time surely. It's a great rest I'll have now, and great sleeping in the long nights after Samhain, if it's only a bit of wet flour we do have to eat, and maybe a fish that would be stinking.

(*She kneels down again, crossing herself, and saying prayers under her breath.*)

CATHLEEN (*to an old man*): Maybe yourself and Eamon would make a coffin when the sun rises. We have fine white boards herself bought, God help her, thinking Michael would be found, and I have a new cake you can eat while you'll be working.

THE OLD MAN (*looking at the boards*): Are there nails with them?

CATHLEEN: There are not, Colum; we didn't think of the nails.

ANOTHER MAN: It's a great wonder she wouldn't think of the nails, and all the coffins she's seen made already.

CATHLEEN: It's getting old she is, and broken.

(*MAURYA stands up again very slowly and spreads out the pieces of* MICHAEL'S *clothes beside the body, sprinkling them with the last of the holy water.*)

NORA (*in a whisper to* CATHLEEN): She's quiet now and easy; but the day Michael was drowned you could hear her crying out from this to the spring-well. It's fonder she was of Michael, and would anyone have thought that?

CATHLEEN (*slowly and clearly*): An old woman will be soon tired with anything she will do, and isn't it nine days herself is after crying and keening, and making great sorrow in the house?

MAURYA (*puts the empty cup mouth downward on the table, and lays her hands together on* BARTLEY'S *feet*): They're all together this time, and the end is come. May the Almighty God have mercy on Bartley's soul, and on Michael's soul, and on the souls of Sheamus and Patch, and Stephen and Shawn (*bending her head*); and may He have mercy on my soul, Nora, and on the soul of everyone is left living in the world.

(*She pauses, and the keen rises a little more loudly from the women, then sinks away.*)

MAURYA (*continuing*): Michael has a clean burial in the Far North, by the grace of the Almighty God. Bartley will have a fine coffin out of the white boards, and a deep grave surely. What more can we want than that? No man at all can be living forever, and we must be satisfied.

(*She kneels down again, and the curtain falls slowly.*)

An Experiment in Theater

THORNTON WILDER:

The Happy Journey

Thornton Wilder (1897–   ) was born in Madison, Wisconsin, and attended schools there as well as in China and in California before entering Oberlin College in 1915. His parents having moved to New Haven, Connecticut, Wilder spent his last two years of college at Yale, from which he was graduated, after military service, in 1920. While a teacher of French at Lawrenceville Academy, he completed his first novel, *The Cabala* (1926). His second novel, *The Bridge of San Luis Rey* (1927), brought him international recognition and the first of three Pulitzer prizes. Subsequent novels have been *The Woman of Andros* (1930), *Heaven's My Destination* (1934), *The Ides of March* (1948), and *The Eighth Day* (1967). Wilder is equally distinguished for his extraordinary contributions to the development of contemporary theater: *Our Town* (1938); *The Skin of Our Teeth* (1942); *The Matchmaker* (1954). *The Happy Journey* is one of six one-act plays first published in 1931 in a volume entitled *The Long Christmas Dinner and Other Plays in One Act*.

Apart from its very considerable merits as a work of dramatic literature, from the playwright-craftsman's point of view *The Happy Journey* is the most unconventional play in this volume. The one-act play has nearly always been limited to a particular place, as have the individual scenes of a full-length play: the forest of Arden, before the palace of Agamemnon, Lord Windermere's drawing room, a forward section of the main deck of the British tramp steamer *Glencairn,* two park benches in New York's Central Park. But influenced by the Chinese theater and by the motion picture Wilder added another dimension to the play: space, and movement in space. (Some years later, in *Our Town*, a play in the form of a landscape, again using a bare stage, Wilder simulated life in virtually an entire New England village.)

But Wilder is something more than a skillful crafts-man and innovator. His plays are evocative and deeply moving without ever becoming sentimental or bathetic. Few of us can see or read *The Happy Journey* without recalling events, characters, situations, and even turns of phrase from our own intimate past. Nothing unusual happens; the play is not obviously *dramatic* and yet it evokes both laughter and tears. Despite the casualness of it all, there is an underlying suspense, a confrontation, and a resolution.

The Happy Journey

Characters

THE STAGE MANAGER.
MA KIRBY.
ARTHUR (*thirteen*).
CAROLINE (*fifteen*).
PA (ELMER) KIRBY.
BEULAH (*twenty-two*).

No scenery is required for this play. The idea is that no place is being represented. This may be achieved by a gray curtain back-drop with no side-pieces; a cyclorama; or the empty bare stage.

(*As the curtain rises* THE STAGE MANAGER *is leaning lazily against the proscenium pillar at the left. He is smoking.* ARTHUR *is playing marbles down center in pantomime.* CAROLINE *is way up left talking to some girls who are invisible to us.* MA KIRBY *is anxiously putting on her hat* [real] *before an imaginary mirror up right.*)

MA: Where's your pa? Why isn't he here? I declare we'll never get started.

ARTHUR: Ma, where's my hat? I guess I don't go if I can't find my hat.

(*Still playing marbles.*)

MA: Go out into the hall and see if it isn't there. Where's Caroline gone to now, the plagued child?

ARTHUR: She's out waitin' in the street talkin' to the Jones girls.—I just looked in the hall a thousand times, Ma, and it isn't there. (*He spits for good luck before a difficult shot and mutters.*) Come on, baby.

MA: Go and look again, I say. Look carefully.

(ARTHUR *rises, reluctantly, crosses right, turns around, returns swiftly to his game center, flinging himself on the floor with a terrible impact, and starts shooting an aggie.*)

ARTHUR: No, Ma, it's not there.

MA (*serenely*): Well, you don't leave Newark without that hat, make up your mind to that. I don't go on journeys with a hoodlum.

ARTHUR: Aw, Ma!

(MA *comes down right to the footlights, pulls up an imaginary window and talks toward the audience.*)

MA (*calling*): Oh, Mrs. Schwartz!

THE STAGE MANAGER (*down left. Consulting his script*): Here I am, Mrs. Kirby. Are you going yet?

MA: I guess we're going in just a minute. How's the baby?

THE STAGE MANAGER: She's all right now. We slapped her on the back and she spat it up.

MA: Isn't that fine!—Well, now, if you'll be good enough to give the cat a saucer of milk in the morning and the evening, Mrs. Schwartz, I'll be ever so grateful to you.—Oh, good-afternoon, Mrs. Hobmeyer!

THE STAGE MANAGER: Good-afternoon, Mrs. Kirby, I hear you're going away.

MA (*modest*): Oh, just for three days, Mrs. Hobmeyer, to see my married daughter, Beulah, in Camden. Elmer's got his vacation week from the laundry early this year, and he's just the best driver in the world.

(CAROLINE *comes down stage right and stands by her mother.*)

THE STAGE MANAGER: Is the whole family going?

MA: Yes, all four of us that's here. The change ought to be good for the children. My married daughter was downright sick a while ago——

THE STAGE MANAGER: Tchk—tchk—tchk! Yes. I remember you tellin' us.

MA (*with feeling*): And I just want to go down and see the child. I ain't seen her since then. I just won't rest easy in my mind without I see her. (*To* CAROLINE) Can't you say good-afternoon to Mrs. Hobmeyer?

CAROLINE (*lowers her eyes and says woodenly*): Good-afternoon, Mrs. Hobmeyer.

THE STAGE MANAGER: Good-afternoon, dear. —Well, I'll wait and beat these rugs until after you're gone, because I don't want to choke you. I hope you have a good time and find everything all right.

MA: Thank you, Mrs. Hobmeyer, I hope I will. —Well, I guess that milk for the cat is all, Mrs. Schwartz, if you're sure you don't mind. If anything should come up, the key to the back door is hanging by the ice-box.

CAROLINE: Ma! Not so loud.

ARTHUR: Everybody can hear yuh.

MA: Stop pullin' my dress, children. (*In a loud whisper.*) The key to the back door I'll leave hangin' by the ice-box and I'll leave the screen door unhooked.

THE STAGE MANAGER: Now have a good trip, dear, and give my love to Beuhly.

MA: I will, and thank you a thousand times. (*She lowers the window, turns up stage, and looks around.* CAROLINE *goes left and vigorously rubs her cheeks.* MA *occupies herself with the last touches of packing.*) What can be keeping your pa?

ARTHUR (*who has not left his marbles*): I can't find my hat, Ma.

(*Enter* ELMER *holding a cap, up right.*)

ELMER: Here's Arthur's hat. He musta left it in the car Sunday.

MA: That's a mercy. Now we can start. —Caroline Kirby, what you done to your cheeks?

CAROLINE (*defiant-abashed*): Nothin'.

MA: If you've put anything on 'em, I'll slap you.

CAROLINE: No, Ma, of course I haven't. (*Hanging her head.*) I just rubbed 'm to make 'm red. All the girls do that at High School when they're goin' places.

MA: Such silliness I never saw. Elmer, what kep' you?

ELMER (*always even-voiced and always looking out a little anxiously through his spectacles*): I just went to the garage and had Charlie give a last look at it, Kate.

MA: I'm glad you did. (*Collecting two pieces of imaginary luggage and starting for the door.*) I wouldn't like to have no breakdown miles from anywhere. Now we can start. Arthur, put those marbles away. Anybody'd think you didn't want to go on a journey to look at yuh.

(*They go out through the "hall." MA opens an imaginary door down right. PA, CAROLINE, and ARTHUR go through it. MA follows, taking time to lock the door, hang the key by the "ice-box." They turn up at an abrupt angle, going up stage. As they come to the steps from the back porch, each arriving at a given point, starts bending his knees lower and lower to denote going downstairs, and find themselves in the street. THE STAGE MANAGER moves from the right the automobile. It is right center of the stage, seen partially at an angle, its front pointing down center.*)

ELMER (*coming forward*): Here, you boys, you keep away from that car.

MA: Those Sullivan boys put their heads into everything.

(*They get into the car. ELMER'S hands hold an imaginary steering wheel and continually shift gears. MA sits beside him. ARTHUR is behind him and CAROLINE is behind MA.*)

CAROLINE (*standing up in the back seat, waving, self-consciously*): Good-bye, Mildred. Good-bye, Helen.

THE STAGE MANAGER (*having returned to his position by the left proscenium*): Good-bye, Caroline. Good-bye, Mrs. Kirby. I hope y' have a good time.

MA: Good-bye, girls.

THE STAGE MANAGER: Good-bye, Kate. The car looks fine.

MA (*looking upward toward a window right*): Oh, good-bye, Emma! (*Modestly.*) We think it's the best little

Chevrolet in the world. —(*Looking up toward the left.*)
Oh, good-bye, Mrs. Adler!

THE STAGE MANAGER: What, are you going away, Mrs.
Kirby?

MA: Just for three days, Mrs. Adler, to see my married
daughter in Camden.

THE STAGE MANAGER: Have a good time.

(*Now* MA, CAROLINE, *and* THE STAGE MANAGER *break
out into a tremendous chorus of good-byes. The whole
street is saying good-bye.* ARTHUR *takes out his pea shoot-
er and lets fly happily into the air. There is a lurch or two
and they are off.*)

ARTHUR (*leaning forward in sudden fright*): Pa! Pa!
Don't go by the school. Mr. Biedenbach might see us!

MA: I don't care if he does see us. I guess I can take
my children out of school for one day without having to
hide down back streets about it. (ELMER *nods to a pas-
serby. Without sharpness.*) Who was that you spoke to,
Elmer?

ELMER: That was the fellow who arranges our ban-
quets down to the Lodge, Kate.

MA: Is he the one who had to buy four hundred steaks?
(PA *nods.*) I declare, I'm glad I'm not him.

ELMER: The air's getting better already. Take deep
breaths, children.

(*They inhale noisily.*)

ARTHUR (*pointing to a sign and indicating that it gradually goes by*): Gee, it's almost open fields already.
"*Weber and Heilbroner Suits for Well-dressed Men.*" Ma,
can I have one of them some day?

MA: If you graduate with good marks perhaps your father'll let you have one for graduation.

(*Pause. General gazing about, then sudden lurch.*)

CAROLINE (*whining*): Oh, Pa! do we have to wait
while that whole funeral goes by?

(ELMER *takes off his hat.* MA *cranes forward with absorbed curiosity.*)

MA (*not sharp and bossy*): Take off your hat, Arthur. Look at your father. —Why, Elmer, I do believe that's a lodge-brother of yours. See the banner? I suppose this is the Elizabeth branch. (ELMER *nods.* MA *sighs: Tchk-tchk-tchk. The children lean forward and all watch the funeral in silence, growing momentarily more solemnized. After a pause,* MA *continues almost dreamily but not sentimentally.*) Well, we haven't forgotten the funeral that we went on, have we? We haven't forgotten our good Harold. He gave his life for his country, we mustn't forget that. (*There is another pause; with cheerful resignation.*) Well, we'll all hold up the traffic for a few minutes some day.

THE CHILDREN (*very uncomfortable*): Ma!

MA (*without self-pity*): Well, I'm "ready," children. I hope everybody in this car is "ready." And I pray to go first, Elmer. Yes.

(ELMER *touches her hand.*)

CAROLINE: Ma, everybody's looking at you.

ARTHUR: Everybody's laughing at you.

MA: Oh, hold your tongues! I don't care what a lot of silly people in Elizabeth, New Jersey, think of me. —Now we can go on. That's the last.

(*There is another lurch and the car goes on.*)

CAROLINE (*looking at a sign and turning as she passes it*): "Fit-Rite Suspenders. The Working Man's Choice." Pa, why do they spell Rite that way?

ELMER: So that it'll make you stop and ask about it, Missy.

CAROLINE: Papa, you're teasing me. —Ma, why do they say "Three Hundred Rooms Three Hundred Baths"?

ARTHUR: "Miller's Spaghetti: The Family's Favorite Dish." Ma, why don't you ever have spaghetti?

MA: Go along, you'd never eat it.

ARTHUR: Ma, I like it now.

CAROLINE (*with gesture*): Yum-yum. It looked wonderful up there. Ma, make some when we get home?

MA (*dryly*): "The management is always happy to receive suggestions. We aim to please."

(*The children scream with laughter. Even* ELMER *smiles.* MA *remains modest.*)

ELMER. Well, I guess no one's complaining, Kate. Everybody knows you're a good cook.

MA: I don't know whether I'm a good cook or not, but I know I've had practice. At least I've cooked three meals a day for twenty-five years.

ARTHUR: Aw, Ma, you went out to eat once in a while.

MA: Yes. That made it a leap year.

(*The children laugh again.*)

CAROLINE (*in an ecstasy of well-being puts her arms around her mother*): Ma, I love going out in the country like this. Let's do it often, Ma.

MA: Goodness, smell that air, will you! It's got the whole ocean in it. —Elmer, drive careful over that bridge. This must be New Brunswick we're coming to.

ARTHUR (*after a slight pause*): Ma, when is the next comfort station?

MA (*unruffled*): You don't want one. You just said that to be awful.

CAROLINE (*shrilly*): Yes, he did, Ma. He's terrible. He says that kind of thing right out in school and I want to sink through the floor, Ma. He's terrible.

MA: Oh, don't get so excited about nothing, Miss Proper! I guess we're all yewman beings in this car, at least as far as I know. And, Arthur, you try and be a gentleman. —Elmer, don't run over that collie dog. (*She follows the dog with her eyes.*) Looked kinda peaked to me. Needs a good honest bowl of leavings. Pretty dog, too. (*Her eyes fall on a billboard at the right.*) That's a pretty advertisement for Chesterfield cigarettes, isn't it? Looks like Beulah, a little.

ARTHUR: Ma?

MA: Yes.

ARTHUR (*"route" rhymes with "out"*): Can't I take a paper route with the Newark *Daily Post*?

MA: No, you cannot. No, sir. I hear they make the

paper boys get up at four-thirty in the morning. No son of mine is going to get up at four-thirty every morning, not if it's to make a million dollars. Your *Saturday Evening Post* route on Thursday mornings is enough.

ARTHUR: Aw, Ma.

MA: No, sir. No son of mine is going to get up at four-thirty and miss the sleep God meant him to have.

ARTHUR (*sullenly*): Hhm! Ma's always talking about God. I guess she got a letter from Him this morning.

MA (*outraged*): Elmer, stop that automobile this minute. I don't go another step with anybody that says things like that. Arthur, you get out of this car. (ELMER *stops the car.*) Elmer, you give him a dollar bill. He can go back to Newark by himself. I don't want him.

ARTHUR: What did I say? There wasn't anything terrible about that.

ELMER: I didn't hear what he said, Kate.

MA: God has done a lot of things for me and I won't have Him made fun of by anybody. Get out of this car this minute.

CAROLINE: Aw, Ma—don't spoil the ride.

MA: No.

ELMER: We might as well go on, Kate, since we've got started. I'll talk to the boy tonight.

MA (*slowly conceding*): All right, if you say so, Elmer.

(ELMER *starts the car.*)

ARTHUR (*frightened*): Aw, Ma, that wasn't so terrible.

MA: I don't want to talk about it. I hope your father washes your mouth out with soap and water. —Where'd we all be if I started talking about God like that, I'd like to know! We'd be in the speakeasies and nightclubs and places like that, that's where we'd be.

CAROLINE (*after a very slight pause*): What did he say, Ma? I didn't hear what he said.

MA: I don't want to talk about it.

(*They drive on in silence for a moment, the shocked silence after a scandal.*)

ELMER: I'm going to stop and give the car a little water, I guess.

MA: All right, Elmer. You know best.

ELMER (*turns the wheel and stops; as to a garage hand*): Could I have a little water in the radiator—to make sure?

THE STAGE MANAGER (*in this scene alone he lays aside his script and enters into a rôle seriously*): You sure can. (*He punches the left front tire.*) Air all right? Do you need any oil or gas?

(*Goes up around car.*)

ELMER: No, I think not. I just got fixed up in Newark.

(THE STAGE MANAGER *carefully pours some water into the hood.*)

MA: We're on the right road for Camden, are we?

THE STAGE MANAGER (*coming down on right side of car*): Yes, keep straight ahead. You can't miss it. You'll be in Trenton in a few minutes. Camden's a great town, lady, believe me.

MA: My daughter likes it fine—my married daughter.

THE STAGE MANAGER: Ye'? It's a great burg all right. I guess I think so because I was born near there.

MA: Well, well. Your folks still live there?

THE STAGE MANAGER (*standing with one foot on the rung of* MA's *chair. They have taken a great fancy to one another*): No, my old man sold the farm and they built a factory on it. So the folks moved to Philadelphia.

MA: My married daughter Beulah lives there because her husband works in the telephone company. —Stop pokin' me, Caroline! —We're all going down to see her for a few days.

THE STAGE MANAGER: Ye'?

MA: She's been sick, you see, and I just felt I had to go and see her. My husband and my boy are going to stay at the Y.M.C.A. I hear they've got a dormitory on the top floor that's real clean and comfortable. Have you ever been there?

THE STAGE MANAGER: No. I'm Knights of Columbus myself.

MA: Oh.

THE STAGE MANAGER: I used to play basketball at the

Y though. It looked all right to me. (*He reluctantly moves away and pretends to examine the car again.*) Well, I guess you're all set now, lady. I hope you have a good trip; you can't miss it.

EVERYBODY: Thanks. Thanks a lot. Good luck to you.

(*Jolts and lurches.*)

MA (*with a sigh*): The world's full of nice people. —That's what I call a nice young man.

CAROLINE (*earnestly*): Ma, you oughtn't to tell 'm all everything about yourself.

MA: Well, Caroline, you do your way and I'll do mine. —He looked kinda pale to me. I'd like to feed him up for a few days. His mother lives in Philadelphia and I expect he eats at those dreadful Greek places.

CAROLINE: I'm hungry. Pa, there's a hot dog stand. K'n I have one?

ELMER: We'll all have one, eh, Kate? We had such an early lunch.

MA: Just as you think best, Elmer.

(ELMER *stops the car.*)

ELMER: Arthur, here's half a dollar. —Run over and see what they have. Not too much mustard either.

(ARTHUR *descends from the car and goes off stage right.* MA *and* CAROLINE *get out and walk a bit, up stage and to the left.* CAROLINE *keeps at her mother's right.*)

MA: What's that flower over there? —I'll take some of those to Beulah.

CAROLINE: It's just a weed, Ma.

MA: I like it. —My, look at the sky, wouldya! I'm glad I was born in New Jersey. I've always said it was the best state in the Union. Every state has something no other state has got.

(*Presently* ARTHUR *returns with his hands full of imaginary hot dogs which he distributes. First to his father, next to* CAROLINE, *who comes forward to meet him, and lastly to his mother. He is still very much cast down by the recent scandal, and as he approaches his mother says falteringly*):

ARTHUR: Ma, I'm sorry. I'm sorry for what I said.

(*He bursts into tears.*)

MA: There. There. We all say wicked things at times. I know you didn't mean it like it sounded. (*He weeps still more violently than before.*) Why, now, now! I forgive you, Arthur, and tonight before you go to bed you . . . (*She whispers.*) You're a good boy at heart, Arthur, and we all know it. (CAROLINE *starts to cry too.* MA *is suddenly joyously alive and happy.*) Sakes alive, it's too nice a day for us all to be cryin'. Come now, get in. (*Crossing behind car to the right side, followed by the children.*) Caroline, go up in front with your father. Ma wants to sit with her beau. (CAROLINE *sits in front with her father.* MA *lets* ARTHUR *get in car ahead of her; then she closes door.*) I never saw such children. Your hot dogs are all getting wet. Now chew them fine, everybody. —All right, Elmer, forward march. (*Car starts.* CAROLINE *spits.*) Caroline, whatever are you doing?

CAROLINE: I'm spitting out the leather, Ma.

MA: Then say: Excuse me.

CAROLINE: Excuse me, please.

(*She spits again.*)

MA: What's this place? Arthur, did you see the post office?

ARTHUR: It said Lawrenceville.

MA: Hhn. School kinda. Nice. I wonder what that big yellow house set back was. —Now it's beginning to be Trenton.

CAROLINE: Papa, it was near here that George Washington crossed the Delaware. It was near Trenton, Mama. He was first in war and first in peace, and first in the hearts of his countrymen.

MA (*surveying the passing world, serene and didactic*): Well the thing I like about him best was that he never told a lie. (*The children are duly cast down. There is a pause.* ARTHUR *stands up and looks at the car ahead.*)

There's a sunset for you. There's nothing like a good sunset.

ARTHUR: There's an Ohio license in front of us. Ma, have you ever been to Ohio?

MA: No.

(*A dreamy silence descends upon them.* CAROLINE *sits closer to her father, toward the left;* ARTHUR *closer to* MA *on the right, who puts her arm around him, unsentimentally.*)

ARTHUR: Ma, what a lotta people there are in the world, Ma. There must be thousands and thousands in the United States. Ma, how many are there?

MA: I don't know. Ask your father.

ARTHUR: Pa, how many are there?

ELMER: There are a hundred and twenty-six million, Kate.

MA (*giving a pressure about* ARTHUR'S *shoulder*): And they all like to drive out in the evening with their children beside 'm. Why doesn't somebody sing something? Arthur, you're always singing something; what's the matter with you?

ARTHUR: All right. What'll we sing?

(*He sketches.*)

In the Blue Ridge Mountains of Virginia,
On the . . .

No, I don't like that anymore. Let's do:

I been workin' on de railroad
   (CAROLINE *joins in.*)
All de liblong day.
   (MA *sings.*)
I been workin' on de railroad
   (ELMER *joins in.*)
Just to pass de time away.
Don't you hear de whistle blowin', etc.

(MA *suddenly jumps up with a wild cry and a large circular gesture.*)

MA: Elmer, that signpost said Camden. I saw it.

ELMER: All right, Kate, if you're sure.

(*Much shifting of gears, backing, and jolting.*)

MA: Yes, there it is. Camden—five miles. Dear old Beulah. (*The journey continues.*) Now, children, you be good and quiet during dinner. She's just got out of bed after a big sorta operation, and we must all move around kinda quiet. First you drop me and Caroline at the door and just say hello, and then you men-folk go over to the Y.M.C.A. and come back for dinner in about an hour.

CAROLINE (*shutting her eyes and pressing her fists passionately against her nose*): I see the first star. Everybody make a wish.

Star light, star bright,
First star I seen tonight.
I wish I may, I wish I might
Have the wish I wish tonight.

(*Then solemnly.*) Pins. Mama, you say "needles."

(*She interlocks little fingers with her mother across back of seat.*)

MA: Needles.

CAROLINE: Shakespeare. Ma, you say "Longfellow."

MA: Longfellow.

CAROLINE: Now it's a secret and I can't tell it to anybody. Ma, you make a wish.

MA (*with almost grim humor*): No, I can make wishes without waiting for no star. And I can tell my wishes right out loud too. Do you want to hear them?

CAROLINE (*resignedly*): No, Ma, we know 'm already. We've heard 'm. (*She hangs her head affectedly on her left shoulder and says with unmalicious mimicry.*) You want me to be a good girl and you want Arthur to be honest-in-word-and-deed.

MA (*majestically*): Yes. So mind yourself.

ELMER: Caroline, take out that letter from Beulah in my coat pocket by you and read aloud the places I marked with red pencil.

CAROLINE (*laboriously making it out*): "*A few blocks after you pass the two big oil tanks on your left . . .*"

EVERYBODY (*pointing backward*): There they are!

CAROLINE: "*. . . you come to a corner where there's an A and P store on the left and a firehouse kitty-corner to it . . .*" (*They all jubilantly identify these landmarks.*) "*. . . turn right, go two blocks and our house is Weyerhauser St. Number 471.*"

MA: It's an even nicer street than they used to live in. And right handy to an A and P.

CAROLINE (*whispering*): Ma, it's better than our street. It's richer than our street. Ma, isn't Beulah richer than we are?

MA (*looking at her with a firm and glassy eye*): Mind yourself, Missy. I don't want to hear anybody talking about rich or not rich when I'm around. If people aren't nice I don't care how rich they are. I live in the best street in the world because my husband and children live there. (*She glares impressively at* CAROLINE *a moment to let this lesson sink in, then looks up, sees* BEULAH *off left, and waves.*) There's Beulah standing on the steps looking for us.

(BEULAH *enters from left, also waving. They all call out:* "Hello, Beulah—hello." *Presently they are all getting out of the car, except* ELMER, *busy with brakes.*)

BEULAH: Hello, Mamma. Well, lookit how Arthur and Caroline are growing.

MA: They're bursting all their clothes.

BEULAH (*crossing in front of them and kissing her father long and affectionately*): Hello, Papa. Good old papa. You look tired, Pa.

MA: Yes, your pa needs a rest. Thank Heaven, his vacation has come just now. We'll feed him up and let him sleep late. (ELMER *gets out of car and stands in front of it.*) Pa has a present for you, Loolie. He would go and buy it.

BEULAH: Why, Pa, you're terrible to go and buy anything for me. Isn't he terrible?

(STAGE MANAGER *removes automobile.*)

MA: Well, it's a secret. You can open it at dinner.

BEULAH (*puts her arm around his neck and rubs her nose against his temple*): Crazy old pa, goin' buyin' things! It's me that oughta be buyin' things for you, Pa.

ELMER: Oh, no! There's only one Loolie in the world.

BEULAH (*whispering, as her eyes fill with tears*): Are you glad I'm still alive, Pa?

(*She kisses him abruptly and goes back to the house steps.*)

ELMER: Where's Horace, Loolie?

BEULAH: He was kep' a little at the office. He'll be here any minute. He's crazy to see you all.

MA: All right. You men go over to the Y and come back in about an hour.

BEULAH: Go straight along, Pa, you can't miss it. It just stares at yuh. (ELMER *and* ARTHUR *exit down right.*) Well, come on upstairs, Ma, and take your things. —Caroline, there's a surprise for you in the back yard.

CAROLINE: Rabbits?

BEULAH: No.

CAROLINE: Chickins?

BEULAH: No. Go and see. (CAROLINE *runs off stage, down left.*) There are two new puppies. You be thinking over whether you can keep one in Newark.

MA: I guess we can. (MA *and* BEULAH *turn and walk way up stage right.* THE STAGE MANAGER *pushes out a cot from the left, and places it down left on a slant so that its foot is toward the left.* BEULAH *and* MA *come down stage center toward left.*) It's a nice house, Beulah. You just got a *lovely* home.

BEULAH: When I got back from the hospital, Horace had moved everything into it, and there wasn't anything for me to do.

MA: It's lovely.

(BEULAH *sits on the cot, testing the springs.*)

BEULAH: I think you'll find this comfortable, Ma. (BEU-LAH *sits on down stage end of it.*)

MA (*taking off her hat*): Oh, I could sleep on a heapa

shoes, Loolie! I don't have no trouble sleepin'. (*She sits down up stage of her.*) Now let me look at my girl. Well, well, when I last saw you, you didn't know me. You kep' saying: *When's Mama comin'? When's Mama comin'?* But the doctor sent me away.

BEULAH (*puts her head on her mother's shoulder and weeps*): It was awful, Mama. It was awful. She didn't even live a few minutes, Mama. It was awful.

MA (*in a quick, light, urgent undertone*): God thought best, dear. God thought best. We don't understand why. We just go on, honey, doin' our business. (*Then almost abruptly.*) Well, now (*stands up*), what are we giving the men to eat tonight?

BEULAH: There's a chicken in the oven.

MA: What time didya put it in?

BEULAH (*restraining her*): Aw, Ma, don't go yet. (*Taking her mother's hand and drawing her down beside her.*) I like to sit here with you this way. You always get the fidgets when we try and pet yuh, Mama.

MA (*ruefully, laughing*): Yes, it's kinda foolish. I'm just an old Newark bag-a-bones.

(*She glances at the backs of her hands.*)

BEULAH (*indignantly*): Why, Ma, you're good-lookin'! We always said you were good-lookin'. —And besides, you're the best ma we could ever have.

MA (*uncomfortable*): Well, I hope you like me. There's nothin' like bein' liked by your family. —(*Rises.*) Now I'm going downstairs to look at the chicken. You stretch out here for a minute and shut your eyes. (*She helps* BEULAH *to a lying position.*) Have you got everything laid in for breakfast before the shops close?

BEULAH: Oh, you know! Ham and eggs.

(*They both laugh.* MA *puts an imaginary blanket over* BEULAH.)

MA: I declare I never could understand what men see in ham and eggs. I think they're horrible. —What time did you put the chicken in?

BEULAH: Five o'clock.

MA: Well, now, you shut your eyes for ten minutes.

(MA *turns, walks directly up stage, then along the back wall to the right as she absent-mindedly and indistinctly sings*):

> There were ninety and nine that safely lay
> In the shelter of the fold ...

AND THE CURTAIN FALLS

Great Plays in MENTOR Editions

☐ **THE GENIUS OF THE EARLY ENGLISH THEATER edited by Sylvan Barnet, Norton Berman, and William Burto.** Includes Marlow's *Doctor Faustus*, Shakespeare's *Macbeth*, Johnson's *Volopone*, Milton's *Samson Agonistes*, and three anonymous plays, *Abraham and Isaac*, *The Second Shepherd's Play*, and *Everyman*. Includes critical essays. (#ME1889—$2.50)

☐ **EIGHT GREAT COMEDIES edited by Sylvan Barnet, Morton Berman, and William Burto.** The complete texts of eight masterpieces of comic drama by Aristophanes, Machiavelli, Shakespeare, Molière, John Gay, Wilde, Chekhov, and Shaw. Includes essays on comedy by four distinguished critics and scholars. (#ME1840—$2.50)

☐ **EIGHT GREAT TRAGEDIES edited by Barnet, Berman and Burto.** Eight memorable tragedies by Aeschylus, Euripides, Sophocles, Shakespeare, Ibsen, Strindberg, Yeats, and O'Neill. With essays on tragedy by Aristotle, Emerson and others. (#ME1911—$2.50)

☐ **THE OEDIPUS PLAYS OF SOPHOCLES translated by Paul Roche.** A dramatic and forceful new verse translation of *Oedipus the King*, *Oedipus at Colonus*, and *Antigone*. (#MJ1794—$1.95)

☐ **THREE GREAT PLAYS OF EURIPIDES translated by Rex Warner.** The classic tragedies of *Medea*, *Hippolytus*, and *Helen* in a brilliant new translation. (#ME1869—$1.75)

Buy them at your local

bookstore or use coupon

on next page for ordering.

Ⓢ

Outstanding Plays in SIGNET and SIGNET CLASSIC Editions

☐ **THE SAND BOX and THE DEATH OF BESSIE SMITH by Edward Albee.** Two of the playwright's earlier works also hailed by critics for their unique and startling power.
(#Y7376—$1.25)

☐ **THE AMERICAN DREAM and THE ZOO STORY by Edward Albee.** Two remarkably successful off-Broadway plays by the author of the prize-winning play, *Who's Afraid of Virginia Woolf?*
(#W8735—$1.50)

☐ **PYGMALION and MY FAIR LADY.** George Bernard Shaw's brilliant romantic play and the internationally acclaimed musical adaptation by Alan Jay Lerner, together in one special edition.
(#CJ1466—$1.95)

☐ **THREE BY TENNESSEE: SWEET BIRD OF YOUTH, THE ROSE TATTOO and THE NIGHT OF THE IGUANA by Tennessee Williams.** Three of the Pulitzer Prize-winning author's most brilliant plays.
(#CE1328—$2.50)

☐ **A STREETCAR NAMED DESIRE by Tennessee Williams.** The Pulitzer Prize-winning play of a woman betrayed by love. Illustrated with scenes from the New York, London, and Paris productions.
(#E9372—$1.75)

SIGNET CLASSIC Collections of Plays

☐ **CHEKHOV: THE MAJOR PLAYS** by Anton Chekhov, Complete texts in English of *Ivanov, The Sea Gull, Uncle Vanya, The Three Sisters,* and *The Cherry Orchard.* New translation by Ann Dunnigan. Foreword by Robert Brustein. (#CE1483—$2.50)

☐ **TARTUFFE and Other Plays** by Molière, translated with an Introduction by Donald M. Frame. *The Ridiculous Precieuses, The School for Husbands, The School for Wives, The Critique of the School for Wives, The Versailles Impromptu, Don Juan* and *Tartuffe* in a brilliant new translation by one of America's leading French scholars. (#CE1300—$2.50)

☐ **PLAYS** by George Bernard Shaw, Introduction by Eric Bentley. *Man and Superman, Candida, Arms and the Man,* and *Mrs. Warren's Profession.* (#CE1480—$2.95)

☐ **IBSEN: FOUR MAJOR PLAYS,** Volume I, translated and with a Foreword by Rolf Fjelde. *A Doll House, The Wild Duck, Hedda Gabler,* and *The Master Builder.* (#CE1397—$2.25)

☐ **IBSEN: FOUR MAJOR PLAYS,** Volume II, translated and with a Foreword by Rolf Fjelde, *Ghosts, An Enemy of the People, The Lady from the Sea,* and *John Gabriel Borkman.* (#CJ1449—$1.95)

Buy them at your local

bookstore or use coupon

on next page for ordering.